THE JANITOR MUST DIE

John Fulton

Copyright © 2016 John Fulton

All rights reserved.

ISBN: 0999381806
ISBN-13: 9780999381809

Table of Contents

1 - Soy Un Perdedor

2 - Ground Zero

3 - Fight or Flight

4 - Office Survival

5 - Elevator Music

6 - End of the Line

7 - One Man Army

8 - Going Commando

9 - Blue Shift

10 - Critical Failure

11 - Poker Face

12 - King Sacrifice

13 - Floodgate

14 - Kairos

15 - Terms

16 - War Machine

17 - Floaters

18 - Katabasis

19 - Epilogue

Edition 1.9

For my brothers, who defy expectations every day.
For my mother, who introduced me to the greats.
For my father, who taught me God has a sense of humor,
and for anyone else who's ever tried to do the right thing,
even when they didn't know what the hell was going on.

1

Soy Un Perdedor

Nora was dreaming of thunder and screaming death when she opened her eyes and realized the radio was on.

She felt the coarse, unyielding duffle bag under her cheek, and felt the driving bass line pound against her throbbing brain. White-hot panic faded to mere irritation. Tina was DJ'ing again.

Nora blinked against the bright yellow sunrise streaming in the minivan windows. She put her palms against her head and let out a groan that even she couldn't hear clearly. She wished she had brought a pair of those noise-canceling headphones Tina was always yammering about, or at least a pair of earplugs so she could enjoy the break of dawn. She reached into her pocket with an olive-skinned hand and pulled out her phone. The time was 6:34am.

She briefly tried to recall how many time zones they'd crossed, but quickly gave up. AC/DC and lack of sleep was a bad combination to calculate to.

Pushing herself upright, she cast a glance out the minivan's left window and swept back a sheet of dark brown hair. It had a long white highlight which ordinarily crossed the top of her forehead and flowed down to her shoulder on the right, but her nap had rearranged it into a spiderwebbed mess. Bracing her hands against the ceiling, she straightened her back with a crackle. She was somewhat taller than average, and sleeping on the short middle seat had left her feeling like she'd been folded into a box.

They were gliding down a winding freeway cut into a range of brown scrub-dotted hills. Dawn was just peeking over the ridgetop to their right, and as she watched, the van slipped into a long shadow that lay over the wide rolling valleys stretching away to their left. The chilled air made a strange contrast with the warm red and brown of the desert.

The van swerved, just enough to draw her attention back to the music—and to the two individuals in the front seats.

In the passenger seat rocked a fun-sized ball of energy with short spiky hair. It was deep black, and raked with bright red streaks. Tina was singing at the top of her voice and periodically cranking up the volume. No one was in danger of hearing her.

The driver, his limp blond hair bobbing to the music, preferred to express himself through the steering wheel. Oddball's narrow face was fixed in a muscle-straining grin. His head wandered from side to side like a loosely tethered balloon. Nora couldn't quite decide if he was swerving to the beat or if it was delayed steering correction.

A thin wisp of curling white smoke leaked from his mouth. He switched hands on the steering wheel and brought a limp blunt to his lips, inhaling deeply.

Nora's eyes narrowed and she slapped her blanket aside.

Oddball swerved and Tina came close to banging her head on the dash. A passing car beeped angrily. Oddball giggled and waved at it in the rearview mirror.

Nora took a moment to fasten her seatbelt and cinched it tight. Grabbing the driver's seat with one hand and reaching out with the other, Nora made a gesture and cranked the volume down. Her fingers never touched the dial.

Tina stared at the radio for a moment, then turned it back up.

Nora turned it down again.

Tina gave the radio a funny look. Oddball looked around, confused.

"I can't...see the music!" he blurted. "I can't—Tina, fix phftheuh...the thing..."

"I didn't do anything! It turned itself off!" Tina yelled, fiddling with the controls.

"Back here Tina."

Tina spun around to see Nora wearing her most unamused Annoyed Face. Sharp, ice-blue eyes and a hard scowl briefly pierced the cloud over Tina's mind. Though the oldest person in the vehicle was Oddball by a large margin—at thirty he outstripped them all by at least half a decade—

Nora was the nominal leader, and she was obviously unhappy.

"Oh...hi!" Tina said cheerfully. "You're awake!"

Nora fought to keep her voice even. "Tina," she said. "Why is Oddball driving?"

"Because it was his turn."

"Dudes!" Oddball moaned. "Turn up the music! Come on!"

Nora resisted the urge to put him through a window.

"Yes," she said, combing a hand through her hair, "but didn't we agree that he's only allowed to drive when he's not *stoned out of his mind?*"

"He's not stoned, he's speedballing!" Tina replied. "I mean, just a little bit—totally safe. See, one stops the other—"

"Pull over," Nora snapped. "I'll drive."

"But I'm driving!" Oddball said, suddenly noticing there was discussion.

"Yeah," Tina said, hurriedly dragging her seatbelt across herself. "He hasn't hurt anyone yet—"

A tractor-trailer horn blared by them and Nora grabbed the seats once again. A sort of shimmer had developed around her hands, like a mirage on the desert. Tina clipped her seatbelt home and grinned at her.

"See?"

"Fantastic!" Nora barked. "Pull over! NOW."

"It's *my* van," Oddball said. He blew smoke all over the windshield and giggled lustily.

Tina suddenly pointed out the driver's side window. "Oh look! There's the diner!"

Nora could see the diner in question over the guardrail to their left, at the near end of a lonely strip mall sitting on the empty valley floor. They hadn't passed it yet — but there was no road to it either.

She groaned. "Great. We missed the exit!"

"Exit?" Oddball said, cranking his head back to look at her. "Where?"

The van wobbled and Nora saw them cross the median and swerve towards the slope. Acid flooded her system and her eyes widened. She only had time for a single shout of protest before the van crossed the incoming lane and punched through the guardrail, becoming airborne.

Time in Nora's head seemed to both race and crawl. Oddball's hair flew upwards; Tina bumped into the passenger window. Smoke and bits of ash swirled through the air, and a large soda unassumingly levitated itself from the cup holder and spun like a top. It seemed to hang in mid-air for an instant, then it sailed back and smacked her in the face. Ice-cold liquid brought her back to the present just as they hit the ground with a tremendous jolt. She could almost feel her spine being shortened by the impact.

All she could hear was the van speeding up like a jet taking off. She was pressed back into her seat, as if she was on an out of control roller coaster.

She focused, shunting power to her hands. The air rippled like water under a sound wave. Pulling herself upright, she leaned over Oddball's shoulder, stretched out her right hand, and forced the brake pedal to the floor.

The left tire dug in. The vehicle flipped onto its side and rolled.

Dinah wiped down the counter by the register and looked wistfully out the window. The small diner was at the end of a small strip mall, but, this being the desert, there was virtually nothing but space for miles and miles. Through the floor-to-ceiling windows in front she could see the rising sun washing over the valley. She swept back a few wisps of wavy dark hair that crept into her vision, and tucked the graying strands behind her ear.

A few customers had come in for takeout—mostly workers from either the nearby industrial park or the research lab further into the desert. Most of them were familiar faces with warm groggy smiles and words of thanks. Nobody could beat Dinah Morrison's cooking early on a Monday morning.

However, the character sitting in the far corner by the window this particular morning was very unfamiliar. He was perhaps in his early twenties, wearing what seemed to be unevenly faded black jeans a size and a half too small, matching retro sneakers, and a black leather jacket with a gray fabric hood. His tousled black hair reached nearly to his shoulders, and his eyes were concealed behind a pair of sunglasses. He had the attitude of a man bored with the world, leaning back in his chair, one foot propped over his knee.

"Excuse me?" Dinah called. The man didn't seem to notice. "Do you want anything?"

There was a crashing sound, and a minivan flipped into the parking lot, rolling like a tumbleweed. It came to rest in a parking space, hung for a moment on its left wheels, and came down right side up with a bang that popped the remaining side windows.

Dinah dropped the cloth and covered her mouth in shock.

The man got up slowly, stretched, and calmly walked to the door.

Dinah picked up her phone. "Should I call an ambulance?"

"There's no need," the man said with a wave of his hand. "Not yet, at least."

Crossing the parking lot, Loyd could see that the van was totaled. Oddball's Mom wouldn't be happy—but it was close to giving up the ghost anyway. He was more concerned about its contents.

His gut tightened as he saw the right-side sliding door open—and he let out a sigh of relief as Nora stumbled out and coughed. She seemed a bit shaken, but unhurt.

As he came up to the vehicle, the passenger door popped open next to him, and Tina burst out. She took a moment to regain her footing, then pumped her fist.

"That was AWESOME!" she blurted. "Did you see it? We almost DIED!"

Loyd turned back to Nora, but she was already pushing past him. He didn't try to hold her back.

She stalked around the smoking grill of the van, ripped open the driver's side door, and dragged Oddball out by his collar, slamming him back into the side of the van.

"Are you *insane?*" she roared. "You could have killed us! Do you realize that? *Killed.* As in *dead!*"

Oddball stared dumbly at her, then defocused. Nora curled her lip and let him slide to the ground.

Loyd stood watching with his hands behind his back. Tina stood next to him holding a smartphone.

"You're filming this?" said Nora.

Loyd held up a hand. "Nora…"

Tina giggled. "Yeah I'm filming this—hey!" The phone was ripped from her grasp and flew into Nora's upraised palm. Spinning to face the desert, she hurled it towards the horizon.

Without another word, she stormed past them into the diner.

Tina bit her lip. Loyd noticed and gave her a quizzical look.

"Uh…" Tina began. "That was *her* phone."

Dr. Vance's feet clunked loudly on the thinly carpeted floor as he strode quickly through the corridor, a brown folder full of aging documents held tightly against his side. He quickly threaded his way through the slowly waking facility as sleepy clerks and custodial workers finished the night shift, carrying half-empty cups of coffee.

Vance swallowed and rubbed his eyes with a dark-skinned hand. He'd forgotten his own morning shot of uncontrolled substances and a heavy sense of urgency was the only thing keeping his eyes open. Scratching his close-cropped curly black hair, Vance peered out of his glasses and shot bleary glances down each hallway as he passed them. Close to exiting his thirties, Vance was a tall thin man with a carefully managed beard and mustache, but the rest of his drawn and rumpled appearance betrayed days, perhaps weeks of long days and longer nights.

He took a quick glance around as he entered an intersection and took his bearings. Hadn't he seen?—There. He saw his white-coated target vanish around a corner and broke into a short jog. As he turned the corner, he tripped roughly over a sleepy-looking custodian folding a "wet floor" sign into his cart. The custodian adjusted his gray company cap and blurted something apologetic, but Vance waved him off, shaking his head.

"It's fine," he mumbled, still focused on the scientist some distance up the hallway. Thankfully, Dr. Stein had stopped to observe the commotion.

Dr. Stein was not an old man by any stretch of the imagination—only a few years older than Vance—but he was easily the more drawn and rumpled of the two. He was a tall thin man with a patchy thin beard, his stringy black hair capped by a blazing white bald spot.

He was currently wearing his perpetually-frustrated-pursed-lip smile, which, combined with his height and hooded eyes, gave most people the impression he was a very arrogant and unpleasant person to deal with. Dr. Vance, however, was not one to judge a man on his appearance—he disliked Stein purely on first-hand experience.

A shadow passed over Stein's face as he recognized Vance.

"Bob!" Vance called out.

Stein turned and continued walking, faster now.

Vance strode quickly to catch up, leaving the janitor to trundle his squeaking cart away.

"Bob," he said, "I've got to show you something."

"Dr. Vance!" Stein said in a bright, unnaturally cheery voice. "How can I help you?"

"I've got something you need to see," Vance said, hefting his folder. "It's important."

"Can it wait?" Stein looked down at his watch. "We've only got a few more hours until the experiment starts."

"No," said Vance. "No, it can't wait. The experiment is exactly what I need to talk to you *about*."

"Well, I'm not sure I want to talk to *you* about it," Stein quipped, "after you went behind my back like that."

Vance's hackles raised and he felt hot anger flush through him. "I did what?"

Stein stopped and poked his clipboard into Vance's chest. "Yes—The Administrator told me about about the little talk you had yesterday."

"I assumed he would," said Vance. "That was the point."

"The point of going over my head, you mean," Stein retorted.

"The point of asking how an 'experiment' like this was approved," Vance said, trying to control his temper. He held up the folder he'd been carrying and tried to hand it to Stein.

"Seriously," he said, "what does this look like?"

Stein waved him off. "For the last time, it's a simple spectrometry reading. What, have you got some kind of irrational fear of Columnar Basalt?"

Vance opened the folder and held up a black and white photo. "Does Columnar Basalt do that?"

Stein blinked at the photo, then took it from Vance's hand and studied it closely.

"Now look," said Vance, "at first, I thought this had to be made up—some kind of hoax—but when I showed it to the Administrator, he went ballistic. Told me that if I valued my job, I'd forget about the whole—"

"Where did you get this?" Stein said.

"Deep storage archives," Vance said. "It was buried so deep it doesn't even exist on the computer database at all. Look at this—spectrometry, radiation—this thing looks like a prop from the X-Files—"

"It sure does," Stein interrupted, casting Vance a suspicious look. "In fact, it looks almost *exactly* like that."

Vance's eyes narrowed. "What's that supposed to mean?"

"What, you think I'm *stupid*?" Stein snapped, crunching the photo into a ball and tossing it aside. "What, you went down to FedEx and said, 'Hey, I need an eight by eleven glossy of this crappy photoshop I made?'"

Vance's jaw dropped. "You think I made this whole thing up?" he sputtered.

"I do," Stein snapped, "and if I have my way, it'll cost you your job."

"My *job*?" Vance barked. "Bob, people could *die*! You think I care about—"

"Shut up," Stein waved him off. "Just stop. You're off the project." He jammed his finger into Vance's chest and leaned in, his head tilted down like a vindictive teacher. "I'm going to have a little talk with the

Administrator about you."

Vance's eyes smoldered dangerously. "You do that," he growled.

He turned away quickly, and crouched to snatch the crumpled photo off the floor. As he stood, he smashed straight into a freckle-faced intern carrying two cups of hot coffee, soaking him in scalding liquid.

"I'm so sorry," the intern mumbled, trying ineffectually to mop off Vance's dripping lab coat with a couple of brown paper napkins. Vance plucked his shirt away from his burned skin and gritted his teeth.

"Wow," Stein said, a self-satisfied smirk seeping onto his lips, "That looks like it hurt. Why don't you take the day off—take some time to appreciate what it's like to be unemployed."

Vance clamped his jaw shut and took a couple of deep breaths. Stein walked on.

"Oh—" Stein called back. "Find a janitor to clean that up before you go."

The Janitor was, at that particular moment, engaged in a battle of wits with a vending machine.

And losing. Badly.

He glowered sullenly through the glass at the toaster strudel, straining his sleep-deprived mind for any possible weaknesses in the fortress of metal and plastic. Its colorful side panels mocked him in perverse glee.

Today had started particularly badly. After spending too much time playing Call of Duty the night before, he'd been late for work and had a splitting headache. He'd only been late by four minutes—but it was enough to piss off his supervisor, who had promptly chewed him out and left him wishing there was a "skip dialogue" option for real life. He had expected to get breakfast at work, but shortly after arriving realized he'd left his wallet at home and only had a buck fifty in his coveralls. The drink machines were out, and now the snack machine had eaten his money.

Not that he'd given up easily. He'd tried banging it, slapping it, reaching up through the trapdoor at he bottom, and even considered leaning it over despite the label warning him not to.

He'd quickly reconsidered after a single attempt. It was far too heavy.

Josh pulled off his gray company cap and bonked his forehead into the plexiglass shield. His olive green coveralls were fairly new, but were already collecting stains around the ankles and sleeves.

He groaned down at his shoes.

"Please," he muttered, "On my hands and knees. *Want. Breffist.*"

Klunk.

The strudel dropped into the retrieval bin with a smack.

Catching something in the corner of his eye, Josh rolled his head so he could look left, and saw a man leaning against the machine, easy as could be. He was tall, his head shaved clean, with a pair of aviator sunglasses resting above a rugged, wry looking smile. The man took a sip from his coffee.

Josh contained his surprise to a startled blink, and squinted at him. "And how long have *you* been there?"

"Not long," the man replied.

Josh noticed he was wearing a pair of olive green janitor's coveralls, like his. Must be new on the shift, Josh thought. He blinked again, and found raising his eyelids the second time more difficult than he had anticipated.

"Are you going to take that," said the other janitor, "or should I?"

The man's sunglasses made assessing his expression difficult.

Keeping his eyes on the stranger, Josh slowly slid down the side of the vending machine, fumbled around the retrieval box for a few seconds, and backed off, greasy prize in hand. Flipping his hat securely back onto his head, Josh sat down with a dull thump at one of the small round tables scattered through the small room.

"Thanks," he said.

"You're welcome," said the sunglasses man.

Silence. Josh chewed his upper lip.

"So," said Josh. "When did you start here Mr..." He glanced at the man's name tag. "...Bishop?"

"That's what they call me," said Bishop. "And you are?"

Josh's face went blank for a moment, and then he remembered he hadn't bothered to fill out the name tag on his coveralls. This was a new pair; the last had succumbed to a particularly nasty incident in the cafeteria.

"Oh," he said, "sorry—I'm, uh, Josh."

"Nice to meet you," Bishop said. He smacked the side of the machine. Another strudel thumped into the retrieval bin.

Josh stared at the vending machine as Bishop retrieved the plastic-wrapped package.

"Missed breakfast huh?" Bishop said. "Me too."

He inserted several coins and punched a few buttons. The machine made a satisfied electronic whine and the empty ring turned, moving the next pastry forward.

"It's been a long morning already," Bishop continued, "and it'll be a long day too."

Josh raised an eyebrow. "How did you do that?"

Bishop crossed to the seat opposite him. "Do what?"

Josh pointed to the machine. "*That.*"

Bishop glanced at the machine, then back at Josh. "Same way you did."

Josh stuck his tongue in his cheek and tried to figure out Bishop's game. He looked from the machine, to the man—one as implacable as the other. Grinning wryly, he tore open his strudel package.

"Okay," he said. "Have it your way."

He got up and walked past the door, heading towards the toaster oven in the kitchenette at the back of the room.

"What happened to your hand?" Bishop said abruptly.

Josh stopped and looked down. Sure enough, a long trail of half-dried blood was wrapping around his hand, semi-congealed into a dark crusty mess. Josh stared at it for a moment in surprise. He hadn't even noticed.

"I, uh...This scientist tripped over me in the hall," he said finally. "It must have happened then."

"I see," said Bishop. "He was in a hurry. Watch the door." He took a sip.

"Yeah, he was," said Josh. "Wait, what?"

The door next to him burst open and the knob slammed into Josh's hand.

"OW!" Josh barked.

Mr. Ruiz stormed in, inadvertently stepping on Josh's strudel. He cursed under his breath, but when he spoke, his voice came out oddly flat and wheezy.

"What the hell is this?" The coffee-toned Head Custodian said, jabbing a thick finger at the fallen pastry. "I pay you to clean, not to litter."

Josh held his throbbing hand and tried to look at Mr. Ruiz without looking him in the eye.

"No sir," he said, "just an accident."

"Dogs have accidents," Mr. Ruiz wheezed. "You're the janitor. Clean it up."

Josh cast a side glance at Bishop. Mr. Ruiz followed his gaze and stared watery-eyed and slack jawed at the man.

"Who the hell are you?" Ruiz wheezed, tossing a limp arm towards Bishop.

"New," Bishop said, taking a sip of his coffee.

"Yeah? W—" Ruiz lost his chain of thought and looked back at Josh. "Coffee spill down the hall."

"There is?" Josh said. "I was just there."

"Then why are you here?" Ruiz snapped. "When you're done, go check the restrooms by the Sector C Test Labs. Their guy is sick today."

"Yes sir," Josh replied.

Ruiz snorted and lumbered back through the door. Josh heard him wheezing all the way down the hall. He looked down at the splattered remains of his strudel and sighed. Re-setting his cap on his head, Josh scooped it up, dumped it into the trash, and prepared to head out the door.

"I've got it," Bishop said, tossing him his pastry. "You let that hand scab over or it's going to get infected."

Josh paused for a moment, then looked down at his hand. The scab had opened and a renewed red line was working its way down his hand.

"Uh...I guess," he said. "You're sure?"

"Don't worry—he won't be back for at least fifteen minutes." Bishop finished off his coffee, planted the cup in the garbage can, and walked out.

As Josh watched him leave, his hand unconsciously crinkled the plastic wrap in his hand, and he looked down at the strudel as if seeing it for the first time. He turned to the vending machine.

"Huh," he said to himself. "Breffist."

Nora slammed the door to the women's room, unzipped her jacket, and turned on the cold tap in the sink. She let the cool water flow over her hands, and then splashed it suddenly into her face, leaning on the countertop. Her hands formed into fists and shook as she tried to control her breathing. Her heart was still pounding in her ears, and she felt like her head was about to burst. She squeezed her eyes shut and pushed her palms into her temples.

"Stupid! Stupidstupidstupid!" she hissed, spitting each word like an oath. She began raking her fingers through her hair again, trying unsuccessfully to make it behave in an ordered fashion. No matter how many times she combed through it there always seemed to be a few white strands in the dark area or a few dark strands in the white, and the more she fussed with it the more tangled it got.

She cursed under her breath. Why had she thought this was a good idea? Take those idiots on a break-in to a high-security test lab? Sure.

"Just shoot me now," she muttered. Her hands wouldn't stop shaking.

"Nora?"

She spun around. Loyd stood there with a concerned look on his face, folding his sunglasses into his jacket.

"Are you all right?" he said.

"What the hell are you doing in the women's room?" she blurted.

"Just checking on you," he replied. "Are you okay?"

"*Okay?*" Nora snapped, "No I'm not *okay*! Your idiot stoner friend drove us off a cliff!"

"It's fine," Loyd said, waving his hand. "I'll push the clerk and she'll let us use her car."

Nora glared at him. "What part of 'I almost died,' do you not understand?"

Loyd was silent for a moment, then he shrugged.

"But," he said, sliding her phone onto the countertop, "You didn't."

Nora bit back something foul and turned to stare at her reflection once more.

"Stupid," she muttered.

His arms enfolded her from behind, and she stood up, her hands instinctively reaching up and grasping his. She shivered slightly—but not from the cold.

"It's been a stressful morning for all of us," Loyd said.

"Stop that," said Nora.

"Stop what?"

She twisted to face him. "This isn't a game—I need to know you're taking this seriously."

"I am. And you need to relax."

"I need to *relax*?" she retorted. "I—What are you doing?"

Loyd had brought her hands in front of her and was rubbing them.

"You're hands are shaking," he said.

"Yeah," said Nora, "I was just in a car crash. I'm full of adrenaline."

"Are you sure that's it?" Loyd said, gazing deep into her eyes. His gaze was magnetic—she felt she could see every ripple of his green irises.

She ran out of words for a moment, and tore them away, looking intently at the taupe towel dispenser. "I...yeah," she said, "I'm pretty sure it's adrenaline."

You're so close to me.

"Have I ever told you how beautiful your eyes are?" Loyd said. Nora's eyes immediately darted back—and then they were locked in. She felt lightheaded, her ears buzzing.

This isn't the time.

"What are you doing?" she whispered.

"Nothing," he said.

He brought his hands up and began massaging her temples. She leaned back. That buzz was in her skull now, vibrating her brain into jelly.

Suddenly, she pulled away and clapped both hands to her head.

"Dammit!" She muttered. "Why did you do that?"

"What?" Loyd replied, sounding hurt. "You needed to relax."

"Relax?" Nora blurted, leaning over and shaking her head. "It's going to take me ten minutes just to wake up again." She rubbed her temple and stumbled. She felt like someone had just dropped a huge soft blanket on the campfire of her mind, and now she couldn't see anything. Anything except Loyd.

"You need to relax," Loyd repeated. "Calm down. You were shaking."

"What I need," Nora turned to him fiercely. "Is for you to take this seriously!"

"Well, I am." he said. "Now can we still make out?"

"No!" Nora snapped. "We have to go stop the end of the world, remember?"

"Well that does change things," Loyd said, leaning against the wall, a little smile playing on his lips. "I mean, you don't want to die a virgin, do you?"

Nora stared at him openmouthed.

"You…you're impossible," she replied, and stomped out.

Loyd waited for a moment, and heard the door open once more.

Nora snatched her phone off the counter and walked out, passing him a single flustered glare as she left.

He smiled slowly, and followed her out.

Josh shook his head and tried not to gag at the putrid mess on the stall floor. Poison gas wasn't as bad as what the cafeteria's meatloaf did to the scientists' bowels. The splash covered nearly the entire stall floor, and it was one of the big handicapped stalls too.

Mop, dirty water, spray bottle of all-purpose cleaner, plunger. As much as he hated this job, his parents had raised him doing chores like this, and after ten minutes of breathing through his mouth and frustrating attempts to pick up the fecal matter instead of just squish it around, Josh's attention was absorbed by his work. When he looked up and saw Bishop leaning against the stall frame he nearly hit the ceiling.

"Jeez!" he blurted. "Didn't your parents ever teach you to knock?"

"No," said Bishop.

Josh tried to decipher that for a moment.

"I'll take that as an apology." he said, and went back to mopping.

After a few moments, he looked up again, and Bishop was still there. He stopped and leaned on his mop.

"Is there something you're supposed to be doing in here?" he said.

Bishop just stared at him.

"Because I've got this covered."

After a moment, Josh pulled his eyes away and returned to mopping. Bishop watched as Josh's mop smacked and swabbed across the now spotless floor.

"You're good at your job," he observed.

Josh looked up at him from under his eyebrows. "I'm a janitor. Anyone can be good at this."

"I suppose that's so," said Bishop, "but not everyone *is*."

Josh paused at that, then shrugged.

"Well, you know what they say," he said. "They say 'crap,' I say 'how much,' and 'what color.'"

He muttered to himself. "How high, how far—"

"—All the way." Bishop finished.

Josh stopped again and stared at Bishop, hard.

"Is there something I can help you with?" he said. "What are you, from management or something? I didn't think we had diarrhea quality assurance."

Bishop smiled. "Something like that."

"Can you be more specific, or would you have to kill me or something?"

"Or something."

Josh's eyes narrowed. He went back to mopping again.

"Well, if I'm doing okay, you might want to go bother someone else." Josh gestured towards the door. "Like that Dr. Vance fella. He sounded like he was on to something big."

Bishop smiled wryly. "I saw—So," he took a breath. "How does someone like you become a janitor?"

Josh jabbed at a stubborn brown spot. "What, you run background checks too?"

"Already did that." Bishop said. "I want to know your side."

"I'm starting to think you're in the mafia or something," Josh quipped. "What, you don't think the custodial arts is a worthy profession?"

"I doubt it was your first choice."

Josh rubbed the spot with his shoe and shook his head with a strained grin as he realized he had been trying to rub out a chip in the floor tiles. "It wasn't. So what do you want? Story of my life?"

"No," said Bishop. "I just have one question."

"Well I already know Jesus, if that's what you were going to ask."

"Do you know Nora?"

Josh's world came to a full stop.

Without knowing exactly what he was going to say, he finally turned to face the other man.

He blinked. Bishop was gone.

"The what?" Dr. Stein barked.

"The wiring," said the Haz-Mat-suited Foreman. "We've got a massive burn out. We'll need to bring out the backup lights and generator."

Dr. Stein clenched his fists and turned red. The Foreman stood casually, standing out like a yellow paper cutout against the shadowy background of the test chamber. Whether the Foreman was used to Stein's typically thorny manner or simply appreciated the inch-thick glass window between them was unclear.

"Of course we'll need the backup lights," Stein snapped. "Why didn't you warm them up the way I told you?"

The Foreman remained silent.

"Well?" Stein snapped.

"The wiring in here is fifty years old," the Foreman said, gesturing to his clipboard. "We should have run—"

"Oh for God's sake," Stein yelled, "why is this so hard—"

"Dr. Stein?"

Stein spun around with such speed and violence that the intern jumped back in surprise.

"What?" Stein snapped.

"S...Sir, there's...someone on the phone for you. The one in your office."

"Who?"

"I don't know, they just sent me down—"

Stein shoved his clipboard into the trembling intern's hands and jabbed his finger at it.

"Make sure they do it right this time. I'll be back."

Stein turned towards the Foreman, raised his eyebrows and pointed a finger at him like a mother towards a disobedient child. The Foreman's visor stared impassively back.

The intern watched Stein stomp down the hall with an odd mix of awe and revulsion on his face.

"Jeez," he said nervously. "Who pissed in his coffee?"

"No one I know," said the Foreman. "But they dream about it."

Stein threw open his office door and picked up the phone from its charger.

"Dr. Stein," he said.

"Has Dr. Vance spoken to you?" said the voice on the other end of the line.

"Ehh...yes," said Stein, "I thought you might be calling about that."

"You're damn right I'm calling about that," Dr. Bird snapped. "I don't think I need to remind you this is a very precisely timed project. Our Mutual Acquaintance is crawling up my ass about this thing being on schedule. If we're going to keep our jobs, I need something to tell him besides that we've got people sticking their noses where they don't belong."

Stein drew in a deep breath and let it hiss out through his teeth.

"I understand sir," Stein said.

"I'm not sure you do," Bird growled. "There's more to this Vance character than meets the eye—I don't even know where he *got* those files."

"Then our deniability is secure," Stein replied forcefully. "Besides, by the time he blows the whistle, it'll be over. What do we care?"

"Idiot," Bird snapped. "It's not what you know—it's what they can *prove* you know. We're taking a big risk here, and if we screw it up now, You-Know-Who will hang us both out to dry, understand?"

"Then don't worry," Stein said. "Because I won't. I've taken care of everything."

"You'd better," Bird said. "Because I'm coming down there to see it in person, and if even a hair is out of place, I'll ditch you so fast it'll make your head spin."

He hung up, leaving the dial tone droning through Stein's head like a saw. Setting the phone down on its charger, Stein glared at it for a moment, then with a single, vicious blow, slapped both across the room.

With an unceremonious screeching of metal, the door to the storage unit rose and slid back into the ceiling. Inside stood a nondescript white van with a ladder mounted on top. The paint on the sides was unevenly shaded, and Nora could almost make out the shape of a long-removed logo beneath it.

"Perfect," Nora sighed. "Nobody could possibly get suspicious about an old white van with no markings."

Tina grinned. "I bet the plates are forged."

She looked at Loyd. "Come on, tell me the plates are forged."

Loyd grinned. "Yep."

"*Yesss*." Tina pumped her fist and did a little jig. "We're like secret agents or something!"

If the outside was uninspired, the interior of the van managed to be a bit more encouraging, if also lacking in originality. It was stacked with huge black waterproof cases and racks of electronic equipment. Nora picked up a small case and looked at the logo on the front; "HC" in angular stenciled letters, with the name "HUNTERCORP" stamped below it.

She smiled wryly. "Mr. E always did have a sense of irony."

Loyd reached in and pulled a case over.

"Told you it would be here," he said. "Christmas came late, but it did come."

He popped the clips, and opened the lid.

Christmas it may have been, but Nora found most of the gear curiously useless. Surveillance equipment, files, funny looking gadgets with no instructions, injectors filled with colored transparent fluid, and guns—boxes and boxes of them.

Tina, however, was noticeably excited, hopping from one side of the van to the other and examining the racks of electronic equipment.

"Oh my GAWD!" she squealed. "Do you know what this *is*?"

"No," Nora replied, scanning the bewildering array of incomprehensible glowing displays.

"*THIS*," Tina announced proudly, pointing to one of the rack modules, "Is a genuine HC model 2034 Signal Interceptor suite!" She gasped and clapped her hands to her cheeks, "And it's with the optional signal processor!"

She leaned dreamily to one side. "I think I'm having a perfect moment."

Nora tried to pretend she was paying attention and caught sight of what looked like a printer on the opposite side of the van.

"Come on," she said. "I need you to make goo-goo eyes at that printer for a sec."

After a few minutes of instruction, Nora made a quick run to the nearby hardware store for some black spray paint. By the time she got back, Tina had made a stencil that they used to paint a rather drab, if fairly clean looking HunterCorp logo on the side of the van.

The girls stood back and took a hard look at their creation.

"Are you sure it's the right size?" Nora wondered out loud.

"Are you sure it's straight?" Tina replied.

Nora stared at it for a moment. First it seemed fine, then again it seemed off. She squinted, and it only got muddier.

"We won't park by a real one," Nora said.

"Yeah," said Tina, "That sounds like a good idea."

Loyd, digging in the file case, unrolled a crinkled blueprint and squinted at it.

"Found it," he said.

Nora dropped what she was doing and crossed the room to his side. "What does it say?"

"Looks like he was thinking of going in that way," said Loyd, pointing to a spot on the plan view. He turned to Nora. "Think you can manage that?"

Nora scowled. "If he thought it was the best way in—we don't exactly have the time to find another."

"I suppose not," said Loyd.

Nora walked around to the driver's side and opened the door. Oddball sat there, lighting a joint. He suddenly noticed her, and turned to see a fierce glare stamped onto her face.

"NO," she snapped.

2

Ground Zero

The test chamber buzzed with activity. The circular room was nearly fifty feet across, and more than a hundred high, the ceiling fading into darkness. The deep shadows were lit only by the blinding pinpoints of spotlights hanging off the ceiling above, half on and half dark. Extra work lights had been brought in, looking oddly fragile on their telescoping mounts. Tangled lines of black power cables snaked across the white-painted concrete and steel floor like the web of some massive prehistoric spider. The chamber had changed significantly since its conversion from a Cold War ICBM silo. Empty of its deadly cargo, most of the now-extraneous catwalks and gantries had been removed over the last few months, leaving only jagged metal fittings with chipped gray paint.

Dr. Stein squinted against the low-mounted lights sending flares across his vision, and he peered into the dark shadows off to his right as he overlooked the test chamber. The many levels ringing the silo itself had been retrofitted to carry hundreds of sensors meant to measure every wavelength of radiation, every photon of light—everything and anything the Specimen emitted during the procedure would be recorded and logged. He stood on one of these balconies now about a third of the way up the silo, watching as a team of lab-coated scientists and workers made the final preparations to the floor brackets that would hold the Specimen in place. A moment later he saw the Foreman in his yellow Haz-Mat suit and gas mask exiting the massive shadowy tunnel to the storage area to his right. His crew and the Specimen were nowhere in sight.

Stein felt his temper start to rise, and headed for the stairs, tucking his clipboard under his arm.

He arrived on the chamber floor to find a lively discussion in progress between the Foreman and the technicians. Adjusting his hard hat, Stein stalked over to the group.

"What's going on?" he interrupted. "Where's your team? The Specimen should have been up here a half hour ago."

"They're working on it," the Foreman said. "We've got a prob—"

"I'm sorry," interrupted Stein, "were you about to say you have a problem?"

The Foreman was silent for a moment. "It makes noise."

Stein stared at him, confused. "I'm sorry?"

"Your box," the Foreman said. "It buzzes."

"It *buzzes*?"

"Yes sir," the Foreman said. "I don't know that kinda rock that thing is, but I think we should have some people check for gas before we move—"

"No no no," Stein interrupted, "Let me make this simple for you— you're late. We're a half hour behind schedule, and my ass is on the line. I don't have time for this."

"I understand sir," the Foreman said. "It's just a safety check. We need to know what this thing is."

"Frankly," Stein said, "you don't."

The Foreman folded his arms.

"Then," he said, "I'm afraid I'll have to take this over your head. We're breaking several safety protocols as it is."

Stein glared at him for a moment, then pulled a sheet of paper from his pocket and handed it to the Foreman. The Foreman stared at it for a good long moment, looked up at Stein, then back at the paper.

"What is this?" he said.

"Signed by Administrator Bird," said Stein. "If you think you can go higher than that, be my guest."

Stein stared into the Foreman's tinted goggles, and tried to look confident. His opponent's expression was as implacable as ever.

When he spoke, Stein thought he caught the slightest edge in his voice.

"Yes Doctor," he said. "One humming rock, coming right up."

"Josh!"

A loud friendly voice sucked him back to the present with a jolt. He whipped his head around to look behind him.

It was a tall man with short dark hair. He was wearing slate gray fatigues, light gray body armor, and a blinding smile. Hefting a pair of large black duffle bags, he kicked up his stride a notch, settling in beside Josh. A pair of McKnight Security shoulder patches marked each shoulder —a black spade with a white chess knight on it. The name tag on his chest read FOSTER.

"Hey man," Foster said, "how's it going?"

"I'm...fine," Josh said. "I'm just—how are you?"

Foster squinted at him.

"You look like hell," he said. "You miss breakfast again?"

"No, actually," said Josh, blinking. "Hey, do you know a guy named Bishop?"

Foster looked at the end of the hall and thought for a moment.

He shrugged. "What does he look like?"

"He's like, shaven," Josh said, gesturing with a hand over his head, "and he wears those old classic sunglasses. They're called...uh..."

He tried to snap his fingers and squinted.

"Aviators?" Foster said.

"Yeah! Those," Josh said. "Have you seen him?"

"Nope," Foster said, shaking his head. "Why?"

"Oh," Josh said. "Uh, no reason. I just...I met him this morning, and he's kind of..."

"Kind of what?"

Josh shrugged, "I don't know. Maybe I'm just tired."

"Okay," Foster said. "Let me know if something comes up. Oh, by the way—we had another meeting today."

Josh hid a scowl. "Oh you did?"

"Yep," Foster quipped. "I'm telling you, the boss likes your style. It's only a matter of time before he opens up a spot, and when they do—"

"Foster—" Josh sighed. "Look, you know I don't blame you—"

"I know," Foster said with a grin. "I wouldn't blame me either—

because frankly it wasn't my *fault*—"

Josh chuckled.

"*But*," Foster continued, "you came all the way out here because I said I could get a *security* job, and that's what I'm going to get you."

Josh pursed his lips and looked at the floor.

"Okay," he said.

Foster put a hand on his arm and the two came to a stop. Foster's voice softened a bit.

"Hey," he said. "I'm serious. Things are going to get better."

"I know," Josh nodded. "I just…" He glanced at the bags on Foster's back. "What are those?"

Foster studied him for a moment, then let out a small grin. "Have you got a few minutes?"

"Soooo?" Tina said. "What happened?"

In the dim light of the console rack, Nora stuffed the last of her white hairs underneath a maroon headband using her pocket mirror.

"What do you mean 'what happened?'" she replied, moving on to checking the fit of her glasses. She wore a white lab coat over a businesslike blue blouse and skirt with black leggings. She frowned. At first, she'd thought being able to ditch the skirt and instantly change her appearance or slip into an air vent was rather clever, but now she was beginning to wonder if they looked conspicuously mismatched. Also, the glasses were too narrow, and they had left the real lenses in, giving the world a slight warp that hurt her eyes. She made a mental note to get fake lenses of some kind for next time—providing there *was* a next time.

"Come on." Tina turned away from the console next to Nora, a mischievous grin smeared across her face. "How was it?"

"How was *what*?" Nora went over the contents of her shoulder bag once more. A purse might have been more inconspicuous, but she needed the extra space. Pepper spray disguised as a pen, gloves, night vision goggles—"

"You don't want to tell me," Tina teased. "It must have been good."

Nora gave an exasperated sigh. "What are you talking about?"

"*Loyd,*" Tina said. "Come on! How was he?"

Nora hoped Tina couldn't see her face flush in the dim light.

"Aaaah!" Tina crowed in triumph. "You're pretending you don't know what I'm talking about, but you you know what I'm talking about."

"God—Tina, this is not the time," Nora looked regretfully at the cracked screen of her phone and then pushed a small radio receiver into her ear.

"Come on!" Tina pouted. "You guys were in there for like ten minutes!"

"Five," said Nora, "and there was no way in hell. I need to focus."

"What for?"

Nora turned and gave Tina a hard look, the belt receiver held under her chin as she untucked her blouse.

"I just told you. I need to focus. Or have you already forgotten the part where we might all die?"

Tina shook her head sadly. "And now you're gonna die a virgin."

"I'm—" Nora cut herself off, stared at Tina, and cut an angry sideways glance at the driver's seat.

"Screw you," she said.

Tina giggled as she turned back to the consoles.

Nora took a deep breath, tried to calm her shaking hands, and made sure the ID was secure on her coat as the van slowed and turned off the interstate. They must be approaching the gate.

Josh's eyebrows drew together and he gave Foster a look. Foster looked offended.

"What?" he said.

"It's so...short," Josh said.

"So? It's gotta be short, or it gets awkward to use real quick. Especially in tight spaces."

"I get that," said Josh, "but how is it going to pick up any muzzle velocity?"

He pointed to the blunt muzzle of the assault rifle in Foster's hands. "Half the powder'll burn up outside the muzzle," he continued, "not to mention ruin your night vision."

"Damn," Foster muttered. "We have *got* to get you a girlfriend."

The two were standing in a small security office just inside the heavy blast door that separated the main facility—the "Grid" as it was called—from the more claustrophobic and submarine-like Test Labs. The office was small, little more than a booth with a glass window, revealing the white ribs of the tubular corridor beyond.

Foster tapped the end of the rifle. "Yeah, the flash is kinda heavy, but the suppressor cuts most of it."

He flipped the boxy weapon over. "Besides, it's a bullpup. Barrel goes all the way through it, except for bolt travel."

Josh scowled at the boxy polymer-sheathed weapon, unconvinced. "It looks like someone punched a bunch of holes in a suitcase, then put a gun inside and screwed some rails on the outside to make it look 'tactical.'"

Foster rolled his eyes. "If you want the longer barrel, you can add one. This is what they're issuing, so it's what you've got to learn to use."

He offered the weapon to Josh. The janitor looked up at him and raised an eyebrow.

"Don't worry about it," Foster said. "This is the security office. I'm king here."

Josh cautiously reached out and took the rifle. It was hefty, but lighter than he'd expected—its grips solid, but oddly comfortable. Carefully averting the muzzle from Foster as he shouldered it, he pointed it at the floor and looked down the squared holographic sight.

"Balance is nice," he said, "even with that huge mag hanging back there."

"It's caseless," Foster said. "Half the weight, half the size—and ambidextrous, perfect for lefties like you."

Josh's eyebrows went up, "Really?"

"Well, *almost* caseless," Foster admitted, "Some kind of plastic or something. The whole system is based around carrying the largest amount of ammo in the smallest package possible, and it ejects down instead of to the side."

"Oh, okay."

"That's not really what I wanted to show you though," Foster said, standing up and turning towards the duffle bag sitting in the far corner. "*This* thing, on the other hand—this is going to change *everything*."

"I see you've been practicing your movie trailer voice," Josh said, pulling the magazine from the rifle and squinting through the smoke-tinted plastic.

Foster snorted. "Just put that down and look at this."

Josh carefully set the weapon on a nearby office chair and turned to Foster just as the other man finished unfolding what looked like a gray and white full-body brace. His eyes widened.

"Is that…?" He trailed off.

"Whatever you're imagining," Foster grinned, "it's better."

"I dunno," Josh said, "I'm imagining quite a bit."

"It does that too," Foster said. He finished locking the legs and hoisted the stiff frame upright.

"Wow," Josh said, "I'd heard we were working on an Exoskeleton, but I didn't know—is this like a…this isn't just for like, carrying cargo stuff around, right?"

Foster shook his head, "Naw—they have those too, but this model is built for combat. You can't throw a truck, but if it's small enough you can flip it."

"That's crazy," Josh said. "How long does the battery last?"

"That's the real breakthrough," Foster said. "The biggest problem was trying to give it enough juice so that it would go as far as a soldier could."

"Right, I know," said Josh. "So how far did they get it to go?"

Foster folded his arms. "If you treat it right—six days, maybe a week on a single charge."

Josh gave him a sideways look. "You're shitting me."

"You caught me," Foster said, "it's more like six weeks."

Josh's eyebrows jumped. "They got it up from three hours to *six weeks*? What's it got—graphene batteries or something?"

"I dunno man," Foster said, shaking his head. "Technology marches on, am I right?"

"Marching?" Josh scoffed. "More like hitchhiking in a Ferrari. What idiot let you get your hands on one?"

"Live demonstration," Foster replied. "Later today. You should come."

"What time?"

"Ehhh, kind of up in the air at this point," Foster said. "I'll let you know."

Dr. Vance exited the main blast door of the facility into the wide main access tunnel, and caught a shuttle out. The gates to the tunnel exit weren't nearly as heavy as those to the Grid itself, but plenty big on their own, and took several seconds to fully open.

Realizing his phone probably had reception now, he immediately whipped it out, jabbed a number, and listened nervously, willing the dial tone to connect faster.

"Come on. Come on…"

Someone picked up. "Yes?"

"They blew me off. The experiment's going ahead."

There was a pause.

"I figured," said the voice on the other side. "They've got too much invested to back out now. Find Martin, and let me know the second you're online."

"Yes sir," Vance said as a white van passed the shuttle going the other way. "Don't worry. We won't miss a thing."

Nora scanned a small map of the base in the dim golden glow of the van's overhead lights and reviewed her route. Reaching the control room itself ought to be easy—it was all the way on the far side of the base, through the grid and in the missile silo sector, but there were only two checkpoints; one at the main grid entrance, and one at the tunnel leading to the test labs—mostly repurposed missile silos.

The corner of her mouth crinkled and her eyes narrowed.

Easy Peasy.

As long as her ID passed muster. The guards at the main gate, and even the tunnel entrance had accepted Loyd's, but they hadn't checked hers. Imperfections in the plan were to be expected, but not knowing where they were meant that she had to treat *everything* as if it were a disaster waiting to happen.

Trust. She told herself. *Mr. E set this up. Mr. E believed we could do it.*

She took a deep breath and closed her eyes. She wished Loyd was the one doing this part. He was always better at talking his way into places he wasn't supposed to be—being able to Push people helped.

She swept her hair back and snapped it into a hair band, examining the result in her pocket mirror. She scowled. A few white strands had snaked their way out from under the headband and been pulled into the ponytail. She pulled as many visible strands out as she could and stuffed them under the maroon elastic. She turned her seat around and tapped Tina on the shoulder. Tina half turned away from her monitors.

"How do I look?" Nora said.

"Like the Progressive insurance lady."

Nora glared at her. "Tina, I've got thirty seconds."

Tina squinted at her, wrinkled her nose for a moment, then reached out, twirled her finger around a white hair and yanked it out.

"OW!" Nora's eyelids twitched, "Tina!"

"You're good," Tina said with a grin.

Nora heard static pop in her ear, and Loyd's voice came through. "We're coming up on the blast door. Get ready."

She snatched up her messenger bag and pushed a tab on her earwig transmitter. "Got it."

Suddenly a thought occurred to her.

"Hey Loyd—if you're coming in, who's driving Tina out to the parking lot?"

"Don't worry," Loyd said. "I found Oddball's stash and hid it."

"*What?*" Nora snapped.

"Aw," Tina groaned.

The van came to a stop, and Nora pushed open the back door and stepped out, slamming it shut.

The tunnel was wider than she'd expected, almost fifty feet wide, and at least the same to its arching rock ceiling. Power conduits and cable scaffolding ran down the apex, obscured by the harsh white glare of the unshielded bowl lights that ran the length of the tunnel. It felt somewhat odd walking into the van in daylight, and then exiting it underground— The van's lack of windows was practical, but disorienting.

Nora turned right from the back of the van and saw the main entrance, a concrete edifice built into the rock wall that stretched up to the arch in the ceiling. It was fairly simple—a small guardhouse, a red-and-white striped vehicle crossbar, and the blast door itself, a gigantic steel square painted white and installed into the wall. She carefully scratched her neck and then pressed the talk button on her earwig.

"How long until Tina has control of the cameras?"

"Not long," Loyd said, nudging her elbow. She started.

"What are you doing?" She hissed.

"Coming with you," he said. "Why?"

Nora glanced down the tunnel.

"I thought you were going in through—" she lowered her voice, "—The air duct."

"No," he said. "I go in the main door. *Then* we split up."

Nora stared at him, "Since when?"

"Since always," Loyd said. "Now let's go. You're making the guards nervous."

Nora glared at him for a moment—then shouldered her bag and pasted a warm smile on her face as she approached the guard. She handed over her ID. He glanced at it, then waved her in.

"Have a nice day miss."

"You too," she said, as the door slowly swung open.

The rough-hewn rock room ahead of her was not much wider than the access tunnel—perhaps a hundred feet—but the ceiling was vaulted to fit the three-story facade of the lab facilities themselves. It wasn't much to look at; just a towering white wall with a garage door on the right and a pedestrian door to the left. The smaller door was graced with steps and a metal awning.

"See you in five," Loyd said. Walking ahead, he disappeared through the door. Nora loitered a moment to create distance between them, and admired the breathtakingly boring corporate signage. On the blank desert of whiteness a sign had been painted; the HunterCorp logo and the message, "Welcome to the Diablo Mesa Research Center." Above these, a couple of Federal branch department seals were painted in homage to the previous owners.

She decided it had been long enough to cast doubt on any connection between her and Loyd. Stepping onto the porch, she opened the door and entered the structure.

Most of the tunnel grid was either office or lab buildings arranged by department. The only exception to this rule was the main storage area, which was its own grid reached by tunnel, and the refitted missile silos, which until recently had been dormant. According to Mr. E, however, In the last few months the silo nearest the grid—Launcher 2—had been completely refitted with sensors for a secret project. A project they intended to derail.

That meant that she would be bypassing the Aeronautics and Propellent labs and heading for the very far side of the grid, to the Physics Department. Taking a quick glance at the signs and comparing them to her map, she made a few turns and headed straight through the line of buildings on the left side of the grid.

There wasn't a lot to see—just narrow white hallways and junctions, lab-coated scientists, workers in green or red coveralls, and the odd security guard in slate and gray. After fifteen minutes or so of walking, she found the room she was looking for—an unused closet near a T-junction. She looked both ways, then reached out and grasped the doorknob.

Doors were funny things. It was always harder to move something she couldn't see—the object in this case being the inside knob. But she found it immensely satisfying being able to open a locked door in one swift movement, as if it had never been locked at all. It was strange enough without freaking people out, and she'd often done it as a party trick, explaining it was "all in the way you turned it." This door took her a couple of tries to feel out the knob's location, but on the third try it turned smoothly, and she entered, swinging it closed behind her and flicking on the light.

Loyd was sitting in a chair at the far end of the narrow space, with his feet up on a card table set up in the middle of the room. Apparently this sector's custodial crew enjoyed their Chinese takeout—there were empty oil-stained cardboard cartons all over the table and shelves ringing the room, and everything smelled like sweet and sour chicken.

"I got the stuff—Took you long enough," Loyd said, getting to his feet. He began unzipping a large black duffle bag sitting on the floor at his feet. "I was starting to get worried."

Nora swept the empty takeout cartons onto the floor and dropped her messenger bag with a loud thump. "Did you tell Tina I was a virgin?"

Loyd stopped digging in the duffle bag and looked up at Nora. "Hmm?"

"You heard me," Nora said, laying out the map. "She told me while we were in the van."

"She did, did she?" Loyd pulled out two Glock pistols, a taser, three blocks of C4, and a thermite grenade, stacking them on the table next to the map.

"Thermite's for you, in case I can't disable the Specimen with the explosives," he said. "Don't look at it, or you'll burn a hole in your eyes."

Nora stared at the stack.

"Where did you get the guns?"

"Mr. E had them in here," he said.

Nora shook her head. "Well we don't need them. What, are you going to war?"

"We're trying to stop an event that could claim thousands of lives," Loyd said. "If there's anything worth killing for, that's it—just in *math* terms."

"We don't need them," Nora said. "We do this clean. Zero body count."

"You know I won't do anything unnecessary," Loyd replied.

Nora gave him a look. "You and I have different definitions of 'necessary.'"

"We have ten minutes," Loyd said. "There's no time to argue about this."

Nora shot a glance out the narrow window slats.

"Okay," she said, and grabbed both pistols.

Loyd looked down at the taser, then back at Nora. She grinned. "I call Glocks."

Loyd sighed and pursed his lips. "How *did* you stay a virgin this long?"

"Krav Maga," Nora said. "Let's go."

Approaching Stein's office, Nora took a quick moment to glance both ways down the hallway.

She smiled—there it was. She walked up underneath the security camera in its glass bubble, and held her hand palm up, as if she was grasping the camera itself in its socket. After "feeling around" for a moment, she felt she had a secure grip on the camera, and twisted, ever so slowly…

There was a sharp grinding sound as the electronic motor tried to compensate, and failed. The camera was jammed facing a blank wall.

Nora walked up to Stein's door, twisted the knob, and entered.

The office was a mess; the desk wearing a snow cap of paper, punctuated by brown folders and neon manuals. Bookshelves covered two walls, and academic accolades the other. She re-locked the door, and went to work, starting with the desk's right file drawer.

It took her several minutes to find what she was looking for, owing to Stein's haphazard filing system, but suddenly, she had it—an old, fat manila envelope labeled "Project Odyssey." She quickly stuffed it into her shoulder bag, and scanned the drawer for anything else interesting. A couple of files caught her eye—She grabbed them, and then zipped the bag shut.

The Foreman's hands were held high as he directed his crew.

"More, more—stop! Right there."

The Monolith settled into place with a soft ringing thud that reverberated through the entire harness. A series of steel braces had been set up around the hexagonal pillar of black stone, locking it into place on the silo floor. It stood straight up, exactly where its nuclear-tipped predecessor would have resided, despite its smaller size—perhaps four feet wide and thirty high. Composed almost entirely of what appeared to be rough volcanic black stone, the rock was formed into six evenly-spaced sides terminating in flat, perpendicular surfaces, as if it had been expertly snapped from a massive pencil lead. Worn, intricate carvings covered its surface, but the object itself looked oddly natural.

Inorganic, but more in a way that suggested eons-old geometric crystal rather than skilled workmanship.

The Foreman and his workers left quickly, some casting strange glances over their shoulders. It only took Loyd a few seconds to realize why—the low thrum buzzed through the room, like the sound of some huge electronic beehive. He stepped cautiously from the shadows.

"Hey!"

Loyd jumped and spun around.

Nora entered the janitor's closet, stuffed the shoulder bag into one of the shelves, and exited as fast as she had come, locking the door behind her. Looking both ways, she proceeded down the hall towards the test chamber. She glanced at her watch and swore—there wasn't much time.

She pressed her earpiece.

"Loyd?...Loyd, are you in position?"

She glanced up and immediately let her hand fall—a security guard with a pair of coffee cups was talking to a janitor just up ahead. The janitor laughed at something and broke off, heading away down the hallway to the test labs, while the security guard walked up the hallway towards her. She noticed he was wearing combat fatigues, rather than the normal security guard uniform. He was probably part of some sort of response team. He also had two cups of coffee.

Nora had missed her morning coffee.

She kept her gaze on the floor as he passed by and adjusted her headband for good measure, forcing herself to keep walking at the same easy pace.

She heard the guard's footsteps stop. A chill went through her.

They began again, but did not diminish.

He was following her.

She forced herself not to look back, and went on as before. Getting to the end of the next hallway, she made a quick right, another right, crossed her own path, and then made another couple rights, getting back on track. She took a quick glance behind—no one.

In a few moments, she was at the Test Labs security gate—just a guardhouse built into the wall, the heavy door itself, and a card reader on the wall next to it. She pulled the card from the lanyard around her neck, and swiped it through the reader in one quick stroke.

It blinked red at her, and beeped angrily.

Nora felt an icy pulse shoot through her chest. She swiped again.

Beep. Angry red blinking.

She was suddenly aware of eyes on the back of her head, and turned around a bit faster than she had intended to.

There stood the security guard, coffee cups in both hands, staring at her.

She opened her mouth to say something, and ended up just pointing at the card reader and shrugging. She swallowed hard and looked at his hands. They were full, and therefore he was at at disadvantage. He was a bit taller than average, which meant she was finished if he got close enough to grapple with her, telekinesis or no. At the same time, if he was too far away, he could simply drop the cups and put her down with the pistol on his thigh. He was a tall, sturdy looking specimen. She might be able to knock him down, or at least knock his weapon away…

She swallowed a lump in her throat.

The corner of the guard's mouth crumpled thoughtfully, then he calmly stepped up to her, and offered her one of the cups.

"Hold this please?"

It took Nora a second to pick up on what he had just said. "Hm?—Oh! Sure."

She took one of the cups from him, and watched as he withdrew a key card from his pocket, and swiped it.

The reader chirped and turned a happy green. Metal rang on metal as the massive door split at the middle and ground open. The guard gestured to the long, circular reinforced corridor beyond with his free hand.

"Ladies first."

Nora thanked him, handed back the coffee before he could say anything else, and walked as fast as she thought she could get away with down the circular corridor, keeping her eyes away from the second guard who stepped out of the security booth—a tall woman with pitch dark skin. The first guard offered the second a cup of coffee as Nora clicked past. She let out a long breath, and felt the tightness in her chest relax slightly.

Men.

Nora approached the Control Room just as a technician opened the door. As he stepped inside, she briefly caught a glimpse of the high ceiling and huge monitors hanging from the walls. She pushed her earpiece.

"Loyd. There's a lot of movement over here—we might not have as much time as we thought."

Static. Nora's brow furrowed.

"Loyd?"

She felt that icy hand tightening in her chest again. Reviewing her map, Nora headed for the test chamber.

Hurrying down the hall, her clearest thought was, oddly enough, how much she hated high heels. This particular pair had been bought secondhand, and they were a tad small—big enough to justify wearing them for the sake of the disguise, but small enough to make her wish they weren't. The glasses were starting to make her eyes itch. She took them off and soaked tears from her eyes. She heard a cart squeaking up the hallway ahead of her and looked at the floor. She hoped there wasn't a security camera in this hallway.

Josh cursed himself for not asking Ruiz which restroom needed to be cleaned. At the time he'd only wanted the conversation to be over, and expected the sick custodian to have noted down which lavatory needed to be taken care of. Unfortunately he had not—which meant that Josh either needed to clean all six, or he would have to call Ruiz and ask him specifically which one needed attention. Ruiz probably didn't know, which meant he would be irritated and then tell Josh to clean all six anyway.

Josh toyed with the idea of giving himself a chemical burn and calling it a day, but that seemed at least as problematic as his other options, with the added discomfort of being mildly dishonest. He sighed, and headed towards the front desk, letting his head droop until he was looking at the floor sliding past. Maybe he could bum a coffee off of Foster and pump a few endorphins into his brain before starting.

He heard the clicking of heels and abruptly realized they were almost on top of him. He jerked his head up and—

The bottom of his mind fell out, and he stared openmouthed at the female scientist in front of him.

She cast a passing glance at him—then turned and froze like an animal in the headlights of an oncoming truck.

Time crawled and raced. Josh's mind went blank.

Nora recovered first. Josh felt the hairs on his arm stand up, as if the air had become charged, and before he could say a thing she had punched him in the face. He saw stars and galaxies, and then he was out.

Nora immediately regretted slugging Josh. Her knuckles had made contact, not just the kinetic bolt, and that meant her wrist now felt exactly as if she'd punched a concrete wall. As he slumped to the ground, she gritted her teeth and quickly glanced up and down the hall. Empty.

"*Ssshit!*" she hissed.

"Nora?" It was Tina's voice. "Did you just deck that guy? What's wrong?"

Nora reached up and tapped her earpiece.

"We're...We're good," she said, haltingly. "I just need to take care of something real quick."

"Damn gurl, what did he ever do to you?"

"Can you get in touch with Loyd?" Nora grunted, dragging Josh into a sitting position. He was substantially heavier than she was expecting. She needed to find a closet. Somewhere nearby. Where had he come from? There had to be—

"I looped the camera, so you're fine, but there's people coming down the hallway, so get moving."

"And go where?" Nora snapped, trying unsuccessfully to pull Josh over her shoulder.

"There's a utility closet around the corner behind you," Tina said, "Hurry up! You want to get caught?"

Nora just growled in response.

"Come on," she grumbled, glaring at Josh's blank face. "You're not even supposed to *be* here."

Administrator Bird folded his arms. He was short, fat, and balding, with hair like cotton balls sticking out every which way. He adjusted his glasses and looked around the test chamber Control Center, watching the three gargantuan displays built into the wall. Each showed a different angle of the test chamber itself, and the Specimen contained therein. Half a dozen technicians sat at consoles arranged in front of him, facing the screens.

Dr. Stein suddenly entered the door to his right, looking flustered. On seeing the Administrator, he instantly cleared the clouds from his expression and smeared a winning smile onto his face.

"Dr. Bird!" he chirped. "How...unexpected!"

"I'm doing very well, thank you," said the Administrator, rubbing a few crumbs from his brown suit. "Is something wrong?"

"No," Stein said. "In fact, we're ready to proceed as soon as you are."

"Good," said the Administrator. "Please begin."

Stein nodded and approached the technicians. "All right then—ready to make history? Let's start."

"Recording active," A technician said, flicking a switch on his console. "We're getting a nice clean feed."

Stein sat at a station and tapped the mic in place. "Foreman, can you hear me?"

"Just fine thanks—stop banging that thing," came the irritated response.

"Are you ready?" Stein continued.

Silence. He directed his attention to one of the monitors, where the Foreman could be seen on the silo floor next to the Monolith. He was kneeling next to an open plastic case.

"What's going on?" Bird snapped. Stein spoke into the mic.

"Foreman?"

The Foreman withdrew an oblong shape from the case—a hexagonal rod, almost like a miniature of the Monolith itself.

"Uh..." said the Foreman, "those carvings you talked about—are they supposed to glow?"

"That's none of your concern," Stein said. "Please approach the specimen."

The Foreman did so at a half-crouch, as if nearing a cornered beast.

One of the technicians squinted at his monitor. "Doc?" he said. "I'm getting a strong signal—"

A sharp, sudden quake rattled through the room. Mugs jumped and the monitors flickered. Stein reflexively gripped his chair.

"Doctor Stein?" came the Foreman's voice. "The buzz is getting louder. *Much* louder."

"Yes, we can tell," Stein snapped. He swallowed hard and looked at the Administrator.

Bird just nodded, his eyes on the monitors. "Proceed."

Stein hesitated for a moment, then went back to his mic.

"All right," Stein said. "Do you see the hole in the surface facing you?"

"Unfortunately yes," said the Foreman.

"You're going to approach the keyhole," continued Stein, "and insert the object at the proper orientation, like we discussed."

There was a pause.

"This is a joke," said the Foreman. "Right?"

Bird abruptly pushed Stein aside, and spoke into the microphone.

"Foreman," he said, "this is Administrator Bird—You have five seconds to comply."

The door behind them burst open, and Nora entered, a pistol in each hand. "Everybody freeze, NOW."

Nora waved her weapons at the dozen or so pairs of eyeballs staring back at her, and immediately regretted not bringing a mask. She swallowed.

"Jesus, don't shoot!" Stein blurted. The technicians continued staring, hands held high.

"Nobody moves, and nobody gets hurt!" she shouted. "Everybody stay calm—"

The door on the opposite side of the room suddenly burst off its hinges in a shower of splinters, and two armed figures burst in. Both wore security gray, and were loaded down with body armor, helmets, gas masks, weapons, and what looked like a heavy-duty full-body brace.

The lead guard raised his carbine, his voice crackling through a speaker on his mask.

"FREEZE! DON'T MOVE!"

Nora saw the second guard's lunge out of the corner of her eye as the officer leaped over a desk and tackled her at the knees. She felt metal make contact with her legs. One gun went off, the other flew clear of her hand, and she hit the floor hard. In an instant, she felt a knee on her back and a hand on her neck, pushing her into the floor. Someone was screaming over the intercom.

"Are you seeing this!" the Foreman shouted. "Somebody talk to me!"

The floor was shaking, the vibration growing louder and stronger. The guard kneeling on her cast a glance towards the monitor bank. The rumble consumed every other sound, pounding against Nora's skull. The lights flickered out, leaving only short snapshots of bright color seared onto the darkness like purple ghosts. Technicians scrambled away from their seats. She heard wind battering against the walls like a hurricane.

No.

She screamed it. "NO!"

The monitors shorted out to black, shuddered, and then the entire front wall peeled back like dried paint. The black storm shredded the entire front of the room like a cheese grater, circling the bright glow beyond and sucking everything towards it—Nora saw a technician jerked into the air and swept away screaming, limbs flailing like a rag doll. The Monolith was standing—no, floating—on its own, circled by a black windstorm of debris. The carvings on its surface danced and glowed. Violent explosions of sparks popped from the destroyed equipment in front of her.

Nora was still staring out into the maelstrom when the guard yanked her upright and muscled her out of the room.

3

Fight or Flight

Fluttering doves filled Josh's vision. He was standing in a bell tower, admiring the view. It seemed vaguely familiar, though he couldn't tell why. Every time he tried to focus on some detail far below, things seemed to get fuzzy. The bell tower was ringing. It had been ringing for hours, but he hadn't noticed until just a second ago.

He pushed his hands against his head to keep it from flying apart. He could feel his heartbeat hammering the inside of his skull.

He squeezed his eyes shut and tried to block out the music. The pounding beat flashed through his brain, illuminating the crowd around him. Subwoofer stacks taller than his head stood high over a sea of hands, beating against his chest like the tides of the sea sped up a thousandfold. The speaker grew larger, consuming and blotting out the light around them like a megalithic black hole.

He couldn't remember why his ears were burning until he saw her face—not shocked, as she had been in the hall, but laughing, hair flying. Something was off. It wasn't a pure replay…something was off…

"Why did you hit me?" he said.

Someone grabbed his shoulder, spun him around, and punched him in the jaw.

The earth shook, and he fell against something hard in the dark. The door burst open.

He tumbled out into the brightness of a hallway, and landed hard. He rolled onto his side with a grunt. The wind was strong, and the lights were flickering. He tried to get his bearings in the half light, but all he could hear was the wind. People were running past him, screaming, dropping things, shouting orders.

He tried to stand, but the world went bright and blurry, and he crouched down again. A blonde scientist screamed something at him in passing, then dashed down the hall. He stared after her, tasted metal, and touched his lip—it was bleeding.

Down the hall to his right, the lights started popping out in showers of sparks, plunging the hallway into darkness.

A flash of light was marked by a sound like a bomb had gone off, and a cloud of dust billowed out of the dark. There was another flash, and Josh saw a massive jagged hole at the end of the hallway eating its way towards him. The roar of a hurricane blasted against his skin. He suddenly felt like a man on a ship at sea, as if gravity had suddenly switched directions—down, up, sideways. He screamed and threw himself down the hall, away from the howling maw, half running, half climbing.

This has got to be a dream. I have to be dreaming.

Foster yanked the fire alarm, and instantly an ear-piercing wail shot through the base. He refocused his attention to his partner, who was quickly shoving Nora down the hallway. He dashed to catch up.

His partner turned to him and shouted, her voice muffled by the mask. "Any others?"

"I didn't see any," Foster replied.

He turned and began walking backwards, covering the pair.

"Son of a *bitch*—" he spat. "We were *this* close!"

His earpiece coughed. "Full report Foster, what the hell is going on down there?"

"They did it sir. The singularity is active."

"How wide?"

The far end of the hallway started peeling away, wind rushing over them.

"At least a hundred feet and growing," Foster shouted, "You'd better get down here Boss."

The hallway was plunged into blackness, and Foster heard the sounds of electronic equipment beeping and powering down.

"Goddamnit," he cursed, and clicked his weaponlight on.

Only halfway sure of which direction was up, Josh scrambled through a corridor suddenly flooded with heavy red emergency lighting. Catching a glimpse of a lab coat disappearing around a corner up ahead, he lunged towards it as gravity gave a sudden lurch, tossing debris from the floor to the wall. Colliding with the wall, he tumbled around the turn and slid to a stop.

"Wait!" he gasped, crawling forwards, trying to catch up. Making it to his feet, Josh pumped everything into his legs and flew down the corridor. A small group of people had piled up against the security entrance ahead of him. As the reinforced door slid open, they fought and shoved their way through, leaving it open behind them.

Yes!

The doors began to automatically slide closed.

"No!" he shouted.

Pushing his legs into overdrive, shoving every last ounce of strength through them, he shot towards the door, watching the red-lit opening slowly, inexorably narrowing…

Jesus Christ please don't let me die.

He hit the two-foot gap at a sprint, rattled through, and felt the doors pinch his shoe as he hit the floor palms-first. Pure split-second reflex ripped his foot clear. The gate shut with a sharp metallic thud.

Josh took mental inventory for a moment, patted down his legs to make sure he was all there, and scrambled to his feet. The red hazard lights blasted the white walls bright scarlet, and left deep black shadows lying behind every corner. He thought he could hear people in the distance, yet the intersection was curiously deserted. Josh felt the sudden animal dread of a straggler in the dark.

He tried to calm himself by taking deep breaths through his nose, and glanced down the hallway ahead—the quickest route to the surface.

As he did so, a thought struck him, and he turned back to face the doors.

Had he truly been the last person out?

He peered through the thick guardhouse window and tried to see if anything else was moving.

"Hey!"

He spun around and a flashlight shone in his face. Holding a hand up, he squinted against the light. Despite the shock, Josh felt himself relax as the security guard lowered his flashlight.

The guard shouted something that was lost in the overhead alarm, but Josh made a guess and patted himself, making an "OK" sign. The guard stepped in and spoke into Josh's ear.

"Anyone behind you?" he yelled.

Josh shrugged. "I didn't see anyone!"

The guard nodded and pointed him down the hallway.

"Head towards the main exit!" he shouted.

Josh hesitated for a moment.

"What is it?" the guard said. "Get moving!"

"Are you sure you don't need a hand?" Josh replied.

The guard gave him a strange look and shook his head.

"Get moving!" he yelled, and waved Josh off.

Josh gritted his teeth, took one last look at the doors, and headed down the hallway.

"Go," he muttered to himself. "Go. Just go."

Nora could only half perceive the fleeing crowd around her by the dim flashing hazard lights. Her world was a pitch dark blur interrupted by flashes of red and the clipped blare of the alarm.

"Here," the covering guard said, his digitized voice almost clear above the noise. "Move to the wall. Boss is on his way."

Her guard's grip dug into her arm as they adjusted course and moved to the right side of the corridor, coming to a halt. The flowing crowd formed an eddy around them, continuing onwards and beginning to thin somewhat. Nora twisted to loosen the woman's grip, only for her to grab Nora's hand and suddenly bend her wrist. A lance of pain shot up her arm.

"*Stop*," the woman's voice growled.

Nora stopped. Her accent was strange, but the intent was clear.

Something moved towards them, causing a ripple in the crowd. Nora watched three more fully armed men emerge and join the circle. Nora suddenly noticed that, while each wore McKnight shoulder patches, their name tags had been removed, and instead each had a callsign scrawled onto the brim of their helmet.

From the trio of newcomers, the leader stepped towards Nora and ripped off her hairband, letting her crumpled white bangs fall over her eyes. Nora picked out the word "BOSS" scrawled above his goggles. When he spoke, his voice was surprisingly deep, to the point she thought it might have been altered by the mask.

"Looks like our intel was good," he growled.

Nora wondered if they had cuffed her as a matter of protocol, or because they knew what she could do with them free. She was lucky they hadn't found the safety pin she'd clipped inside her sleeve—still, getting it out was going to be a pain.

"Caught her in the control room," said the first guard, who had apparently dubbed himself MISSIONARY. "Looked like she and the research staff were having a disagreement."

Boss cocked his head. "A 'disagreement?'"

"She pulled a gun on them," the female guard—MOTHER—said in her unplaceable accent. "Two, in fact."

Nora felt Boss's eyes drilling into her.

"Well," he said, "Isn't that interesting."

"We don't have time for this," Mother broke in. "We may already have an outbreak on our hands."

"Security's on it," said a trooper. "We've already got people at the doors." His name was Ronin.

"Check on them," Boss said, turning to Missionary. "Catch any others?"

"Nope. Just her."

"There weren't any others," Nora interrupted. Boss cast her a glance, and she realized she had probably conveyed the opposite. Boss turned back to Missionary.

"How close can you get to ground zero?" he continued.

Missionary shook his head. "Ground zero is a sucking hole—if they're not with the evacuees, they're not in this universe."

"Boss," Ronin said, "I'm not getting a response from the door."

Despite the noise, Nora felt a chilling silence within the circle.

The last man, Big Red, finally spoke for the first time.

"Shit," he muttered, adjusting his grip on his rifle. "I friggin' hate Mondays."

"Split up," Boss snapped. "Mother, Missionary—Babysitting duty. Ronin—Hey!"

Ronin had slowly migrated away from the circle and stepped down the hall a few feet, apparently studying something in the crowd.

"Boss..." he said slowly raising a finger. "Does anybody else see—"

A voice—she thought it was Missionary's—suddenly exploded next to her.

"RONIN!—UP! LOOK UP!"

A ceiling tile struck Ronin on the head, prompting him to turn his gaze skyward an instant before a black shape dropped through the ceiling and tackled him to the ground. Nora saw a pair of long hooked jaws open wide and clamp shut like a trap, thrashing back and forth. Ronin screamed.

Before any of them had a chance to raise their weapons, Boss had barreled through the circle and lashed out with an armored fist, grabbing the creature behind the head. There was a metallic ring as a long blade flipped out from his arm brace and locked straight. She heard something inhuman shriek as he punched the blade through it— once, twice, three times. She lost count. He ripped the thing off Ronin and tossed the body away like a smashed tent. A jolt went through her as it hit the floor. She looked straight at the twisted shape on the ground and felt her panic rise as her mind failed to make the thing coalesce into something she could recognize. The faster ideas came, the faster they were tossed away.

Bird? she thought. *Bug? Alien? Dog? Demon? Dinosaur?*

She felt her reason slipping away and primal fear replacing it. A need to run, a need to hide, a need to see the sun.

"Mother" blocked Missionary's move towards the fallen soldier, handing Nora off to him and kneeling at Ronin's side. Pulling out a long white injector from her vest, she popped off the safety cap and stabbed him in the thigh.

"Heads up!" Big Red yelled. "Contact front! X-Rays mixed with friendlies! They're coming out of the ceiling!"

Nora followed his finger down the hall, over the heads of the fleeing personnel, and only saw blackness beyond the flickering emergency lights, slowly going out one by one. With a sudden shock, she realized the lights weren't simply going out—they would become partially obscured by something, and then abruptly explode into showers of sparks.

Mother muttered something under her breath in a language Nora didn't understand.

"Missionary," Boss said. "Talk to me soldier."

"I see 'em sir," Missionary said, calm fury settling his voice.

Boss folded his blade and stood, unslinging his assault rifle.

"Red, Missionary—" he barked, "—gas 'em. Watch your fire."

Missionary pulled a gas canister from his vest, yanked the pin loose, and let fly, hurling it over the heads of the crowd. It vanished into the black mass beyond. Red's grenade followed swiftly.

"Boss!"

It was Big Red, hand on radio.

"They're all the way up to the main entrance!" he shouted. "We're about to be cut off!"

Boss hesitated, and cast a long look at the melee behind them. Green smoke had already started to obscure the scene. Something was moving in the mist. Something she couldn't recognize. She tried to to look at the thing Boss had killed in the dark, but there were too many people in her way.

More shapes were staggering into view, falling to the ground and twitching as people dodged past them.

"Boss!"

Boss turned to Mother.

"Can he move?"

"I'll carry him," she replied.

"Do it," he said, "I'll take point. Red—watch our rear. Missionary—" He jabbed a finger at Nora. "Hold on to her."

Nora cast a look backwards as she was hurried off. She saw human figures staggering, and something else—long, clawed legs writhing in the dark. Banshee cries chased them up the corridor.

The thinning crowd ahead of them suddenly exploded into screams of terror, scattering like a flock of birds.

"Left! On the left!" Mother shouted.

Another jolt went through Nora as what seemed like the entire squad fired their weapons—a shocking, staccato explosion that shattered her nerves like a mirror. She screamed as the air itself reverberated and pounded against her. Something huge and inhuman crowed and hit the floor with a thud. Boss stomped what she assumed was its skull flat with a loud *crunch*, then waved them on.

She heard Missionary hissing vague curses though his teeth as they passed. He gave the mangled body a wide berth. Nora cast an unseeing glance at it. She didn't understand. Disaster should have meant her death—many deaths. But she had been expecting an explosion or something, not—what was happening?

Someone slammed into her, and she turned back to find the squad forcing their way through the panicked crowd. Shellshocked employees were running into them, screaming, shouting, grabbing at them for help, eyes wide with panic. The guards pushed them aside, offering no assistance besides the occasional finger pointed towards the exit. Nora slipped and fell, her hand splashing into something wet and sticky. Missionary hoisted her upright again, and then she saw the body—lying facedown in a torn lab coat dark with blood.

They came up on a half dozen security guards armed with shotguns and pistols. Boss pointed back and yelled something over the alarm. The leader nodded and waved his men forwards.

Nora caught Boss casting a look behind him, watching them disappear into the green smoke—then, without a second glance, he turned and they strode on towards the exit.

Josh was making slow progress. A third of the lights flickered wildly, and another third had winked out entirely, leaving him stumbling around in the half-dark. As he approached a junction, he saw several people dash through, and hurried to follow.

"Hey!" he yelled. "Hey, wait up!"

Turning the corner, he saw them enter a short inter-building bridge, when the lights shorted out. He heard glass breaking and sheet steel pop as it warped. There were several screams of terror, and then another sound drowned them out—A screech like a hawk the size of a tiger. A ferocious, rattling sound that stopped him in his tracks.

He whirled and sprinted back the way he'd come. Ducking into a restroom, he frantically tried to push the slow door shut, and then backed slowly away into the darkness, flicking on his phone's flashlight and shining it around the dark corners.

It was empty, except for an A-frame ladder leading up to a gaping hole in the ceiling tiles.

That meant—

His light fell on the toolbox, sitting on the counter by the sink. He leaped for it and frantically threw open the lid, tossing away the tray and digging among the heavy metal implements inside.

Ha!

He pulled a crowbar from the toolbox, tested its weight, and found it surprisingly handy.

Glancing into the mirror, he froze.

It was hard to be sure in the dim light, but he thought he had seen something drop from the ceiling. He rubbed his eyes, opened them wide, and leaned over to look at the floor by the ladder.

At that instant, something bit him on the ankle. He jumped and immediately tripped over what looked like a two-foot long madman's conception of a black scorpion. It had clamped onto his left leg. He screamed, thrashed and kicked, whacking the creature on the ground, trying to scrape it off with his other foot.

Somehow he kicked it loose, and it went skidding under the sink, hissing furiously. Bracing against the wall, it made a quick turnaround and launched back at his face. Josh slapped it away with a blow from his crowbar and scrambled for the door, yanking it open and wriggling out into the eye-wrenching red of the hallway. Something latched onto his ankle once more—one of the scorpion's huge foreclaws had clamped down like a vise on his pant leg. Josh panicked, imagining that his whole foot was being cut off. He shook and kicked with his other foot, falling over in the process. The thing hissed and he saw it suddenly contract and curl up, lashing out with its stinger. His eyes bulged and he whipped the creature against the wall, finally pinning it there with his foot. It writhed and hissed furiously, its tail slapping an angry beat against the wall and floor like a beached fish. Josh managed to prevent himself from instinctively pulling his foot away, freeing the creature. His mind raced.

Reaching out with his crowbar, he tried to hit the scorpion with the hooked end, but found it difficult to reach his feet. He grimaced and promised himself he would do more crunches if he ever made it out alive. Leaning forwards, he swung and bounced the crowbar off the bug's head. It hissed at him. He hit it again and grimaced. He couldn't get the leverage to really smack it.

Flipping the crowbar around, he decided to try the pointy end.

"Yeah, it's not working for me either," he grunted. "Here, try this."

Reaching forwards, he stabbed the scorpion between the head and the carapace and started twisting the blade around. The bug rattled and jerked, chittering and thumping the walls. With a final, vicious twist, Josh cranked it into the head, and the bug stiffened, legs twitching slowly.

Prying the pincers off, he tested his ankle movement. Everything seemed to be in place. He turned to the carcass and stared at it.

"It's all so *real*," he muttered.

A bloodcurdling shriek tore down the hall and he jumped, nearly dropping the crowbar in the process. He briefly heard something clumping in the dark.

"Oh come on!" he muttered to himself. "What now? Mutant horses?"

The lights ahead were gone, the only illumination from the adjoining passage on the left. Josh held his breath. Holding the crowbar out ahead of him in a two-fisted death grip, he strained to sift any sound of movement from the blaring alarm.

Blauuuump…Blauuump….Blauuump—

He thought he saw something move in the grainy darkness, and stiffened.

"Please be something with two legs," he whispered.

Two skeletal black forelegs emerged into the light, followed by a frilled skull with jaws like vertical hooked shears. Cocking its head to the side, it looked him over with three blank, pearlescant eyes, and let its split lower mandibles hang open. It was easily six feet tall.

"Shit," he spat, and powered back through the restroom door.

The thing let loose an earsplitting shriek. Josh skidded on the tile floor, reversed direction, and threw himself back against the door just in time to pin the creature's skull against the frame. It screamed again, pushing and scrabbling. Josh braced his feet and fought rising panic.

You panic, you die, he thought. *You panic, you die, Godpleasedon'tletmedie.*

The thing gave a push and managed to shove its head inside and curl it around to face Josh—the neck was long and flexible, allowing it to take a sideways snap at him. He jumped back, and it was in. He whacked it in the jaw with the crowbar, and dodged deeper into the restroom, the monster hot on his tail.

Bouncing off the long countertop, he threw himself forwards, tripped, hit the floor, and became a quadruped, scrambling underneath the nearest stall partition and jerking his legs clear of the snapping jaws. The creature jammed its pincers in after him, then withdrew and began probing with its long clawed forelegs. Josh stepped up on the toilet and glued himself to the back of the stall. Glancing over the wall into the partition next to him, he hesitated, gritted his teeth, turned to thrust himself over the gray sheet steel.

Something smacked his feet from under him. He lost his grip, felt the wall slide past his hands, and fell straight into the bug's open jaws.

CRUNCH.

Josh's head spun. The stench of death filled his mind, and something wet was in his left eye.

Suddenly, he realized the bug wasn't moving.

Something came to rest on his shoulder and he exploded, thrashing against the bladed jaws until he'd managed to flip himself over and put his back to the wall, pinning the bug's mangled skull with his foot.

He stared at it. Honestly, it was hard to even tell if it was conscious—the lidless mercury-silver eyes had no pupils. One of the forelegs rose and fell limply, curling like a squashed spider's. The skull looked bent, and Josh soon noticed a pool of opaque black liquid forming beneath it.

Flipping the stall door open with his hand, he dragged himself through and climbed to his feet, taking a look at himself in the mirror. His left shoulder and arm were soaked in stinking black gore, and a long cut bled freely on his forehead—the blood was getting in his eye. He staggered to the sink, plopped his dirty cap on the counter, and turned the faucets on to rinse the mess from his hands.

Something nudged his shoulder and he started.

It was Bishop, aviators perfectly in place, holding Josh's dropped crowbar.

"What the hell?" Josh barked. "Don't do that!"

"I'm sorry," Bishop said. "You dropped this."

"Uh…thanks," Josh replied, pointing to the counter. "Put 'er there."

Bishop set the bar down as Josh continued scrubbing his hands and glanced over at the stall.

"That was quite a sight," he said.

"You just stood there and watched?" Josh shot back.

"It's been a long time since I saw someone kill something like that," Bishop continued.

Josh planted his hands against the counter and groaned loudly.

"That's right," Bishop said, patting him on the back. "Deep breaths."

"Don't touch me," Josh said, pushing his hand away. "Who are you anyway? What's going on?"

"You can't stop here," Bishop said. "You have to keep moving."

"Why?" Josh said. "Is that…underground hurricane going to suck everything into hell or whatever?"

"No," Bishop said, "but there's someone you need to find, and fast."

Josh stopped, "Who?"

"I think you'll know her when you see her."

Josh stared at him for a moment.

"Wha…" He ran out of words. "So she…really hit me?"

Bishop cocked his head, then flicked his finger against Josh's forehead.

"OW!" Josh barked. "What did you do that for?"

"Are you awake?" Bishop said.

"I have a *cut* there!" Josh growled.

"Take the first left when you walk out," Bishop said, turning towards the exit. "Just follow the lights."

"What?" Josh said, squinting out of his blood-caked eye. "Where do you think you're going?"

Bishop ignored him and rounded the corner. Josh snatched up his hat and crowbar, limping after him. Hooking the rapidly closing door with his hand, he stepped into the hallway.

He looked both ways, peering into the dark. Bishop was nowhere to be seen.

"Oh come on," he muttered. Noticing the adjoining left hallway still had lighting, he looked down to the end and saw blinking bulbs continuing for some distance.

He took one last glance behind him, adjusted his grip on the crowbar, and started jogging.

The going had been slow, with Mother lugging Ronin and his equipment.

Nora squeezed her eyes shut and tried vainly to block out the ringing in her ears as Missionary hurried her along, one arm looped through hers.

They had made a detour and suddenly found themselves alone, with only the occasional dead body to keep them company. It was by no means silent with the alarm overhead, but compared to the chaos of before, it was unnervingly calm.

Nora had tried not to think about what would happen if they failed. To be honest, she hadn't really known—Mr. E had never explained it. She just knew that there would be consequences if they did. Earth-shattering consequences.

Reality-shattering consequences.

She had hoped she wouldn't be around to find out what that meant.

As they came to a left turn Boss raised his fist and pulled up short. The others jerked to a stop. For a moment, Nora wondered what they were doing—

"Oh *shit!*" Missionary hissed.

At first, all she could perceive was a constant rumbling thunder, like a stampede somewhere in an adjacent hallway. She hadn't heard it while the other evacuees had been running beside them, but now that they were alone she could hear it, rising, mixed with a curious high-pitched chittering—and then the sound burst into sudden clarity from the hallway to their left.

All heads immediately turned towards it. Weapons snapped to invisible vectors trailing off into the scarlet gloom—ending in a roiling black mass of rangy limbs pouring into the hallway. Nora caught her breath. It filled the corridor from floor to ceiling in seconds—and then vanished as it hit the overhead light and it popped in a flash of sparks.

"Weapons free!" Boss growled.

Four muzzle flashes blasted the darkness away, and a cacophony of screams exploded from the mass. Nora wished she could turn away, wished there was some way she could close her ears to the barrage of sound as streams of white tracers lanced into the black. Blazing automatic fire lit up the approaching wall of claws and chitinous limbs in strobing flashes, branding ghostly images of snapping jaws and flashing blades onto the back of her eyes. Limbs and splashes of black gore pinwheeled through the air as if a giant weed-eater had been taken to a hedge. Carapaces burst on impact, splattering gore everywhere.

"Missionary! Red!" Boss bellowed, "Frags and gas!"

Nora felt herself shaken as Missionary pulled something from his vest, passed it to his free hand, and hucked it down the hallway.

"Frag out!" he yelled hoarsely.

"Gas Out!"

Nora tensed for an eternal instant—and the grenade went off, the shockwave slamming into her as the crack of the explosion thundered down the hall. She pried her eyelids open and looked. At first it seemed like nothing had happened, and then she realized that the mass was shifting differently—its advance had been stalled, the front ranks reduced to piles of bloody mulch. The rear was now forced to dig through the bodies of their compatriots to continue the fight. Green gas filtered up through the bugs, and they too began to wilt, going into spasms; flipping and jerking, curling up like massive contorted burrs as they tumbled through breaks in the wall of the dead, only to join its ramparts.

"More—Behind us!" Mother shouted, bringing Nora back to reality. "We've got to go!"

"Right! Right!" Boss stabbed his hand to the side. "Knock it down! Go! Go! Go!"

Nora felt herself drawn away by Big Red as Missionary crossed the hallway to the right, braced himself, and kicked the sheetrock wall in with a single blow. Turning, he grabbed Nora and pushed through the new door he'd made.

The others streamed in behind him and rapidly began piling file cabinets and other furniture to block the entrance. Already she could hear the enemy nearly on top of them, growling and hissing. Red jammed his weapon through a narrow gap in the barricade and hosed the attackers, to furious hissing.

"The next room!" Boss shouted, and they piled through the far door. Boss shut it firmly as Red backed through.

The lights suddenly flickered and sprang to life, bleaching the room a greenish white. It was one of the labs, wide and full of tables packed with instruments.

Boss pointed towards Mother.

"Lieutenant, find—"

"Sir," Red interrupted, "Security's on the line."

Boss put his hand to his earpiece. "Who am I talking to?"

"Sergeant Donelson," Red said, "In Security Control."

"On the surface?" Boss said. "What happened to?—"

He stopped himself and put his hand to his ear. "Control, this is Hazard Actual...Lieutenant calm down and—"

Nora watched as Mother laid Ronin carefully onto his back, reaching a hand under his helmet to check his pulse.

"Then that means you're in charge," Boss said. "Nothing with more than two legs gets past that gate, understand?—I said *do you understand?*"

Another pause.

"Good," he said. "Hazard out."

He put his hand down and turned to Missionary. "Security retook the main door, but Lieutenant Patterson is dead."

He pointed out the door they had come from.

"That means some of us need to stay and tangle this flow up here. Lieutenant, Missionary, take Ronin and—"

"Booker's dead." Mother interrupted.

The alarm blared. No one spoke.

"Missionary," Boss said in a low voice, "Take...Take the girl and join the evac—Mother, Red, you're coming with me."

"Aye Boss," Missionary said, grabbing Nora's arm.

"Oh, and Foster," Boss said.

"Yeah Boss?"

"Don't take any chances."

"Aye sir."

Nora was staring at Ronin's body when she saw an armored hand suddenly reach in front of her and snap its fingers.

"Hey," Missionary said. "Wake up. We gotta go."

She blinked and stared at him.

"Gimmie your arm," he said, reaching out for her elbow. Nora pulled away, and he grabbed her other arm instead.

"Hey!" she blurted. He paid no attention, hefting his weapon in his right hand, and looping his left under her arm.

"Listen," he muttered, "you wanna live? You come with me. Let's go."

He kicked open the opposite door, looked both ways, and stepped out into the next corridor.

"Freeze!"

Josh pulled up short and held up his hands as a flashlight beam stabbed him in the face. A security guard stepped out from the shadows, a leveled M4 in his hands.

"Show me your hands!" he shouted. "Put the weapon down!"

"What?—Oh!" Josh slowly set the crowbar down. "I just, uh—"

"Is that your ID?" the guard said. "Let me see it."

Josh slowly reached down and pulled the tag from his coveralls, holding it out for inspection. The flashlight beam shifted to the laminated card, allowing him to see somewhat.

Another flashlight beam poked his retinas.

"Agh," Josh muttered. "Can you...We're all on the same side—"

"Keep your hands up," a second voice ordered. "Don't move."

Josh was starting to feel nervous, like a kid with his back to a dark closet.

"Uh, guys," he said. "Listen, we—" He looked over his shoulder.

"I said *Freeze*—"

"Don't move!"

"Okay!" Josh said. "Okay! I'm not moving!"

The first officer scraped blood off the tag and compared it to Josh's face several times.

"Who is he?" the second guard said, "and what's that smell?"

"Uhh..." the first guard squinted at Josh and shined the flashlight in his face again.

"Whoa—Is that your blood or someone else's?" the second officer demanded.

"Mine," Josh replied.

"Bullshit," said the first guard. "That's way too much for you to still be walking around."

"Well, not all of it's mine," Josh admitted, immediately regretting it.

"What?" The first guard said. "I thought you said it was yours?"

"No, you don't understand," Josh tried to explain. "Look closer—it's not red, see…?"

Both guards stepped back.

"What *is* that stuff?" said the second.

"There's a…" Josh floundered for words. "Look," he said, "I'm a janitor, okay? I was working, and I got this stuff on me. I'm just looking for the exit."

"Oh yeah?" the second guard snapped. "Then what was the crowbar for?"

"Sir," said the first guard. "I'm going to need you to come with us."

Josh's brows drew together. "What's going on?"

"Quarantine Protocol is in effect," the second guard replied. "Keep your hands where I can see them and try not to touch that stuff on your clothes."

"Is it dangerous?" Josh said.

"You're going to be fine," the first guard said, pulling a set of handcuffs from his belt. "Now please come with us."

"What are those for?" Josh asked.

"They're for your safety," the guard said, kicking the crowbar aside.

Josh and the guards exited the building facade into the bare and sparsely-lit tunnel section in front of the main door. It was packed from wall-to-wall with terrified civilians and the occasional security officer.

"Oh great," said the first guard. "We're going to have to push our way through that?"

"Quit your whining," said the second, yanking Josh's arm.

"Ow," complained Josh. The guard's yanking was rubbing the cuffs on his wrists. He looked down at them. He'd never really been cuffed before. It felt wrong.

Several guards were herding the mass of nervous civilians through to the series of company buses parked just outside in the main access tunnel. The first guard raised his flashlight, and started pushing his way through. Josh felt a nudge on his back, and began walking forwards into the crowd. He sighed. At least he'd made it out.

As he looked back up, he suddenly felt a chill along his spine, and turned around.

Bishop materialized out of the crowd, wearing a guard's uniform, and tapped the second guard on the shoulder.

"Excuse me," he said, "could you look there please?"

The guard, as if noticing something, turned and looked intently at the ceiling.

Josh stared at Bishop openmouthed as he produced a key, unlocked the handcuffs, and allowed them to drop to the floor with a clatter.

"Don't get on the buses," Bishop said, and turned to point back the way they had come. "Take the first left, and then straight on."

Josh regained speech control. "What?"

Bishop jabbed his finger towards the door. "Straight, and then a left," he said. "Now hurry, before the other one spots you."

Josh spun and saw the first guard starting to look around. He was several people ahead, and had apparently lost them.

"Wait a minute," Josh turned back to Bishop. "Who—"

He was already gone. Josh scowled, cast a glance over his shoulder, and pushed his way back towards the door.

Nora clenched her fists and concentrated, pulling her arms apart for the third time.

Nothing. She gritted her teeth. Holding the safety pin in her bloody hand was difficult enough without trying to find a tiny plastic tab.

Think dammit! Think!

Her mind was spinning. First underground hurricanes, now floods of giant mutant ants from hell. She kept expecting to run into Cthulhu around the next turn. Maybe she already had.

She had to get away. Find her friends. Know if they were still alive.

It didn't seem like it would be too hard—escape, followed by blending into the crowd, and then she'd slip away among the survivors. Tina still had to be receiving her—though nobody had talked in a quite awhile.

If they had any brains, they'd have split already, she thought. That would complicate trying to find them.

She immediately remanded herself for thinking that. Of course they'd stay. They were a team. A team out to save the world. Who wanted to run away from that?

Me.

Missionary turned a corner and stopped short, jerking his weapon to his shoulder.

Nora looked up, saw it was Josh, and quickly lost interest.

Oh good. She thought. *Now we can all die together.*

Josh threw up his hands.

"Whowhowhoaholdupdon'tshoot!" he sputtered.

"Josh?" the armored man's voice grated through his mask. Josh recognized the exoskeleton.

"Foster?" he said.

"Yeah," Foster said, flipping his mask up. "You're going the wrong way man. The exit is that way."

"I know," Josh said. "I mean, uh…"

Foster wrinkled his nose. "What's all that stuff on you?"

"Uh," Josh couldn't figure out how to answer that.

I fell on a bug, he thought. *It was shitty.*

He glanced at Nora. She looked more than a little shellshocked and didn't seem to be paying the least attention to him. He wasn't sure whether to be angry or relieved.

"I, uh," he began again. "I think I...there was a..."

"A bug?" Foster finished. "Are you okay?"

Josh blinked. "Yeah, I'm fine," he said. "How did you know I fell on a bug?"

"Because we're drowning in the bastards," Foster said. "Listen man, stick with us—I don't want to bury anybody else today."

"People are dead?" Josh replied. "Are you sure I'm not on drugs or—"

Josh found his thought process cut short as Foster grabbed him by the collar and looked into his eyes.

"Jeez!" He snapped. "What are you doing?"

"You're fine," Foster said. "You're officially deputized."

Josh felt the butt of Foster's USP .45 being shoved into his hands, and tried not to drop it as Foster turned away and dragged Nora up.

"What's happening?" Josh muttered.

"I said you're deputized." Foster repeated. "Say it back to me."

Josh stared at him blankly. "I'm deputized?"

"Good enough," Foster said. "Hold her."

He shoved Nora at Josh, who automatically looped an arm through hers and averted the muzzle of his pistol. She turned her head lazily and gave him a cold look. He swallowed hard.

"Josh, meet Nora, meet Josh," Foster muttered, hefting his carbine. "Let's go. Stay right on my tail."

"Uh, maybe I...should..." Josh tried to think of something to say, and couldn't. He turned to look at Nora again and found her looking back. Her expression was strained but otherwise impenetrable.

He forced a smile. "So...how was your morning?"

Josh felt an explosion of pain as her knee connected with his groin, and he dropped to his knees.

She was off and running before he had recovered enough to speak.

"That bad, huh?" He hissed through his teeth.

Nora turned to see Foster sprinting after her. She saw a stairwell door on her right and quickly shouldered through it. Spinning to face the door, she worked frantically at the cuffs. She had spent the past ten minutes trying to jam the tip of the safety pin into the zip tie's ratchet, and she thought she'd finally—

The cuffs loosened. She ripped her hands free. She made a fist with her right and took a deep breath. Energy built like a charge within her. She cocked her arm back like an archer and held it taut, waiting.

The door's narrow window darkened slightly. The instant she heard the latch rattle, she let fly. A bolt of kinetic energy split the air, slamming the door in her pursuer's face.

She heard a grunt of pain and grinned in spite of herself.

Foster kicked the door so hard that it rebounded off the wall and nearly came off its hinges.

Foster stepped through and looked up. Nora was already two flights above them, pounding up the steps as fast as she could. He turned to see Josh stumbling in after him, doubled over.

"She got away," Josh croaked.

"Not yet she hasn't," Foster replied. "Let's go."

He leaped forwards and took the steps two at a time.

Deciding he didn't want to be left at the bottom of the stairs with whatever was lurking in the hallway, Josh took the steps as fast as he could—which wasn't very fast at all. He arrived at the top of the steps to find Foster halfway through the doorway to the third floor. He spoke up.

"Hey—"

"Shh!" Foster cut him off, holding up a hand.

Looking for what Foster was looking at, Josh's gaze roved around the inside of the wide beige-carpeted hallway beyond. This floor was mostly boardrooms. The walls were old and wood-paneled, and the air was musty and dry. The alarm's blaring reached them only faintly from the lower floors—either this floor's circuits hadn't been updated, or the alarm had malfunctioned somehow.

Foster stepped carefully out into the hallway, his footsteps almost completely absorbed into the carpet. It felt strange, Josh thought, the tranquility of the moment—like disturbing a tomb in an earthquake.

Foster turned to face Josh and swept his hand to the left. "Take those." He whispered. "I'll take these." He pointed right.

"Wait," Josh said.

"What?"

"Have you got any more mags?" Josh said, holding up his pistol.

"You're not supposed to *shoot* her." Foster replied.

"That's not what I'm worried about." Josh glanced back down the stairs.

Foster looked at him thoughtfully, then pulled two pistol magazines from his vest and handed them over. Josh stuffed them into his pockets.

"Thanks," he said, and turned to the left. Keeping the weapon raised, he opened the nearest door.

The long boardroom was empty. Checking under the table, he noticed the door at the opposite end of the room was open. He headed for it, treading softly.

He found himself in another boardroom. At first, he didn't notice anything strange, but after a moment he noticed that the drop ceiling had been noticeably wrecked near the far end of the room—panels ripped out and scattered over the floor.

He immediately crouched, clicked on the USP's attached flashlight and scanned the floor for scorpions. He was in no mood to get into another wrestling match with an overgrown mutant lobster. The things were probably radioactive or something.

He was still wrapping his mind around those things. The smaller one was obviously some sort of mutant scorpion, but he had no idea what the other thing was. Some kind of crazy pterodactyl-spider-bug. They were loud too—not very bug-like. Like something out of a nightmare. All of it was.

He was starting to wonder if he weren't hallucinating the whole thing.

This state of mind was not improved when he stood up just in time to see Nora fall through the ceiling.

She hit the tabletop, rolled off the far side, and jumped to her feet assuming a fighting stance.

They sized each other up.

"That looked like it hurt," Josh said.

Nora tried to hide a wince.

"It did," she replied.

Josh glanced at the door and wondered what he should do next. He glanced up at the new hole in the ceiling, then looked back at the dusty girl in front of him.

"How did you get up—"

She cut him off with a punch to the jaw—from six feet away. The bolt of kinetic energy smashed into his already bruised nose and he stumbled back, dazed.

He threw up his arms, and felt the next two bolts slam into them. Opening his eyes, he saw her leap onto the table and launch herself onto a chair to his right—

—Which rolled out from under her. She flipped and landed with a thud.

Josh almost threw himself across the room, and shoved the chair aside. He dragged Nora upright and wrapped her in a bear hug from behind, keeping hold of her wrists.

"Just calm down for a second!" he barked.

He saw the air shimmer, felt the hairs on his arms stand up—and then she snapped the back of her head into his nose. His vision exploded into bright blobs, and the world spun.

Nora pushed away from Josh and scrabbled away on all fours, launching herself towards the doorway. As she pushed herself to her feet, still moving forwards, she slammed head-on into something large and metal. Stars and nebulas burst in front of her eyes, and she fell to the floor, clutching her head.

A pair of steel-braced combat boots appeared in front of her, and a reinforced glove met the back of her neck, forcing her flat.

Foster let out an awed sympathetic groan tempered by a repressed half-chuckle.

"Oooooh—*Damn* that looked like it hurt."

Nora clutched her aching head and growled helplessly into the carpet.

4

Office Survival

Josh groggily sat up. His nose felt it had a baseball growing inside.

"Nice job," Foster said, pulling Nora to her feet. "Glad both of you are using your heads. That's what I like to see." He stepped over to Josh and offered him a hand.

Josh took it, taking a moment to scoop up his pistol.

Foster tugged Nora out into the hallway and Josh followed, slowly, willing his head to stop pounding.

"Look," Foster said, directing his lecture to Nora. "I realize you and your Dad have issues, but he's my boss, and for some reason, he seems to want you to make it out of this alive. So—"

"If he cares so much he should've come himself," Nora interrupted.

Foster chuckled. "My point here, is that you want to live, I want to live, Josh over there wants to live—"

"The Company's screwed you," Nora interrupted. "Don't you understand? We're all dead. All for—"

"We're not dead," Foster replied. "Not yet we're not. In fact, if you don't try to pull off any more stunts before they seal the main door, we've got a pretty good chance of getting out of here alive."

"Dere gonna seal da main door?" Josh blurted. He had tried pinching his nose to stop the bleeding, but he hadn't figured out exactly where to do it, and the front of his face was streaked red.

"Yep," Foster said. "We're on the clock people, so—"
He froze.

Josh felt a chill go through him. He adjusted his grip on his pistol.

"Fozter?" he said.

Foster looked up at the ceiling.

"Do you hear that?" he said quietly.

"I do," Nora said. "It sounded like there were rats in the ceiling."

Foster turned to her, "Rats?"

Josh heard the crunch of foam tiles and spun around just in time to see the ceiling behind them collapse under the weight of hundreds of scorpions. The bugs poured onto the floor like living molasses, quickly filling the hallway from wall-to-wall.

Foster yanked a gas grenade from his vest, ripping the pin out and tossing it into the bugs' path. The sound of the fuse burning merged with the hissing of several hundred dying arachnids.

"Run!" he shouted. "Run! To the stairs!"

As they reached the door, Josh stuck his hand out to yank the knob, but suddenly he froze, turning to the elevator next to it, a look of confusion on his face.

"What are you doing?" Nora said.

Foster reached past him, yanked the stairwell door open—and was immediately swarmed by a wave of scorpions.

WHOMP!

Josh heard the pulse smack into his ear as the air shimmered. Scorpions exploded off Foster and slammed into the wall behind him, but he staggered backwards and fell into the approaching swarm, flailing wildly.

"Foster!" Josh shouted.

Turning to face Nora, he saw she was stabbing the elevator recall button with one hand while slashing the other at the incoming horde. She cast another arc of rippling force. Some of the scorpions were peeled off the floor and sent skidding, others stopped in their tracks, gripping the carpet with their claws and hissing.

On impulse, Josh stomped on the nearest bug, and it cracked open under his heel, black and grey guts squelching out the sides like a jelly donut under a sledgehammer. He stomped another one, and another, as fast as he could, trying to work his way towards Foster. Most stuck to the floor, but others leapt at him like crickets, stopping him in his tracks as he paused to peel them off. Nora slapped them back in midair, or tried to knock them off of him. He tried to pick off the bugs nearest to Foster, taking potshots at the slithering mass. The shots rang impossibly loud, even over the constant hissing.

Foster screamed—Josh looked up and saw him staggering, helmet missing, covered in black bug guts. Foster ripped another writhing thing off his back, and its tail lashed out, striking him in the wrist.

"We're coming! Just gimme a sec!" Josh shouted.

Foster crushed the scorpion in his hand against the floor and looked up at Josh. Veins stood out on his face, but his movements were slow and feverish, his eyes bleary. He gave Josh a lopsided grin and waved him off, shaking his head.

Josh's stomach tied itself in a knot.

"Foster!" Josh shouted. "Look at me!"

He took aim but something latched onto his ankle and he panicked, leaping and stomping, trying to shake it off. He flipped the scorpion under his heel and crushed it, making it hiss like a squashed fungus, then put a bullet through its head.

"Josh!" Nora called. Josh turned and saw the elevator had arrived. He looked back at Foster, and suddenly saw he was clutching at something on his chest. Foster vanished into a plume of green fog.

"Foster!" Josh called. He realized he could hear scuttling above him, and looked up just in time to step clear of another massive break in the ceiling.

Thwomp!

The pouring bugs scattered like a house of cards, and Nora grabbed Josh by the shoulder, pulling him inside the elevator and jabbing continuously at the CLOSE DOOR button. With a few jabs of her fists, she blasted most of the invading scorpions clear as the doors began to close. Josh fired several rounds through the gap, but even so they leaped against the narrowing slit, rattling like hail.

A single wriggling shape shot through the doors as they sealed, trying to scuttle up Josh's leg. Nora kicked it loose, and it slapped into the far wall, falling to the floor. Like lighting it flipped upright, its stinger held high.

Josh jumped into the air and stomped on the scorpion with both feet. It let out an abrupt squelch, like the air being forced out of a bike pump all at once, and then Josh stomped it again, over, and over, and over again, until it was barely more than a black reeking smear on the floor.

He turned and punched the elevator wall, recoiling at the pain, kicking it with his feet.

"Shit!" he roared. "Shit! Shit! Shit!"

He looked up at Nora. She was still looking at the smashed carapace, her arms folded tightly across her chest.

"What did you do that for?" Josh shouted. "I could have gotten him!"

Instead of answering, she slid down to the floor and curled into a ball, shuddering silently.

Josh looked away, chewing his lip. He had a sick feeling in his stomach he couldn't shake, like the bottom had dropped out, but everything had clumped up and stuck inside anyway.

With shaking hands, he raised his pistol and removed the magazine—half a mag left. He slid it home with a snap, and took a deep breath. The two spare mags in his pocket burned against his leg like an accusation. The last gifts of a dead man.

"He might have had a chance," Josh said softly. "With the gas and all."

Nora didn't reply.

To Officer Donelson, security was one of the most boring jobs in existence. After three years as a guard at this desert facility, most of it spent alone in this control room, Donelson sometimes felt like he'd been transferred to a desolate planet—a prison, spreading as far as the eye could see.

Every day, he'd shown up to work with a badge on his chest and a gun on his thigh, and he'd never fired it once in anger. Never a shooting, never a fire—he'd scared away some punks painting graffiti on the walls a few months ago, but that had been it for almost the entire year to this point. It had been so exciting at the time—the chase, coordinating with his buddies over the radio. They'd all gone to the bar and celebrated afterwards, making jokes about how they'd all be promoted, now that they were heroes.

But that's all they were. Jokes. Everyone knew they'd been in practically no danger at all.

Nothing like this.

Now his watery, blurring eyes snapped from monitor to monitor, his hands gripping the armrests so hard he had to keep stopping himself from tearing them off as he watched the world come apart live on CCTV.

In less than two hours, his job had gone from blue-collar rent-a-cop to the last line of defense. It had all started when he'd gotten a call two hours ago from Lieutenant Patterson, the Security Chief at the facility. He'd kept it mystifyingly curt, saying that there had been an "incident" inside the test labs, and that from now on they were to take all orders from an asset using the callsign "Hazard" as gospel truth, and that they were to do so because it would be both *"advantageous,"* *"useful,"* and help out with their *"monkey nuts"* problem.

It had taken a couple tries for Patterson's odd speech pattern to ring a bell in Donelson's mind, but as soon as it had, he had enthusiastically acknowledged the order.

The codebook in his desk didn't provide much more context than that, besides confirming Patterson's order was legit. Whoever "Hazard" was, according to protocol, he was now in absolute control.

Or at least, as much control as anyone could be.

The bright, bluish screens showed him people running, employees piling onto trucks in the tunnel while security guards blazed away in the dark at things that refused to coalesce into something he could recognize. Fires burning, sparks flying—everywhere he looked something was going desperately, horribly wrong. One of the cameras panned slowly across a hallway that had been splattered red, and he turned his head away, rubbing the bridge of his nose.

Security is already down there, he reminded himself. *This is your job. Stay here.*

It felt so strange—he knew where each location he could see was, but the carnage displayed on each screen seemed unreal, the very color of blood tricking his mind into imagining it was all some sort of prank or movie. These things didn't happen in real life. They didn't happen to normal people. Not to him.

Another camera screen blinked out. Nearly a dozen had gone down in the first five minutes—mostly around the test chambers, which was where he assumed the...*incident*, had started. That rate had slowed significantly, but every now and then another one would flicker and die, leaving only a NO SIGNAL message on the monitor.

He wondered why emergency services hadn't arrived yet. That was just as well, he supposed—he still didn't know what he was going to tell them had happened. Active shooter? Terrorist attack? Fire? It was nearly impossible to tell with the lighting in there. He could barely see people running around and screaming—or at least he thought they were screaming. There was no audio. Hell, it could be the goddamn zombie apocalypse for all he knew.

The radio crackled, and he recognized the voice of Sergeant Hendricks. "ICP this is Guardian Two-One—Come on Control, pick up!"

Donelson snapped up the radio and mashed the talk button. "Guardian this is Incident Control," he said. "I'm reading you loud and clear."

"Hazard's approaching the front door. Can you see them?"

Donelson scanned the monitor banks for a moment, then found the camera outside the main tunnel entrance and magnified it. From the camera's point of view, mounted next to the checkpoint booth that housed the door controls, he could clearly see the arched tunnel entrance embedded in the hillside.

"The doors are still closed."

"I know," Hendricks' snapped. "We're right in front of them. Can you see *inside*?"

Donelson grimaced and pulled up the interior camera. *Stupid.*

The doors were away up the hillside from his location in the main office building by the lakebed. Guardian, Hendricks' unit, had been thrown together out of nearly a dozen guards armed with anything and everything they could dig out of the armory. Hazard team, and whoever was left of Patterson's unit, was still inside.

The interior camera showed three personnel buses lined up in front of the blast doors, with security guards piling out and heading for the rear of the convoy.

"They're at the door," he said. "Looks like something's chasing them."

"I know that," Hendricks replied. "Can you see what it is?"

"Nope—Lighting's still shit."

"Dammit."

"All units!" the radio crackled. "This is Hazard One-One. Open the gates—we're coming out!"

"Okay, get ready!" Hendricks hollered, presumably to a guard. "Open it up! Now! Now! Now!"

Donelson switched to exterior cameras, and saw the main doors crawl apart into the walls. As soon as the gap was wide enough, the lead bus lurched forwards, and was quickly followed by the other two. As the last bus pulled out, he saw perhaps a dozen figures spill out behind them—mostly security guards, all of which looked like they'd taken a beating, and two—no, three—men in full body armor and exoskeletons. As soon as they exited, one of the armored men began pointing and giving orders—Donelson guessed that was Hazard Actual—and they seemed to be in some sort of discussion when the last Hazard member collapsed to his knees, just outside the door.

"Close it!" Hendricks shouted. "Close it now!"

It happened so fast Donelson almost didn't see it—something large and black lunged out from between the doors and locked its jaws around the man, dragging him back through the door. The guards, half of which were facing the wrong direction, sprayed shots through the door before one dove for the man and snagged his feet before they disappeared through the doorway. The group became a dog pile as more guards closed in and tried to get a grip on the man, some jamming the muzzles of their weapons through the doorway and firing blindly into the darkness beyond.

Donelson could barely hear the commotion over Hendricks' radio.

"Stop the doors! Stop the doors!"

"Red! Reach for me!"

"I can't hold him! Somebody grab him! Grab him!"

"He's slipping!"

"Shit! Shitshit—"

"Get out of the way!"

The radio was all shouting and screams of pain for a few seconds. Donelson suddenly saw dozens of long black limbs snaking their way up through the still-open crack of the door, pulling through vicious snapping mandibles. Hazard Team adjusted their fire and pushed them back. The guards pulled back their comrade, his arm shredded and bloody, and backed away from the doorway. Donelson couldn't see the Hazard operative.

"CLEAR!" Hazard Actual bellowed. "Frag out!"

Donelson thought he saw the motion as Actual tossed the grenade through the door, and men dove to either side. A burst of smoke and dust shot out, chunks of black debris cutting though the smoke like gravel under spinning tires.

Donelson heard Hendricks clear his throat. "Holy…What the hell were those things?"

"Lock it down." Hazard Actual growled.

"They were like—"

"Lock it down NOW."

The door closed the last few feet, and sealed with a thud.

The elevator came to a stop, and the doors opened. Josh brought the pistol up to eye level, gripping it tightly in his sweaty hands. He cursed under his breath and wiped them against his coveralls, keeping the weapon raised, and carefully looking both ways before exiting into the darkened hallway.

"Is it safe?" Nora whispered.

Josh quickly looked around the half-light of the t-junction. Where they were, the lights had almost gone out completely. To his left the lights flickered intermittently, and to his right was pitch black. The best-lit hallway was straight ahead, leading towards the exit.

"Is it safe?" Nora repeated.

"No," Josh said, swallowing the stone in his throat. He started walking forward. "This way."

The hallway was lined with windowed labs and offices on their right, and on their left was the occasional window to the "outdoors"—just gray stone tunnel wall with a safety net hanging across it.

The door. Josh commanded his scattered wits. *Find the door.*

As they approached the junction, Josh heard footsteps. Big, heavy footsteps. At first he thought it was two people, but it was too coordinated for that—

He turned to the nearest door on his right and quietly pushed through into one of the labs, Nora right on his heels. Quickly closing the door behind them, he crouched next to the wall, below the windows and out of the way of the dim light shining through the shades. The room was full of rows of long countertops with sinks and scientific apparatus.

Nora, crouched next to him on his left, tugging on his arm.

"What is it?" she whispered. He turned to put his back against the wall and put a finger to his lips, listening hard.

His heart jumped as he realized the footsteps had stopped.

Not this way, not this way—

They started again, still slow and steady, but still getting closer. He froze and took in a breath, forcing himself not to look up and try to see where it was. Mentally he tracked the creature's position as it thumped down the hallway like a soft-shoed horse. His shivering hands held the USP .45 in a death grip.

It's going past you. It hasn't seen you. It's going to walk right past you if you just stay still.

Josh turned to see Nora sitting like him, with her back to the wall, eyes squeezed shut. She swallowed and her throat jumped.

He let go of the gun with his right hand and touched her sleeve lightly. She started slightly, and pushed his hand away.

Distracted for a moment, a heavy footstep shocked him back to the present. He held his breath. The footsteps had stopped right next to them.

Josh could see the jagged, lethal shape casting its shadow through the shades and onto the floor. The large angular head was searching, turning back and forth, holding for a moment, then moving again. He swallowed and adjusted his grip. This was one of the big ones.

He studied the shape of the head. It looked bony, but that didn't mean it was bulletproof. The thin neck was out of the question, unless he was grappling with it at point blank. He scowled. He didn't want to do that again. What about the body?

He held still as the footsteps began again, moving down the hall.

Josh began to let out a sigh of relief.

Then, twenty feet to his left, he heard the window glass shatter, and the creature clambered over the wall and into the room, turning to face them with a loud banshee screech like an asthmatic sea gull.

Josh didn't think. There wasn't time to think. He reached across Nora, forced himself to place the glowing front sight center of mass, and pulled the trigger.

The report was much louder than he'd thought it would be. He'd never fired a gun indoors, though he'd heard several that day from afar off.

Not waiting to see the effect of his first shot, he fired as fast as he could. The creature rushed towards them as if nothing had happened.

Nora half-leaped, half-clambered over him trying to get away, and sprinted lengthwise down the room, away from the bug. Josh somehow managed to hold onto his gun and roll himself into one of the aisles between countertops. He leaped to his feet as another earsplitting call pounded his ears. The thing had to be right on his heels—

It passed his row, and suddenly he realized it wasn't after him. Nora had dashed straight back until the room ended, and then made a right turn and kept going, the shadowy black creature in hot pursuit.

Josh saw his opportunity, lined up the green dot, and pulled the trigger.

Nothing happened. He twisted the pistol sideways. The slide had locked back—empty.

Frantically stuffing his hand into his pocket, he pressed the mag release with his other hand and heard the empty magazine clatter to the floor as he drew the fresh one out of his pocket.

Nora screamed, and he looked up to see her sweep a rack of test tubes off the countertop and into the face of the creature, who bulled right through it and tackled her.

Josh felt the mag snap home, ripped the slide back, and focused on the front sight, squeezing the trigger.

The creature screamed at the first shot, reared on the second, and toppled back as the next two punched through its skull. Writhing on the floor, it crawled backwards, scything its claws through the air as if trying to wave him off. It was hard for Josh to tell if he'd hit something vital—but he was surely causing it pain. He stepped up to where Nora lay and stood before the creature as it lurched upright, its legs staggering and shaking. He could see hard-strung tendons underneath the chitinous armor. It moved with a sharp birdlike quickness, constantly twitching, as if it was jacked up on amphetamines.

It opened its split jaws obscenely wide and hissed at him. Josh aimed at the roof of its mouth, approximately where he thought the brain case was, and shot it. A splash of aerosol black gore burst out the back of its head, and it went limp, its skull hitting the floor with a dull thud.

He felt Nora's bloody hand on his arm.

"Are you okay?" he said.

"I'm fine," she said, peeling the hand off his shoulder and looking at a small cut on her palm. "I'm fine. Just a scratch." There was another cut bleeding down her cheek.

"You sure?" Josh said. He turned and looked her up and down, but couldn't see any other injuries.

"I'm sure," she replied, removing her lab coat and pulling at the hem, ripping off a strip of fabric. "Just…a bit shaken up."

"I would be." Josh clenched his hands to try and stop them from quivering.

Nora glanced over his handiwork. "So…you killed it?"

Josh looked at the bug again. It didn't move.

"I'm thinking yes," he concluded.

"Huh," she snorted. "I guess so."

Somewhere down the hall, he heard a banshee scream. Something thumping down the hall.

Lots of somethings.

Nora stopped wrapping her hand and looked up. "Oh God no."

Josh scanned the back of the room and saw a door. "This way!"

He pulled it open and they slipped inside the adjoining passage, closing it behind them. Through the window Josh could see shadows gathering beyond the window shades.

"Back! Back!" he hissed. "Keep going!"

They sprinted down the passage to the far door, which opened into a wider main hallway. Josh heard the thunder of footsteps increasing. "Back! Go up!" he said.

"Up where?" Nora sputtered, but Josh had already pushed past her to a door labeled STAIRS.

Her eyes widened and she reached out a hand. "Wait—!"

Josh opened the door. The stairwell was empty. "What?"

"Wha—" Nora glared at him. "Why did you do that?"

"Because we've got to get out of here!" Josh shot back.

"Don't you remember what happened with the last one?"

Josh looked up the stairs, listened, and then looked back at her and shrugged. "It's clear. Let's go."

He took the stairs two at at time.

Nora hesitated—then heard something banging on the door to the lab down the hall. She swallowed hard, and entered the stairwell.

Josh was waiting for her on the landing, crouched next to something. When Nora saw what it was, she inhaled sharply and looked away.

It was a body.

Donelson turned to Vance. Vance looked blankly back.

"Well?" Vance said.

"You didn't see it?" Donelson said.

"*I* didn't see it," said Dr. Martin. His accent carried a noticeable English tinge.

Donelson sighed, tapped a few keys, and the screen's image wound back at high speed, shadows and light fighting for space in the frame.

Donelson tapped the spacebar and brought them to a sudden halt, then tapped it once more to play it forwards. He pointed to the screen. "There—wait for it."

Vance rubbed his chin and squinted through his glasses at the image onscreen. Dr. Martin, of a much pinker, and somewhat rounder and balder persuasion, stuffed his hands into his brown jacket pockets and frowned in concentration.

Donelson turned to face them again. "Well?"

Vance shook his head. "It's too dark."

"Okay," Donelson said, "I'll narrate—see that?"

He pointed to a slightly lighter blur on the screen. "That's a guy. There's his hat, there's his shirt or whatever—"

"Okay," Vance said.

"—And here he goes in the door—" Donelson continued,

"Is that a men's room?" Martin asked.

"Yeah," Donelson said. "Now watch what happens."

He scrubbed forwards and paused as the bug tried to push its way inside.

"Oh whoa!" Vance said. "He's got one after him!"

"Uh huh," Said Donelson. "Now watch what happens next."

The bug pushed its way in, and the door closed.

There was a pause.

"Is that it?" Vance said.

Donelson was winding forwards again. "Wait for it."

The door opened, and Donelson paused.

"*There.*"

Vance stared at it the monitor a moment, then his scowl slowly disappeared.

"Wait," he said. "He...What?"

"So that lucky fellow down there just gets away?" Martin said.

Donelson slapped the desk with his palm and pointed a triumphant finger at him. "Yes! So you saw it too?"

"Saw *what*?" Vance said. "So he managed to kill one of those things? That's great, but they're really not that tough on their own." Mentally he chafed at Dr. Martin's use of the word *fellow*. In his opinion the older man had spent far too much time in his study, and some days Vance thought it showed a bit more than necessary.

Martin snorted, "Not if you are *armed*, of course."

Vance folded his arms and shrugged. "I still don't see why this is significant."

"It's not," said Donelson. "Not yet."

He switched cameras. The next clip showed Josh being detained by security.

"Wait," Said Martin. "So we have him in custody?"

"Nope," Donelson said. "Watch this."

He pulled up another camera. It was overlooking the crowd of employees moving towards the main door. The two guards, with the man between them, marched into the crowd and became separated. Abruptly, the guard still with the man looked up at the ceiling curiously.

"Where did he go?" Vance said.

"There!" Martin pointed. "He's just...he's walking back inside?"

"What, did they just let him go?" Vance said.

Donelson shrugged. "I can't tell—look, now they're freaking out."

Both guards were pushing frantically through the crowd, as if searching.

Vance shook his head. "I don't understand. That doesn't make sense at all."

"It gets worse," Donelson said. "That's just the old stuff—this is where he is *now*."

He pulled up the elevator camera, showing Josh and Nora.

"You've got to be *kidding* me," Vance hissed. "Where's the radio? We need to call Hunter *now*."

"Where's the man they sent her up with?" asked Martin.

"I dunno," said Donelson. "There's damage to the system. One moment they were all heading towards each other, and now your officer is missing and this guy is with your prisoner there."

"So you don't know what happened?" Martin said.

"A guard and a prisoner come in one side, a stranger enters the other, and the prisoner and the stranger walk out the other side cool as can be," Donelson said. "What do *you* think happened?"

"Oh, God," Nora muttered, covering her mouth.

Josh held a finger to his lips and glared at her. She quietly closed the stairwell door behind them and looked out the narrow window.

Josh listened hard. Every now and then he'd hear a short chitter or squeal—inquisitive, or perhaps they were signaling each other. The stampede, however, had died down. Every now and then he heard a thumping sound traveling along the wall, but it always seemed to be single individuals, scattering back throughout the maze of rooms and hallways. He made a mental note not to fire again unless he absolutely had to—they could probably handle a couple of those things at once, but not more than that. Not with one pistol and…whatever it was that Nora had.

He wondered briefly if she could shoot, and rolled the mangled body onto its back to get at the man's belt buckle. After a moment, he managed to free the belt, and swung it around his waist.

"What are you doing?" Nora whispered.

"What does it look like?" Josh said. "I'm looting a body."

Josh cinched the belt tight and slotted his USP into the empty holster. That made him one large flashlight, a pair of handcuffs, some pepper spray, and—most importantly—two whole mags of .45 slugs richer. The holster was right-handed, so for him it was backwards, but he planned on carrying it mostly in his hands anyway.

He felt sorry for the man, in some place he'd pushed to the back of his mind, but once he had realized the guard was no longer in any pain he'd made a conscious effort not to think about how how he'd gotten that badly mangled—His last sight of Foster was still fresh in his memory.

That, and the dead bug they'd left on the floor two rooms back. He'd killed one. On purpose this time.

It wasn't much, really, in the grand scheme of things, but it *felt* different. If you shot them, they died. No tactical calculus there. At some point in the last twenty minutes or so he'd stopped thinking like a civilian in an evacuation line and started thinking like a survivor—a warrior, a caveman in the unforgiving wild. Civilization had ceased to exist in the thousand yards of sheetrock, steel, carpet, and solid rock that lay between them and the surface. That kind of thought could have triggered panic, or maybe despair. It was still there, seething beneath the surface—but that wasn't all he felt. One one level, he felt like he was about to explode—on the other, he felt totally calm. He'd stopped thinking of the bugs as triggers for his imagination and started to think of them as obstacles, with strengths and weaknesses. They might just make it out of here.

Find ammo, smash door, protect wo-man, he thought to himself. *Boom Shakalaka.*

It was bothering him that he couldn't find the man's gun. It wasn't next to him, or even still in his holster. He'd rolled the body over, but the man hadn't been lying on it.

It was fine. He didn't need a second gun.

He took a quick glance at the man's face, and noticed his eyes were open. He closed them, and yanked the ID tag from his shirt, muttering a few words under his breath.

Nora came up the stairs behind him, the increasingly bedraggled lab coat tied around her waist.

"I'm gonna be sick." she muttered, covering her mouth.

"Good," said Josh. "Maybe it'll throw them off our scent."

Nora looked up. "What?"

"Let's go," Josh said, and bounded up the steps. Approaching the second-floor door, he looked in through the window, opening it carefully.

It was a wide office space, packed from wall-to-wall with workstations. He walked into the room softly, peering into each cubicle over the his pistol sights.

There was an audible click behind him. He froze.

"Freeze," said Nora.

Josh turned around slowly, lowering his weapon. Nora was holding the dead guard's USP with both hands, leveled at his chest.

Well, that answered the question of where the gun went, he thought. The only question now, based on how awkwardly she held it, was whether she was more likely to shoot him on purpose or by accident.

"Is it chambered?" Josh said.

"Don't move." Nora snapped.

"What about the safety?" Josh said. "Is the safety off?"

"Of course the safety's off!"

"Okay." Josh said, forcing himself to nod slowly. He took a long, easy glance around the room. He hadn't had time to check the corners properly.

"Give me your gun," she demanded.

Josh thought for a moment. "No."

Nora's eyes flashed. "Give it to me *now*!"

Josh held a finger up to his lips and pointed at the stairwell door.

"You remember what just happened?" He said in a low voice. "You fire that gun and they'll be all over us in ten seconds."

Nora glared at him, but did nothing.

"Look," Josh said, quietly. "If you're looking for answers, you're asking the wrong janitor."

Nora scowled. "What the hell is that supposed to mean?"

"Bishop." Josh said. "Or whatever his real name is. Aren't you working with him?"

Nora stared at him, confused.

"No!" She hissed. "What are you talking about?"

Josh studied her face hard for a moment. She *seemed* surprised.

"I don't know." Josh said. "He was snooping around this morning, asking about me and you."

"What does he look like—wait a minute." Nora shook her head. "No. You're not getting out of this one. Why are you here? Why are you working for my Dad?"

"I don't work for your Dad!" Josh blurted. "I work for *HunterCorp*. Does your Dad OWN HunterCorp?"

Nora's expression didn't change. The fog in Josh's head cleared.

"Oh." He said. "So when Foster said—"

"Who's Foster?" Nora interrupted, without changing expression.

Josh stared at her, unsure how to respond. Something caught in his throat. He looked away and kept his voice even.

"Foster's the guy we left behind."

He looked up, met Nora's eyes, and saw them melt slightly. She lowered the gun.

"Oh." She said simply.

"He got me the job here." Josh continued. "After I got expelled from Arbor."

Nora's forehead wrinkled. "Foster went to Arbor?"

"Yeah." Josh said. "Sat in the back, with me."

He passed a hand over his chin. "He had a beard then. Wore sunglasses all the time."

"And he worked for HunterCorp then?"

"McKnight Security," Josh said, "After the Marines, of course. I think HunterCorp owns them. They paid his way."

"And Bishop works for Hunter?."

Josh heard something like footsteps down the stairwell behind them. Nora hadn't noticed yet. It was still a couple of walls away, but to him it was still more than enough reason to keep moving.

"Like I said," Josh replied, letting an urgent edge slip into his voice. "I thought he was with you. Looks like I was wrong—but if either of us want to live to find out who he *does* work for, we'd better get a move on. That means the gun points somewhere *else*, got it?"

Nora chewed her lip and held his eye for a moment, then nodded sharply.

"Okay." Josh said, turning to leave. "Let's go."

5

Elevator Music

Josh stepped into the elevator and pushed the button for the bottom floor. Swapping his half-empty mag for a full one, he automatically checked if there was a round in the chamber, and held it loosely in his hands, ready to take out whatever appeared beyond the doors when they opened.

Nora watched him, and attempted to pull back the slide on her weapon.

It didn't move.

She pulled again—nothing. Finally she took a firm grip on the slide and yanked it back hard.

A cartridge flipped out the ejection port, bounced off the wall, and landed on the floor between them.

Nora shot him a look, swept her highlight over her ear, and stuffed the gun into one of the pockets of her lab coat, knotting the sleeves securely around her waist.

Josh glanced at the cartridge where it lay on the floor, then back at the door.

They stood in silence. Josh tried to think about where they were going, or about the elevator music, or about anything else. Anything at all —

"Are you going to pick that up?" he asked.

"Be my guest," Nora said.

"Are you sure?" said Josh. "That's a whole shot—"

"Nope. All yours," Nora said.

Josh considered debating the point, but pocketed the round.

Find ammo, He thought to himself. *Protect wo-man.*

The lights suddenly flickered and blinked out, accompanied by the low whine of motors shutting down. Josh felt the car stop moving.

"Oh great," Nora muttered.

Josh clicked on his flashlight and squinted at the glare coming off the brushed metal doors. He pointed the beam at the ceiling.

"What are you looking for?" Nora said.

"The emergency exit, I think," Josh said. He reached up and pushed aside a transparent plastic ceiling tile. His brow furrowed.

"What's wrong?"

"I found the door," Josh said, "but it looks like it's locked from the outside—and it's a little high."

"I can fix that," Nora said, moving under it and raising her hand towards the door.

"Oh?" said Josh, noticing the subtle ripple in the air around her hands. "Uh…okay."

He watched her fingers feel around in the air for a few moments.

Josh folded his arms. "So…What else can you do?" he said. "You can punch someone across a room, break zipties, kick people in the nuts…"

"I didn't use it for that," Nora said.

Josh grimaced.

"Oh, okay," he said. "That makes me feel a lot better."

Nora twisted her wrist, and Josh heard the snap of a bolt unlocking. Nora pushed outwards and the door flipped open, revealing the pitch black of the elevator shaft. She smirked at Josh.

"I guess you should probably rest before trying to climb out," she said. "I mean, seeing as you're *injured* and all."

"Actually I'm just scared of the dark," Josh said with a quick smile, pointing upwards. "If you really want to go first I can give you a boost though."

The corner of Nora's mouth twitched, but she said nothing. Looking up, she crouched slightly, Josh felt a static buzz in the air. Suddenly she leaped straight up, grabbing the edge of the door and pulling herself through.

Josh watched her feet pass through in time to see her do a full handstand inside the shaft, then flip gracefully over and disappear momentarily.

He took a deep breath.

"Cute," he said. "Cute, funny, *and* talented. Of course she is."

"What was that?"

Josh looked up to see Nora peering down at him.

"Nothing," he said. "How does it look up there?"

"It looks like nothing," Nora said. "Hand me your flashlight."

Josh looked down at his pistol light for a moment, confused, then remembered the flashlight on his belt—a huge long metal bar, the kind you could use as a club if you really wanted to. He pulled it out of the belt clip and held it up. Nora reached down and it leapt up into her palm.

She clicked it on and waved the beam around the interior of the shaft.

"Looks like there's a door here," she said. "Do you need a hand up?"

"Nah," Josh said, looking up at the opening, then hid a scowl. It wasn't much more than a foot above his head, but the edges didn't seem to have much in the way of easy grips.

"One pull up," he muttered to himself. "Easy. Just one pull up."

He wound up like a spring, and jumped.

He touched the metal rim, then fell back.

Nora lost interest and began looking around the interior of the shaft.

Josh decided that standing on the handrails was the best way to get enough height. Jumping up, he pushed off the rail with his foot.

He slipped.

Nora heard a thump and a muffled curse.

She stepped to the edge of the exit and shined the flashlight down at him.

"Are you sure you don't want help?" she said.

"Yep," Josh replied, putting his hand up to block the light. "Can you—can you point that thing towards the wall or something? I can't see."

She tilted it up, the light shining onto the wall of the shaft above her.

"That's good," said Josh, looking up at her, "Right th—"

His eyes widened, and Nora stared at him quizzically. "What?"

"Don't move!" he whispered, slowly reaching for his USP.

Nora heard something rustling in the darkness above her, and a chill buzzed down her spine. With her left hand on the flashlight, she formed a fist with her right and clenched it.

Wait for it. She thought. *Don't move—*

Something hissed, and she spun around on reflex, throwing out her hand and releasing the pulse.

It missed. The scorpion hit her face an instant later, clawing and hissing. She stepped back, lost her footing, and fell, bouncing off the cable mechanism and sitting down hard on the steel roof. She screamed, trying to pull the cold, writhing creature loose. It hissed again, so close she could feel the musty, bitter air against her face.

Josh's looked wildly around the elevator like a caged rat, listening to Nora's screams. He leaped up, grabbed the edge firmly, and with a single, massive effort, pulled himself up until he was halfway out of the hatch, with the rim cutting into his stomach.

He reached out, and grabbed a metal brace. Once he had a foot on the rim, he virtually leaped out onto the roof of the elevator.

The shaft was pitch dark except for the flashlight's beam shining where it lay, casting a monstrous shadow on the wall as Nora struggled and wrestled the two-foot black arachnid gripping her arm. The tail curled back and whipped forwards, over and over again. Nora jerked her head back and forth, trying to pull herself away as each strike lashed at her neck.

Josh grabbed the thing by the legs on each side and yanked hard, once, twice—it came loose. Lifting it bodily, he swung it as hard as he could. The bug went sailing across the shaft, slamming into the wall. It scrabbled for grip, failed, and fell out of sight between the wall and the elevator.

After a moment, Josh heard it bounce off a girder with a loud *bong*.

He turned to Nora. She lay in a heap, staring up at him. She was slightly pale, but otherwise looked all right.

"Are you okay?" he said.

She just stared at him for a second, then burst into laughter.

Josh smiled along, trying to figure out what was so funny. "Uh…I guess he's gonna feel that in the morning."

She nodded, still laughing, and held out her hand. Josh took it and pulled her to her feet.

"I'm really sorry," he said. "Some guys just won't take no for an answer, y'know?"

"Good thing you were here," Nora said. "You're such a good *friend*."

She said the last word with a weird growl that made Josh stop for a moment.

"Uh…yeah," he said. He tried to look closer at her expression, but it was hard to discern in the dim light. "I mean…are you sure you're okay?"

"Sure…Yeah…" Nora rubbed her forehead and staggered. Josh quickly steadied her.

"Are you sure it didn't sting you or something?" he said.

"Sting?" Nora slurred. "What're you talking…bout—*AH!*"

Just then she had turned her head, and suddenly grimaced.

"I think I've got a…a knot in my neck. Can you—" She pointed to the back of her neck. "—Can you look—"

"Sure," Josh replied, and she turned around. His gut turned.

He almost didn't need the flashlight to see it. There was a huge blotch on the back of her neck, and it was growing fast.

"Oh no," he muttered.

He tried to pull the collar of her shirt down a bit so he could see how far it went, but she flinched.

"Don tuch it!" Nora yelped.

"Sorry," Josh said. "Uh…I don't want to scare you, but—"

"Don tuch it," Nora mumbled. "I'll be fine…"

She reached down to pick up the flashlight, but Josh beat her to it, snatching it up and putting a hand on her shoulder.

"Whoa, don't move for a sec," he said. "Let me take a look at this."

"NO," Nora snapped, ripping herself away. She turned around and shoved him, staggering. "Just don tuch it. It's a fine."

"I think you're bleeding," Josh said. "This is serious."

"*You're* a bleedig," Nora retorted. "Go…go poop yourself. I'll be fine."

She tried to take the flashlight, but Josh pulled it away. He gave up trying to convince Nora of anything and decided to try getting them out of the elevator shaft. Using the flashlight, he discovered they were between floors, but the set of doors to their left were only a couple feet above the elevator roof. After a short search Josh saw something that looked like a latch. He pushed Nora into a sitting position next to the cable assembly.

"I'm going to be right back, okay?" he said. "Just sit right here for a second."

"You're tuching bhe." she said, pointing to him with a wandering finger. "Ima…tell my boyfren…about you."

"You do that," Josh said. "Just give me a second."

Stepping around the cable assembly, he reached up and fiddled with the latch until it finally loosened. With some effort, he jammed his fingers between the sliding doors and pulled them apart. The hallway was fairly well lit—apparently the power was stable here. He turned back and stepped carefully to Nora's side.

"Okay," he said, "Ready to go—are you okay?"

Josh could see shining wet streaks running down Nora's face. She sniffed.

"I'm sorry," she moaned. "It wasn't my *fault*. I *tried*!"

"It's okay, let's talk about this later, all right?" Josh replied, taking her hands in his. "Ready? Come on—"

He pulled her to her feet, but she didn't move.

"I don wanna," she muttered. "Jus tell me the trugh."

"That's fine," Josh said, "It's this way. Come on…"

He tugged her over to the door, slowly, catching her as she tripped over cables and metal bars.

"Where ar we going," she mumbled.

"Somewhere you can lie down—but not yet! Not yet!" he warned as she started to sit. "Come on, just a bit further—"

Letting go of her hands, he pushed the doors open and clambered out into the hallway, setting the flashlight down and glancing both ways before beckoning to her.

"I'm up here," he said. "Can you see me?"

"I'm not ready," she said. "Can't you respeck that?"

"I know you're not ready," he said, "but it's important. We're sitting ducks here."

She shook her head. "No. You said we don't have to, and I'm not ready."

"Ready for *what*?" Josh snapped. "It's like, a step further!"

Nora gazed dully at the three-foot ledge. "It's a *big* step."

"Okay, yeah," said Josh. "But I've got you. Just give me your hand."

His heart skipped a beat as he thought he heard something rattling above, and he reached through, grabbing Nora's hand and pulling her up. "Come on…"

"No," Nora shook her head in a wide arc, like a pouting toddler.

Josh sighed and reached out, turned her around and pulled her back against the open doorframe, slipping his arms under her hers and locking them around her chest. Leaning back, he lifted her out of the elevator and set her down in the hallway.

She turned around and slapped him.

"Ow!" Josh blurted. "What was that for?"

Nora wagged her finger at him. "I tol you don *tuch* me!"

Turning away, she wove her way down the corridor.

Josh, noticing a first-aid kit on the wall, removed the plastic case from its mount and opened it, trying to make sense of the various plastic-wrapped objects inside.

"Hey," he called out, as loud as he dared. "Do you want to stop and sit down for a second?"

"No!" Nora shouted, rubbing her neck. "I have to find a masseuse!"

"A what?" Josh called back absently. He quickly jogged after her.

"A massufangin!" Nora mumbled loudly, and leaned against the wall to stop the world from spinning. Her USP slipped from her coat and clunked to the floor.

"I don't think they have any of those down here," Josh said, closing the first aid kit. He picked up the pistol and kept it ready, glancing behind him every few seconds. The truth was, he was much closer to panicking than he wanted to admit.

Nora placed her forehead flat against the wall and made a loud guttural sound, like a lion hocking up a loogie. Josh sighed. They needed somewhere to hole up. Somewhere sealed off, where he could take care of her and was easily defensible. Somewhere with running water.

A few turns later, Josh pushed Nora into the women's restroom seated on a swivel chair he'd commandeered from one of the offices. Despite everything, it had felt strange deciding which restroom to pick, and he'd finally gone with the women's on the idea that if Nora woke up it wouldn't feel as odd. It was a pain fitting the chair through the door, but he wasn't about to look for one without armrests—they were the only thing keeping her from falling out. He nudged her to the middle of the room, and swept the restroom stall by stall.

Clear.

Josh chewed on his cheek and tried desperately to think of something constructive to do. Truth be told, he wasn't sure how fatal whatever she'd been stung with was. He had no idea how much venom had made its way into her bloodstream before he'd thrown the scorpion down the elevator shaft. If he was really lucky, she'd wake up with a few hours with a headache and otherwise feel fine. If he was unlucky—which was much more likely...

He didn't want to think about that.

Tipping Nora's head up, he tried to pull one of her eyelids open with his fingers.

"Nora?" he said. "You still with me?"

"Noh," she said. "I have boyfren stupit."

Josh sighed. "Good. Now—Nora?"

Her eyes rolled back into her head, and she rolled over.

Expletives rolled through his mind like fire alarms.

Oh shit.

Ohshitohshitohshit.

He flipped open the first-aid kit and scattered the contents across the countertop. By this time his inner monologue was going strong.

What's the point? He fumed. *Nobody has antivenom for a newly discovered species of demon space bug!*

Shut up or say something constructive. He retorted.

He picked up random tubes filled with fluid, some green, some red, and tried to read the curiously obscure labels; "ReGel—FIRST AID COMBAT REGENERATIVE AGENT INJECTOR," "ANTIVIRAL AGENT INJECTOR," "FIRST AID ANTIBACTERIAL AGENT."

No antivenom.

He threw his hands up. "What the hell is this stuff?"

He racked his brain for any shred of advice he have ever heard about poisonous bites, but the only thing that came to mind was sucking it out of the wound and spitting. He made a face. The idea made him nauseous.

He shot a glance at Nora's limp figure.

No. Not doing it.

Moving behind the couch, he took another look at the sting. It looked swollen and was starting to turn green.

Josh swallowed hard and squeezed it on both sides. A small drop of something greenish brown emerged.

He made a face, screwed up his courage, and set to work.

Twenty seconds later he was emptying his stomach into the nearest toilet.

"Stupid idea," he coughed, "Stupid."

He squeezed his eyes shut and punched the metal stall with a shout of rage.

For Christ's sake do something!

His mind raced.

A half-formed thought popped into his head, and he burst out of the stall, rushing over to the first-aid kit and rummaged through it.

There.

He scanned the small print on the "antiviral" red tube, looking for side effects, or its intended use—anything.

"SIDE EFFECTS: nausea, vomiting, dizziness…"

Check, check, and check. He thought.

He flipped the tube and looked for its name. If he was going to use it, he wanted to know what it was *supposed* to be used for.

"INTENDED USE: Counters effects of compound injection via stinger."

Josh scowled. What *kind* of compounds?

The kind you don't talk to the FDA about.

Suddenly everything fell into place. The vague wording, the simple injection method, its unusual placement in a common first aid kit. Admission of knowledge hidden in plain sight. No one would ever question its existence until it was needed—

He scanned the pictorial instructions on the side, flicked the safety cap off the back, and darted over to Nora, holding the injector like a hammer, orange safety tip down. He was suddenly glad she was wearing very thin clothing—well, *more* glad.

He held the injector up and aimed at her left thigh.

Make it count…

He swallowed, remembered the instructions, and stabbed the injector into her leg.

He felt a positive click as it hit, and the tube hissed.

"One, two, three…" he counted to ten, and let go, looking up at Nora's face.

Nothing.

He didn't know what he had expected to see—of course it would take time to work. Hours, probably.

Sitting back on the cold tile floor, he leaned back against the wall opposite her, and let the tube clatter to the floor.

"Please work," he prayed under his breath. *"Please, please please work."*

Nora was developing a fever.

Josh wasn't sure whether to be happy or concerned about that. On the plus side, it meant that her body had recognized something attacking her and was hitting back. That was what an antiviral treatment was supposed to do, right?

Unless it was antivenom. He had no idea how that worked.

The more he thought about it, the stranger the scorpion's behavior became in his mind. It looked like the thing had been waiting in ambush. Had it just been targeting her incidentally? Or was it some sort of bio-engineered monster that intentionally sought out humans?

He stood slowly, and looked into the darkened U-shaped tunnel leading out to the main hallway. A natural choke point. Perfect for defense.

He looked up at the ceiling and sighed. Drop ceiling. Perfect for getting buried in two-foot-long poisonous arachnids.

There was nothing for it—they were going to have to keep moving.

He began packing up, assessing his meager supplies.

Adjusting the gun belt around his waist, he stuck one USP into the backwards right-handed holster, and set the other on the counter for the time being. The one and a half mags went into his front pockets, which, plus the two on his belt, the full USP, and Nora's mostly-full USP, made him feel fairly safe, at least in the ammo department.

The first-aid kit was clearly not meant to be belt-mounted, but he was going to have both hands full, so he awkwardly looped it on and made do. The remaining antivenom injector and two "ReGel" injectors went into his zippered side pockets. He wasn't entirely sure what they did, but they said "first aid," and the pictorial instructions implied that their main purpose was to stop bleeding. If nothing else, they would give him time to strap some gauze or something onto a wound.

Turning around, he took a deep breath and contemplated the best way to pick Nora up. If he tried to fireman carry her, he figured, he'd be able to move, but not shoot, or at least not very well. Dragging her seemed too slow. Carrying her horizontally would leave his hands full as well.

He frowned. There weren't a lot of good ways to get this done.

Obviously she couldn't just ride piggyback because she couldn't hold on. For a second he thought he had a brain wave and considered cuffing her hands and looping them over his neck—then she wouldn't *have* to hold on—but a second later he dropped it because it would cut off his air supply, not to mention be extremely awkward to explain when she woke up.

He finally settled on trying to carry her in front. He knelt by the couch, worked his hands underneath her back and knees, and tried to stand up.

He utterly failed the first time and fell forward.

"You're heavier than you look," he muttered.

The second time, he lost his balance and fell on his back, with her on top of him.

"Oh no, of course not," he grunted, replying to her imagined retort. "I meant that as a compliment. You look—" He wrestled himself upright. "—Great. You look great. Beautiful even."

He struggled to his feet.

"That's good Josh," he muttered to himself. "Very smooth. Compliment the girl *after* you find out she's spoken for."

Now that he was standing, carrying her was much easier. He walked over to the counter and retrieved his pistol.

Suddenly, he realized she was probably light enough to move to one of his shoulders. He knelt down and tried to stand her on her feet, but this didn't work, so he just lunged upwards and flopped her over his right shoulder.

He groaned as the weight nearly pulled him over, but after a second of shifting her weight around, he steadied. Looking out into the darkened U-turn, a brief shiver passed through him as he found himself imagining the things hiding in the shadows.

Another thought flashed through his mind. It didn't quite banish the evil thoughts from his mind—but it did change their context somewhat. Here he was, with a weapon in one hand and a girl in the other, preparing to brave the shadowy passageways and make their way to safety.

"Boom-Shakalaka," he grunted, cocking the USP's hammer. "I Josh da Barbarian. Josh stop for nothing!"

A nervous chuckle forced a grin onto his face. He shifted Nora's weight, and stepped out into the passage.

6

End of the Line

Josh was quickly discovering his role as a barbarian hero came with a certain amount of thematically appropriate baggage. A pre-made labyrinth, for one. Half the doors seemed to be locked, and half of the rest were broken—these were kind of a wild card, as broken could mean "open" or "wedged shut." About every five minutes he was having to put Nora down and pry something open. He came to look forward to these, however, as thematically appropriate barbarian-scale musculature hadn't come with the job, leaving him to work with his normal-scale, wiry build. He decided to take Foster up on his invitations to the gym more often—and then felt a pang as he remembered that wouldn't be happening.

More than once, he was forced to stop and wipe tears from his eyes. They never quite seemed to dry.

Surprisingly, he found the alien presence in this particular area was rather sparse, and he only stomped one lone scorpion before finally reaching the rock-walled lobby. There had been a couple hundred people there the last time he'd seen it. How long ago had that been? Two hours? More?

The blast door leading out to the main access tunnel—wonder of wonders—was open.

Looking both ways down the dimly-lit half-cylinder, a chill went down his spine as his body adjusted to the cooler air. It wasn't just the cold though—He felt his his nerves had been strained taut for so long that they were beginning to pull out of place. The short break after he'd injected Nora had helped, but coming down off the shock of almost losing her, combined with all the other crap he was trying to not think about, was quickly exhausting him. He felt like if he blinked too hard, or stopped putting one foot in front of the other, that he'd simply collapse and pass out.

Awake. He told himself. *Focused. Stay focused.*

He hissed through his teeth and blinked away a bead of cold sweat. Where were all the bugs?

Had they found a way out? Did they communicate somehow, passing the word down? He'd heard hundreds in the corridors below.

Where had they all gone?

Maybe the doors of the tunnel were shut, and they were looking for more exits. Or maybe the tunnel doors were open, and they'd all escaped. All the others were open.

Seeing that he had perhaps a half mile to walk to get to the end of the passage, he glanced around and spotted a medium-sized cargo truck parked against the far wall about fifty feet down. Sure, it would attract more attention, but he was pretty sure the bugs hadn't figured out how to open car doors. It had an oversized back like a moving van's, but Josh didn't really care what was inside. Discovering the passenger door to be unlocked, he pulled it open and looked inside.

"Oh—Jeez…" He looked away and tried not to throw up. The stench from inside was overwhelming, like death—but not quite. There was an abrasive edge to it, like something else at work. Looking back, Josh examined the scene further, forcibly holding down the contents of his clenched stomach.

A man in blue coveralls sat slumped against the steering wheel, his face pale as wax and beaded with sweat. His skin was webbed with dark veins tinted an unhealthy bluish green, and his dull eyes were stretched wide open. For a second, Josh thought he was bleeding from the mouth, but the fluid dripping out of the corner of his sagging lips held no trace of reddish tinge—It was flat black.

Letting out his breath slowly, Josh looked down and saw the keys were still in the ignition.

Josh set Nora down slowly and looked both ways down the tunnel. Leaning over, he grabbed the man's sleeve and pulled him onto his side. The man's head lolled back, and Josh stifled a gag.

There was a large bruised sting on the man's swollen hand.

Despite his clammy skin, he obviously hadn't been dead very long, and the body was far from cold. Josh managed to yank him from the cab, dragged the body to the far wall, and left it there. He took a brief moment to search the man's coveralls, but all he found was a couple of key cards and his wallet. He took the cards, but left the wallet intact.

Something banged into something metal up the corridor, and he froze.

It didn't repeat, but he figured he'd long overstayed his welcome. Quietly stealing back across the tunnel, he picked up Nora and loaded her into the passenger seat, trying hard not to slam the door as it closed.

It was still louder than he had hoped, but he put his faith in the vehicle's construction to protect them and entered the driver's seat. Pausing to check both pistols were chambered, he prepared to start the truck. Just as he was about to turn the key, however, he stopped.

Picking up his flashlight, he clicked it on and carefully leaned Nora's head forward to check her neck, peeling back the adhesive dressing he'd slapped over it.

There they were—darkened veins, like the long diffused ink of an old tattoo.

She was still shivering and felt almost hot to the touch—the fever was intensifying, sweat beading on her skin.

Nora muttered something.

Josh instantly switched priorities and lifted Nora's head up. "What? Did you say something?"

The veins on her face had begun to web and soaked the light up like a sponge. One eyelid slowly lifted halfway, then dropped again.

"Nora?" Josh tried to keep the urgency out of his voice. "Hey—can you hear me? What were you about to say?"

Nora groaned and slumped forwards. Josh pushed her head back up. "It's me, Josh. Can you hear me?"

She didn't answer.

Josh shot a look at the body across the corridor, and set his jaw. Fastening Nora's seatbelt, he settled back into the driver's seat, made sure the truck wasn't in gear, and turned the key.

"All preventatives administered," Vance said, stepping into the Control Room. "We'll keep the survivors under quarantine for the time being. We had a couple of noncompliance issues, but I doubt security will have any real problems."

"Hunter'll be happy to hear that," Martin replied, his eyes still fixed on the monitor bank.

"Tell me about it," Vance said. "There were quite a few stings—to think we almost didn't stock up for this. Now *that's* bullet-dodging my friend."

"You did your best. We all did."

"Our best might not be good enough."

"Then worrying does us even *less* good," Martin replied. "Get something to eat or drink, maybe some sleep—we've got a long day ahead of us."

Vance frowned, but with a final sigh he turned and left. Martin sat down and began tapping his fingers on the desk.

Donelson gave him a sideways look. "Relax, huh?"

Martin stopped himself and smiled wryly. "Hmm—I think I'll go for something to drink as well."

He stood up to leave and paused at the door. "Do you want anything?"

Donelson shrugged, "7Up and a Mars bar."

"Right."

The engine chugged to life, but didn't move when he released the brake.

Josh looked down. It was a stick shift.

"Crap," he muttered.

Looking down at the gearshift beside him, Josh felt a curious mix of warm familiarity and stumped panic. He had driven his grandpa's tractor once or twice, which had been stick shift, but that had been a long time ago, and Grandpa had done most of the actual shifting. The engine chugged away in the back of his mind, needling him with the fact that he would probably be attracting visitors if he didn't get a move on in the next thirty seconds or so. Eyes flicking back and forth, Josh suddenly remembered why there were three pedals, gingerly pushed on the one he hoped was the clutch, and gingerly pushed the stick into first gear.

A horrendous grinding sound prompted him to immediately return it, which led to more grinding. He stomped on the clutch and held it down.

"SHIT!" he banged his forehead on the steering wheel. "Shitshitshit."

He thought for a moment, and tried moving the gearshift again.

No grinding.

He shifted it into first, and gingerly let the clutch up.

The truck lurched forwards, and he stomped on the brake. The engine died.

Josh sighed, and turned the key again.

As the engine turned over, Josh briefly wondered if there was something else he should be doing, and then the truck jolted forwards violently and died again.

Josh sucked in a breath through his teeth, and closed his eyes for a moment.

Think before you leap. Think. Think. OH—right.

He depressed the clutch, moved the stick out of gear, and turned the key.

After a couple seconds of playing musical chairs with the pedals, Josh finally got the vehicle into first and trundled it out into the wide tunnel thoroughfare, clipping the cargo container in front of him on the way out.

Josh gritted his teeth and reminded himself that insurance rates were the least of his issues at the present moment—he had successfully gotten the vehicle to move. Besides, he didn't need the left headlights anyway.

As the truck chugged down the tunnel, he squinted ahead through the dim light. The harsh overhead bowl lights seemed to have been cut out some distance ahead, and all that was left was the dim red hazard lights on each wall and his remaining headlights. He couldn't tell how far it was to the door, but Josh couldn't help a slightly optimistic feeling.

On the home stretch. Just a little farther—Unless the doors are locked, and then we die alone. Fantastic.

After a little while trundling along in first gear, Josh decided it was probably worth attempting to bump it up a bit. After a little grinding and experimentation, he managed to get the truck into third and attain pretty brisk pace—

Something darted into his headlights, and he hit it at full speed with a loud thud that shook the vehicle. He reflexively stomped on the brakes.

The engine died, and Josh felt the pedal fighting him as the truck screeched to a halt.

Pausing for a moment, Josh re-swallowed his spleen, and managed to engage the parking brake. The headlights cast an odd pattern now that they were splattered with whatever he had hit, casting a blotchy high-contrast pattern over everything. It was nearly impossible to see ahead.

Drawing his weapon, Josh made sure the safety was off, and shakily pushed the door open, jumping to the ground.

This is stupid. Stay in the truck!

What if I hit somebody?

Did it look like somebody?

Despite having a pistol that already mounted a light, he had decided to bring the big flashlight with him. Supporting his gun hand with the wrist of his flashlight hand, Josh directed the beams to the crumpled mass in the middle of the road.

It was ridged and black, and beneath it was an opaque and quickly widening puddle on the ground in front of him.

Idiot.

The headlight still needed to be wiped off. He quickly cast the beam around him, seeing nothing but piles of boxes and shipping crates on each side. Crossing the grill, he holstered the flashlight, pulled his non-gun sleeve over his hand and rubbed the sticky headlight furiously.

There was a crash behind him—he spun around and raised his weapon.

The scorpion froze in the light, midway down the side of a crate. Josh took a moment to aim—it moved.

He pulled the trigger twice, the muzzle flash lighting up the tunnel.

The scorpion popped off the ground and flopped across the road, scrabbling in a mad circle across the floor.

He shot it once more for good measure. It stopped moving.

Letting out a long sigh of relief, he turned just in time to see jaws launch out of the darkness and clamp onto his thigh.

"Whoa!" Donelson jumped forwards in his chair and began pushing buttons. "Got a live one!"

"What?" Martin turned away from his papers and squinted at the screen. "What's going on?"

"It looked like gunshots, but now—" Donelson leaned closer to the screen. "I think it's...Hey, it's that guy!"

Searing pain shot through Josh's leg and he jerked the trigger. The pistol went off. Josh found himself lifted by his injured leg and dragged to the ground, feeling as if a pair of steel pincers were tearing into his thigh. Fire burned through his veins, and he found himself kicking, hitting, trying to wave off or shoot the thing attacking him all at once.

It let go and screamed into his face as he jammed the muzzle against it's head. He pulled the trigger over and over again, fighting to control his aim.

BAM! BAMBAMBAM!

In the wildly pitching beam of his flashlight, he saw splashes of gore and viscera explode out the back of it's skull. It twisted away, writhing and gurgling on the ground.

Josh's leg wouldn't stop burning.

He screamed in pain, fighting his contracting muscles to try and sit up, crawl backwards, move, *anything*.

Tearing his eyes away from the blood gushing from his leg, he shone the flashlight wildly in all directions, trying to spot any other attackers in the shadows.

There's more. There's always more—

He quickly unfastened his belt and awkwardly tried to knot the stiff nylon around his thigh, holster and all, trying to stem the bleeding. He couldn't tell how big the gash was, but...

His vision began to go spotty, and he was having trouble sitting up.

"No..." he muttered. "Nononono..."

Breathe. Come on, focus.

Everything was getting blurry.

The injector.

He coughed. *I can't.*

A thought tugged at the edges of his blurring consciousness, blaring like an alarm in his head. *Now. Do it NOW.*

With numb, shaking fingers, he fought back the darkness closing on the edges of his vision and scrabbled at the pocket zipper until it opened, stabbing in his senseless fingers and pulling out whatever he could grab. Tubes spilled over the wet floor, and Josh realized he was sitting in a widening pool of blood.

He somehow managed to orient the tube in the right direction and stabbed it into his leg. He hoped it was one of the ReGels. He could barely feel the prick of the needle.

"Owh." he murmured. *One, two, three, four...*

Josh's eyes flew open, and he sucked in a deep breath. He was shivering and cold, but he felt like he was burning up inside. He seemed to have a fever. He tried to move, and his leg gave a painful twinge. He gritted his teeth.

His pistol sat on his lap, the flashlight still shining across the floor. He picked it up and clicked it on and off. The beam was still strong—he couldn't have been out long. In fact, the more awake he got, the shorter he began to suspect his blackout was. That would explain why he hadn't bled to death—

As the beam of white light crossed his injured thigh, Josh did a double take.

Reaching out carefully, he pushed aside the shreds of bloody fabric, and scraped away the half-coagulated blood, revealing a jagged and lumpy scar composed of healthy pink tissue.

The wound was gone.

Carefully, he flexed his leg, bending his knee back and forth. A couple of minor twinges, but nothing debilitating.

"Holy shit," he muttered, then again. "Holy *shit!*"

He grimaced and carefully drew his legs under him, gingerly testing his healed limb. It complained, but not much. Glancing at the floor, his eyes briefly widened in astonishment at the size of the pool of blood he'd been lying in. He wasn't sure how much one had to lose before dying, but if it was more than that, he would have been surprised.

Bringing his mind back to the mysterious noises in the darkness, Josh quickly glanced at the dead bug. It was lying in it's own puddle of precious bodily fluids. He wondered if he had been lucky enough that somehow only the one bug had heard his gunshots.

After a couple seconds of waving the flashlight around, he didn't see anything. There was no point in staying any longer. He got the truck in gear and lurched down the tunnel. Glancing at his fuel gauge, he noticed the needle was hovering just above empty. He scowled.

Speaking of gas...

He shifted in his seat, feeling an uncomfortable pressure in his bowels.

Frrrrrp.

He grimaced. He felt like he was trying to pass a rock or something. Also, he felt very hungry for some reason. He checked Nora's forehead and found her fever had died down a bit, and she still had a pulse.

Frp. Frrp. Fp.

Josh tried to remember what he had eaten that day. It couldn't have been much.

Bfrp.

He wanted pizza.

Frzrp.

Like, a whole family-sized meat pizza with bacon, and sausage, and cheese, and anchovies…

Fbrp. Frrp. Frrrrrrrrrrrrp.

He didn't even like anchovies. He decided to add pepperoni instead.

He tried to peer into the darkness ahead, and suddenly realized his bladder was full.

That's when it hit.

He stomped on the brakes, accidentally killing the engine, and spent precious seconds frantically looking for the nonexistent "park" gearshift, hissing a stream of uncouth nouns and adjectives. He finally just stomped on the parking break. Throwing open the door and climbing down off the truck as quickly as he dared, he tried to hold in the seething volcano threatening to rupture his innards. Fumbling for his zipper, he waddled into the darkness near the tunnel wall, and finally managed to sweep his coveralls clear before the mountain blew it's top.

"What do you mean he's up—"

"Just look! He's right there!" Donelson jabbed his finger at the screen, gesturing wildly for Martin to come closer, "Look! See? The truck's moved, and he's getting out."

"I can't see," Vance said.

"Try this," Donelson said, switching to infrared.

All three of them gave a collective gasp of surprise and disgust.

"Oh God!" Vance blurted, and averted his eyes.

"So…" Donelson muttered. "He'll live?"

Vance nodded rapidly. "Yes. We, uh…reduced that side effect, but never quite eliminated it—"

Martin cut in. "And there's still nothing coming up the tunnel?"

"Nope," Donelson said, switching cameras, "Not a damned—"

He stopped and looked closer.

Vance frowned, "Whoa—what's that?"

After spending five minutes trying to find something to wipe his ass with, Josh reluctantly sacrificed his underwear to the cause and left them behind to die.

He still wanted pizza.

Two minutes later, the truck coughed and stalled, and he had to restart it. A minute after that, he reached the main doors, and the truck died. Josh tried to get it going again, but the engine just turned over a few times and then muttered out.

Josh sighed, and with the pistol twitching in his sweaty grip, opened the door and stepped out. He'd put his belt back around his waist and holstered the extra pistol in it, along with the flashlight and a crowbar he'd found in a tool box underneath the seat.

Twenty feet in front of the truck, the corridor's half-circle terminated in a massive pair of sliding steel doors riding on a track flush with the concrete floor. The doors were actually fairly well lit; it was still gloomy here, but a pair of bowl lights were still on overhead, and he didn't have to use the flashlight except to read small print on the signs.

Josh took a closer look at the dark pile of debris centered at the door seam and confirmed his suspicion; bug carcasses. Whole bodies were crushed flat between the huge steel frames, with broken and burst insectoid carapaces and long thin limbs hanging half in, half out. Some of them were fifteen feet above the ground. Black gore covered the ground in a sticky sulfuric oil slick. He covered his mouth with his sleeve and turned to the guardhouse on his right.

The long structure was embedded in the wall to the right of the forty-foot-wide doors. It jutted out somewhat—the main doors didn't roll all the way into the wall, so it didn't block the driving path—and was made of mostly light materials, with large windows halfway up the sheetrock walls.

The single window facing back down the corridor was blocked after thirty feet by a large shipping container, and his truck parked next to it in the middle of the road. The broken stub of a traffic boom gate stood uselessly by the door whose window had been smashed out.

Josh glanced back towards the truck. The vehicle and cargo container took up a substantial part of the passageway, but the far side of the corridor remained clear. He scowled. Too clear. If he took cover in the guardhouse and got cornered, something could sneak around the truck and be almost right outside his front window. Of course, there was nothing there now, but two things about this tunnel had been bothering him ever since he entered it.

One, what if the door wouldn't open?

Two, whether it opened or not, how screwed would he be when the aliens heard the noise and came running down the tunnel?

If the sheer mass of bodies now piled by the door were any indication, the correct answer was "screwed as hell."

Then again, they hadn't heard the truck, so who knew what might trigger another rush for the door.

He pushed the thought from his mind, and carefully pulled open the guardhouse door.

Glass crunched under his shoes as Josh stepped inside. There had been quite a fight in here—there was blood everywhere, some of it red, some of it black. He waved the flashlight beam across a couple of desktop workstations, the weapons locker, and finally the duty guard's station, with the bar gate and door switches mounted on the wall next to it. One of the monitors was split into quarters, showing four security camera views. CAM1 showed a view farther down the corridor from the ceiling, CAM2 showed the guardhouse area, CAM3 displayed the inside of the guardhouse, where Josh saw himself standing next to the console, and CAM4, according to the label, would have shown the outside world, but didn't. All it showed was a blizzard of static. For all he knew, there was a snowstorm outside. It wouldn't have been the weirdest thing to happen that day.

He gave the door button a hard look. He hadn't planned beyond reaching the doors, much less what would happen once he got out. With any luck, security or the military was here and turning anything with more than two legs into a thin black paste—but what if they were after more than that?

He'd been bitten, and Nora had been stung. There had to be dozens of walking wounded tracking otherworldly pathogens and toxins all over the place.

It would be a quarantine nightmare.

And if that was the case, what were the chances that they all ended up in shallow graves in the desert?

He found himself weighing the morality of fighting back if someone took a shot at him, or just turning himself over to be…neutralized. Better to live than to die—but better to die than start an epidemic.

He swallowed hard and pulled himself back onto more clear-cut ground as another possibility occurred to him. What might happen if he were to open these doors only to discover the surface swarming with alien horrors with a preference for live prey? Looking down at the pistol in his hand, he thought of the arms cabinet behind him, and wondered just how much firepower they kept on hand for wayward tourists.

Turning quickly, he glanced over the double doors. A locker that size could hold a couple of full-length shotguns, a scoped rifle, maybe a brace of assault rifles, or even one of those caseless carbines Foster had showed him, plus enough ammo for a decent-length firefight.

A padlock held the taupe sheet metal doors closed, and the front was splattered red.

"So much for safety locks," Josh muttered grimly. He jammed the straight end of the crowbar into the space between the loop and the lock, and levered down as hard as he could. The lock snapped off with a *ping*, and fell to the floor. Josh grinned wolfishly and pulled the doors open.

His smile died abruptly.

The locker was nearly empty, except for a brown cardboard box, a long shotgun barrel (with no shotgun attached), and a lone padded nylon pistol case.

Trying to contain his disappointment, he unzipped the pistol case and pulled out a small stainless finish snub .38 special revolver.

He sighed. "Great—now they can't take me alive."

A disturbing thought took root in his mind, and he glanced back towards Nora, still unconscious in the truck.

If they take us…

He quickly pushed the thought from his mind and rifled the box for the revolver's ammo. Loading the weapon, he slipped it into a chest pocket. The case had no handles or belt loops, and was therefore almost useless. He found a couple of extra cartridges and a speed loader inside, and dropped them into the same pocket.

Something chirped.

He froze, his pocket halfway zipped.

The sound came again. An electronic beep, like a radio or intercom. It was outside the guardhouse door.

"Hey," The radio crackled. "Hey buddy, pick up."

7

One Man Army

Josh's voice crackled over the intercom. "Hello?"

"I'm almost surprised that worked," Vance muttered.

Donelson waved a hand furiously at him, his other hand pressing his headset firmly against his ear.

"Sir, you reading me?"

"Uh...hm" Josh paused. "Not to ruin your day, but you should know I'm not whoever you're calling."

"Look up," Donelson said, "See the security camera? You're on video."

There was a pause as Josh looked up.

"I see," Josh said. He glanced at the door.

"So," he continued, "Do you think you could—"

"Hang on a sec," Donelson said, "I need to go talk to someone. Give me a sec, okay?"

Josh's reply was wary. "Uh...yes?"

"Good, I'll be right back. Out."

Donelson set down his headset and stood up.

"I'm gonna go tell the Boss about this guy," he said. "Don't let him go anywhere."

"Of course," Martin replied absently. Vance pointed his thumb at the screen. "But what do we do if—"

The Lieutenant was already out the door.

Dr. Martin squinted at the screen. A clipboard sat on the desk in front of him with a sheet of note paper half filled with hastily scribbled notes.

"What have you got there?" Vance said abruptly. Martin started.

"Hm? Oh! Yes..." he said. "Just...observing..."

"Looks like you're scoring something," Vance said, pointing to a series of tally marks running across the top of the page.

"As a matter of fact, I am," Martin said. "The Sergeant here—"

"Lieutenant," Vance corrected.

"—Of course," Martin continued, "My apologies—was helping me review all the footage we can find of this...custodial character."

"What for?" Vance said. "We already know where he is."

"Yes..." said Martin thoughtfully. "But we don't know *why*."

Josh dug wearily in the pile of broken insectoid limbs and body segments, kicking and shoving oozing carapace sections and pulped chunks of gristle away from the human body underneath. It smelled like hell—literally, he mused, attempting to ignore the sulfuric stench the bodies emitted. He sat back, his hands covered in black gore, took a breath. Squinting at the mess, he tried to see how much progress he'd made.

After digging in the pile of broken bug corpses for several revolting seconds, he'd finally uncovered the top half of the man's body, and determined conclusively that he was dead. He was still somehow in one piece, but seriously mangled, especially at the shoulder and neck, where the armor was weak. Josh considered briefly that a lot of his good fortune seemed to be at the expense of someone else, but quickly pushed the thought aside. If he'd been dead, he would've wanted someone else to find a use for his gear.

In fact, he thought, considering his literally intoxicated companion, there was still a possibility he'd need to arrange for it to be passed on to her. He wondered how long it would be until the guy on the radio got back from whatever errand he was taking care of.

Testing for a limb still connected securely to a carapace, he managed to pull a couple of bodies loose and roll them aside, where they began to form widening pools of sulfurous black liquid. He squinted and wrinkled his nose. The smell was so bad he could almost see it. Taking a deep breath, he grabbed the one intact shoulder strap on the man's vest, and pulled hard—slow and steady. The man's legs caught for a moment, then broke loose. Josh pulled the body out and dragged him by the armpits to the guardhouse.

Before he went any farther, he decided to consolidate resources. He and Nora obviously weren't going any farther in the truck—it wasn't nearly as close to the door, and didn't have near as nice a field of fire.

Josh carried Nora to the guardhouse, set her down at the guard's station, and checked her pulse—low, but not as low as before, or so he thought. She still wasn't awake yet.

His radio coughed.

"Hello? Hey buddy, acknowledge."

Josh lifted the now-untangled earpiece from the contractor's vest and pushed the talk button.

"Yeah, I'm still here. You guys ready to open the door?"

"No can do pal. We're under quarantine protocol."

"You're under *what*?"

"Quarantine protocol. Nothing goes in, nothing comes out."

"I know what quarantine means," Josh growled. "What I have a problem with is you not understanding that—" He'd been about to say they weren't infected, but to be honest he wasn't sure how true that was.

He took a breath. Time to try a different tack. Maybe quarantine meant keeping out monsters, not viruses.

"Come on," he said. "Do I look like I've got four legs and a can opener for a face?"

"No. I can see you both on the security cam."

Josh looked up and saw the security camera in the corner opposite the guard's seat.

"Exactly," he said. "So what's the hold up?"

It sounded like there was some intense discussion on the other end of the line.

Josh had assumed up to this point that they could override the door if he tried to open it—but now he was considering hitting the button just to see if it worked.

"Look..." Donelson was back on. "Pal, if we open that door, all hell's going to break loose."

"I only need a couple of seconds. You don't even have to open it all the way—"

"I know that, and you know that, but my...uh...*supervisor*...is saying we need more time."

Josh's mind raced. He'd known how big those doors were. He'd known how likely it was that they would be locked. But to have come all this way only for—

"Okay," he said. "Is there another way out? Or are you guys just welding all the doors closed at this point?"

Silence.

"I'll see what I can do," The radio said. "Don't go anywhere."

"I'll be right here," Josh said tonelessly.

Static.

Josh sucked in a breath.

"Supervisors," he muttered.

He glanced at Nora and suddenly wondered what the going rate was for a CEO's daughter.

On the other hand, maybe they already knew—the guy on the radio had said he could see *both* of them.

His brow furrowed. Then why were they giving him the run around instead of telling him they were on the way? Did they think *he* still didn't know who she was? Was that bad, or good?

Josh glanced around the area, his thoughts churning.

Foster trusted them. He thought. *Foster followed orders.*

Foster's dead now.

He shifted his newly-healed leg and felt a small lance of pain. He grimaced. There weren't exactly any better deals on the table—he certainly wasn't going back into the Grid.

He took a deep breath. *Fine.* Then his best option was holding out here. He needed to be in a position to negotiate with whoever showed up —no matter how many legs they had.

And...

He looked down at contractor's mangled body. Thanks to his friend on the radio, he might just have the tools to do it.

Going back to the truck, Josh got the first aid kit, a map out of the glove compartment, the truck's toolkit, and a second first aid kit he found under the seat.

After transferring his loot to the guardhouse, he put the truck in neutral, tried once again to start it, and managed to cough it into reverse and move it about twenty feet back and to the left before it died again. That was good enough—now it was parallel to the container and blocking the tunnel except for a twenty foot wide bottleneck.

After completing his setup, Josh went back to the guardhouse and resumed raiding the guard's equipment. He had mixed feelings about the job—on one hand, the dead man reminded him of Foster, and Josh tried to treat him with respect, but on the other, he felt an enormous amount of relief with each military-grade weapon system he managed to untangle and wipe off.

"I know—It's not fair," Josh muttered to the body as he rolled it over and unstrapped the vest. "But I want you to know I appreciate it."

From the body he retrieved a caseless assault rifle equipped with a flashlight and a red dot sight, a SPAS-12 automatic shotgun, and another USP .45. With the exception of the soldier's exoskeleton, which was locked up and bent, everything seemed to be in working order, though more than a little sticky. He was getting used to the smell anyway. Josh wondered if there was a sink or water fountain in the guardhouse. Water caused rust, sure, but blood would cause jams.

The ammunition situation was not awesome, but fair. When he found it, the rifle's bolt was locked open—it's owner had burned through the entire magazine before he died. He found two more mags in the vest, and about two dozen shotgun shells. The USP didn't seem to have been used, but, being a backup gun, it didn't have much to offer either—two more mags to add to his current inventory.

The one place he seemed to have more than enough was explosives. The guy was simply lousy with stuff that went boom or whoosh. Josh removed and counted three fragmentation grenades, three gas grenades he assumed were smoke or tear gas, a flashbang, and two claymore mines —wide, rectangular slabs of plastic explosive with hundreds of ball bearings embedded in the front side, all sealed in a plastic case with a handy label that said "FRONT TOWARDS ENEMY."

Despite himself, Josh let out a maniacal chuckle, imagining what something like that would do to a solid wall of bugs.

His smile faded somewhat as he unpacked one of the mines. First, he would have to figure out how to arm it.

"Oh shit," Donelson muttered.

Vance leaned in over his shoulder. "What's he doing now?"

"He found Red's claymores."

"His what?"

"So much for soldier proofing," Josh muttered. He'd found a small laminated slip of paper illustrating the priming process, but he still wasn't sure he'd gotten it right. He stood up, popped a crick in his back, and looked over his handiwork.

It was a fairly simple setup. The two mines were placed side-by-side in the choke point between the shipping container and the cargo truck. The bugs, when they came, would naturally focus there, and with any luck he'd wipe out most of them with a concentrated double-barrelled strike.

He scratched his neck. His coveralls were doing a pretty good job of keeping the blood on the vest from soaking all the way to his skin, and the gunpowder smell offset the coppery-sweet blood smell, but it still had the air of something someone had died in, and it made him uncomfortable. He'd found a sink in the restroom inside the guardhouse and rinsed as much bodily fluid as he could out of the fabric, and used duct tape to fasten the destroyed right strap back together again—sort of. It was an obvious hatchet job, but he didn't have much choice. At least it didn't smell like rancid bile and sharts, the way bug guts did.

"And I thought they smelled bad on the outside," he muttered, and turned from the claymores to the guardhouse. He hadn't checked on Nora in awhile. As he tried to wipe the remaining sticky black clots off his face, his radio crackled.

"Hey bro, you okay?"

Josh squeezed his mic. "Still here, unless you want to open door for me."

"Glad to hear it. Look. We're getting some guys together to get you out, but you're going to have to hold—"

"Whoa, hold on a second," Josh interrupted. "Why do you need more guys? Just open the door. It'll take ten seconds."

"Look, the last time we opened those doors, we barely got them closed again. They weren't exactly made to have alien guts all through the works, and if that happens again we may not be able to seal it."

"But there's nothing here *now*!"

"Oh there will be, trust me."

Josh's blood ran cold, and his ears instantly switched focus from the radio to the environment, straining through the atmospheric murk of of the tunnel for anything that sounded like a threat. For a moment, he couldn't hear anything at all—then with a shock, he realized it had been there for minutes now; a scratchy, seething burble of footsteps, like a pot being brought to boil. He peered into the darkness beyond the truck and container. The lights were too dim for him to make anything out.

Josh pushed the talk button.

"What's going on?"

"Right," said Donelson. "Now, I want you to listen carefully."

"What's that noise? Is that what I think it is?"

"You've got a lot of heat incoming," said Donelson. "Now, listen to me—"

"It's what?" Josh choked. "How many?"

There was a series of pops and movement whiffles on the other end. A new voice ground through the radio.

"Son? This is Boss, Hazard Team Leader. I'm in charge of this operation."

"What's that noise?"

"Bugs Mr. Murphy," Boss said calmly. "Lots and lots of bugs."

"What am I supposed to do?"

"We've been delayed," said Boss. "Now I want you to listen to me very carefully. If you've gotten this far you obviously know how to handle yourself—"

"No! No I don't!" he blurted. "I'm not a soldier. I'm just a guy who knows which ends of a gun goes bang. That doesn't make me—"

"Shut up and listen," Boss barked. "We are on our way, but you have to hold out until we get there, understand?"

Josh felt his teeth rattling together in his mouth and clamped his jaws together, trying to make them stop.

The claymores aren't set up right, He thought. *I'm not ready. I'm not ready. I'm not ready—*

"You're not gonna die," Boss growled, "You're a cornered animal. A dangerous animal, and you're going to fight like one. Hear me?"

Josh stood rooted to the floor, like a man watching a car bearing down on him.

"Talk to me son."

Josh cleared his throat. "Got it."

"Good man. Hazard out."

The radio coughed, and he was alone.

Josh set to work.

He double-checked the claymores, couldn't find anything wrong with them, shifted a couple of crates to create some makeshift cover near the door, and made one last check on Nora in the guardhouse. He felt her pulse—still slow, but steady—and headed for the door.

Abruptly he stopped, and dug the small revolver out of his pocket. It wouldn't be any use to him—if he ran out of this much ammo, he was dead anyway. He stuffed the weapon into one of her coat pockets, dumped the spare ammo into her opposite pocket, and dragged her into the restroom at the back. Propping her up in the corner, he closed the door securely.

He pressed the talk button. "Hey bro, you still with me?"

"Yeah, I'm here," Donelson replied.

"Okay listen up. There's a bathroom at the back of the guard station. The girl is inside, unconscious. If I go down, that's where to find her.

Okay?"

"Yeah, I got it," Pause. "Why don't you both hide there?"

"I'm not risking that," Josh said, "If we get buried you're going to have a hell of a time digging us out."

"I dunno man," Donelson replied, "You stay in the open, that's a death sentence—"

"It's not me I'm worried about," Josh said. "I've made my mind up. Just let me know when the cavalry's here."

"You bet. Good luck."

Josh took up his position behind the crates and peered past the claymores into the darkness. He still couldn't see them—but he could hear the rumble, echoing down the hallway like an incoming train. If this group was anything like the swarms he'd seen that morning, it was going to be more than enough.

It suddenly seemed like an eternity had passed since then—only hours ago his worst fears were getting chewed out by scientists or petty supervisors, and contemplating a disappointing future career literally cleaning up other people's crap. Now his worst nightmare took the "chewing" part literally, and was making crap *out* of his co-workers.

As he plugged the claymore wires into the hand detonators, his fingers itched in anticipation, and a nervous chuckle slipped out. The fear remained, but something else was creeping in the edges of his consciousness, taking the edge off.

He set his jaw. Maybe he would die. But then, he'd never been so alive.

The echoing thunder of feet crew closer, filling the tunnel. He could barely hear himself think.

Where were they all coming from?

All of a sudden he saw it—the wave blotting out the gray walls to each side, a roiling sea in the muddy darkness. They were the big bugs—no scorpions he could see. His hand involuntarily tensed—he focused on his fingers, willing them to remain loose.

Wait for it...

The container and truck blocked the flanks of the approaching wall of spikes and jaws. The sound crashed in on his ears and pounded his skull. He waited a few more seconds, ducked behind the crate, and mashed the first detonator.

Nothing.

Ice shot through his veins. He squeezed trigger number two.

Several things happened all at once.

The mine went off, blasting the crate backwards. It struck him in the face and threw him onto his back. Ears ringing, he tried to regain his bearings, cursing and hefting the rifle to his shoulder. Looking over the crate, he peered through the smoke and tried to see if the mine had done any good.

He felt like he'd dislocated his neck, and everything sounded underwater. He could hear the screams and chattering of the bugs beyond. He couldn't tell if they were confused or enraged, but it was clear there was plenty of them left. The cargo truck's windows and headlights had all been blown out. He couldn't see beyond the smoke and dust, but it looked like the wave had not only been stopped, but blocked—probably by the dead and wounded who had either been thrown back or disintegrated in the front. Even more had probably been dropped in their tracks towards the edge of the mine's range; he didn't imagine there were a lot of things that C4-powered buckshot couldn't penetrate. He wasn't sure claymores were meant to take on solid crowds so close together though—meaning he had no idea how far back the damage actually extended. He leveled the rifle and pulled the trigger, unloading his magazine at about carapace level into the smoke and dust. The weapon vibrated like a jackhammer in his hands, orange flashes chopping though the darkness and smoke in front of him.

It locked dry. Through the watery soup of guttural chittering he heard hundreds of somethings banging on metal, tried to figure out what the noise was—and then he saw the cargo truck had grown a massive spiked fro. It looked like a chia-pet from hell.

"Oh...SHIT!" he hissed.

Josh shot a glance to his left and saw the same thing happening to the shipping container—the bugs were simply boiling over the obstacles like a wave of brambles.

"SHIT!" he sputtered. "SHITSHITSHITSHITSTIT!"

Josh dumped the empty mag and shoved a new one home, slapping the bolt handle out of it's notch. It snapped forwards with a loud metallic *chak*.

He pulled the weapon snug against his shoulder, whipped the muzzle towards the container, and started with the bugs in the lead, hosing the mass all the way to the back. The bugs in front jerked and burst like piñatas, flipping off the metal cargo crate and splattering to the ground. The aliens behind them couldn't even fall—they died standing up, collapsing like a pile of jumbled sticks.

Josh changed mags and turned to give the truck a matching overhaul, but by this time they were pouring over the hood and onto the floor. He turned the front rank into mush and burned the remainder on the truck.

The rifle's muzzle flash was burning itself onto his vision. He could barely see what he was shooting at. He caught movement to his left, and realized the center had untangled itself and he could see the first bugs starting towards him. He was about to be skewered from three directions at once.

Weapon dry, he fumbled for the shotgun slung against his chest, and blasted the closest bug's jaw out the back of it's head, backing up as quickly as he could fire. He was instantly glad he'd carried the weapon chambered—he'd even left the safety off.

Why didn't that fricking claymore go off?

Josh yanked open the guardhouse door and ripped the pin from a grenade, tossing it out the windowless door and ducking behind a desk. Heartbeats later, there was a ear-shattering *BAM*, and the scattered frontrunners jerked and flipped to the ground screeching.

A few seconds later, he threw a second grenade that went off inside the mass pouring over the container. The air was filled with smoke and pinwheeling bug parts.

Josh forced himself to carefully aim his last frag and landed it smack in the choke point. Ducking behind the desk, he pulled the gas grenades from his vest. He was briefly interrupted as the explosive went off, the shockwave slapping against his back. An enterprising alien tried to squirm underneath the door's middle bar, growling furiously—Josh pumped two servings of buckshot into it.

The window next to him cracked and shattered, showering him with glass, and he forced himself to rip the pin from a gas grenade as he stood up, throwing it past the bug trying to climb in the window and into the main mass. He hefted the shotgun one-handed and blasted the bug back out the window, and slung his last gas grenade out to the left, trying to get it back into the main mass. He still wasn't sure what the gas was, but it seemed to be helping, or at least confusing them. In fact, a lot of them were falling down and writhing on the ground—but there was always more where they came from.

He'd been counting shells, and the shotgun was due to run dry any second now—he dropped it against his chest and drew the USP, popping shots through the windows as the mass of bugs pounded against them.

The slide locked open and Josh dropped the mag, slotting the new one home before it even hit the ground. a nanosecond later his thumb managed to release the slide, and he was emptying his second mag into the bug ramming the bent door bar. Three windows burst into shards almost at once, and Josh knew he was dead.

Suddenly, time slowed to a crawl. The noise and chaos faded to nothing as a calming presence flooded his consciousness. Everything faded from his thoughts except for one concept—one thought that sprang into his mind fully formed as if dropped into his brain by a neighboring consciousness.

DUCK.

Josh dropped to the floor and clamped his hands over his ears.

The grenades had been surprising—but this was traumatic. All Josh was aware of was a feeling like he'd been punched from all sides at once, his skull reeling and the air beaten from his chest. The air was instantly filled with smoke, dust, fragments of glass and steel, most of which seemed to be striking his face. Despite covering his ears, Josh felt as if someone had jammed a nail into both sides of his head. Everything rang. There was nothing but a thin high-pitched underwater whine. He was choking, sucking on nothing, trying to shout. All he saw was blurs of light crossing his vision. Something was lying on top of him. A bug.

He thrashed in panic and screamed—or thought he did, he couldn't hear it—but suddenly realized it was dead. It was heavy, and he was covered in steaming gore, but it was dead.

He shifted a foot loose and awkwardly placed the heel against the bug's body. It took an extra half second for him to regain motor control and kick it off him—it felt like his mind had been knocked loose from his skull and was just sort of floating around nearby as he rolled over and crawled forwards on his elbows, trying to get clear.

A bright light split his vision and he saw spots. His eyes narrowed reflexively and he tried to force them open and see what was going on. Was the door open?

He looked out the destroyed guardhouse door, making out a massive pillar of light shining through the jumble of smashed bug bodies.

Am I dead?

He thought he heard the chatter of automatic weapons fire. A figure loomed up over the pile of bodies, a massive, dark figure silhouetted against the light.

Dammit. He thought. *I don't wanna be dead.*

8

Going Commando

Josh felt the darkness close in on him, and wondered if maybe he might blissfully pass out, like people in the movies.

It didn't happen.

He had the vague sensation that he was being dragged somewhere, felt the sun on his face, and lost track of time for a moment—but the sun kept burning in through his eyelids and keeping him from slipping away. He groaned and tried to bat it away like a fly or someone with a feather duster—then a grip like steel locked around his wrist and pinned it to the stretcher beneath him. He opened his eyes.

What the hell?

He was looking up into the sun as it burned holes into his eyes, he blinked, turning his head back and forth and trying to get away from— rough hands gripped his head and pulled his eyelids back. The sun was back—no, it was a flashlight. Someone in black was shining a flashlight in his eyes. All he could hear was a constant, cutting ring, like his brain's own personal dial tone cutting through the burning red mist in his head.

We're sorry, your call cannot be completed as dialed. Please check the number and dial again...

People were muttering, but he couldn't hear anything they were saying. His ears were still underwater.

We're sorry, your call cannot be completed as dialed. Please check the number and dial again...Goodbye.

Even the phone didn't want to answer his questions.

He woke up to the vibration of a vehicle in motion. He wasn't sure if he'd passed out or not—he thought he could remember them lifting him into the vehicle, but the more he thought about it the less sure he was—

The vehicle's breaks whined and it jerked to a stop. The door by his head opened and suddenly he saw a face.

Or more of a mask, really. Not a face. But there was a face beneath it, he was pretty sure. And it was upside down. The mask and the upside down part threw him for a moment, but then he remembered he was lying on a stretcher, and the soldier was obviously grabbing the handles at his head.

It was a soldier. It had to be—he didn't know of too many emergency personnel who dressed in all black and wore balaclavas and smoked military goggles to work.

He wondered which branch they were from. He couldn't see any patches.

Josh could hear again, at least on his left side, but he was extremely tired. They lifted him up and he felt every single step as they thumped over to a tent. The olive green flaps swept over him, and the sun was replaced by the bitter glare of a bright overhead medical lamp. He squeezed his eyes shut, but someone peeled them back open with a latex-gloved hand. Another flashlight beam stabbed into them. It was a medic, with a light green face mask and clear plastic goggles—the first eyes Josh had seen from the outside. For a moment Josh's mind latched onto them, and he felt he could see every detail of each green iris—the beam poked into his eye again.

"Can you hear me?" It was a female voice. It wasn't particularly kind, but it wasn't harsh either.

"Ow," Josh muttered.

The medic looked up across him to her compatriot. "Positive response."

She looked down at Josh again. "Can you hear me?"

"Yes," Josh croaked.

"Everything's going to be just fine, okay?" said the medic. "Just hang in there."

"Okay."

There was a thump as they moved him from the stretcher to a flat plastic table that shifted oddly under him. The two medics began stripping off his vest and shoes, finally rolling him over and peeling the coveralls off.

"No no no—" he tried to wave them off. "I'll do it—"

"Please stay down," said the male medic, pushing him back down.

The female medic gingerly pulled back the shredded bloodstained fabric hanging from his thigh. Josh began to feel very self conscious.

After a moment, the medic reached down and wiped some of the clotted blood away.

"Major laceration," she said. "Recently healed."

She looked up at her partner. "Make note of that."

Someone touched Josh's shoulder and he felt a burning sensation.

"Aagh!" he barked. "Watch it!"

The medic looked down and carefully peeled back the edges of another tear near his left shoulder. Josh tried to lift his head, but someone pushed it back down again.

"I see it. Another laceration—possible shrapnel," the female medic said. "That one's still open. Irrigate and pass him on."

Josh's pain stress quickly turned to anxiety. "Irrigate? What are you—"

He felt a sharp pain lancing at his shoulder. It felt like someone was squirting something into the wound. The attendants held him down.

The squirting stopped, and the pain faded to a numb throbbing. Josh sucked air in and pumped it out, vainly yanking at his limbs. No good. They might as well have cuffed him to the table.

"Jesus," one of the attendants burbled. "That's gonna need stitches."

The female medic leaned over Josh's head. "Let's move him on down the line. Ready? One two—Push!"

Before Josh could figure out what they were talking about, they shoved him hard, and what he had assumed to be a plastic tabletop turned out to be more like a surfboard on a set of rollers. He slid through a barrier of plastic flaps, and into the next station, where he was hosed within an inch of his life with soap and cold water. They rolled him back and forth to make sure every nook and cranny was flushed as he shivered in the cold air. He was still busy thinking about what they meant by "stitches" when they power washed his nuts.

They scooted him on to the next station, where two more medics leaned over him. "I want you to look at me, okay?" Said the first. Josh immediately looked at the second as he moved towards Josh's shoulder, threading a hooked needle.

"Wait! Wait a minute!" Josh blurted. "I hate needles! Don't you have anesthetic?"

"Just look at me okay?" said the first medic. "Look at me and in a minute it'll all be over."

Ten minutes later, Josh was sitting against a wall wrapped in a speckled gray wool blanket. He was in a sort of triage area or something that they had set up in the facility's center, surrounded by dozens of other relatively uninjured and cleaned employees. He felt thoroughly scrubbed, stabbed, and exposed, and it was going straight to his pride, which was waffling between utterly mortified and totally crushed.

They wouldn't let him have his clothes back, not even to rifle through the pockets—much less the weapons he had been carrying. He was irritated about both—but he found himself more concerned about the weapons than he had been expecting. He felt vulnerable without them. Exposed.

Well, technically he *was* exposed, wearing nothing but a gray kilt and a shoulder dressing. But in a different way.

He forced himself to take a deep breath and calm down.

Everything's fine now. You've done it. Escaped. All downhill from here.

At least it was warm inside. He had never gotten used to how cold the desert was in winter.

He leaned his head back against the wall with a thump, looked up at the massive bright skylight three stories above him, and took a deep breath. In and out. He was tired, but there was no way he was going to sleep in public without underwear, so he decide to look around and make everyone else uncomfortable.

He recognized the room as the ground floor of the Welcome Center's atrium. This was the part that was hidden by the berms outside. For some reason, this building and it's administrative sibling across the street looked like they had been built like bunkers. Exceptionally tall ones. The room he was in was perhaps the size of a small football field and bracketed on each end by curving information desks and hallways, with several banks of solidly occupied cushy chairs and fake desert plants. Pastels and faded earth tones were blocked over the entire area, now crammed with knots of sad looking flesh-colored lumps wrapped in speckled gray blankets and wet hair, with the occasional guard dressed in flat black wandering the aisles. The ceiling appeared to have two large cutouts evenly spaced to create a wide balcony ringing the space and an equally wide bridge smack across the middle. Escalators led down from this upper floor at angles, emptying towards the information desks. The effect was that of a closed-off mall filled with people who'd been at a pool party gone horribly wrong.

The black-clad guards seemed relaxed. Josh tried not to stare, but his curiosity was severely piqued. He couldn't figure out if they were too lightly armed for fighting armies of space lobsters, or too heavily armed for guarding a bunch of cold naked people. Every last one of them wore balaclavas and shaded goggles or sunglasses, and the velcro patches where their rank would have been were fuzzy and bare—even their unit patch was a simple round black circle bordered in gray text, as if they had asked the artist to intentionally leave it blank to screw with people. No one was close enough for him to read the words.

He turned his mind to other frustratingly opaque subjects—Like where Nora was. They'd known there was two of them, right? They'd seen him put her in the restroom on the cameras—but had he told them she was in there?

I did. Yes.

Wait. Did I?

He saw something move out of the corner of his eye and immediately whipped his head to the right, craning his neck towards the information desk. Over by the end of the room, a medic joined her comrades tending to a man in his fifties who looked vaguely like a large frog.

Triage had apparently not been able to move anyone from here yet. Josh let his breath out with a whoosh.

He heard a joint pop, and turned to see Nora standing almost next to him, clutching a blanket to her chest that wrapped around her from armpits to knees. She sat stiffly on the floor across from him, looking a bit like a soaked black-and-white cat. She was shivering, but her face was stern enough to give the impression she was trying to set a patch of the carpet on fire with her eyes.

Josh folded his hands in front of him and tried to keep his eyes from flickering to her clavicle.

He opened his mouth, then closed it again. He was thrilled to see her—especially considering a moment ago he'd thought they'd accidentally left her behind—but she was obviously concerned with something else, and he wasn't sure how to gauge his response.

"Did..." he thought for a moment. "Uh...how are you?"

"Great," Nora said, scowling from behind her scrambled white highlights. "Just frigging perfect."

Nora's fingers restlessly shifted their grip on the blanket. Josh tried to think of something else to say.

"Oh," he said.

There was another pause. Josh twiddled his thumbs.

"Did, uh...you get the complimentary friendship bracelet too?" he said, holding up his wrist to reveal a piece of orange plastic tape knotted loosely around his wrist, "They told me it means 'delayed'...which, hey, is better than *dead*."

He chuckled. Nora didn't. His chuckle died.

"Oh—there's yours," he pointed to her wrist. "You were leaning over on it so I...couldn't see it..."

He looked at the ceiling.

"They actually have one for 'dead' too," Josh started again. "And another one for—"

Nora looked up suddenly and locked eyes with him.

"You do know we're going to prison, right?"

Josh blushed on eye contact, and looked to the side with what he hoped was a thoughtful scowl.

"Maybe. Maybe not," he said.

"They need to pin the blame on somebody," Nora said. "That's going to be us."

"Not *me*," Josh blurted, then pulled back and reassessed, glancing to both sides. No one was acting like they heard, but there were at least a dozen people within earshot. And Nora was glaring at him again.

He shifted around until he was sitting cross-legged and leaned forwards.

"I mean," he said in a much quieter voice. "You were incognito at the time. How many people really know you were there? Besides me of course."

"They *caught* me stupid," she said. "They knew my name, *everything*."

Josh scowled. "Oh."

He shifted again and felt a draft on his cold wet legs. Nora sighed and returned to looking at the floor.

Josh looked down at the blanket, frowned for a second, and looked up.

"Would you like some pants?"

Nora looked up, confused. "What?"

"It would be just for a second," Josh said. The soldier—or at least Josh assumed he was a soldier—stared at him impassively through the lenses of his sunglasses. They blended in with his black uniform, as if he was a statue made entirely from one material. Even his voice didn't sound human—he was speaking through the voice changer installed over his balaclava, which gave it a harsh crackle and pitched it lower.

"Nobody goes in or out," the guard stated. "I'm sorry sir."

He raised his hand from the grip of the M4 hanging on his chest, and held it out like a brick wall.

"Please go sit down. We'll address your concerns soon."

The guard's somewhat skinnier partner leaning on the pillar next to him chuckled from behind his gas mask.

"Hey man, if my morning had been this bad, I'd need a good shag too."

Josh flushed and turned to Nora, whose face had grown dangerously dark. He could've sworn he saw her eyes flash visibly. She opened her mouth to speak, but Josh cut her off.

"Look," he said, "I'm the custodian here. I've got an employee record and everything. I just need two pairs of spare coveralls from the janitor's closet, and that's it."

He thought for a second. "You can even watch us change if you have —" Nora was poking him. He turned to face her.

"What?" he said.

"I don't *want* anyone watching me," Nora hissed. Josh rolled his eyes and sighed. He had wanted to go alone so they looked less…suspicious, but Nora wasn't thrilled about the idea of disrobing in front of several hundred people.

"We're pushing it as it is," Josh whispered back. "They might not let us do it at *all*."

He heard digitized sniggering behind them. Apparently the masks didn't interfere much with their hearing. When he turned around, they had resumed their stoic posture. He put his hands on his kilted hips and shrugged.

"Well?"

The first soldier shook his head. "No can do."

Josh dropped his chin to his chest for a moment, then picked it back up. "What if I tell you the key code to the janitor's closet. Could one of you go get them?"

Nora sighed. Josh ignored her.

The soldier shook his head again. "I'm sorry."

"What's this?" Another soldier appeared and stepped up behind the two guards. Josh caught sight of two chevrons on his sleeves.

"Something seem to be the problem?"

"No problem Sergeant," the first guard said. "I was just—"

"Not you," the NCO said, pointing to Josh. "Lover boy here."

Josh stared opened mouthed at the NCO's aviators for a moment, then regained speech control. "Who—Oh! Uh…Yeah. I'm the…Janitor. Here.

Uh—and I have some spares—spare coveralls—in the closet on this floor, and I was wondering if me and my friend here—"

"No problem. I totally understand," the NCO said, turning to the first soldier. "If you would, Corporal, escort these two to the closet, allow them to change behind the door, and escort them back. If anyone asks why, tell them to talk to me."

The corporal hesitated for a second, his expression hidden.

"Yes Sergeant," he said crisply, and shot a look at Josh and Nora.

Raising the hazard tape between them, he jerked his head toward the hallway. "Lead the way."

As Josh ducked under the tape, he heard the second guard murmur in disbelief. "Lucky son of a bitch."

"You have no idea," he muttered to himself, and stepped down the hallway.

Nora drew up on his right, and the Corporal stayed a decent three or four paces behind. Taking a sly glance backwards, Nora quietly slipped her arm into Josh's. Josh shivered and gave her a look.

"What are you doing?"

She gave him a radiant smile. "Play along."

"Why?"

"Just do it."

Josh adjusted his jaw and looked away.

They made a left turn, and he glanced back at her.

"So!" he said. "How was decon?"

Her brow furrowed. "Deacon?"

"Decontamination. Scrubbing."

"Oh," she said. "They were looking at my neck."

Josh swallowed. "They were?"

"Yeah," Nora swept her hair back and leaned forwards to reveal the sting. "They were pretty interested in it."

Josh squinted at the brown-ringed puncture. It looked better, he supposed. He heard Nora talking and looked up. "Hm?"

Nora gave him a funny look, but continued. "Well, apparently there were...other people who had been stung."

"I can imagine," Josh said. "What happened to them?"

"I don't know," said Nora. "But it didn't sound real great."

"It didn't look real great," said Josh. "So they asked you about it?"

"No," said Nora. "I woke up while they were still talking and picked it up from the things they said—Wait a minute, you know what happens to people who get stung?"

"I came across a few victims on the way out," Josh said. "And then there was you of course."

"Oh," Nora said.

"Honestly I'm just happy to see you alive," Josh said. "It was touch and go there for awhile."

"That's what they're so confused about though," Nora said. "They looked like they were expecting things to be a lot worse, but almost everyone who's been stung so far seems to be recovering fine."

Now it was Josh's turn to look confused. "Really?"

"Yeah," Nora said. "They said a lot of the employees were complaining that the security guards forced them to take some sort of injection earlier, and maybe that had—"

Josh stopped short. "Injections?"

"Yeah," Nora said. "That's why they're so confused—I never got one."

"Yes you did," Josh said. "*I* gave one to you."

Nora stared at him. "You gave me...What did you give me?"

"A shot," Josh said. "Found it in the first aid kit."

"A shot of *what*?"

"I..." Josh tried to come up with an answer, and found it more difficult than expected. "Sting...stuff."

"For a sting?"

"It said it was for stings!"

"What kind?"

"I don't know!" Josh said. "Look, it was either that or—well it worked, didn't it?"

Nora opened her mouth, then closed it again, and then her eyebrows drew together and she stared at the wall opposite.

"Hmph," she said.

They walked on for a few steps, then reached a T-junction. Nora pulled off to the right, and Josh pulled to the left.

"This way?" Nora pointed left.

"Yeah."

"Oh."

A few minutes later, Josh was punching numbers into the closet's keypad. It opened with a tiny electronic *zip*, and they stepped inside.

The janitor's "closet" was actually rather spacious, perhaps the size of an average apartment kitchen after accounting for the utility shelves, massive square metal sink, and the rolling bucket and mop wringer, among other grimy and caustic odds and ends. Making a beeline for a shelf on the far side of the room, Josh pulled open a worn cardboard box, saw the folded green canvas inside, and chortled triumphantly.

He heard the door close, and turned around.

Nora was standing inside the closet, locking the door behind her.

Josh felt his face drain of color and felt his ears burning.

"What are you doing?" he hissed.

She stretched one arm out and pointed to the wall across from her. A large air vent was located next to the sink.

Josh look from her, to the vent, and back.

"We're breaking out?" he whispered.

"Remember when I said *we* were going to prison?" Nora said. "That meant—" She pointed rapidly between them, "*We*, as in, myself and *you*."

"Why me?" Josh sputtered. "What did I do?"

"You're on the cameras." Nora shot back. "You helped me." She jerked her thumb towards the door. "Do those guys look like local cops to you?"

"You know who those guys are?"

"I don't *need* to know—we leave *right now*, or we spend the rest of our lives in a black site in Alaska."

Josh hesitated for a moment, then began digging in one of the other boxes.

The guard was hard at work attempting to stuff a pair of earbuds underneath his goggle straps when he heard something thump inside the closet.

"Shit."

Nora frowned and stepped down from a box, one fist holding her blanket together and one holding a screwdriver.

"This one's too small—" She glanced towards Josh and abruptly shut her eyes. "Oh! Sorry!"

"Look *that* way!" Josh barked.

Nora pursed her lips and held out the tool. "This one doesn't fit."

She heard him rummaging in the cardboard box, and a plastic handle was pressed into her hand.

"Try that."

The guard cocked his head to one side, listened a moment, then went back to his MP3 player.

"No no no," Josh said, zipping up his coveralls. "You've got to *push* into it, like—never mind, let me do it."

He reached for the screwdriver, but Nora pulled it away.

"I'm fine," she snapped. "Leave me alone."

"Look," Josh said. "I'm sure you could learn, and I'd be very happy to teach you, but right now you can either change while *I* watch, or let *me* deal with the screws."

The corporal looked up and pulled the earbuds from his head. Nothing.

He stepped closer and knocked heavily on the door. "Hey, open up!" No response.

He backed up a step, picked up his boot, and kicked the lock in. Barreling inside, he swept the room with his rifle, his eyes stopping on the open vent.

Three turns down, Josh scowled and tried not to look at Nora crawling ahead of him. She giggled.

"Stop that," Josh said.

"What are you mad about?" Nora retorted. "Now we're even, right?"

"Even nothing," Josh said. "I looked away. You *saw* I looked away."

"Not fast enough."

"Well maybe next time you should have given me a heads up!"

Nora reached a t-junction and stopped, fiddling with the cuffs of her coveralls. They were a bit big, and the metal zippers were cold, with a tendency to yank out a hair every so often.

"Where are we going, anyway?" Josh said.

"Uh," Nora glanced both ways. "Out. I haven't gotten past that part."

"What?" Josh snorted. "You just saw and air vent and went 'well that's gotta lead *somewhere*'?"

Suddenly Josh felt the thin metal creak as it shifted under his hands. They froze.

Nora glanced back at Josh. "Uh—"

The vent fell away as it broke under him, dumping them both through the drop ceiling. For an instant, Josh flailed as he saw a table rush up to meet him, and then he flipped forward and landed hard on his back. They crashed through the weak structure. Nora's skull thudded into his stomach, blasting the air from his lungs.

Blinking as he recovered, Josh suddenly found himself looking down the barrels of an assortment of rifles, shotguns, and SMGs. Josh tasted brass.

"Stay down," a soldier growled.

Josh held his hands up and tried to grin.

"It's not what it looks like," he said.

"It had better not," said another man, stepping into the circle. He had longish black hair and was wearing a ballistic vest over his hooded leather jacket. "Otherwise I'll be *very* upset."

Josh felt Nora start with surprise.

"Loyd?" she said.

Nora's eyes locked onto Loyd and tunnel vision reduced everything else to a peripheral blur. His smile came as a shock, and she felt herself tense up as he burst into laughter.

"Look at you!" he said, spreading his arms wide. "I came as soon as I heard you made it out,"

He crouched in front of her. "If I'd known you were this stir-crazy I'd have come sooner."

Nora tore her eyes from Loyd's and rolled them around the room full of black-clad soldiers.

"They with you?" she croaked.

"Hm? Oh! Of course—" he looked up and waved at the men. "Go ahead and stand down boys. We're all friends here."

They slowly lowered their weapons. Nora sat up and turned to check on Josh. He was looking around slowly, a picture of tight-lipped, wide-eyed suspicion.

Loyd stood and reached down his hand to Nora.

"Come on," he said. "There's someone you need to see."

Nora hesitated for a second, then took it.

They exited the building onto a wide skybridge. It was almost forty feet wide and several hundred feet long, linking the welcome center and the Main Office. The walls were steel frames with windows, and the ceiling punctuated with skylights, so Nora had plenty of time to drink in the view as they crossed the bridge. On her right, the road passing below them shot out into the desert until it met the interstate a half mile into the endless desert plain, and on her left it trailed away up the mesa about a quarter mile until it ended in a walled divot in the rock—the entrance to the underground facility. The buildings connected by the skybridge both had foundations with huge berms thrown up against all four sides.

The part of the Welcome Center they had just left was almost entirely white and brushed metal, like a modern art museum built on top of a fallout bunker. The building they were crossing to, however, had a superstructure much more in tune with it's bunkered foundation—a thick, squared-off office structure built of concrete. Besides the glass-walled lobby off to their right and the skybridge itself, there were hardly any windows on the ground floor wider than arrow slits.

A thumping roar overhead drew her eye to a large black helicopter crossing over them. Nora followed it's path as it circled and disappeared behind the office building.

"Blackhawks?" Josh said. "*Stealth* blackhawks?"

Nora slid her eyes his way. "What?"

"The chopper," Josh said. "Didn't you see it?"

"I saw it," she said. "What about it?"

Josh chewed his lip.

"Nothing," he said. "I'm just trying to figure out how far down the rabbit hole we are."

"Farther than you know," Loyd said suddenly. "Much, *much* farther."

The massive brutalist building finally swallowed them up, and they went down a couple more hallways, rooms full of people to either side. Several arguments seemed to be in progress between the civilians and the police or soldiers or whoever they were. People wanting to leave, people wanting to call their families, people wanting to know where their co-workers were—the chorus of unintelligible humanity and the clipped, digitized responses from their overseers blending into a stormy cacophony.

Loyd led them up a flight of stairs to the next level, and they entered a door marked SECURITY. Passing the empty reception desk, they entered a soundproof room with a heavy door. The label read CONTROL ROOM.

It was sealed off—no windows, just banks and banks of monitors, which were almost the only thing visible in the dark. Several black silhouettes stood in the center of the room, like cutouts against the grid of bright rectangles.

As one of them turned to see who had come in, the light fell on his face, and Nora's jaw fell open.

"Mr…" she choked on something that wasn't there. "Mr. E?"

9

Blue Shift

"Oh my God!" Nora wrapped the man up in a bear hug. "You're alive!"

Mr. E gave a triumphant laugh and hugged her back. "It's good to see you too."

Nora loosened her grip and pushed back to get a good look at him. He looked to be all in one piece—new glasses, a scruffier beard, but besides that he was exactly the same roughly-shaven middle-aged college professor she remembered, down to the olive green field cap.

"This isn't funny," she said, failing to wipe the smile from her glowing face. "I'm so mad right now, I swear—why didn't you tell us you survived?"

Mr. E held up his hands in mock defense. "Whoa, maybe next time I should just *stay* dead."

"No," Nora shook her head vigorously. "Uh-uh. You do that, I'll kill you."

They both laughed.

Josh laughed halfheartedly, then noticed Loyd watching him. He suppressed a fabricated cough and decided to see if he could decipher the uniform patches of the men surrounding them. Most of them wore black fatigues, body armor, and carried assault rifles. One or two had their masks pulled up—these in particular were casting wary looks at him. He avoided eye contact and jammed his hands in his pockets.

"So," said Mr. E. "I see you and Loyd managed all right in my absence."

"Just followed the plan," Loyd said with a shrug. "Nothing to it."

Mr. E shook his head in astonishment. "Unbelievable. You kids never fail to amaze me."

"I don't understand," Nora said. "I thought for sure we'd screwed the whole thing up."

She glanced quizzically from Mr. E to Loyd, and noticed the joviality seep from their faces. They exchanged glances.

"I mean…it went off," she said.

"Yes," said Loyd. "but things are far more contained than they *would* have been."

"That's right," Mr. E said. "Once we deactivate the artifact, we can extract it, and make sure it gets the respect it deserves."

"Right. Of course, but—" Nora said, glancing around the control room. "—Who is 'we' anyway?"

Josh noticed a change in the atmosphere of the room. Several of the agents shifted slightly just as Nora had said *we*.

A stiff smile formed on Mr. E's face. "Ehh—yes…" he said. "There's quite a few things I want to catch you up on as soon as possible—but first, let's get you both something decent to wear."

One of the men stood and approached Easton, whispering something in his ear.

"Have you found Tina and Oddball?" Nora said.

"We'll talk soon," Easton said. "There's something I need to deal with —Loyd? Get them…whatever they need. I'll be with you shortly."

Loyd led the way down the hall, and opened the door to one of the security offices.

"Clothes in there," he said with a sweeping gesture.

Josh entered. Loyd closed the door behind him, pulled Nora close, and kissed her firmly on the mouth.

They stood there for a moment, foreheads pressed together.

"I thought I'd lost you," Loyd whispered.

"I'm okay," Nora replied. "There's nothing to worry about now."

Loyd laughed. "I'm not letting you out of my sight. Not till this whole thing is over."

Nora smiled mischievously. "You won't have to."

The door opened and Loyd quickly pulled it shut again. Josh's protest was muffled by the door.

"Go on," Loyd said.

Nora stuck her tongue in her cheek and grinned. She felt reckless and slightly lightheaded. And why not? She'd just lived through hell. *Carpe Diem.*

"This morning," she said, "I—"

With a loud snap, the latch was turned and the door yanked open. The mood vanished like a haze, and was instantly replaced by embarrassment. She pushed back and looked at the floor.

"Can we help you?" Loyd said in a silky voice.

Nora looked up at Josh. He looked like he'd stepped on a nail. He blinked, then forced a wide smile onto his face.

"I didn't find anything," he said, slightly louder than necessary.

"No?" said Loyd.

Josh stared at him for a long moment.

"Where's the bathroom?"

Loyd pointed down the hall. "Two doors down."

"Thanks," Josh said, and stepped between them.

For an instant, Nora thought she caught his eyes flicker over to meet hers—and then he was past and down the hall.

She watched him go for several seconds.

"Nora?"

She started and turned to Loyd. "Huh?"

Loyd's brows had drawn low.

"Is...are you all right?" he said.

Nora shivered and folded her arms. "I...uh...yeah," she said. "I'm good—Mr. E said something about clothes?"

"...Yeah," Loyd said, pointing down an adjoining hall, "This way."

Josh stared hard into the mirror. His face was clean, but even the scrub-happy decon personnel couldn't hide the battered flesh beneath. His face sported several browning cuts in addition to the main one on his forehead, all held together by thin adhesive strips. His felt the stitches on his shoulder scrape on his coveralls every time he moved, and he had a large bruise under his right eye.

He leaned forwards, examined the purple blotch carefully, and grimaced. This one was different, he remembered—it was one of the few that had been inflicted by a human.

Or at least, a human he cared about.

"I'm very disappointed in you," he said to his reflection. "This girl has been nothing but trouble from the minute you met her. Don't be an idiot."

He looked up at the ceiling and sighed.

"Okay," he muttered. "Focus. Come on. What's going on here?"

He clapped his hands to his head and squeezed his eyes shut.

"HunterCorp is investigated for—whatever the hell this is. Best case scenario—I'm out of a job. Worst case—" He chewed his lip, then let out a long breath that turned into a bitter laugh. "I end up in the custody of the wannabe Men-in-Black."

He took a deep breath and opened his eyes. "Who the hell are these guys?"

He leaned back into the mirror.

"No patches, no faces, no badges—not even little American flags," he muttered, shaking his head. "Gotta have federal pull, or at least state—no local emergency services."

He cocked his head and rocked back and forth restlessly.

"Or maybe they just never got the call."

He turned around and faced the stalls, scratching his chin.

"Hold up," he said. "What does Nora have to do with this?"

He stood up and paced back and forth.

"Unless she was a spook for the CIA or something when I met her—which I doubt she was…"

He stopped for a moment, then grunted and shook his head. "See, that's just exactly what I *don't know*."

He swept his cap off the counter threw it violently to the floor, turning to the mirror as if demanding answers.

"What the hell *is* she?"

A toilet flushed.

Josh controlled his shock and set his hands on the counter, looking down into the sink in front of him.

Great. Just great. Go on, talk to yourself some more dumbass.

He heard the door open, and glanced at the exit in the mirror to watch the person leave.

Instead, someone clapped him on the shoulder.

He bit back a startled curse and looked up to see Bishop standing next to him in the mirror.

Bishop smiled. "Sounds like you two need to talk."

Josh closed his eyes and sighed. "Oh, so you give relationship advice now?" he said. "Up until this point I was pretty sure you were either my conscience or a spook—"

He turned to face an empty room.

After looking both ways, he sighed.

"I wasn't finished!" he yelled.

There was no reply. He clamped his mouth shut and turned to look down at the sink again.

"Don't worry Josh," he muttered. "You're not crazy. Of course you're not crazy."

Josh stepped out of the restroom, tugged his cap firmly onto his head, and looked around for a vending machine. Seeing one to his right, he approached and looked at the prices, fully aware that there was absolutely nothing in his pockets.

After a moment of staring down a bottle of electrolyte embalmed lemon-lime sports drink, it occurred to him that there might be some change underneath the machine, and crouched down to look.

He groaned loudly. "Oh come on. Who cleans *under* these damn things?"

Someone behind him tapped his shoe, and he shot upright.

Nora looked down at him, straightening a gray long-sleeved athletic shirt.

"No luck?" she said.

Josh stood up slowly. "...No," he said. "Got any change?"

She shrugged. "Maybe."

Josh took in her outfit and noticed something. "You didn't have any spare pants?"

Nora had knotted the coveralls' sleeves around her waist, using the lower half as an impromptu pair of trousers. She looked down at them with a smile.

"Yeah..." she said. "Nothing bug-proof, anyway."

"Oh," Josh nodded. "Practical."

She shrugged, "I probably don't need them—I guess we're in the clear now..."

"No no," Josh said. "Really, I'm touched that you share my sense of fashion."

Nora snorted.

"So," he said. "Not to change the subject, but I've been meaning to ask you something."

Nora's smile vanished. "Oh?"

"Yeah..." Josh chewed his lip. "How—I'm lost. You seem to know at least some of these people."

"Surprisingly," Nora said, running a hand through her hair. "Yes."

"But there's also these other guys," Josh said, "And you don't seem to know who they are, but the people you know *do* know them, so..." He gestured in the air. "Where does that leave us?"

Nora looked at him strangely. "Us?"

The air grew thick.

"Yeah!" Josh said, "Like, are we not going to die? And how did you get here? What were you doing? Because if you know, I'd really like to know." He shrugged. "Just saying."

Nora stared at him.

"Oh," she said. "Okay...sure."

She glanced over his shoulder at the vending machine. "Did you want something to drink?"

Josh blinked. "Yes."

She nodded. "Okay."

As she turned away, Josh let out a long breath and shook his head.

Drink in hand, Nora led the way into the break room, and sat down at one of the circular tables. Josh sat across from her, cracked open his sugary sports concoction, and took a long draft from it.

He set it down hard on the table and drew in a long breath.

"Wow," he said. "I didn't realize I was that thirsty—"

He looked up and realized Nora was halfway through chugging her green tea and still going. It was completely gone in about ten seconds.

She brought the empty bottle down, came up for air, and set it down on the table.

Josh twisted his bottle back and forth for a moment.

"Why does my head hurt?" Nora said aloud.

"Maybe you're allergic to space scorpions," Josh said.

Nora snorted, but it was a laughing snort this time. She leaned back.

"Yeah," she said. "I suppose there's that."

"Either that," Josh said, "or you're going to get scorpion powers."

Nora looked at him and raised an eyebrow. "What?"

"Scorpion powers," he said, forming his hands into claws and hissing. "You'll be able to climb walls and stuff. Develop a sixth sense."

Nora rolled her eyes.

"Not that you need any of that," Josh said. "I mean, you can already climb like...well, I don't know what. And that's one hell of a right hook," He pointed to his black eye.

Nora sighed. "Yeah, sorry about that."

Josh was silent for a moment. "What was this all about?" he said, "I knew you in college for like ten seconds, and then you were gone—now all of a sudden, you're a super powered activist spy burglar or something."

Nora shook her head. "No no no—it's not like that at all."

"Okay then," Josh leaned back, crossing his arms. "Enlighten me."

Nora thought for a moment, then leaned forwards, stretching out a hand towards her empty bottle. Josh felt a strange charge in the air as she moved her fingers like a musician playing an invisible instrument. The air shimmered, and the container slowly floated loose of it's earthly bounds, turning gently in space.

Nora opened her hand, and it flew to her palm like a magnet.

Josh didn't move for a moment, staring at the plastic container, then he looked up at her.

"And?" he said.

Nora's brow furrowed. "And what?"

"What is it?" Josh said. "What does that mean? How does that relate to…" His train of thought came to a stop and he gestured to the room around him. "All of *this*. Do your friends know what these alien things are? Does your—what do *you* have to do with that?"

Nora looked hard at him for a moment. Josh met her gaze and backed off a bit.

"What's wrong?" he said.

She cocked her head. "Nothing," she said. "I'm just not used to—"

She levitated the bottle and spun it, "—You're sure you've never seen me do this before?"

Josh looked at the bottle, then looked at her. "Sure I did," he said. "You beat me unconscious with it. Remember?"

Nora looked hard at him. "Never before that?"

"No," Josh said, a confused look crossing his face. "How long—have you had it all this time?"

Nora stopped spinning the bottle and held it poised in mid air for another second. Then her features relaxed and she set it down on the table.

"I've had it since I was very young," she said, settling back in her seat and crossing her legs. "I don't actually remember when I first discovered I was…different."

Josh's mouth twitched, but he sat back a bit and settled down to listen.

"What does that mean specifically?" he said.

"Mostly this," she said, pointing to the bottle. "When I focus, I can move things with my mind."

She wiggled her fingers. "It's not purely mental—It takes a lot of physical effort too."

"Hmm."

"Dad said I got it from my mother," she said, "but it wasn't until I met Dr. E that I found out where *she* had got it from. She's been gone since I was small, and Dad...well, he made sure I hid it from everyone else."

She smiled mirthlessly, "Dad never had time to talk."

Josh's brows drew together. "But...I mean...so...Where *did* she get it?" he said.

"The Monolith."

Josh's puzzled look intensified. "Huh?"

"I don't know exactly how," Nora said. "Dr. E didn't have time to explain that part before we got separated...and then it was just the four of us, on the run. Me, Loyd—I don't even know where Oddball and Tina are now."

Josh looked down into his drink. "So you spent a year playing Jason Bourne?"

"Has it been a year?" Nora said. "Feels shorter than that."

"I've been here a year," Josh said. "so at least that long."

Nora slipped a glance at him as he looked down. "But how did you end up here? I thought you lived in—"

"I did," Josh said, "After the...uh...thing went down, I didn't really know what to do next. Foster said a friend had offered him a job with his security company, and he vouched for me."

Nora raised an eyebrow. "He vouched for you so that you could get a job as a janitor in another state?"

"It was *supposed* to be security," Josh said. "I arrived just in time for them to close the opening. Apparently there was some kind of administrative kerfuffle between the McKnight Security people and the administration here. Anyway...Foster let me stay at his place, and I took the custodial position instead."

Nora's brow furrowed. "But why didn't you stay in college?"

"Hm?" Josh said, "I, uh..." He cleared his throat, "It's complicated."

"It couldn't have been your grades," Nora said, "You're smart. I remember that."

Josh cocked his head, "You remember that?"

Nora shrugged, "Honestly, that's about all I remember."

Josh snorted, "You mean besides…"

"*Oh*," Nora said. "Yeah, besides the fight, you mean."

"Yeah," Josh said. "Where did you go anyway?"

"I went to the Professor's house," Nora said. "Just in time for it to blow up in front of me."

Josh blinked. "Oh."

Nora looked off into the middle distance.

"That's when I realized I had to do something," she said.

"Something about what?"

"My Dad," Nora said. "The people he works with—The kind of people who thought they could kill my Professor and get away with it."

Josh frowned. "A drug cartel?"

"No," Nora snapped. "*HunterCorp*."

"Hm," Josh said.

"I'm serious," Nora said, "There's rich and powerful people controlling this company who think they can get away with anything. People have died because of that—*your* friends have died because of that."

Josh squinted at her suspiciously. Nora blinked.

"What?" she said. "What's that look for?"

Josh studied her for a long moment. "You mean Foster," He said flatly.

Nora took a deep breath and matched his gaze.

"I have two friends still missing," she said, "and they tried to kill my Professor."

"Obviously, they failed," Josh said. "That's awfully convenient, don't you think?"

Nora stared at him.

"And on top of that—" Josh continued, "—as long as we're talking about it—from what I can see, there's at least an equal chance that Foster died because of what *your* buddies did, not Hunter's."

"You actually *believe* that?" Nora sputtered.

"I'm not saying I believe anything," Josh said. "Not yet."

"But I *know* them," Nora said. "And *I'm* telling you that would never happen."

Josh looked up at her, then back at his drink.

"Okay," he said. "Tell me about them."

Nora studied him for a moment, then cleared her throat.

"Loyd's a Meta," she said. "Like me."

"What's a Meta?"

"That's what they call us."

"Who does?"

"Dr. Easton," Nora said. "He's a college professor now, but he used to work with my—with Hunter, back when the Monolith was a US Government project."

Josh kept his face blank. "So these guys with guns are legit, right? Feds?"

"Huh?" Nora looked confused.

"The guys who hosed us down, took all our clothes—they're federal agents, right?" Josh said.

Nora shrugged. "I don't know. Easton's working for them. That's good enough for me."

Josh scowled. "Hm."

Nora's expression grew irritated. "Okay," she said. "What now?"

"Nothing," Josh said. "Keep going."

"What have you got to be so stubborn for?" Nora snapped. "Now I don't know what you're thinking, but this isn't the time to be flying off the handle and doing something stupid."

"Stupid?" Josh said. "Stupid like what? Trying to escape through an air duct?"

"I don't know," Nora said. "And besides, you know Loyd."

She picked up her bottle and threw it across the room into an open trash barrel.

Josh looked blankly at her. "I know Loyd?" he said.

"Sure," Nora said. "You met him. Remember? At the party."

Josh looked up at the ceiling for a moment, then back at Nora. "Which party?"

"*The* party," Nora said. "The one where…" She trailed off and made some vague gestures towards the world in general, "…The fight. We were just talking about it."

She looked for some flash of recognition on Josh's face. None surfaced.

"*That* party?" he said.

"Yes!" Nora said. "*That* one."

Josh looked down at the table, and blinked. He looked at the ceiling, and blinked again.

Nora frowned.

Josh leaned forwards.

"Did he have different hair then?"

Nora sighed and let her forehead fall onto the table.

"I swear I don't remember!" Josh said. "It's weird, I remember some things like they were just branded into my memory, and others—" He fluttered a hand off into the air. "Poof. Nuthin'."

"Well…it was a stressful evening," Nora said.

Josh snorted. "Understatement of the year."

The door opened suddenly, and the private mood was suddenly gone. Loyd stood in the doorway.

"Nora," He said, pointing a thumb over his shoulder. "Dr. E wants us. Let's go."

"Oh! Loyd—" Nora stood and pointed at Josh. "—You…You two have met right? I introduced you."

Loyd looked from Nora to Josh for a moment.

"Yeah," he said. "Of course."

"Really?" Josh said.

Loyd stuck his tongue in his cheek. "Yeah," he said again, immediately turning around and stepping out the door. "What are we waiting on? Let's go."

Nora turned to Josh. Josh shrugged.

"Come on!" Loyd yelled from the hallway.

Nora looked like she was about to say something, and then abruptly swallowed it.

"See you in a bit," she said.

Josh waved.

She turned around and left.

Nora followed Loyd down the hall and into the Control Room. She squinted as her eyes tried unsuccessfully to find a middle ground between the piercing brightness of the monitors and the grainy darkness surrounding them. Easton stepped forwards to clasp her hand in his, and she picked out a smile on his shadowed face.

"There you are!" he said. "Nora, I want you to meet someone—"

Out of the corner of her eye, Nora caught Loyd leaning over the sitting technician's shoulder and asking him to pull something up.

"Nora?" Easton said.

Nora jerked her head back around in time to see Easton tap the the shoulder of a burly man facing the monitors, who looked up and turned to face them. Like the others, this man was dressed from head to foot in black fatigues and body armor. He would have been a blocky figure even without the extra gear, but with it he took on the appearance of a human tank, complete with a cinder block jaw speckled with bristles. He smiled broadly, though Nora suspected that was the only way he could smile, and stuck out a meaty hand.

"Colonel McCauley. I'm in charge here," he said. "Pleasure to meet you, miss."

Nora gingerly allowed her small hand to be held in his viselike grip, and smiled politely.

"Nice to meet you," she said. "Which branch Colonel?"

"I understand that you were inside the facility when this all went down?" McCauley said, brushing past her question.

"Yes," she said, glancing at Easton quizzically. "We were trying to stop it."

McCauley laughed. "Don't worry, I've got far more important things to think about right now than breaking and entering—I just need a few answers from someone familiar with the layout."

Nora let herself relax a little. "I'll do what I can," she said.

"Good!" McCauley said, pointing to one of the monitors, "Do you recognize this man?"

Nora squinted at the screen in question, and barely recognized herself and a cluster of individuals wearing exoskeletons in a hallway.

"Which one?" she said, casting a quick glance at Loyd. He was looking intently at something on one of the other monitors. The technician was pointing out something on the screen he seemed to find very interesting.

"That one," McCauley jabbed the mushy blur of pixels again.

"I can't tell which one you're pointing to," Nora said. "Besides, they all wore masks."

"Did they target you specifically?" Easton said. "Did they know your name?"

Nora thought back. "Yes..." she said. "They seemed to know everything. It was like they were waiting for us."

McCauley glanced at Easton.

"I don't understand," Nora said. "Are you saying these might be the same guys that tried to kill you?"

"It's possible," Easton said. "But if that's the case—"

"Then Hunter is with them," Nora said coldly.

The Control room went silent for a moment.

"Right under our noses..." Easton said slowly. "Colonel, we need to put everyone on this immediately."

"Wait, what?" McCauley grunted. "How much is 'everyone'?"

"Absolutely everyone," Easton said. "Every last man."

McCauley snorted. "Sure Prof. I'll detach a few squads and we'll have a look around in a minute—"

"You do that, and I'll have your head," Easton snapped.

Nora started. She'd seen the professor angry—or at least, mildly irritated—this easily was far beyond any state she'd seen him in.

McCauley stood up straight and curled his lip. "Don't try to bluff me Prof. Nobody died and made you God."

He pointed to the monitors. "We've got people watching quarantine, people on overwatch, and that's not even mentioning the people we've got watching the front gate to make sure none of those freaky-ass bug things make it out. Two squads. Take it or leave it."

"I don't believe this," Easton retorted. "There's not more than a dozen specimens inside, tops."

"Dozen?" Nora said, casting a hand towards the monitor bank. "You haven't seen? There's loads of them down there, and more coming through the portal every minute—"

"They're not coming through," Easton said. "We're sure of that. HunterCorp has obviously been experimenting with them."

Loyd suddenly spoke up. "He's right," he said evenly. "The quake could have opened dozens of holding cells."

Nora whirled on him. "I saw *hundreds* of them down there," she said. "Maybe thousands. It doesn't matter where they're from—we have to stop them or all hell's going to break loose—"

"All of that means nothing if we can't pin it on Hunter," Easton interjected. "We have the opportunity to end this right here; catch him red-handed." He gripped Nora's shoulders and looked her in the eye. "This is it—we can stop him before any more harm's done. We can finally get the answers you've been looking for!"

Nora swallowed and turned toward the monitors. For most of them, the darkness blotted out everything, static obscuring many others—perhaps a third were still functioning.

Did anyone have the complete picture?

She turned back. "What...what do you want me to do?" she said.

"Mr. E," Loyd interrupted. "Can I speak with you privately?"

Easton turned to him. "Can it wait—"

"No."

Easton sighed and adjusted his cap. "Be ready," he finished, and then followed Loyd outside.

Josh lay on the break room couch looking up at the ceiling, trying to process everything he'd learned from Nora. His mind would keep following a thread until he blinked, and then he would doze off—almost. He'd hear a noise, or imagine he heard one, and find himself listening for things in the ceiling, or stepping over to the door and scanning the hallway for who knows what. He was tired—dead tired—but still restless. He sat up and gripped his knees to stop his hands from shaking.

"You're safe," he muttered to himself. "You're safe. Calm down."

He didn't feel safe.

His father had been in the military. He felt fairly at home around soldiers, even if they were being pushy. Soldiers had rules, and if you figured out the rules, usually everything went fine—or at least worked themselves out. Technically speaking, all of the rule breaking these guys had done so far was in his favor—but it had become pretty clear that this good grace depended solely on the good graces of the Professor character and Nora's boyfriend, whose name escaped him once more. As soon as he got on their bad side, things were going to get painful very fast, perhaps even with Nora backing him up.

He wanted to punch Loyd in the face.

She's with that guy now? Why? He's a dick!—

—And you have more pressing concerns. Like living beyond the next six hours.

He shunted the subject aside and focused. Nora had said that HunterCorp was doing something illegal—had he inadvertently made himself look like a criminal? Perhaps he was among criminals now. Maybe both groups were. Great—twice the conspiracy, twice the fun, and twice the number of people trying to bury him in a shallow, unmarked grave.

He rubbed his eyes and sighed. It felt like he'd been sat down at a high-stakes poker game with no knowledge of what kind of hand he had been dealt.

No, not Poker—Mao. That game where you had to figure out the rules as you went. The catch was that no one told you *that* either, because part of the game was the fun of running rings around the newbies.

He hated that game.

The door opened, and Josh sat up, forcing himself to act natural.

It was Loyd.

"Debriefing," Loyd said. "Let's go."

"Already?" Josh replied.

"I said let's go, didn't I?" Loyd said, raising his eyebrows. "*Vamanos*."

Josh felt pushed, but not sure what to do. He watched Loyd's body language. Was something up? Or was he just being a jerk again?

"Come on!" Loyd said. "McCauley doesn't like to be kept waiting."

"Okay, okay," Josh said, raising a hand. "Chill out. It's not life or death, right?"

Josh stretched. Loyd looked at the wall and shoved his hands in his pockets.

"Lead the way," Josh said.

Loyd pushed through the door, and Josh followed, offhandedly glancing back over his shoulder.

He stopped in his tracks.

There were three black-clad agents standing behind him, their weapons hanging loosely from their hands.

Josh felt the familiar static an instant too late. Loyd's punch blasted him in the gut, and dropped him to his knees.

"You have no idea how long I've wanted to do that," Loyd said.

He crouched in front of him.

"Same guy, wrong place, wrong time," he said. "Your boss is getting sloppy."

"I think you've got the wrong guy," Josh wheezed.

"Maybe," Loyd said, "but it's up to *you* to convince me."

He stood up.

"Keep an eye on him," he said. "I'll visit before we clean up."

Loyd stepped into the control room to see Nora looking over the technician's shoulder at one of the monitors.

"Is this what I think it is?" Nora said, standing up. "Where's Josh? He needs to see this."

Loyd stared at her for a moment.

Nora cocked her head. "What's wrong?"

"I have bad news," Loyd said. "Tina and Oddball are dead."

10

Critical Failure

Josh looked out at the Visitor's Center from underneath the bill of his cap as the Sergeant brought him to a stop in front of two guards.

"This one goes back into Quarantine," the agent said. "The Captain'll take care of him before we leave."

The two guards exchanged looks.

"Uh Sergeant," one said. "Has he been through decon—"

"Just do it, okay?" the Sergeant interrupted. "We've got to put him somewhere until the Spook gets back, and this is where the prisoners go. It'll be five minutes, tops."

There was a short pause, then the guard shrugged. "Yes Sergeant."

The two agents grabbed him by the arms and started him down the staircase to the lower level, practically dragging him most of the way. Reaching the bottom of the staircase, they dropped him unceremoniously to the floor. Someone nudged Josh's bruised ribs with a boot, and he yelped, flipping onto his back.

"Jeez," one guard muttered. "We shoulda just rolled him down."

The two re-ascended the stairs. Josh tried to think of an appropriate retort, but couldn't think of anything worth more broken ribs.

"Dicks," he muttered under his breath.

Seeing as he had nowhere to go, and it hurt to move, Josh decided to remain in place for a moment and consider his new predicament. No matter how much nothing he thought he knew, it seemed obvious their rescuers thought it was too much for him to live.

He wondered if Nora knew what had happened to him.

Suddenly something large and blurry leaned over his head and blotted out the sun.

"Mr. Murphy, I presume?" said an English-accented voice. "Mr. Joshua Murphy?"

Josh squinted and made out a balding roundish man with gray hair and spectacles. Standing with his hands clasped behind him, he managed somehow to look rather distinguished despite wearing only a wool kilt and a frighteningly pale farmer's tan.

Rolling painfully to his knees, Josh stood up straight and winced as his cracked rib shifted.

"Well," he said, "I...what was your name again?"

"I didn't offer it," Dr. Martin said. "but I shall—My name is Dr. Lewis Martin."

Josh chewed his lip for a moment, then stuck out his hand.

"Josh Murphy, as presumed," he said.

Dr. Martin shook it warmly.

"Glad to hear it," he said. "Please, follow me."

He turned and strode off between the islands of shivering exposed humanity like a man used to not wearing pants in public. Dusting off his coveralls, Josh took a deep breath and started stiffly after him, keeping his eyes on the floor. For the first time that day he felt that his situation was perhaps marginally superior to those around him. It made him uncomfortable.

Finally reaching the other side of the room, under the overhanging balcony, Dr. Martin approached a tall black man wearing glasses, who was sitting on the floor studying the carpet pattern.

"Vance!" Martin whispered. "Vance! Look what I found!"

The man looked up suddenly, as if out of deep thought, and Josh recognized the scientist who had tripped over him in the hall that morning. Vance turned to look at Josh, and his eyes widened in recognition.

"Holy…" he nearly stood up, then stopped himself and tried to look relaxed, while quickly looking back and forth.

"You brought him over *here*?" he said. "Look what he's wearing!"

Josh's impression of his clothing putting him in a superior position immediately vanished. Of course they had dumped him with the quarantined civilians. His coveralls might as well be blaze-orange and have "PRISONER" stenciled on the back.

"It's a chance we have to take," Martin replied. "They're coming back for him soon. I know it."

"So what's up?" Josh said. "You guys got a way out of this?"

"A way out?" Vance said. "Aren't you going back *in?*"

Josh stared at him. "What?"

He turned to Dr. Martin, whose had adjusted his glasses and was studying him intently.

"Tell me," Martin said. "You met a man this morning. A stranger with sunglasses."

Josh's mind went into overdrive as his range of responses to these strange men narrowed sharply.

"Uh…" he said. "How—I meet a lot of people."

"We saw you in the break room," Vance said in a low voice, "After I tripped over you in the hall?"

Josh clamped his jaw shut and cast his gaze from one to the other, taking a small step back.

"Passing on information?" Vance said. "Awfully coincidental, you being there."

"Coincidental!" Josh blurted. Now he had something to work with. "What, you think I'm some sort of secret agent?"

Martin let out a frustrated sigh. "George…"

Vance glared at him. "What?"

"If you were one of Easton's, we'd know by now," Martin said, turning to Josh. "There's a chance that you're one of Hunter's," he continued, "but that's unlikely. Therefore we have to assume you're one of Bishop's." He stroked his chin thoughtfully.

"Which is quite interesting," he continued, "because I was fairly certain Bishop was a solo operation."

Josh held up his hands. "Hold up a sec," he said. "I'm not *with* anybody, okay? I woke up this morning as Josh Murphy, *custodian extraordinarie*, and there's nothing more to it."

"Then how come Nora trusts you?" Vance said.

"She doesn't," Josh replied. "Not *that* much. And how do you know who she is anyway?"

"Because we work for Joseph Hunter," Dr. Vance said, "and he wants his daughter back."

"*Dead?*" Nora choked. "What do you mean *dead?*"

"I'm told our guys found Oddball in the parking lot—he'd been shot. Tina is missing, but…" He shook his head and slowly sat down.

Nora stared at him. "But *what?*"

Loyd swallowed and stared at the monitor bank. "They found her jacket. It has blood on it."

Nora sat down heavily and stared into space. "I…" She stopped and covered her face with her hands, squeezing her eyes tightly shut.

"No," she muttered. "There's no body."

"Nora—" Loyd said softly.

"*No,*" Nora said sharply. "If there's no body, they don't know."

"She's gone."

"She's *not* gone," Nora shot back, standing up. "She's *not* gone, and you are going to make sure they *find* her."

Loyd stood and stepped towards her. "It's okay."

"It's *not* okay." Nora shoved him away. "You're going to find her."

"We've already *looked,*" Loyd said. "They've been out there for *hours* now."

Nora folded her arms and looked intensely at the floor.

"Then Hunter has to have her." She shook her head. "That's got to be it."

"If Hunter has her, what makes you think she's still alive?" Loyd snapped.

"Because I know Hunter," she said. "He's not a sadist—he wants to know what she knows."

Loyd opened his mouth, then closed it again.

Nora folded her arms and set her mouth in a hard thin line.

"I'm sorry," she said. "Were you going to say something?"

Loyd stared at the opposite wall.

"Go on," Nora said slowly. "say it."

Loyd turned slowly to face her.

"He killed your mother," he said. "Why can't you believe he's killed my friend?"

"Tina is *our* friend," Nora growled, "and you don't know him like I do."

They locked eyes for a long moment.

Dr. Easton burst into the room, a huge smile on his face.

"Nora!" he said, breathlessly. "I found it!"

Josh stared at Dr. Martin. "She's *what*?"

"CEO Joseph Hunter's daughter," Martin said. "We work for Hunter."

"Everyone in this *room* works for Hunter," Josh said. "Except Emo Kid and his black ops friends, that is. I think they work for Uncle Sam."

"Depends on who you ask," Dr. Vance muttered.

"Oh for God's sake," Josh hissed. "Can't anybody just give me a straight answer?"

"We haven't got time to spell out the whole picture," Vance said. "We don't even know if we can't trust *you*."

"I want to get out of this alive." Josh said. "I want *Nora* to get out of this alive. And if you're not with Professor whatshisface and his little conspiracy circus, then I don't think either of us have much left to lose."

"Easton wants Nora alive as well," Vance said. "What does that prove? Why do you care about her so much anyway?"

Josh tried to turn away and winced as his bruised rib shifted. "I—Look, we spent three hours watching each other's backs, okay? If there's a way to get out of here and take her with, I'll cooperate."

He suddenly noticed Martin staring at him with a curious smile on his face.

"Fascinating," he said, adjusting his spectacles and stroking his chin, "If...then why..."

"He's a plant," Vance hissed. "You shouldn't have brought him over here. Why do you think they let him keep his clothes? Five minutes ago we were invisible—now they've got us."

"Who is this Professor guy—" Josh interrupted, "—Easton, anyway?"

"You really don't know anything, do you?" Martin said.

"No," Josh growled, "I'm not a plant; I'm not a weed; I'm not a rat; I'm just some idiot in the wrong place at the wrong time who wants to go home."

Vance snorted. "Go home?" he said. "What makes you think any of us are going *home* after this?"

"I won't say I wasn't concerned," Easton said, slapping a yellowed folder onto the conference table, "but Loyd was right to trust you with this—He found the files right where you left them, and I've been going through them ever since."

Nora snatched the file over to her side of the table and flipped it open, eagerly flipping through the contents. Easton shook his head.

"I was expecting to find enough to shut HunterCorp down, but—this was a regular treasure trove of information. It was all I could do to focus on finding the one file. I haven't even looked at it yet."

Nora picked up the dossier's first page and picked out the name from the thick blotchy typewritten text;

FILE #112275746362-12747G

Asset designation: "Rosetta."

Full Name: CASSANDRA HUNTER.

She flipped to the next page, only to be confronted by line on line of almost unreadable text covered in patches of black ink blocks.

No.

She flipped to the next page. There was barely a sentence that wasn't broken by heavy black rectangles.

Nora studied her third page and held it up to the light.

"Do you see anything?" Loyd said.

Nora didn't reply. She squinted fiercely at the page, then set it down and dove into the remaining ones, looking for something.

"I'm sorry," Easton said. "It's so—"

"Is this a copy or an original?" Nora said. "Is this all you found?"

Easton shrugged. "I looked through everything. I can look again, but I don't think—"

"This is a copy," Nora said. "I can see the paper through the ink blocks. It has to be a copy."

"Of course it's a copy," Easton said. "The originals were destroyed when—"

Nora's eyes locked on him. "What?"

Easton closed his open mouth and swallowed, glancing at Loyd.

"It's a copy because copies are all that survived the original project," he said. "We've been looking for copies this whole time. Hunter burned the rest."

Nora felt her face drain. A cold burn settled in her chest as her mind rattled around her skull like a beast in a cage, probing for holes in Easton's logic.

She swallowed hard.

"I don't understand," she said. "Why would anyone keep these? They're...almost unusable. He has to—"

"I suppose he kept them for the same reason we were looking for them," Easton said. "Any shred of information was better than none at all."

"That can't be it," Nora said, shaking her head. "It doesn't make any sense. There's got to be more here somewhere—"

"I was there," Easton said. "I saw them burn. There is nothing more."

Nora searched his expression for some hint of doubt, and found none. She looked down at the pages.

"I don't understand," she said.

Easton sighed. "I'm sorry."

Nora started as she felt Loyd's hand on her shoulder, and jerked away, standing up suddenly.

"I need to be alone," she said. "Thank you, but I need to...I need to be..." She was finding it hard to speak. She swallowed hard. "I'll be back."

She walked quickly out of the room, without bothering to close the door behind her.

Easton sighed.

"I didn't want to do this," he said. "There was no need to upset her like that."

"It's her *mother*," Loyd said. "We either give her something, or she turns on us like she did her father."

"*I'm* going home!" Josh said. "I'm going home because *I'm not part of this*. There's nothing I can do about it, and nothing anyone *wants* me to do about it."

"What about Bishop?" Martin said.

"What *about* Bishop?" Josh snapped. "If Bishop wants to play Morpheus, he can play it with someone else. I'm sure there's someone in here who wants to unravel conspiracies and fight giant space ants from hell."

"'Space ants,'" Vance snorted.

"Speaking of which—" Martin interrupted. "I've been meaning to ask you about that; how is the 'space ant' situation inside?"

Josh looked puzzled. "How is it?" he said. "You don't know what those things are?"

"We do—more or less," Martin said. "But I'm afraid that after a certain point we don't really know the…er…saturation level."

"It was plenty high when we left," Vance said. "What else do you need to know?"

"I'm not presuming the answer to be a hopeful one," Martin said. "I would, however, prefer to know how long we have left."

"How long?" Josh said. "How long until what?"

"Until…" Martin hesitated.

"Okay," Vance said. "So how many did you have to fight off at the gate?"

"How many?" Josh said. "I don't know. Hundreds."

He saw both men's faces fall visibly.

"What?" Josh said.

Martin stared at the floor. Vance smiled grimly.

"They've been busy," he said. "Assuming Easton is acting the fool he always has—"

"A fair assumption," Martin mumbled.

"—We have…days. Maybe hours," Vance finished. "Not more than that."

"But how?" Martin said. "It sounds like the creatures were *expecting* this to happen."

"Hold up—" Josh interrupted, "We've got how long before *what*? Before they…dig out or something?"

"'Or something,'" Vance said.

Josh winced as a loud speaker whine rang through the room, and turned to see where the sound had come from. An officer was standing on the information desk at the far end of the room, adjusting his bullhorn.

"Attention," he droned. "Attention please. Quarantine procedures have been completed, and we will be moving you all to a secure safe zone."

"Here it comes," Vance muttered.

Josh tried to swallow. His ears buzzed with adrenaline.

Jumping to his feet, he cast around for a spare blanket—but there were no spares. He knew there weren't. It was too late anyway—Squads of agents were already filing down the aisles, pulling people to their feet and pushing them into lines.

"Please follow the directions of all uniformed personnel, and proceed to designated areas," droned the bullhorn. "We thank you in advance for our cooperation at this time."

Josh was beginning to feel very alone. He could feel hundreds of eyes on him—he already knew the guards were watching, bug now he noticed the other detainees were staring at him too—wondering why he'd gotten to keep his clothes, he supposed.

Josh took deep breaths, trying to relieve the tension in his chest.

"Murphy."

Josh turned to face Martin.

"*Don't,*" Vance hissed.

Martin's eyes said he wasn't paying attention to his companion. "Listen carefully," he said.

"I'm listening," Josh said flatly, trying to control his shaking hands.

"Keep calm," Martin said. "Keep your eyes open, and we'll be in touch."

"You'll be in touch?" Josh sputtered. "You're in lockup, and I'm about to be beaten to a pulp by Emo Kid and the Men In Black Tac Squad!"

"If I'm right," Martin said quietly. "You're safer than we are—now, chin up, and wait for something absurd to happen."

Martin winked and turned away. Josh felt a shock go through him as a gloved hand grabbed his shoulder.

"Sir," said the guard, "please come with me," and yanked him from the line. Before he knew it, a pair of guards had looped their arms though his, and were quickly steering him down an adjoining hallway.

"Uh…" Josh shot a glance over his shoulder at the rows of worried looking half-naked detainees watching him leave.

"You sure you got the right guy?" Josh blurted.

The guards didn't answer.

"Please follow all directions from uniformed personnel," droned the bullhorn, rapidly disappearing into an incoherent smear in the background noise. "We thank you in advance for your cooperation at this time."

An agent shoved Dr. Vance up the stairs of the bus. The metal was cold under his bare feet, and he shivered, holding tightly to his emergency blanket. Swallowing his retort, he followed Dr. Martin down the aisle until they found a pair of seats on the left side of the aisle.

Martin gestured towards the seat. "Do you want the window?"

Vance stared at him for a moment, then shrugged. "Sure."

As Martin settled in next to him, Vance looked out the smeared glass and tried not to shiver.

The soldiers were packing the survivors onto two large buses, both driven by guards.

A soldier tapped sharply on the window. Vance jerked his face back.

Martin clapped him on the shoulder. "Just keep your head down," he said. "They know what's happening."

Vance shook his head. "They're gonna have to be pretty fast."

He heard the door open and looked forwards. An agent climbed into the cab, turned to the driver, and tapped him on the shoulder.

"You're relieved," the agent said.

"Already?" the driver replied.

The agent checked to see if her weapon was chambered.

"Yes," she said. "It's time."

The driver hesitated for an instant—then shrugged and got up from his seat, working his way around the agent and out the door.

The new agent let her weapon hang and formed her hand into a fist. The air around it shimmered.

Vance tapped Martin's arm. Martin looked up.

"And one more thing," the agent said. The driver turned around.

Before he could say a word, the agent jabbed him in the throat. As he staggered, she clapped her hands against his ears. There was a deep pulsing *whoomp* sound as they made contact, and he dropped like a marionette with the strings cut.

Josh was shoved through a door and into a large office, dragging him in front of a large wooden desk. He heard another guard's voice crackle.

"Okay, do it."

The guard on his left forced him to his knees and pinned Josh's arms while the other bent his head to the side. Josh saw a flash of steel out of the corner of his eye, but only had time for a sharp breath before he felt the needle pierce his forearm. He instinctively struggled, and the left guard's grip tightened, threatening to pull his arm from its socket.

"Easy…" he heard the speaker blast in his ear. "Stoppit."

"Okay," said the other, withdrawing the needle.

Josh rolled his eyes as far as they would go and saw the guard examining a dark red liquid the syringe now contained. He realized he was looking at a sample of his own blood.

"Are you gonna stay?" the agent barked. "*Are* you gonna stay?"

He punctuated his question with a sharp wrench.

"Yeah," Josh gasped.

The arms released, and both guards stood on either side of him.

Across the desk from Josh, looking out the floor-to-ceiling window, was Loyd. He stood gazing down on the mass of struggling humanity streaming out of the quarantine area like a man looking down on an anthill he'd just swept open with his shoe.

The NCO stepped up to the window.

"Detainee delivered," he said. "Permission to leave?"

"Send Easton the blood sample," Loyd replied. "Leave the guards here."

"Sir."

The NCO took the syringe case from the guard and walked out, closing the door behind him.

Josh could hear the wind humming through the air ducts in the ceiling. The left guard's vocoder popped quietly as he took a deep breath and coughed.

Loyd's voice came suddenly, quiet and clear.

"It's amazing really," he said. "How many people made it out, I mean—we did a head count, and the first estimates are something like two thirds.

Josh wasn't sure if he was supposed to respond, so he didn't.

"Not that I'm not happy about that," Loyd said, "but it is—*surprising*, wouldn't you say? Considering how fast everything happened?"

Josh shrugged. "Not sure what you mean."

"It's almost like someone *knew* it was going to happen."

Josh swallowed and looked down at his knees. A large red spot had appeared on his sleeve and was growing rapidly. He pressed his hand against it.

He felt sick.

"It wouldn't have to be that many," Loyd continued. "One guy, pulling the fire alarm a few minutes early, and *bam*—fifty more lives saved."

He looked over at Josh and smiled, his eyes sharp as a hawk's.

"Isn't that interesting?"

"That guy took my blood," Josh said. "I'm pretty sure that's illegal."

Loyd laughed and crossed his arms in front of him, "Do I look like I care?"

Josh chewed his lip, "No."

Loyd studied him for a long moment, and then uncrossed his arms, circled the desk until he was directly in front of Josh, and leaned back against the hard wood surface. When he spoke, it was in a much softer tone than before.

"You know," he said, "I never did thank you for saving my girlfriend's life."

Josh looked up at Loyd, managed to keep his face blank, and waited for the other shoe to drop.

"Heard you carried her out on your back," Loyd continued, pulling an e-cig out of his pocket and sticking it in his mouth. "Shot your way out like it was Halo or something."

A puff of water vapor wafted through the air. Josh chewed his lip.

"I carried her part way," Josh explained. "The...uh...Men In Black here were the ones that really rescued us though."

"Not before you took on a whole crowd of those spider things by yourself," Loyd said evenly. "Don't sell yourself short man—you're a badass."

"No," Josh shook his head. "I'm—I'm really not. There was...a guard that helped..."

"Uh huh. And he got offed like *that*," Loyd snapped his fingers. "I've seen the tapes man. Don't lie to me."

"I'm not lying!" Josh blurted, staring up at Loyd with what he hoped was a sufficiently honest look. "I'm not—I don't know what or who you're looking for. What do you want me to say—"

In one casual motion, Loyd pulled a gun from the small of his back and set it gently on the desk next to him, just out of reach.

Josh stared at it, then looked back at Loyd.

"What do you want me to—"

"Do you want it?" said Loyd.

Josh swallowed. "Want what?"

"The gun," Loyd stated, his eyes boring into him. "Go on. Take it."

Josh slowly opened his bloody hand and held it up.

"I just want to go home, okay?"

"Just reach out, and pull it to you," Loyd said. "Go on. I won't stop you. It's not even loaded."

"I—"

Loyd snapped his fingers, and Josh instantly felt something metal pressed against his head. He clamped his jaws together and tried to think.

"It's now or never pal," Loyd muttered around his e-cig, crossing his arms. "You've got ten seconds."

Josh squeezed his eyes shut and his brain went into overdrive.

"Running out of time," Loyd said. "Five, four, three—"

Click.

Josh felt a shock go through him and squeezed his eyes shut.

"Huh," Loyd said, "You really can't do it, can you?"

"Please," Josh sputtered, "Just tell me what you want. You've got the wrong guy."

Loyd crouched in front of him and nudged Josh's chin up until their eyes met. A low buzz hummed through his mind and grew until his vision tunneled to just those green irises staring into his soul.

"Who do you work for," Loyd said slowly.

"The company," Josh droned.

"Who do you work for," Loyd repeated.

"I work for HunterCorp." Josh swallowed.

Loyd placed both hands against Josh's head and squeezed. It felt like someone had driven a nail into each temple. He cried out and tried to peel Loyd's hands from his head. The pain spiked.

"I know when you're leaving things out," Loyd grated, his voice coming from all around. "You don't just work for the company. You work for *Hunter*."

"I've never even *met* Hunter!" Josh shouted. The pain spiked again. He gritted his teeth.

"No good spymaster *talks* to his lackeys!" Loyd shot back. "He sends people like your dead guard friend, or that weird bald sunglasses guy. Quit taking me for an idiot. Who was your contact?"

"I don't have one!" Josh said, "I don't know what you're talking about! Please—"

Loyd shoved him over on his back. He hit the floor and covered his head. When nothing happened, he lowered them and looked up at Loyd.

The other man glared down at him, wiping a nosebleed from his face. He studied Josh for a long moment.

"Hm." He mused. He turned to the guards.

"I'm done," he said. "You two take over."

"Yes sir."

Loyd picked his gun off the desk, stood, and headed towards the door. He stopped as he passed Josh, and backed up until he was in front of him.

"I'd do the honors myself, you understand," he said, "but I've got places to be."

He walked out, and closed the door behind him.

Josh heard the left guard fiddling with his weapon, but he couldn't figure out what it was until he heard the sound of a slide being pulled back and suddenly released with a solid ring of metal on metal.

He squeezed his eyes shut and strained Loyd's statement for meaning, something to say, something that would grab their attention. He felt a cold ring being pressed against the back of his head—

"Whoa whoa whoa—" the guard on his right spoke up. "He didn't say to *kill* him."

"What?" The left guard replied. "Sure he did. What's your problem?"

"He said 'take over,'" said Righty. "Not 'take out.'"

Josh held his breath.

"What's the difference?" Continued Lefty.

"What's the *difference*?" Righty replied. "There's a hell of a lot of *difference* is how much difference. What are you, four?"

"I'm old enough to make you eat that gun, is how old I am," Lefty shot back.

Josh stared at the spot on the desk where Loyd's gun had once been and strained to locate the guards behind him by sound.

They're going to shoot you. You've got to move. You've got to fight.

"Oh good," Righty muttered. "You've graduated to threats. That's mature."

"I—" The guard stopped and growled something under his breath. "Look—you know I ain't threatening you or nothing, all right? Just don't put me in this position, okay?"

"*I'm* putting us in this position? *You're* the one who was gonna wax the prisoner before the Spook was done with him."

Something caught Josh's eye and he squinted though the glare on the window. It looked like someone was standing in the office opposite theirs.

"The Spook *is* done with him. He literally said the word 'done.'"

"That's what interrogators do. He's trying to psych him out."

"Oh he is, huh? Then why didn't he tell *us*?"

"He doesn't need to tell us! Why the hell would he tell us?"

"So we don't *shoot* him!"

Josh heard the door open.

"What the hell is this?" A third voice crackled authoritatively.

"No problem Corporal," said Lefty.

"He's about to execute one of the prisoners." Said Righty.

"On orders?"

The answers came on top of each other.

"Yes—."

"—No."

There was a pause.

"Listen," the NCO's voice came low and enunciated. "If I have to un—"

"The Spook was in here, and he said, 'take care of it!'" came Lefty.

"God dammit, that is *not* what he said!"

"Knock it off!" the NCO's bellowed. "Which 'Spook'—The Kid?"

"Yeah," said Righty, "The psycho one."

"He's not psycho," Lefty muttered.

"Not compared to *you*—"

"Shut up," the NCO growled. His radio coughed as he adjusted something.

"HK Actual, this is HK 1-3, requesting clarification, over."

Static.

"HK Actual, this is HK 1-3."

Josh strained his ears for the response.

"HK 1-3 this is HK Actual, go ahead."

"Actual, The Spook's just finished his interrogation and I've got two dumbasses with conflicting reports on how to process the prisoner. Please advise, over."

"Wait one."

Josh could feel the seconds slipping past like cars on a racetrack. His eyes roved the room frantically in search of a letter opener, a trapdoor in the floor, a stray grenade—anything.

He stared through the window again, and in a flash finally made out the figure opposite. His eyes widened.

It was Bishop, standing there with his hands clasped in front of him, just a hint of a smile nearly visible on his face.

Josh began looking around. Staring at the desk, he suddenly realized it was a significantly more solid affair than he had first assumed—maple, possibly oak. Perhaps not bulletproof, but close to it. Even more significantly, none of his captors were between him and it, meaning if he moved fast enough—

Josh moved before he had time to doubt himself. In one leap, he scrambled up on top of the desk, and rolled into the chair, tipping it backwards onto the floor. Rolling to his feet, he—

—Was immediately tackled by Righty. The deafening crack of a gunshot blasted through the room.

Josh hit the ground like a ton of bricks under another ton of bricks, the wind smashed out of him. He struggled to breath.

"Jesus Christ *hold your fire!*" The NCO's voice barked.

"God Dammit—You shot me!" Righty groaned. He adjusted his hold, but kept Josh's face shoved into the carpet.

"How was I supposed to know you were gonna tackle him?" Lefty retorted. He stepped forward into Josh's vision. "Besides, I hit you in the armor. Let him up, I've got him covered."

Josh felt Lefty get up, and the pressure released enough for him to turn his head sideways and suck in a painful breath. There was nowhere to go. He was flat on his face, with a gun trained on his head.

The NCO's radio popped.

"HK 1-3 this is HK Actual, pick up."

"This is 1-3, go ahead."

"Yeah, Captain says he's not our problem. Use your own discretion."

There was a pause. Josh could hear Righty standing behind him, breathing like a stepped on squeaky toy—long, labored.

"Come again, HK Actual—elimination is authorized?"

Josh tensed. *No. No no no...*

"Nobody up here cares 1-3—deal with it, and move on. We've got a lot of people to process."

The NCO muttered a curse.

"Tell them I'm a friend of Nora's!" Josh blurted. "I'm not supposed to be here! This is a mistake!"

"God dammit," the NCO growled, looking up at his men. "Neither of you saw who did it, right?"

"I don't see no nametags," Lefty said.

"Nobody saw...nuthin," Righty huffed. "I'm shot."

"You're wearing a bulletproof vest. It's just a broken rib," The NCO snapped. "Okay, grease this sucker quick and let's go."

"Got it," Lefty muttered.

Josh squeezed his eyes shut.

Click.

The only sound was Righty's breathing.

"What the hell now?" came the NCO's voice.

"I got, I got it," Lefty muttered. Josh heard the slide rack, and a cartridge thumped to the carpet next to his head.

Click.

Josh gritted his teeth. "*FUGH!*"

The NCO sighed, "Oh for the love of…"

"It's not my frickin' fault! The frickin' gun's jammed!"

Out of the corner of his eye, Josh saw Lefty look up at Righty.

"Dude, toss me your piece," Lefty said.

"Yeah, sure…" Righty replied, slowly drawing the weapon from its holster.

"Whoa, wait—"

WUMP.

Like magic, a Glock semi-automatic pistol landed flat on the beige carpet, inches from Josh's eyes.

For a half second, no one moved. Time crawled, and Josh saw the numbers 9X19 engraved on the slide grow larger and larger in his vision.

He snatched at it just in time for both his hand and the gun to be pinned to the floor by Lefty's combat boot.

"Oh no you don't *bitc—*"

Lefty's comment was cut off by his foot exploding. His subdued mutter abruptly turned into a high-pitched scream, and he fell over backwards, clutching his leg.

Josh ripped his bloodied hand from under the man's boot and rolled onto his back, leveling his weapon at the astonished NCO, who stood frozen in shock, his rifle hanging limply from his hands.

For several furious nanoseconds the the pistol and the NCO's rifle cracked in tandem, Josh forcing himself to keep his eyes open as shockwaves filled the air. On Josh's third shot, a perfect red halo framed the man's head. He dropped in his tracks, rebounding off the wooden desk.

Josh felt his ribs scream as Righty kicked him, and let out an involuntary gasp. He fought to move, scrambling backwards and kicking wildly. Righty took a strike to the thigh, and caught the second kick in his hands.

"Come 'ere mother-*ugh.*"

Josh kicked him in the nuts. As soon as the agent let go, Josh was crawling backwards again—straight into Lefty's lap.

He felt arms wrap around his neck, pulling him backwards. He managed to jam his gun hand underneath Lefty's arm, which gave him the breathing space to realize he'd just done the stupidest thing possible.

"Got 'im!" Lefty shouted. "I got 'im!"

Righty climbed unsteadily to his feet, and slowly drew a long combat knife from his vest. Josh felt a spike of adrenaline and dug his fingers in, trying to pry Lefty's hand loose. The agent's grip appeared to loosen for an instant—then shifted like lightning, locking even closer around his windpipe.

Josh choked for breath, brought his free elbow up, and slammed it into Lefty's side.

"What are you waiting for!" Lefty coughed. "*Cut* 'im!"

Righty took a lurching step forwards, then halted. He sounded like he was trying to breath mud.

Josh grabbed the slide of his pistol with his right hand and pulled it free. He fumbled it into a proper grip, twisted over until he could jam the muzzle against Lefty's armpit, and pulled the trigger.

An earsplitting crack stabbed his eardrums, and the world was blown out to a high-pitched ring. Josh shouted and heard nothing. He felt the grip around his neck relax, and immediately hooked his fingers under the man's arm, tearing it away.

He stopped and looked up.

Righty stood only a few feet away, knife still at the ready. Josh held out the Glock and put the front sight over his mask.

"Don't," he said.

Righty stared at him dully, and staggered. Looking down, he slowly pulled the side flap of his armor vest loose.

Josh noticed the fabric underneath was soaked. The agent touched it with the exposed fingers sticking out of his cutoff gloves.

Righty stared at the dark red smear on his hand, looked up at Josh, and fell like a log, hitting the floor with a resonant thud.

Josh struggled to his feet and realized that, aside from the ringing, he could hear again. He shifted his aim to Righty, and tripped over the NCO as he backed up, nearly falling.

All three lay still.

Josh's breathing slowed.

I'm alive.

"Okay," he said, controlling his breathing. "Think, think—you're alive, you're a fugitive, you've got a gun—what now?"

He heard the door unlock behind him and spun around, gun raised. To his surprise, the door was pulled shut again, leaving a black cylindrical object on the floor. He recognized it an instant too late.

BANG!

The shock rendered him deaf, blind, and stunned, staggering backwards. Guessing at the location of the door he pulled the trigger, loosing a pair of almost inaudible shots. Something hard connected with his jaw, and everything went black.

"Drivers aren't responding," the Lieutenant quipped.

"Oh, you think?" Captain McCauley snapped, gesturing towards the buses speeding into the desert. From their position on top of the Administration building, he could see them both roaring off towards the horizon. He turned to the officer at his right. "Lieutenant, tell air support to get off their asses and smoke 'em. *Now.*"

"Sir?"

"I said *smoke* those bastards," McCauley shouted.

The officer hesitated.

"But—"

"Whoever is driving those things ain't ours, get it?" McCauley growled. "*Do it.*"

"Yes sir."

"McCauley!" Loyd shouted. "What the hell's going on?"

Captain McCauley cursed under his breath and turned to see Loyd, Professor Easton, and that girl they were so concerned about striding across the roof towards him. The Captain crinkled his hard-bitten lips in a scowl. *Great.*

"We're having a problem with Quarantine Protocol," McCauley shouted back, holding up his hand. "Everything is under control."

"You've got *five seconds* to tell me what's just happened, Captain," Loyd growled, coming to a stop directly in front of McCauley's face.

"Bring it up with your supervisor Spook," McCauley said, curling his lip.

"You make me, and you'll regret it," Loyd snapped back.

"Please, gentlemen—" Professor Easton interjected. "I'm sure there's an easier way to solve this—"

"Professor," McCauley barked. "You've got *three* seconds to get your mook out of my face before he gets his shit wrecked."

"How much you wanna bet?" Loyd said.

"*Loyd!*" Mr. E said, more forcefully this time. "I don't have time to untangle you two while the operation is in jeopardy. *Stand. Off.*"

Loyd stepped back, his eyes smoldering. The professor turned to the Captain with a broad smile. "Captain—you were saying?"

McCauley shot a glance at Nora. "She cleared?"

Mr. E turned to Nora and studied her for a moment, then turned back to McCauley. "She's…well, be tactful."

McCauley gave Easton's face an intensive working over. "Be more specific."

"No."

McCauley considered this for a moment, then looked up as the doppler thump of helicopter blades roared over them, the fierce-looking black attack chopper sweeping out over the chem plant in pursuit of the two distant dust plumes pulling onto the tarmac.

The Lieutenant held his hand to his earpiece. "Pilot's asking for permission to engage."

"He's what?" McCauley said.

"He's looking for permission to engage sir."

"Well, give it to him!"

"Yes sir," the lieutenant tapped his earpiece. "You have a go. Repeat —"

A lance of smoke slashed across the sky, and the chopper exploded into ragged flaming chunks.

McCauley heard the girl speak for the first time—a loud gasp of shock.

"What the hell was that?" she blurted.

"McKnight," Loyd growled. "Hunter still has assets in the area."

"They just killed that guy!" Nora said.

"Two," McCauley said. "Apache carries two."

"Two guys?" Nora said.

"You said this area was clear!" Loyd snapped. "You said there was nobody here when you guys showed up except local security."

"There *wasn't*," McCauley retorted. "We scoured this place from top to bottom, and we didn't find *shit*."

"Oh?" said Loyd, gesturing towards the burning pile of scattered debris. "Then explain *that*."

Easton shook his head, "This was supposed to be contained. No mess—"

McCauley threw his hands up. "Professor, this was a crap sandwich from the start. Don't pretend we didn't tell you that."

"Quit making excuses and clean this up," Loyd said. "Now you know where they are—take care of them."

"'Take care?'" Nora said, grabbing Loyd's arm and yanking him around. "What, are you at war? What's going on?"

Loyd pulled his arm away. "Let me deal with this Nora—"

"No," she said. "I want to know what's happening *right now*."

"It's complicated."

"I just saw two men *die* right in front of me," Nora snapped.

"Hunter's eliminating witnesses," Easton said. "If he gets away with those buses, we'll never pin this to him—he'll get away scot free."

Loyd passed Nora a pair of binoculars. She raised them to her eyes and focused on the vehicles as they pulled into the small airport. Dozens of tiny figures were hemmed in by perhaps a half-dozen McKnight security guards armed to the teeth. A cargo plane was pulling out of the hanger.

"We shoot that down," McCauley said, glancing at Easton, "and we could kill 'em all. We don't wanna do that…right?"

"Focus on the ground game." said Easton. "*That's* where Hunter's got to be."

"We already checked."

"Then check *again*!" Easton snapped.

Nora had stepped back, holding the binoculars in numb fingers. She felt dizzy. *Witnesses? Killing…witnesses?*

She turned and ran smack into an agent. She hadn't noticed him standing there.

"Oh!" she said. "Sorry."

As Nora turned away, she suddenly felt a burly arm whip around her throat, cutting off her shout of surprise. In another second she had been dragged backwards through a door, and into the dark stairwell.

11

<u>Poker Face</u>

Josh didn't understand.

He felt awake—all it took was a blink—but now he didn't know where he was.

It was dark, cold, and pitch black. He had a headache, but couldn't move his hands or feet.

After jerking back and forth a bit, he discovered he was securely strapped to a metal chair. He tried to reach his fingers back and pick at the bonds, but they were too far. He gripped the armrests and yanked, trying to see if there was any loose connections.

Nothing.

He suppressed a bout of claustrophobia and focused. Now that he thought about it, he was rather surprised that he was still alive—he'd half expected to wake up dead, so to speak. He was trying to remember why…

Oh right! They were going to shoot me.

He frowned. Something different had happened next, obviously.

Now he remembered. They had all abruptly died.

He had killed them. No—two. One had shot the third.

He had killed two men.

A horrible, terrifying doubt rose like acid inside and tore at him.

This all has to be some kind of mistake.

They were going to kill me.

They didn't.

Because I didn't let them.

You didn't explain.

I tried.

"I *tried*," he muttered fiercely.

He tried to control his breathing and relax. His restraints began to feel strangely tighter, the room itself closing in around him.

They're dead.

Shut up.

They're dead, and you killed them.

"No," he muttered to himself.

Saying it aloud helped—seemed to make it more focused and real. "No. I killed them, but they tried to kill me."

Besides, he thought, he'd only killed two men. They had shot the third. Somehow.

Josh heard a groan in the dark next to him. He froze.

For a moment, all he could hear was his own heartbeat pounding in his ears as they strained through the empty background noise for a scrape, a breath—

There it was again.

"Hello?" Josh said, in a moderate tone.

He would have talked louder, but he wasn't sure exactly what he was disturbing, and it was entirely possible it was just a guard sleeping—in which case he was in no hurry to wake them up.

He waited. Nothing.

"Hello?"

"Guh," said someone.

Someone female.

"Nora?" Josh said.

"Hm?" The voice was groggy, but responsive.

"Nora!" Josh hissed. "It's me! Wake up!"

"What's going—OoooW!" she said. "Why do I keep getting knocked out?"

Josh sucked in a long breath of relief and grinned in spite of himself.

"Don't look at me," he said. "I'm just glad we keep waking up."

"I can't see."

"I think it's just dark."

"Oh."

Josh listened closely, trying to feel out the size of the room. It couldn't be that large—the air was very still, and smelled musty.

"Okay," he said. "Can you do that...thing. That thing you do?"
"What?"
"You know—can you break the straps or something?"
"Straps?" Nora said.
There was some thumping and the sound of Nora grunting as she pulled at the chair. She stopped.
"Straps," she muttered.
"Yep," said Josh. "Can you break them?"
"No," she said, "but I might be able to *unlock* them."
Silence.
"So are you going to do it?" Josh quipped.
"I'm working on it! I'm not friggin' superwoman."
"Oh come on," Josh said. "It took you thirty seconds to crack a zip tie."
"Then give me thirty seconds," she retorted. "I can't even tell what these are *made of* yet."
Josh settled back and shut up. Of course, she was right. There was no point getting in her face about it.
"I don't know about you," Josh said, "but I'm starting to wonder if these government guys are being up front with us."
"Oh?" grunted Nora. "Why's that? Because you're tied to a chair?"
"Among other things."
"What?"
The metallic ring of a door bolt shot through the room. Josh froze.
A blinding rectangular halo of light cut itself out of the darkness in front of them, and a figure stepped through the open doorway, reaching to the side to flick on the light.
Josh shut his eyes a split second too late, and the hot white overhead light blinded him.
"Aagh..." he groaned. "Give a guy a heads up why don't ya?"
The man dragged a metal chair squealing across the concrete floor, set it backwards in front of the two prisoners, and sat on it, folding his arms on the backrest.
Josh blinked spots from his eyes and tried to look straight at him,

hoping to let Nora continue whatever progress she was making. It was hard to match the man's gaze—he was wearing sunglasses and a full-face balaclava. The patch on his gray fatigues read "BOSS."

"Uh..." he said. "Do you work for the...the government...guys?"

The man didn't answer.

Josh cleared his throat and swallowed.

"You killed three men," Boss said suddenly. His voice was low and clipped—he was apparently using a small version of the voice modulator the other soldiers were using.

"No. Absolutely not," said Josh, shaking his head.

The man's sunglasses stared impassively back. Josh swallowed.

"I'm serious—the uh...there was a guy in the other office. He...well, they were going to kill me," he finished lamely, "and...uh...I'm sure you don't want that, right?"

"I haven't made up my mind yet," Boss said.

"They were going to shoot me," Josh said.

"Very perceptive of you," said Boss, withdrawing a bundle of crushed papers from his back pocket and unfolding them.

Josh stared at him for a moment.

"So..." he said. "Why am I not dead?"

"Because I'm not with them," Boss said, "and also because of her."

He nodded towards Nora.

Josh looked at Nora. Nora looked back. He slanted an eyebrow. She shook her head vigorously. *I don't know.*

Josh turned back to Boss. "What?"

"When did you two first meet?" Boss said, looking from one to the other.

Josh swallowed. "Uh...six—" he turned to Nora. "Was it six?"

Nora nodded. "Seven."

"—Seven. Seven this morning," Josh said, looking back and nodding. "Something like that."

"Seven," Boss repeated, nodding along with them. "Seven. Bright and early."

Josh nodded. "Yeah. Still getting the 'bright eyed and bushy-tailed' part down, but—"

Boss's hand lashed out and slammed into Josh's leg, leaving a full syringe of something standing upright in his thigh. Josh choked back a yelp and froze, staring at it.

"What the hell is wrong with you!" Nora shouted.

"He's fine," Boss said, "and he's a liar."

Nora swallowed hard and tried to look behind her.

Josh's eyes were fixed on the syringe's contents.

"What is that!" he croaked.

"I'm not going to tell you," said the interrogator, "but if you lie to me again, you're going to find out—*Now*," he continued. "Why don't we try this from the top?"

"He's just the janitor," Nora forced out. "He doesn't know anything."

"How do *you* know?" said Boss. "You just met him."

Nora slowly closed her mouth and leaned back in her chair.

Boss turned back to Josh.

"You're quite a survivor for a member of the custodial arts," he said. "Ever been in a fight before today?"

Josh clamped his hands onto the armrests and took a deep breath. "What kind of fight—"

"Ever shot anyone?"

"No."

The man stared at him for a moment. "Correct," he said, glancing at the paper, "but this isn't your first violent episode, is it?"

Josh stared at him. "Episode?"

"Expelled from Arbor University for, quote—" said Boss, looking at his paper. "—'Assault and battery of two fellow students.'"

Nora leaned forwards in her chair. "*What?*"

"*Ooooh.*" Boss whistled. "Against two *female* students!"

"In my defense," Josh said, "I didn't know that until afterwards."

Nora looked confused. "That was a girl?"

"You deny the assault charge?" said the interrogator.

"Yes!" said Josh, "No! I mean..." He twisted his mouth into a frustrated scowl. "Look, she was there. Tell her what they say I did."

"What are you talking about?" said Nora.

"The incident in…" Josh paused. "You remember."

Nora stared at him, then shook her head. "You got in trouble for that?"

"I got *expelled* for that," Josh snapped, "because you skipped town before telling your side of the story."

"My dorm *blew up*!" Nora shot back. "I went underground!"

"So leave a note or something!"

"So what you're saying," Boss said, pointing at Nora. "Is that *she* got attacked,"

Josh nodded.

"And you just happened to walk past in time to hear a group of people wrestling in the *women's room*, and decide it was your honorable duty to check it out?"

Josh chewed his lip. "I'm reluctant to put it in those terms—"

"Yes or no."

"Yes."

"And upon discovering two individuals attacking a fellow student," Boss continued, "You decided to fight them instead of call security?"

Josh chewed his lip.

"I was *fine*," Nora growled.

"Good to know," Josh said. "Next time I see someone choking your lights out I'll just let *you* deal with it."

He turned to the interrogator. "What does this have to do with anything anyways?"

"Nothing," Boss replied, balling the sheet of paper and tossing it over his shoulder. "Just curious."

Josh stared at him. "Why?"

"I'm learning what you look like when you tell the truth," The interrogator said, pulling another piece of paper out of his pocket. "I asked you questions about something I already know—now I'm going to ask you about something I don't."

Josh swallowed hard. He glanced at Nora, but Nora wasn't looking at him. She was staring intently at Boss.

"See," Boss said. "I already know quite a bit about you. I know your name is Joshua Murphy. I know you were expelled trying to protect Nora Hunter. I know that you're here because Shane Foster said he could get you a job."

"What?" Josh blurted.

"I know that you ate a toaster strudel for breakfast, and that you don't talk back to your overbearing supervisor," Boss continued. "But what I *don't* know—" He set his hands on Josh's armrests and leaned in until Josh could feel the man's breath on his face, "—Is who you *really* are."

Josh's blood ran cold, and he suddenly felt as if someone had stripped off his skin and found someone else underneath.

"You know," said Boss, "it was really cute at first—the whole 'wrong guy in the wrong place' act. Perfectly executed. Brazen, but just plausible. I'm a hard man to fool, and you fooled me."

"But everything you said is true!" Josh said.

"It was perfect," Boss continued. "Too perfect."

"What is!" Josh shot back.

"Does Nora know?" he said. "Who you really work for?"

Josh shook his head vigorously. "I don't know what you're talking about!"

"You think the security cameras are blind around here?" Boss barked. "We saw everything. *Everything!*"

"Why does everyone keep talking about the friggin' security cameras?" Josh sputtered.

"You knew how to escape the security guard's handcuffs," Boss growled. "You knew just where to go to run into Nora and her escort."

"Foster?"

"You convinced her to trust you when she had a gun to your head," Boss said, his voice steadily raising in power, "You knew to duck when the truck exploded at the doors, *just* before rescue arrived."

"I don't know how *any* of that happened!" Josh replied. "I was guessing!"

The interrogator gave Josh's chair a swift kick. Josh saw the light soar over him, and leaned forwards as the chair slammed into the concrete, his head barely bouncing against the unyielding floor. Boss stepped over him and grabbed him by the collar, shouting in his face.

"Don't lie to me!" he roared. "You've had firearms training!"

"My Dad taught me to shoot!" Josh gurgled.

"You knew what serum to give Nora."

"It was the only thing that looked like it would work!"

"You rigged military grade explosive devices!"

"IT HAD PICTURE 'STRUCTIONS!"

"DAD!" Nora shouted. "STOP IT!"

The room came to an abrupt halt. Josh could hear his heartbeat again. Boss stood up slowly, staring at Nora.

Nora felt the eyes beneath his sunglasses boring into her—and then he reached up, and in one swift movement, pulled the mask from his face.

He was a man with short graying brown hair, and a lean face chiseled from granite. His sharp blue eyes were too open to describe as a squint, but Josh got the impression that he was angry or surprised, and their natural state was a tad narrower. A scowl curled the corner of his mouth.

When he finally spoke, it was in a smooth growl that wasn't terribly loud, but had surprising carrying power.

"Who told you?" he said.

"No one," Nora replied. "I know your voice."

Joseph Hunter smiled in spite of himself, "So you do listen."

"I listen," said Nora.

"Then why are you here," he said.

"Why are you beating the shit out of your own employee?"

Josh considered seconding her, but a sharp glance from Hunter shut his mouth. He knew that look.

"Because he doesn't *work* for me," Hunter said. "He works for the people that sent you here."

"No one sent me here," Nora retorted. "I came here after you killed Professor Easton."

"And now he's alive again," Hunter said. "How convenient."

Nora swallowed.

"Either way, you tried to kill him."

"I was trying to keep you safe," Hunter growled, "I wanted you to know the truth—"

"What truth?" Nora interrupted, "The same truth you told me about Mom?"

Hunter rolled his eyes. Nora leaned forwards.

"Oh right—" she said. "You didn't tell me about her. Or about the Monolith, or anything else!"

"It's called *compartmentalization*—"

"Compartmentalizing? Or just burying it so deep that no one will *ever* know what happened!"

"Because that's what you came for," Hunter nodded sardonically. "The truth."

"I came here to *stop* you," Nora growled, "To keep you from exploiting something you don't understand."

"*Exploit?*" Hunter shouted, "Of *course* I exploited it. You've seen what comes through that portal—there's a whole planet on the other side packed to the gills with biological killing machines; an entire civilization reduced to *dust* by a threat older than recorded history. You can't beat an enemy you won't understand. Easton never understood that."

"So why not just destroy the object?" Nora interrupted.

"Don't you think we thought of that?" Hunter said. "Or did Easton tell you this whole thing was about *money*?"

"Well," Nora sneered. "It did make you rich, didn't it?"

Hunter's back straightened a notch.

"*Money*," he spat. "I made millions with my own two hands—Easton's people had billions *given* to them and they're *still* stealing their designs from us. The only thing we've ever shared is that damn rock down in the basement—I had the door, and they had the key. We couldn't have turned the thing on if we'd wanted to."

Josh saw Nora pause as an odd expression crossed her face, then it was gone, and the angry mask returned.

"And what happens to those people you kidnapped?" she said. "Your own employees? What are you hiding down there that requires you to silence hundreds of your own workers?"

"Do have any idea," Hunter growled. "What those goons would have *done* to them? Those workers are like family—"

"*Family?*" Nora interrupted. "If you wanted me to think you cared about *family*, you should have stuck around and taught me so."

A muscle in Hunter's jaw twitched. He crossed his arms.

"If I hadn't done what I did—" he began.

"I don't *care* why you did what you did—" Nora interrupted again, but this time he powered over her.

"—*None* of us would be here today!" He finished.

Nora clammed up and stared at the opposite wall, her face like stone except for the occasional angry twitch.

Josh, still on his back with his feet in the air, weighed the risks of asking whether someone was willing to set him up upright or staying out of conversation altogether. In the end, his throbbing head won out, and he spoke.

"Excuse me," he rasped. "Not to…interrupt or anything—but can someone please pick me up?"

"So," Hunter said, lighting his cigarette. "What do you think?"

"I don't know what to think," Vance replied, shaking his head at his wall of clues. "It's like a riddle, wrapped in a mystery, tied in an enigma… rolled in a blanket—"

"I get it," Hunter interrupted.

"—Packed in a box full of little styrofoam peanuts," Vance finished.

"Oh please," Martin muttered, chewing absently on the end of a pen. "Surely it's not so complicated as all that."

He glanced at Hunter's cigarette. Hunter noticed and showed Martin his hand.

"Just nerves," he muttered. "I'll get rid of it."

"I'm sure you *wouldn't* think it's that complicated," Vance snapped at Martin, "not when *your* solution is 'literal interpretation of eight-thousand-year-old-poetry-in-a-dead-alien-language.'"

Martin shrugged. "If it fits all the available evidence, I don't see the issue—and it's not a dead language."

Vance scowled at him. "At what point does it mention aviator sunglasses?"

Martin sighed. Vance spun around and pointed to the wall behind him. It was covered in grainy photos, half-decipherable messages scribbled on crumpled notebook paper, and starbursts of string crisscrossing and intersecting like the framework of some complex molecular compound.

"Unkillable custodian…" he began, "…Mr. Shades, plus mutant ninja college students, *plus* black ops cleanup crew, all present for the first day of an alien invasion, equals *what*?"

"We already know most of the links between these," Hunter reminded him. "Professor Easton and his overlords were bound to come for the Monolith sooner or later."

"But they've never hit anything this *big* before," Vance said, "and they've known we had it for years—why now?"

"They knew *who*," Hunter said. "They didn't know *where*."

"So you're saying they wanted to shut us down?" said Martin. "But what about Nora? Surely she didn't know about—"

"As far as I know, she didn't," said Hunter. "It's obvious they pumped her full of misinformation about what it is and what we did with it. What's really strange is that is that Easton's boys are acting like they didn't know it *either*."

"What," said Vance. "You mean the Locust?"

"Exactly," Hunter said, gesturing with the glowing tip of his cigarette, "Look at them—light weapons, riot gear, laid out half their equipment without even setting up a perimeter. If they'd forgotten to close the doors after extracting Nora and Mr. Murphy they'd be swimming in bugs right now."

He snorted and took another draw, "friggin' amateurs."

"And Bishop?" Vance said.

Martin opened his mouth, but decided not to say anything. Vance raised an eyebrow, but Martin only shrugged and rolled his eyes.

Hunter removed his cigarette and let out a long breath of smoke, still squinting at the wall of clues.

"That's the other big question," he said. "What does Bishop and *this* guy have to do with this?" He tapped a finger on Josh's photo.

"We've known nothing about Bishop for six months," said Vance. "What makes you think that's going to change now?"

"Because this time we've had gotten to see him work," said Martin. "Even putting aside any interpretation of the texts in our possession, we have far more concrete data on Bishop now than we've ever had."

Hunter turned to him. "All right then—what's your interpretation?"

Martin looked at the wall and chewed his lip. "I haven't concluded anything yet, if that's—"

"Ballpark," said Hunter, stubbing out his cigarette in the island sink.

Martin thought for a moment, casting a glance at Vance.

"Prophetic interpretation aside," he began, "Bishop's motives have always been murky because he almost always makes his move far before anyone is watching him, and even afterwards determining who benefited the most from his actions is very much a guessing game. The fact that we knew of his existence at *all* before this particular incident is something of a fluke—"

"The *point*," Hunter muttered.

"The *point*," Martin said, "is that Mr. Murphy's preeminent goal in every observed incident has been to protect Nora at cost to life, limb, and reputation. Bishop, who very rarely associates with anyone, was seen openly talking to Murphy in full view of a security camera. What does that suggest?"

"That he wants us to think he's protecting Nora," Vance said,

Martin sighed, "My dear fellow, I feel you have perhaps missed the forest for the trees."

"So you're saying he's got plans for Nora?" Hunter said,

"It's possible," said Martin, "but more obviously, I think that he has no interest in either she or her guardian dying, and has taken steps to prevent it."

"That doesn't necessarily make us friends," Vance said.

"Not with Bishop," said Martin, "but I think it's highly unlikely that

Murphy himself has any ulterior motives."

"I don't know about that," said Vance. "You remember what happened to Foster."

"Foster himself said that it was his own mistake," Martin said, "and Foster has known Murphy longer than any of us. Certainly long enough to notice anything that might give him doubts."

Hunter's thoughtful scowl loosened a bit. "Then perhaps we should bring Foster back in," he said. "Have him ask a few questions."

"I have another idea," said Martin. "Not necessarily a conflicting one—but I would very much like to ask Mr. Murphy his own explanation of what we saw."

Hunter shook his head. "I already asked him."

Vance snorted, "On this one, I agree with Martin," he said. "You've done bad cop—now let us try good cop."

"Foster's good cop." said Hunter.

"Foster has a conflict of interest," said Martin. "We already know his opinion. Besides—" Martin shot a glance at Josh's photo. "—We've assumed up to this time that our janitor understands more about Bishop than we do. Perhaps we should put that to the test."

Josh heard Nora let out a long breath. She was trying to ignore the unnatural feeling of being stuck in one position, clenching and unclenching her fingers in rapid fanning motions. Hunter had left the light on when he left, thankfully.

"So…" Josh said. "Is that the way your Dad vets all your guy friends?"

"If he had his way," Nora muttered. "Pretty much."

Josh chuckled. "Well, I bet it keeps the creepers away."

"Along with everyone else," Nora muttered.

"Well yeah," said Josh. "I'm just saying—"

"I'm sorry—" Nora interrupted, "—Did you miss the part where he *stabbed* you?"

Josh halted all trains of thought and tried to figure out which one had the bomb on it.

"Uh…" he said. "No—"

"People are dead now," Nora continued. "It's *his* fault, and it's the people who run this company's fault."

Josh stared at her. "What did they do?"

"For the love of—!" Nora sputtered. "Haven't you been paying attention?"

"To *what*?" Josh shot back. He was starting to lose his own temper.

"The experiment!" Nora said, slowly, enunciating. "The one that let out all the aliens?"

"They did that?" Josh said. "How do you know?"

"Because I came here to *stop* it!" Nora straightened in her chair. She seemed to be looking down her nose for just an instant, but Josh wrote it off as unintentional—he had more important information to process.

"Look," he said. "I've been here for almost a year now. Dangerous stuff happens, yes—but nobody ever got killed. Before you and your pals showed up, I had a job, I had friends—"

"You're not listening—"

"Just—just hold on for a second and hear me out." Josh said.

"No!" said Nora. "Why should I?"

"Because it's MY *FRIGGING LIFE* YOU RUINED!" Josh hopped in his chair, shifting it sideways.

"I DIDN'T *NEED* YOUR HELP!" Nora shouted back. "You could have walked on past, but *no*—"

Josh clenched his hands into fists and gritted his teeth, wishing he could take back his outburst. Sure, he was mad—but yelling only got people to stop talking if they gave a shit what you had to say.

"…My *life* was in danger, and I wasn't sticking around to find out who wanted it." Nora continued. "How was I supposed to know you would get in trouble?"

"Okay, fine, please—" Josh said. "Just—tell me what you were here to stop."

"What?" Nora snapped. "I told you! The Monolith?"

"See, I don't know what that is," Josh replied.

"I told you!"

"No. You didn't," Josh said, "You said it was an alien thing, and Foster said it was a rock, and that's *it*. Now, you were saying it caused the whole hurricane-zero-gravity vortex of death?"

"*Yes*." Nora said. "You didn't figure that out already?"

Josh rolled his head around and tried not to scream.

"Okay," he growled. "You know what? Don't tell me. Who cares? *I don't!* I don't care, I don't care..."

"This is important!" Nora hissed. "Don't you want to survive this?"

"To be honest, I'm not sure what difference my opinion will make at this point," Josh replied.

"We can't just give up."

"*I can*," Josh snapped. "I'm not in this for your little Daddy-Daughter spat. I was in this because you were going to *die* if I didn't."

"Die?" Nora snorted. "I got away from both you and your buddy."

"Uh huh," Josh barked, "and you ran straight into a swarm of those scorpion things, which is why Foster is *dead* now."

Nora paused. "You blaming that on me?"

"No," Josh stated. "I'm saying that if it hadn't been for him, you'd be dead right now—I don't expect you to feel guilty about it, just a little more respectful of the fact that whatever you do next could cost you, or *me* my miserable little life. And I'm not excited about dying today."

"We're not going to die," Nora said. "Professor Easton will find us—"

Josh laughed aloud, but before Nora had a chance to ask why, the latch clanked, and light flooded the room. Hunter stepped in.

"You're coming with me," he began, looking at Josh. "Got some questions need answering."

"Mr. Murphy! Good to see you so soon," Dr. Martin said warmly, holding out his hand.

Josh automatically shook it, looking around the strange room warily.

Dr. Martin turned to Shona. "I'm sure we don't need those anymore

Sho—*Lieutenant*," he said, and turned back to Dr. Vance.

The "Lieutenant," out of her heavy equipment, holstered her sidearm and produced a key. Josh sized her up as she unlocked his cuffs. The tag on her uniform read 'Mother.' He thought he had seen the tall, dark-skinned woman hanging around Foster, but it was very difficult to pin down when—perhaps months ago. He made a mental note of the stern glint in her eye and decided to tread carefully.

She backed away and stood beside the lab door. Feeling reluctant to turn his back to her, Josh stayed as close to the countertop circling the room as he could, and turned to face the two intellectually-minded characters in the room.

Dr. Martin seemed friendly enough, leaning against one of the far counters with his arms folded, but he had a strangely gleeful glint in his eye that Josh didn't find entirely comfortable. He felt more kinship with the frustrated looking Dr. Vance, who was adjusting his glasses and glaring at the wall covered in paper and string.

"Josh," Dr. Martin said, "—May I call you Josh?—I understand you have some questions about who we are and who we're working for."

Josh didn't speak for a moment.

"Well..." he began, "...I thought you were going to ask *me* questions."

"Would you prefer that?" Vance muttered.

Josh stuck his tongue in his cheek and stared hard at him.

"We do have a few questions," said Martin, "but unlike most of the people you've met today, I'm willing to trade for them."

Josh snorted. "You're going to let me go?"

Martin shook his head, "Just information for information—but your answers may make a difference in how things proceed from here."

Josh took in a deep breath and let it out long and slow, "Doc, if I even make it to tomorrow I'll consider myself unreasonably lucky."

"Then we have more in common than you know," Dr. Martin smiled. "Which brings us to my first question."

He turned to set down a small leather-bound volume on the center island, and moved towards Vance. Josh was momentarily distracted by the book.

"We've been going over some of the security footage," Martin said. "Copied as much as we could before we evacuated down here—"

"Where are we?" Josh said.

"We're below ground again," said Martin. "The...*men in black*, as you call them, are currently unaware that this section of the base exists, or at least that it is occupied. The size of the tunnel network is working in our favor."

Josh noted the tunnel he'd been brought though was round, not squared. He wondered if they were a safe distance from the Monolith.

"I see," said Josh. "I assume I haven't been out very long?"

"An hour or so," said Dr. Vance. "They gave you something to wake you up."

Josh nodded—slowly. "That explains the headache I guess."

"Yes—as I was saying," Dr. Martin began again. "We've been going over the security footage, and we were wondering if you could clear up a few things for us."

Josh hesitated. "What kind of things?"

Vance opened a laptop on the island, pushed some folders aside and turned it around to face Josh. Dr. Martin gestured to a stool.

Josh looked at it, then stopped himself from turning to look at the Lieutenant.

"I think I'll stand," he said. "Thanks."

Martin shrugged, reached over, and hit the spacebar.

Josh couldn't quite tell what was going on at first—it was dark and grainy, and the only illumination was the rotating hazard lights.

Then he saw a figure stepping cautiously into the hallway—himself, he realized—and a moment later his avatar froze in terror as he saw something move at the other end of the hallway.

Almost before he realized it, he saw himself shove back through the door with the bug hot on his heels.

A few moments later, he opened the door, apparently unharmed, and disappeared into the hallway.

Vance leaned forward and tapped the spacebar, looking at Josh intently. "Well?"

Josh searched Vance's expression, then turned to Martin. "Well what?"

Martin shrugged. "What happened?"

"Uh…" Josh swallowed. "I killed it." Strictly speaking, that was true.

"How?" Vance said with a shrug.

"Uh," Josh's mind raced. He wasn't sure if he was walking into a trap, or opening the door to an important revelation.

"I fell on it," he said. "I'm not exactly sure…I think…" He trailed off, "I think I broke it's neck."

He looked up and saw two pairs of eyes squarely fixed on him. He forced himself to look back blankly.

"So a six-foot creature corners you in the restroom," Vance says, "and you…fell on it?"

"It all happened very quickly," Josh said, "I was trying to climb over a stall at the time, and it grabbed me, see, and…"

Martin was smiling at Josh with a knowing grin that made him uncomfortable.

"My my," the Doctor muttered, "Isn't that interesting."

Josh shook his head.

'Fell on it.' Right. Idiot.

"Look," Josh said, "If you guys are just going to go over your boss's questions, I'm not going to bother. I've done a lot of crazy things today, and a lot of crazy things have happened to me."

"Oh, we *know*," said Vance. "What we don't know is *why*."

"Well, I don't know either," said Josh. "All I want is to get out of here before my luck runs out. Okay?"

"Are you certain it was luck?" Martin said.

"I don't know!" Josh sputtered. "It sure as hell wasn't *me!*"

"Maybe it was," Vance said. "How badly did you want to survive?"

Josh stared at him. "What kind of question is that?"

Martin let his forehead fall into his palm.

"Lewis," Vance snapped. "I'm asking you, let me work. As I was saying —"

"I was fighting for my life," Josh said. "How bad do you *think* I wanted to survive?"

Martin sighed and walked over to the wall of clues.

"Exactly!" Vance said. "Now, you've seen Nora's abilities, right?"

"Yeah," Josh said warily.

"Well, abilities like those can lie dormant for years—"

Dr. Martin stuck his hand between the two, a small photo held in his fingers.

"Have you seen this man?" he said.

Josh's jaw dropped. "That's Bishop!" he said. "Who is he?"

Vance squinted at him. "'Bishop?'"

Martin slammed a fist against the countertop.

"*HA!*" He barked.

"Okay, okay," Vance said. "You can stop right there. I'm not paying you a dime until the blood test is ready."

"Blood test?" Josh said, "You guys took my blood *too*?"

"Only a little," Martin said.

Josh scowled at them incredulously. "Why does everybody want my blood?"

"To find out if you're a Meta," said Vance.

"What difference does that make?" Josh sputtered, looking at his forearm. He found two small round band-aids sitting next to each other.

"Not much," Martin quipped.

"He killed three men by making them *shoot each other*!" Vance snapped. "If that's not psychic, *nothing* is."

"Bishop has mutant jedi powers?" Josh blurted. "Then he's your guy— why are you talking to me? He's obviously your Meta."

"'*Bishop*,'" said Martin, "is a ghost; a spectre; a wisp of vapor that appears and vanishes at will—we're not even sure he's corporeal at *all*."

Josh blinked. "Come again?"

"His name isn't Bishop," Vance said. "That's the codename *we* gave him."

The scientist threw up has hands, "Now he's just laughing at us."

"Well, it's a cracking good joke," Martin quipped. "An alien with a sense of humor!

"Hold up," Josh said. "So is he a Meta or an angel or what?"

"No," Martin replied, "but if I was a betting man, I'd say he's fond of Rube Goldberg machines. Luck has nothing to do with it, Mr. Murphy—*Destiny* has come calling. And despite your assertions to the contrary, I believe you have answered it."

"Now you're just being dramatic," Vance huffed.

12

King Sacrifice

"Play it back," said Loyd. "Just the last part."

The agent seated in front of the monitor bank tapped a few keys. The footage on the middle display snapped back, temporarily resurrecting the three dead guards and returning them to their positions, standing nonchalantly in a semicircle, with Josh flat in front of them.

After a few seconds, Lefty placed the muzzle of his flawed weapon against Josh's head, and, as before, it failed to fire.

Despite knowing what was coming next, Easton flinched as Righty stiffly tossed his weapon short. Josh grabbed at it, Lefty pinned it to the ground and—

"Oooh," the agent groaned. "That had to hurt."

Easton turned away. Loyd remained staring at the screen, arms folded and a determined look stamped on his face.

"Can you please turn that off?" Easton said.

"This isn't right," Loyd said. "Something's not right."

McCauley snorted. "You're damn right. Who let those idiots past basic?"

"That would have been your department," Easton said.

"My responsibility is *ops*, not *training*," McCauley shot back.

"Oh for Christ's sake," Easton gestured to the screen. "Do you know how much it costs to train you people? You think that money just *appears* out of nowhere?"

"Like I said," growled McCauley, "Not. My. Department."

"I had to schmooze senators, representatives, I had to schmooze presidents—"

"He's got to be a Meta," said Loyd. "Or have help from one."

"What?" Easton said. "Why? It was an accident."

"Not if the guards were Pushed," said Loyd. "A charade for the cameras."

"Why would...*whomever*, want to do that?"

"To make us look like idiots," said McCauley.

"To keep us off Hunter's scent," said Loyd. "You know how he is—keeps everything decentralized. It's *his* company—if he knew about our plans even a week ago, there's no telling how many sleeper agents he could have had in the base personnel alone."

"And any of them could have been a Spook," said McCauley.

"That explains why he went to such lengths to recover his employees," said Easton, stroking his scraggly chin.

"It would," said Loyd. "And it explains why *this* guy—" He pointed to Josh, "—is always so close to Nora."

"Where *is* Nora?" said Easton.

"By the airport," said McCauley. "We lost the tracker down a maintenance shaft behind the control tower. Recon is en route."

"Screw that," said Loyd. "Hunter's jumpy—tip him off and he'll vanish. We have to come down all at once or not at all."

He interlocked his fingers and pushed away, cracking his knuckles. A faint glimmer disturbed the air around them. "At least a platoon."

"Sir." The officer at the desk pointed to one of the monitors. "I've got movement in the tunnel."

McCauley leaned forwards and squinted at the flickering, indistinct image.

"Can't tell," he said. "Looks like the swarm is moving."

"Exploring," said Loyd. "Don't worry. They've got nowhere to go."

"That is...quite a lot of them, isn't it?" Easton said. "Fascinating—McCauley, have you found Hunter's nerve gas stockpiles yet?"

McCauley shook his head. "Nope. You guys were supposed to find that out and tell me where to look."

Loyd looked up at the ceiling. "McCauley, I'd have thought that the military taught you there was no 'I' in 'team.'"

McCauley snorted. "You've obviously never been in the military."

"Come on." said Hunter. "Talk to me."

Nora looked up, a thin, sarcastically wide smile forming on her face. "What about, *Daddy*?"

"Anything," Hunter said. "Ask me anything you want to know."

"I did," said Nora. "I asked you over and over again. And do you remember what your answer was?"

Behind the ice-hard irises, Hunter's eyes twitched.

"'Can't tell you Punkin,'" Nora said. "Got to keep you safe.'"

"I was telling the truth," Hunter replied. "That was my job—"

"Keep me safe from what?" Nora said. "Your imaginary industrial spies, searching for the secrets of your success? The hundreds—maybe *thousands* of people you've indirectly killed by selling weapons?"

Hunter fought down a curl of his lip and looked to the side.

"Oh," said Nora. "That's not to mention not telling me my mother had honest-to-God *superpowers*, which I inherited? That would have been a nice one to know growing up!"

"I wanted you to know you weren't different," snapped Hunter. "I wanted you to know you were one of *us*."

"But I'm *not*," Nora retorted. "Am I?"

"Yes you *are*." Hunter spread his arms wide. "Why does it matter if you've got a few extra bells and whistles?"

Nora grimaced and shook in her chair. "Why do I need to have a *reason* to know who my mother was? Why do I need some sort of excuse to find out why I can—move things *without touching them*?"

"I told you what you needed to know, when you needed to know it," Hunter said. "Anything more would have made you a target."

Nora nodded. "To your imaginary enemies. Right—"

Hunter stood and flung his chair across the room with an ear-rattling metallic crash.

"Just who do you think the bastards playing soldier upstairs *are*?" he shouted. "The God-damned *Postal Service*?"

"They're here because you broke the law!" Nora snarled back.

"They're here because I won't play their game," Hunter growled.

"Don't sit there and say you didn't wonder—even for just a second—what they planned to do with all those witnesses. Don't you *dare*!"

"You killed two men," Nora said.

"I've killed men for thirty years. And not just by selling weapons. I've killed them in person. I've killed them with rockets, knives, guns—my bare hands—" He pointed through the wall to the other room. "And your guardian angel there has killed three of them."

Nora swallowed, "You're a murderer."

"They started it," Hunter replied.

"You're lying to yourself," Nora said. "Everyone knows you killed Mom."

"I'm sure they told you that," Hunter said. "Probably the only way they could get a smart girl like you on board with a fustercluck like this—"

The dampened echo of an explosion thumped overhead. Hunter looked up.

"Let me go," Nora said, a thin smile framing her smoldering eyes. "They'll go easier on you."

Hunter shook his head, "No, they won't."

"What was that?" Martin looked up at the ceiling.

"Oh no," Vance muttered. He quickly slapped his laptop shut and stuffed it into a bag.

"Whoa—wait a minute," Josh said. "What about Bishop? Is that it?"

"We're going to have to move," said Martin, pulling together a sheaf of paper from the desk.

"But I've still got questions!" Josh asked. "Just tell me—do you know who Bishop works for?"

"We'll have time later," said Martin.

He picked up the small leather-bound book from the desk, and was about to stuff it in his bag when he hesitated, then pushed it into Josh's hands.

Josh flipped it over and found no markings on either side. He could feel it was packed with loose papers and scrawlings. He looked up at Martin quizzically.

"For later," Martin said, quickly zipping his bag closed. "In case we don't meet again."

Josh took a deep breath to calm his nerves and awkwardly stuffed the small book into his chest pocket.

"So," he said. "Who's coming to dinner?"

"By the sound of that explosion, I'm going to guess the ones with guns, not claws," said Vance.

"For now, anyway," Martin added.

Josh started looking around the room for a weapon. He heard the door open and spun around. It was Hunter.

"Pack it up," he said. "We need to be gone."

"I'm on it, I'm on it," Vance said, ripping cards and photos from the corkboard and stuffing them into a shoulder bag as fast as he could.

Hunter turned to the Lieutenant, who had just finished clipping a helmet to her head. She took a quick glance at her rifle's chamber and slapped the bolt into battery.

"Shona," Hunter said, "get everyone out and up to Foster's position. I'm going to keep 'em busy until you get clear."

A flash of cold lightning shot through Josh, and he spun to face Hunter.

"*Foster?*" He blurted.

Hunter gave Josh a passing glance as he punched a mag home into his sidearm, and holstered it.

"That's right," he said.

It took a moment for Josh's mind to remember how to form words.

"I thought he was *dead!*"

"Ordinarily, he would be," Vance said. "Even *with* his emergency injector, that much venom should have put him in a coma, at least."

"It's been a very strange day," Martin added.

"Was he drinking caffeine before he was stung?" Vance muttered absently, "That might have affected the way his body chemistry interacted with the toxins—or perhaps that's milk—"

"Foster can vouch for me," Josh said. "He knows me. Where is he?"

"Son," Hunter muttered. "If it hadn't been for Foster, I'd have just waterboarded you and got it over with."

Josh shut his mouth.

He saw the Lieutenant's eyes staring intently at him through her goggles.

"We could use another man," she said.

Hunter looked Josh up and down, then turned to Martin and Vance. "You trust him?"

The two moved their heads simultaneously—Vance left to right, Martin up and down.

Hunter sighed and turned to the Lieutenant.

"You sure?"

"He'll be with us," she said, "or he'll be dead."

It took Josh a moment to realize they were being serious.

"Sounds fair," he said.

The Lieutenant drew her sidearm and tossed it to him. "One mag," she said. "You stay right up with me."

Josh nodded, did a brass check, and pointed it at the floor. Trust issues notwithstanding, the rough grip felt good and solid in his hands.

He heard several clicks behind him, and turned to see Vance showing Martin how to rack his USP's slide.

"It's rather stiff," said Martin. "Are you sure I won't set it off?"

"It's fine, just pull it back real hard or it won't cock," Vance said.

Josh turned to see Hunter pulling a large black case from one of the shelves next to them and pulling out what looked like a massive backpack harness. Slipping his arms through the metal framework and clamping the two halves of the chest harness together, Josh watched as he stepped into his bulky metal exoskeleton and quickly strapped in until each limb had its own armored shadow. The Lieutenant was already halfway into hers by the time Hunter tapped a button on his forearm's screen, and Josh heard the suppressed whine of capacitors charging. Pulling a helmet complete with goggles and an angled metal faceplate from the case, he slipped it over his head and turned to the Lieutenant with a voice that crackled through the vocoder.

"Update."

"Motion sensors tripped in the well and local access hallways." she said, the helmet giving her own voice the robot treatment as well. "Back door still clear."

"Stay frosty," Hunter grated. "They're stupid, but they're not *that* stupid."

The Lieutenant hefted a heavy riot shield with a small glass window bolted into the front. *"Hineni..."*

"...Send me," Hunter responded, pulling his own shield from the case.

They clanked shields, and in a second Hunter was through the door and thumping down the hallway to the right.

"Stay behind me," The Lieutenant said crisply. "We're picking up one more."

Josh pushed through the door to the interrogation room and stopped dead in his tracks.

The Lieutenant pushed past him, saw the empty chair, and muttered a curse under her breath as she whipped a flashlight beam from one corner to the other.

Josh heard the faintest creak behind him—and turned in time to see Nora drop down behind him, hit the floor with a soft thump, and launch herself into the hallway, shoving past the startled scientists.

Josh sprang into the hallway and pushed through. "'Scuse me—"

He tore down the corridor, his eye catching Nora a split second before she vanished around a corner forty feet ahead.

Somewhere beyond, a spattering of gunfire grew to a roar. Gritting his teeth, he cranked it up a notch.

McCauley clumped off the last step in the metal staircase onto the floor of the three-story shaft and sucked in a triumphant breath through his nose. Grinning in spite of himself, he watched the Second Squad leader peel off his file and walk up to him. Hunter was not going to go down easy, he knew that—and he hadn't expected him to. It didn't matter. They had him, like a fish in a barrel. All they had to do was dump enough bullets and bodies into the hole, and Hunter would die.

The men wouldn't like it. But they didn't have to. Besides, the survivors would thank him later—someday it would be worth something to have been in this room.

Someday soon.

"First Squad is inside," the NCO said.

"And what are you doing outside?" McCauley snapped.

"Waiting on you, sir," said the NCO.

"Not anymore you're not," McCauley said. "Get moving. Backup is right behind you."

The shadows on the floor came alive. Looking up, McCauley could see the silhouettes of Third Squad clattering down the stairs.

The NCO nodded, and jogged back to his men, barking orders. The reserve quickly formed up with the leaders guarding the open door, and the squad quickly filed through.

McCauley lit a cigarette as the Third Squad NCO clattered up to him. "Orders?"

"Follow Second," McCauley said, "See if—"

His radio crackled. It was the Second Squad NCO.

"2-4 to Clubs, acknowledge."

"Clubs here," McCauley barked, pinching his throat mic.

"We've got bodies sir," he said. "Looks like First Squad."

McCauley frowned. "*All* of 'em?"

"They're all bunched up. Looks like they got ambushed."

McCauley let go of the button and hissed. "*Christ...*"

"We're holding here," The NCO said. "Looks like—"

His voice was drowned out by the earsplitting blast of gunfire clipping through the mic. McCauley cursed and ripped the mic from his ear.

"What happened?" The Third Squad NCO was starting to look jumpy.

"Second's pinned down," McCauley shouted, cupping his ear and grimacing.

"What happened to First—"

"*MOVE!*"

Corporal Markovic led Second Squad.

He was new—new enough to still be intoxicated by the power to walk into a building, strip the occupants of their clothes, and make them cower on the floor. They were invincible—even the security guards had offered little opposition. For whatever reason their commanders had made sure they didn't kill too many of them.

But why not? Markovic had thought at the time, *we're just going to have to get rid of them anyway.*

The prospect of going after *Joseph Hunter himself* and finally getting into a real scrap was a feeling he could barely contain, the veteran operatives remarks be damned.

"Finally, some *action*!" He had said.

Now, tripping over the bodies of his comrades in the dark, with a bulletproof juggernaut shredding them from the shadows, he found himself wishing he could land a good hard slap on his younger self's face.

The screams and shouts of alarm seemed to have begun eons ago. Every false twitch meant death—so far not for him, but no less than three of the men who had followed him inside were now dead. The maze of tubular corridors was filled with smoke and the lancing flash of bullets and muzzle flashes.

He gripped his throat mic and forced himself to speak.

"Third squad!" he choked. "Third squad! Sound off!"

"God dammit—where is he?" someone screamed back. "Oh Jes—"

Markovic heard an exchange of gunfire up ahead, and a gurgle over the radio.

"Movement left!" someone barked. "Everybody watch left!"

"Hitman 2-2, I've got Eyes on! Someone down the hall!"

"Wait for backup!" Markovic shouted. "Third Squad, regroup on me—"

The Corporal saw movement ahead and snapped his weapon towards it. An operative jogged out of the smoke and came up short, holding up a hand.

"Friendly!" he barked. "Friendly—"

Fast as thought, an armored figure sprang from the intersecting hallway, grabbed the man, and punched a blade through his side.

Markovic screamed an epithet and sprayed them both with a fusillade of bullets, backpedaling until something tripped him. He fell flat on his back.

Bullets whizzed over his head, and he froze, unsure if his opponent could see him.

"Corporal!" A voice said. "Corporal! Get up!"

Someone shone a light in his face, and he squinted.

"Cut that out!" he said. "Is he still here?"

"He's down the side passage," the man said. "On your feet—we've got a chance to box him in."

"Screw that," Markovic spat. "Let's get out of here!"

"You even think of running," The man grated. "And I'll shoot you my own damn self."

The Corporal recognized him now—it was Sergeant Horvath, Third Squad. *Shit.*

"Yes Sergeant," he said.

"Good—you're with me," Horvath said. "Third Squad is flanking—let's go."

"Everybody's dead here," Markovic said. "What about my guys up the hall?"

"Dead," the Sergeant said. "You're with me now. *Move.*"

He started down the hallway, weapon raised. Markovic followed.

Within a hundred feet, the passage ended in a T-junction. Two men stood on either side of a door.

"He's inside," one of the men hissed, letting go of his shotgun to point vigorously at the door. "What now?"

"Where's the other two?" the Sergeant snapped. The operative pointed back to the left.

"Watching the other entrance," he said. "It's a small room. He's boxed in."

"So nuke it and let's go!" Markovic blurted.

"Shut your face!" Horvath growled. He pointed to the other man, "Martinez, call for backup. Stevens, prep to breach."

Stevens slipped a few more shells into his weapon and checked the chamber. Horvath stood next to the door.

"Stack up," he snapped. Markovic bit back his protest and stood next to the door. Martinez stacked behind him.

"On my mark," said Horvath. "Three, two, one—GO!GO!GO!"

Stevens, shotgun at the ready, raised his boot, kicked in the door—and was immediately punched across the hall with a bone-crunching *wham* as the far wall brought him to a stop.

Horvath fumbled his weapon and shouted in surprise as Hunter barreled out the door. The arm carrying the shield punched into the Sergeant, and Markovic felt Horvath spring backwards and clobber him to the ground. Hunter's rifle roared, and the Corporal screamed, trying to hide beneath his shredded NCO's body. One of his legs burned like fire.

He heard scattered shots and looked up—the armored warrior ducked behind his shield as a hail of bullets exploded from the room he had just exited and ricocheted off the bulletproof material. The juggernaut responded with a hastily thrown frag grenade.

The following explosion immediately silenced the guns and left Markovic's ears ringing, the empty silence testifying that his comrades were dead.

They were dead, and he was all that was left, crawling backwards on one leg, fumbling for his holster with nearly numb fingers, trying to chamber the nearly useless pistol and throw one last spark of defiance at the implacable angel of death now striding down on him.

He released a building shout of fear as Hunter strode down on top of him, raised the pistol, and had it immediately smacked away by the edge of his enemy's shield.

Hunter stepped on his chest and raised the rifle to his eye.

"Don't shoot! Don't shoot!" Markovic choked. "It was just a job man! I was just doing my job!"

Hunter hesitated.

"Dying ain't much of a job." He replied.

WHAM!

Nora had found a weak spot—the ribs under the arm—and hit it with enough force to knock Hunter into the wall. He pushed off and came up swinging blindly—her block took the brunt of it, but too late. The supercharged metal arm powered through the force field and cracked her hard enough to knock her flat.

As soon as Hunter saw her though, he froze.

"Nora!" he said, as if incredulous. "What are you—"

She shot her fist forwards and drove a shimmering pulse smack in his face. His head popped back, but he raised the shield, blocking the follow up shot with a hollow *bang*. Nora barely had time to scramble to her feet before he was on her, arms flung wide—

His hands were faster than they looked. In half a second he had dropped the shield and had one of her wrists locked in his grip. After a frantic couple of seconds, he had the other. Nora screamed with rage and yanked at them. She heard his voice grating through the vocoder.

"Listen to me!"

"Let go!" she shouted, and opened her fist.

The blast was weak, but enough to give his helmet a solid whack. She did it again, and then again with her other hand.

Suddenly, with a terrifying wrench, she found herself spun into chokehold, his arm wrapped around her neck, pulling her off balance.

Josh turned the corner in time to see Hunter's chokehold, but not early enough to know what to do about it. Just as Hunter backed up to the open doorframe he saw something behind the two—one of the black-clad bodies moving, scraping a pistol off the floor and swinging it towards the two fighters.

Josh brought the pistol up.

"No!" he shouted. "Don't you do it!"

Whether the agent heard or not, he leveled the weapon and fired.

Josh snapped off three shots. The man lay still.

Nora felt herself being lifted off the ground and swung into a room ringed with racks of aging electronic equipment. Planting her feet against a server tower, she concentrated, gathering strength as she shoved off.

Sparks exploded from the rack, and they shot backwards, landing hard.

Nora cried out as the chest armor clips jabbed into her back, and rolled off, leaping to her feet as Hunter managed to raise himself to one knee.

As soon as he looked up, Nora swept the helmet from his head, wound up, and hit him with a full pulse. The air crackled, and Nora saw him fall backwards with a thud, the weight of his heavy exoskeleton working against him, his bruised face streaming blood.

She cocked her leg back and snapped a kick towards his ribs, but found it blocked by hard metal. Her shin howled for relief, but it didn't matter now—she could feel the energy in the air, flowing through her veins, warping the air around her hands as she concentrated and let fly, pounding him with wave on wave of thin air turned to flying granite.

He crumpled, wilted, dodged, scrambled backwards, the unstoppable force now turned to a flailing, cowering—

His fist lashed out in a blur, and she felt a massive blow smack into her chest like a piledriver. Before she knew she had left the ground, she felt herself jerked to a stop by the doorframe making contact with her back, and she collapsed to the floor, fighting to breathe.

Through her skewed and blurry vision, she saw Hunter pull himself painfully to his feet, wobble, and collapse back to his knees. He was clutching his chest, hacking something onto the floor. She suddenly realized that broad streaks of red were meandering out from underneath his vest and down his trousers, spreading thick and dark, like paint. The floor was covered in red streaks, and as he hacked again, she saw more red splattered onto the dirty white floor.

Her chest unlocked, and she sucked in a gasping breath, blinking tears from her eyes and rolling to her knees. They sat there, battered and glaring at each other across the room, neither willing to make the first move.

"What are you doing?" Gasped Hunter.

Nora sucked in a breath. "Stopping you."

"Why?"

It took Nora a moment to control her breathing.

"Because no one else is going to die today," she said,

Hunter spat blood and gave her a mirthless grin.

"Are you sure?"

Nora's eyes narrowed. "What are you talking about?"

Josh suddenly skidded in the door next to her, frantically scanning around the room.

"We have a problem," he said, tossing boxes to the side.

"What?" Nora looked up at him. "Something wrong?"

"Ha!" Josh yanked open a sheet metal locker and began tearing out its contents, scattering them over the floor. He froze for an instant, leaning out the doorway.

"What are you doing?" Nora said. "You're—Hey!"

Josh pulled her into the locker, closed the door, and clamped a hand over her mouth.

"Be quiet!" he hissed. "Don't say a word."

Ordinarily, she would have tried to wrench herself loose, but being right up against him she could feel him quaking—something had spooked him, bad.

For a moment nothing happened. Through the grate she could half see the room beyond. She was beginning to get worked up enough to push out and give Josh what he deserved, but—

In an instant, the room was filled with operatives. Shouting, yelling, all with their weapons trained on Hunter.

"Howdy boys," Hunter said. "Make yourselves at home—"

One kicked him. Two forced him facedown on the floor.

"You got him?"

"Yeah, I got him."

"Turn it off! Deactivate the suit!"

Loyd walked into view, not two feet in front of them. Nora tried to say something, but Josh's grip was like iron.

"*No,*" he whispered. "Do it and we're dead."

Hunter looked up.

"You," he growled.

"Hi there," Loyd said, crouching down. "How's your day been buddy?"

Hunter apparently didn't reply, so Loyd continued.

"You know, this is kind of a momentous occasion for me," he said. "I've heard so much about you—was really looking forward to it."

He laughed, "Nora hates you *so much.*"

Nora felt a brief jab of guilt, but her father's laugh drowned it out.

"I'm sure she does," Hunter muttered. "Gotta say though, you've got to be a pretty good liar to keep her going."

"I'm sure you would know," Loyd said.

"Don't try to pull that shit on me," Hunter said. "If you're half as smart as you think you are, you know that Nora doesn't hate me because I tell lies. She hates me because I don't tell her *anything.*"

There was silence for a moment. Nora heard Hunter coughing again.

"Maybe that's why she likes me better than you," Loyd growled. "Because I can tell her *anything,* and she just eats it right up."

Nora's urge to leave the locker had completely vanished.

Easton stepped into the room.

"Loyd—ease off. You two—pick him up."

Two men dragged Hunter up to his knees. Easton crouched in front of him.

"Do you know," Easton said slowly, "how long we've been doing this?"

Nora's eyes flicked to Hunter's. His face was grim and pale, his chest heaving. Nora found herself wondering how long it too for someone to bleed to death.

"More than twenty years, last I counted," Easton said, standing. "Longer than that little girl of yours has been alive."

"Long enough for her to grow up without a mother," Hunter said.

Nora's heart skipped a beat, and the world shrank until it encompassed only the two men beyond the thin sheet metal grate.

Easton forced a smile, and began to circle the room, his hands clasped behind him.

"I hear you've been telling lies about me," Hunter said.

"Lies?" Easton said. "*Lies?* Everything I told her was true—technically speaking."

"You told her I killed her mother."

"Only because that's what happened," said Easton. "Unless you'd like to tell me different."

"To anyone else, I might not," Hunter said, "but if you think I'd let you off the hook, you're a more pathetic man than I thought, and I thought you were plenty—"

Easton spun like lightning and struck Hunter across the face.

"I did my *job*," Easton hissed. "I didn't have to like it. The only variables anyone could have controlled were controlled by you. *You* failed her."

"She was never anything more than a *pawn* to you," Hunter snarled. "Just like my daughter!"

"Everyone's a pawn!" Easton snapped. "I'm a pawn—you're a pawn—we're all pawns of one thing or another. The only difference between me and you is *I've* accepted it!"

Easton crouched in front of Hunter again.

"I'm *proud* of what I've become," he said. "I'm an agent of something bigger than myself—The ultimate good, the best possible compromise between freedom and control; order and chaos."

He spread his arms wide.

"This doesn't have to be personal," he said. "This doesn't have to be the battle of egos. We're all working towards the same goal—and we always have been. Your daughter needs to know that—and only *you* can tell her."

Hunter's expression remained impassive.

"You're a man of conscience," Easton said. "I know you'll do the right thing."

"I already have," Hunter said. "Go to hell."

A muscle in Easton's jaw twitched, but he didn't lash out.

He stood slowly, adjusted his cap, and turned to his men.

"Spread out," he said. "I need Nora and the scientists alive—everyone else is expendable."

13

Floodgate

Josh stood frozen in the cabinet, trying to control his breathing, his heart pounding against his chest, very conscious of the fact that he was in a full-body-press with a beautiful girl, and even more conscious of the fact that outside the thin, ridiculously un-soundproof metal walls of their hiding place, were dozens of men wielding automatic weapons. The knowledge that they would *probably* not shoot first and ask questions later didn't really improve matters in his mind—they might let Nora live, but they would almost certainly take him aside quietly and empty his skull.

While staying in one place might have been an excellent course of action if their hiding place was any good, the cabinet was a ridiculously obvious spot, and almost certain to be checked eventually. To be honest, Josh was surprised they hadn't tried it already.

Maybe Bishop was watching out for him after all.

The thought, whether true or false, helped him relax somewhat. Either way, their best chance was to move somewhere more secure, and to move fast.

Josh swallowed, discovering his throat was painfully dry, and suppressed a cough, swallowing again. Commanding his right hand to reach forwards, he gripped the inside of the lock mechanism and slowly, carefully twisted it. Testing to make sure he couldn't turn any further, he tried to free his left hand from Nora's face so that he could swing it open in a more controlled fashion.

Her grip on his fingers was stronger than he had thought.

"Nora," he whispered. "Let go."

He waited, but she didn't answer.

He reached up with his other hand, and gently peeled her fingers away. She let go. He felt a tremor pass through her.

He carefully put his left hand against the door, his right holding the lock, and slowly, slowly pushed the door open. The hinge whined in protest, and Josh cringed.

Slowly squeezing past Nora, he stepped out one foot at a time, scanning the room and doorways.

No signs of life remained besides the overhead light and the red streaks of blood on the floor, which trailed out one of the doors.

Josh briefly wondered what they were doing to Hunter, but another wayward squeak of the door sent his mind back to focusing on his environment and all the possible specters in the shadows.

As he let go of the door and stepped forwards, he drew his USP and did a brass check, more to settle his mind than anything else. Something slapped to the floor behind him, and he turned around.

Nora had collapsed to all fours, and was staring down at her hands. She slowly peeled her right palm from the bloody floor and stared at the coagulated red fluid.

"Nora," Josh said.

She continued staring.

He swallowed and cast a glance around. He felt almost like someone disturbing a sacred rite—interrupting a mourner with the news that they need to make a grocery run.

Still, he thought, grocery runs were important and life-sustaining, so there was that.

He crouched, and tried to take her hands in his.

"Nora," he said again. "We have to go—"

She yanked her bloody hand away and said something sharp under her breath.

"I'm sorry," he repeated. "Look at me."

"Get back," she snapped. "Let go."

"I can't," said Josh, grabbing a hand. "I wish I could, but right now I can't. We have to go *right now*. Hear me?"

"Stop it!" she snapped, pushing away.

"I can't. We have to go, or they're going to get us, okay?"

Nora grabbed him by the collar and shook him.

"Just stop it!" she hissed. "Just *stop it*! Just *stop*!"

Josh swallowed a rock and tried to pull her upright. She stood, but didn't let go of his coveralls.

That was fine. He wrapped his arms around her and looked up, pulling her along.

She pushed her head against his chest, and he tried not to stop walking. It sat there like an iron weight against his ribs as he leaned out the doorway in front of them and looked both ways.

Focus.

The stale scrubbed air picked at his nostrils, bringing him back to their present situation. He took a deep breath, and tried to guess which way most likely led to the surface. He'd been out cold when they brought him here—he had a vague sense that it was the same day still, but besides that, he'd completely lost track of time, place, and direction. All he had to go on were grids of dimly-lit circular hallways and the occasional doorway.

He looked up and all around the walls, but could see no directional signs whatsoever. This part of the base was obviously not quite as well-traveled as the others.

"God *please* let this be the right way," he muttered, and made a left.

After three or four nerve-wracking minutes, they found themselves at the bottom of a massive rectangular shaft with daylight spilling down through the metal staircase. Josh immediately headed up, gently tugging Nora along.

Reaching a landing just beneath the edge of the wall, Josh noted the grated ceiling, and pulled Nora away from him.

"Stay here," he said, holding a finger to his lips. "I'm going to go check up ahead."

Nora just stared at him dully and slid to the floor.

Josh turned to go, hesitated, and pushed himself forwards, his weapon at the ready.

The horizontal basement-door opening to the outside was still open, but Josh remained cautious—he hadn't seen anyone leave, and there was no reason to believe that all of them were downstairs. Right now, on the brink of escape, they were at their most vulnerable.

Josh wiped the sweat from his hands and rewrapped his fingers around the pistol, forcing himself to measure his steps as he walked up the last staircase. If he walked too fast, they'd hear him—if he walked too slowly, his nerves would root him to the spot.

He took a breath, focused on his front sight, and and raised his eye level just above the top edge of the grate.

His eyes met nothing but the empty salt flats, stretching away to the distant mountains. The rapidly reddening sky was shot with the torn black swirls of clouds. Turning around, he saw they were next to an empty helipad raised slightly from the gritty lakebed, and beyond that rose the towering white sides of an air traffic control tower. The mesa rose beyond it, perhaps a half mile in the distance. He briefly wondered where Shona and the scientists had gone. He didn't remember there being a lot of structures near the runway. The Men in Black would have seen anyone trying to leave over the open desert. Perhaps they had taken cover in the terminal, or the hanger he could see next to it.

Luckily, it looked like a straight shot for them to get there, but he didn't trust it—maybe the others had come through here and eliminated anyone watching the shaft, and then again maybe they hadn't. Josh wasn't interested in taking chances. He quickly glanced around and saw some cover in the form of a couple of large AC units a few feet away.

Good enough.

Some of the tension left his chest, and he turned around, tramping down the steps as quickly and quietly as possible.

Professor Easton watched from the helipad on the roof of the Administration building as construction cranes maneuvered into place over the concrete cap of the Test Chamber, almost a half mile away.

Hunter, lying on a stretcher, watched the medic tending to him uncap a thick injector full of green liquid.

"Oh Jeez," Hunter groaned. "You're not going to give me that knockoff shit, are you?"

"Hold still," the medic said. "This is gonna hurt."

He jabbed the injector into Hunter's thigh and mashed the button with a gaseous hiss. Hunter grimaced.

"Look at it," Easton said over his shoulder. "The first time it's seen the light of day in who knows how long."

"You never gave a shit what I did with it," Hunter rasped. "When I studied it you said I was fooling with things beyond my understanding—when I finally buried it you told them I was wasting it."

He coughed painfully, and took a breath,

"*I* had it," he gurgled. "and you *didn't*. That's all that ever mattered. Just like Rosetta."

Easton cast a dark look his direction.

"It was never yours at all," he said. "It belongs to mankind, not to some money-grubbing exploitation artist."

"Exploitation?" Hunter spat. "Are you even listening?"

A guard stepped up to Easton.

"They're ready to detonate," he said.

"Good!" Easton said, "Give them the go-ahead."

The guard keyed his mic.

"Sierra 2-2, this is Echo—You have the go-ahead for detonation. Repeat, go-ahead for det, over…"

"Last chance," Hunter said quietly. "You blow that cap, and we all die."

Easton cast a side glance at him and cocked his head.

"Joe," he said. "Do yourself a favor, and shut the hell up."

The echo of the blast reached Josh just as he and Nora reached the top step and heard the first crunch of salt under their shoes. Soon a series of pops and cracks could be heard. Josh automatically tensed, looking around for the source. It sounded like it was coming from beyond the Tower, in the direction of the Mesa.

Reaching for the radio clipped to his belt, Josh twisted it on and adjusted the fit of the earpiece. He was immediately deafened by the cacophony of screams and shouting happening on the other side. Yanking it from his ear, he rolled the volume knob down and re-inserted it.

"—What the hell are these things?"

"Three on the right! Right! Somebody get some fire over there!"

"Jesus Christ, get it off! Get it—"

"Echo 1 to Overwatch, we need evac, NOW!"

Confused, Josh tried to figure out who was talking. Had Hunter's people run into trouble? Or was—

His train of thought was interrupted by Nora pulling away. He tried to grab hold of her arm, but she shucked it and stepped back.

"I'm good," she said, her voice unstable, but calmer than before, "Just —I can walk. Let me walk."

Josh hesitated, but finally nodded. "This way."

Turning the corner of the helipad revealed the control tower was jutting out of a long low two-story building—the Terminal, Josh supposed. A hanger stood adjacent on their left. Josh wondered if there was still anything airworthy left inside—he wasn't qualified to fly it, but perhaps there was someone else around who was.

Approaching the back door, Josh noted the half-dozen or so company vans and SUVs scattered around the small parking lot, and approached the nearest one. It was locked. He spent a moment looking for the keys, and then suddenly realized the thumping overhead had gotten louder. He looked up in time to see a black attack helicopter swoop low over the building and arc out into the desert.

Shit.

Josh glanced at Nora.

"This way!" he yelled, and pointed to the terminal's back door. "Let's go!"

He made a dash for the metal door and yanked at the handle. It was locked.

He turned around and cast about desperately for somewhere to hide as Nora walked past him.

"What are you doing?" he said. "It's—"

She opened it without a hitch and stepped inside.

Josh stared at the door, shot a glance at the chopper coming back around, and slipped inside after her, closing it firmly. The loud bang echoed through the hallway, making Josh cringe.

"You wouldn't think that thing would be so loud," he muttered with a nervous chuckle.

Nora didn't respond. Josh's smile died away.

"Okay," he said. "Let's try this way."

The building was deserted. Some of the lights were still on, but they were flickering. Long stretches of pitch black shadowed the way forward. Josh padded down the corridor, listening to the electronic buzz of fans and vending machines as they passed.

He was looking for the stairs, Josh decided. He was going to find the stairs to the control tower, climb to the top, and see what he could see. Obviously, escape on foot—at least before dark—was a complete waste of time, with or without a highly conspicuous and unfortunately keyless vehicle. And if the enemy was carrying infrared or night vision...

Josh swallowed, fighting back a wrenching pang of despair. He felt like a man in free fall, his mind racing. He blinked and tried to focus. Maybe, given enough vending machine food and drinks, they had a chance to wait it out. Surely it could only be so long before the small army of men in black and their miniature air force drew some local attention. They were smash-and-grab-types. For a proper search, they'd need to get provisions, fuel, drones—all things he hadn't seen when he was above ground.

Then all they had to deal with was whatever those guys on the radio had been screaming about.

He pushed the thought out of his mind. They needed to get to that tower.

Finding a staircase, he entered slowly, checked to see that Nora was following, and began climbing. Pushing open the third floor exit, Josh carefully looked around for the chopper before stepping out, and discovered they had exited the left side of the tower onto the roof of the terminal. Looking right, the airstrip stretched parallel to the terminal.

Josh could still hear the thumping overhead, but it had died down to a distant shudder, and was fading fast. Looking across the airstrip, Josh spotted the chopper in the distance, crawling through the evening sky towards the main buildings a half mile up the slope to their right. As he watched it, a dart of white smoke lanced away from it, and then another —Josh followed the missiles as they streaked away—

—And detonated in the midst of a black carpet that seemed to surround the Welcome Center. It was like a living flood, flowing around it and spreading into the desert.

"Oh God," Nora whispered.

Josh didn't say anything. He just watched the black stain creep ever wider, splitting and tearing into smaller swirls. He could just hear the thin, inhuman screams and ululating cries pulsing across the plain towards them, turning his blood to acid in his veins. At that rate, they would reach the terminal within the hour.

There, under the low, claustrophobic storm clouds and blood-red sky, they were trapped.

Josh slowly collapsed to his knees and rolled flat on his back, staring up at the sky. He tried to think of something to do, something to say. Nothing came.

Squeezing his eyes shut, he shouted. An earsplitting, hoarse, animal sound boiling up from the bottom of his lungs.

He followed this with a long string of foul language, most of which was so mangled even he couldn't discern what he was saying.

"It's not FRAGGERIGKING *FAIR!*" he exploded, springing to his feet and kicking an exposed air duct.

"It's not—" he lapsed into unintelligible Angrish once more.

He dashed twenty feet down the roof, as if the view would be somehow different from there, and then crossed to the opposite side. A black smear meandered across the horizon, spilling towards the mountains and over the dry lakebed. They were caught in a massive pincer stretching for miles.

"*SHIT!*" he barked.

He stomped back over to Nora's side as she stared out towards the buildings in the distance, watching two helicopters landing and lifting off the top of the Administration building. The black mass grew and piled up, burying it in a living wave.

The last chopper rose into the air just as the mass spilled over onto the roof. For a moment, everything was chaos, and then the aircraft hung awkwardly in the air and began spinning, small black figures tearing loose and spinning slowly through the air. The vehicle spun, turned slowly onto it's side, and did a swan dive into the black mass below it, exploding in a massive fireball.

For a full second, Josh didn't hear anything—and then the sound reached them. A low pulse on the wind, there one instant, and gone the next, echoing out over the desert.

"Come on…" he muttered. He glanced at Nora. She was still staring dead-eyed out at the scene of destruction, pale and slack-jawed, her shoulders drooping.

"Nora?" Josh said.

She didn't respond. He spoke louder this time.

"Nora."

When she finally spoke, her voice was low and steady—almost disturbingly so.

"Have you ever had one of those moments," she said. "Where you realize, no matter how hard you tried, you've turned out just like your parents?"

Josh glanced down at his pistol and swallowed hard.

"I suppose," he said, slipping it into his holster.

"Well I haven't," Nora said. "Not until just now."

Josh couldn't think of anything to say, so he didn't.

"I thought I was right," she choked. "I *swear* I did."

"We all make mistakes," Josh said, reaching out to lay a hand on her shoulder. "You can still—"

She flinched. He drew his hand back.

The black wave in the distance drew his attention. He watched it approach, mesmerized by the sheer scale of the thing. It was still moving, slowly but surely, spreading over the desert and the facility buildings, splintering them into fragments that vanished beneath the dark tide.

"Terrifying, isn't it?"

Cold shock gripped Josh's chest, and he whirled to see Loyd standing not twenty feet behind them, backed by a trio of men with assault rifles. The last operative seemed to have just emerged from the stairwell.

The air rippled around Nora's hands as she settled into a fighting stance. Josh's hand itched for the grip of his weapon.

"Whoa—" said Loyd, holding up his hands. "Everybody just calm down for a minute. There's no need to escalate this. Yet."

Josh mentally pictured his draw and immediately knew it was pointless. All three men had their weapons leveled, and for good measure one of Loyd's hands was wrapped around a Glock. Whether he was capable of using it, Josh didn't know, but there was plenty of guns to deal with before he got there. He closed his hand into a fist and tried to control his nerves.

Loyd slowly set his weapon on the ground, and stood, holding a hand up to his ear.

"Hear that?" he said. "That's salvation, on it's way."

Josh strained his ears and separated the thud of chopper blades from the background rumble.

"Now," said Loyd. "We can all do the sensible thing and get on the nice helicopter, or we can shoot it out here. Who wants to die first?"

Josh's eyes flicked from soldier to soldier, and saw the same nervous tension in all of them; poised like traps, every barrel aimed straight through his chest.

He glanced at Nora, and to his surprise found her looking back at him, mouth drawn to a hard line, eyes hard.

He swallowed and turned back to Loyd.

"Who doesn't like helicopters?" he said.

"I'll take that," Loyd said, jabbing a finger at the ground. "Please—the gun?"

Josh nodded and slowly reached down towards his holster.

Suddenly, Loyd shouted.

"GUN!"

The Glock flew off the ground and into his hand. A thunderclap smashed the air out of Josh's chest. He hit the deck before he realized he was falling, gasping for air, clawing at his chest with numb fingers.

He heard Nora screaming, and suddenly she was there, her eyes wide with shock and fear. Someone pulled her away, and she was replaced by Loyd standing over him, a cold gleam in his eye. He smiled.

"Draw."

Josh's vision blurred and faded to vapor, and he slipped away.

14

Kairos

"Cuffs!" The agent growled. "Gimmie your cuffs!"

Nora fought like a wildcat, but with an operative on each arm, it was a losing battle. She twisted her head back to where Josh lay, and fought to see through brimming eyes.

"NO!" She screamed over the pounding helicopter blades. "No! Let me see! Take him with us!"

She felt cold steel lock around her wrists, and they dragged her into the troop bay of the Blackhawk. She gathered her legs under her and lashed out at the left agent's legs. He staggered—then turned and slugged her.

The world spun, and Nora tried to mentally separate her nose from the back of her head. She lazily saw the troop bay shift as they dragged her upright and sat her back into a hard seat, and the three agents piled into those next her.

Loyd got in last, lifting a pair of headphones from the rack and slipping them on. He stood, looking out the bay door as they lifted off. Nora tried to lean forwards and see out, but the guard next to her stuck his arm out and pushed her back. She set her jaw and squeezed her eyes shut.

Someone tried to put something on her head, and she thrashed and struggled for a moment until the agents held her down and someone clapped a headset over her ears. The roar of the engines was immediately blunted.

She opened her eyes.

Loyd slowly sank into his seat across from her, and continued looking out, a grim expression stamped on his features.

His voice crackled through her headset.

"You know I had to," he said slowly looking up at her. "He was making a move."

For all of an instant, their eyes locked, and time stood still. Nora felt the world fade away and blur around her. There was a low hum in her ears, growing louder and louder—

Josh's eyes. She remembered Josh's eyes looking up at her, confused, losing focus. She remembered the blood. She looked down. Her hands were sticky with it.

The clouds cleared, and she was back, alone in the storm.

She looked up into Loyd's eyes, and found they no longer mystified her as they once had—she could see right through them, straight into the monster hiding beyond. A monster she knew in herself.

So they were kindred spirits, she thought.

Not anymore.

The last thread between them snapped, and she was free. She took a deep breath, and let it out slowly.

The corner of his mouth twitched as he misread her expression, but his commitment to the act won out. He resumed his somber gaze.

"You understand," he said. "Don't you?"

She let her face relax, go completely blank.

"Yes," she said. "Yes, I understand."

His facade broke for a moment, and he narrowed his eyes, studying her.

Then he cast his gaze back out the window, and didn't look back.

Nora heard thunder overhead.

Josh felt himself falling, and then suddenly he was blinking in the blazing desert sun. He squinted and his inner ear did a flip as he rolled over and found himself on a plain of blinding white salt extending to the black mountains on the horizon.

He tried to swallow and slowly pulled himself into a sitting position. Turning to the side, he noticed his shadow stretching away, and froze.

There were two shadows.

He turned his head around and saw a figure a few feet behind him, standing with his back to the sun. It was difficult to make out his features squinting against the light.

Josh slowly stood and faced the man, shading his hands against the unnatural brightness.

After a moment, he cleared his throat and spoke.

"Hi," he said.

The man cocked his head.

"You noticed," he said.

Josh stared at him for a moment.

"Uh...Yes." he said uncertainly. "Noticed what?"

"Me," said the man.

Josh blinked a couple of times and shifted his weight.

"Um," he said, "would you mind moving over a few steps? It's really hard to look right at you right now."

The man stood there for a moment, then turned slowly, took several long strides to the left, and turned to face Josh once more."

Josh sighed.

"Of course," he said. "It's you."

Bishop raised an eyebrow.

"Something wrong?"

Josh shook his head, "Hmm? No—Well, uh...I don't know yet."

"Do you remember what happened?"

Josh stared blankly at him, then put a hand to his chest. It ached. His fingers came away bloody. He heard buzzing in his ears, and the world suddenly seemed to be spinning again.

Bishop's voice snapped him out of it.

"Josh?" he said. "Are you sure nothing's wrong?"

"I was shot!" Josh blurted.

"Yes," said Bishop. "And how do you feel about that?"

"Why didn't you do something!"

"I did," Bishop said. "How do you feel?"

Josh leaned over and hacked blood onto the white desert floor.

"Oh God...Am I dead?" he coughed. "If I'm dead, why does it hurt so much?"

"It hurts because you're *not* dead," Bishop replied, crouching in front of him.

"Then where—how did I get *here*?" Josh choked.

"You're not here," Bishop said. "You're back there."

Josh spat a string of blood and rubbed his face off with his sleeve. "What? Then why are—what are you doing here?"

"I just want you to know you're doing well," Bishop said. "There's a bit left to wrap up, but you're almost there—"

"I'm doing *well*?" Josh exploded. "What do you mean I'm doing *well* —You looked the other way for a second, and now I'm lying in a pool of my own blood, with a sucking chest wound!"

"That's why I'm telling you," Bishop replied. "Now take a deep breath —"

Very suddenly he placed both hands on Josh's chest.

"Clear," he said.

The jolt that went through his chest felt like Bishop had just hit him with an anvil. Leftover static crackled through his nerves.

He sucked in a painful breath and glared at Bishop. "What the—"

"Clear—"

WHUMP!

The world grew blurry and red. He felt an amazing pressure in his chest, like his heart was about to burst. He wanted to curse, speak, yell— anything. It was all blocked. He couldn't breath.

"Clear!"

WHAM!

His eyes flew open, he sucked in a rattling breath, a hoarse cry grating from his throat.

Drawing another breath into his lungs, he tried to let it out and choked, hacking uncontrollably.

The bright sun had oddly changed temperature from yellow to sickly green, and there was no more wind. He tried to rub his eyes, but someone stopped his hands and pushed them back down. A dark shape interposed itself between him and the sun, and he thought he heard people in the background.

Slowly, the dark shape solidified and it's features became clear.

Foster's looked down into his face, a bright grin smeared across his bruised and bandaged face.

"*HAHA!*" Foster barked triumphantly. "Welcome back you son of a bitch!"

Josh felt the world settle, and squinted at him. He kept expecting to find he was dreaming, but instead everything was real and unpredictable. He could feel the air in the room, the harshness of the light needling his eyes—the sharp pain in his chest.

He looked down at his heart. A large square white dressing was stuck over his sternum. He was lying on a gurney in a small white room. The Lieutenant, standing by the nearby counter with a surgical mask and several trays of blood-specked medical instruments, was setting aside a small defibrillator pack.

Josh looked back up at Foster.

"Am I dead?" he mumbled.

Foster burst out laughing.

"Nope," he said, "but you sure gave it your best shot."

The Lieutenant reached over, popped the cap off an injector, and stabbed it into Josh's thigh.

"Ow!" he blurted.

"How many of those does he need?" Foster asked.

"Enough for him to walk on his own," she said, peeling off her surgical gloves. "Unless you want to carry him."

She turned to Josh.

"The bullet struck your sternum," she said. "It did not penetrate, but it did stop your heart. You're lucky we got to you as soon as we did."

"Look at this thing!" Foster said, holding up the book Dr. Martin's had given Josh. "Not quite bulletproof, but it sure slowed it down."

The small volume had a clean round hole punched in the cover, but inside the bullet had changed direction and torn a ragged hole out the back. A few more puzzle pieces clicked into place, and Josh felt a chill go through him. It felt like only a moment ago Martin had handed it to him—

he had given no thought to what pocket he might put it into, no—

"Holy shit," he muttered, trying not to rub his chest.

"Glad your sense of irony is intact," Foster said, tossing the book into the gurney and adjusting his crutch, which Josh was just noticing for the first time. He looked pale and weak, wobbling a bit on his feet, even with the battered exoskeleton supporting him. His face was covered with taped-together cuts and purple bruising, and his fatigues had been cut away in several places, showing swollen sting marks capped by round adhesive dressings. Foster gave him a lopsided grin.

"We heard the shots and came running," he said. "Well, *they* came running. Talk about lucky."

"Lucky? Me?" Josh said. "What about *you*? How the hell are you *alive*?"

Foster shrugged, "Threw myself down a stairwell, shot myself full of antivenom and passed out."

Josh stared at him, "But...how did you get out?"

"The back door," Foster said, pointing a thumb over his shoulder. "I only blacked out a couple of times."

"He means the maintenance tunnel," The Lieutenant said, grabbing Josh's wrist and checking his pulse.

Another thought resurfaced in Josh's mind.

"So," he said, "did Hunter get out?"

The Lieutenant shot a glance at Foster, whose expression faded visibly. He took a breath.

"We were hoping you could tell us," he said.

Josh looked up at the ceiling.

"They caught both of them."

Foster sighed. The Lieutenant turned the the corner and gave it a brief tongue-lashing in a language Josh couldn't quite identify.

For a moment no one said anything. Foster broke the silence.

"Well," he said nodding at Josh. "We got you back—and that's a long ways from nothin'."

The Lieutenant stripped off her surgical mask and began shoving her hands into a pair of combat gloves.

"We're out of time," she said. "When he can stand, bring him to the hanger."

15

Terms

Despite the massive pair of earmuffs clamped over her head, the roar of rotor blades continued to pound against Nora's skull. Her guards didn't allow her to raise her hands from her lap, so most of the trip had been engaged in periodically peeling her lips apart and waiting for her nosebleed to glue them back together again.

"Yes?" Loyd said suddenly. He was listening to someone—the pilot, Nora guessed. He glanced out the window and peered down through the darkness.

"Yes," he said, more definitively this time. "Set her down."

They banked left, and began circling. Nora tried to peer out the window to her left, but all she could discern on the ground was a collection of hazard lights, several of them spinning wildly. More choppers.

She felt her ears pressurize as they approached the ground. Contact wasn't too harsh, but it was unexpected. Loyd pulled open the side door, and rotor wash flooded the compartment. He gestured to the guards, and they quickly unbuckled her and pulled her upright. Expecting a pause to let the blood drain back into her rubbery legs, Nora almost lost her footing as the agents immediately started forwards and unceremoniously dragged her out the door.

The air had been cold inside the chopper, but now the full force of the night wind cut through her thin shirt, chilling her to the bone. Nora squeezed her eyes to slits against the flying dust as the agents bent over and jogged her clear of the spinning blades.

Nora saw Loyd was leading them across a wide circle of idling helicopters; three Blackhawks, with their fireteams standing in the desert nearby, apparently waiting for orders.

Crossing the circle, Nora shivered and began to wonder if Loyd was hiding any more of her clothes around somewhere.

They were heading for a small knot of people standing about a hundred feet away, in the center of the circle. Most of them were agents, but after a moment Nora picked out a grayish uniform near the center. Her eyes widened, and she focused on it, but another soldier was standing in the way, and it was difficult to make out—

He moved. She identified Hunter's face immediately.

He was standing up. He was alive.

She let out a sigh of relief, and then quickly stood up straight again, flicking a glance at Loyd striding ahead of her. They weren't out of the woods yet.

She recognized the man standing with his back to her as Professor Easton. He had his hands on his hips, and was having a very vigorous discussion with one of his officers about something. Nora strained her ears and tried to hear what he was so worked up about.

"Oh, so it's my fault now?" Easton snapped.

"Yes. You're damn right it's your fault," McCauley shot back, sticking an aggressive pointer finger in Easton's face. "When you said your little pals were going to be the diversion, I thought you mean they were going to pull a fire alarm, not unleash the *Goddamn roach apocalypse.*"

Easton shook his own finger back at him and shook his head rapidly. "No no no—You don't get to say that. Not after botching the witness clean up."

"I botched—" McCauley looked like his head was about to explode. "Yeah, well I can botch looking out for you too pal, so *zip*—"

"You two done?" Loyd interrupted, finally reaching conversational range. "We're behind schedule already, and time's running out."

"Behind schedule?" McCauley sputtered. "Are you kidding? Half my men are dead. Why are we even still *here*—"

"Nora!" Easton blurted, his face lighting up in a smile. He held out his hands in welcome, and stepped forward to embrace her. "There you are—"

Nora spat in his face, stopping him in his tracks.

McCauley burst out laughing as Easton wiped his glasses on his shirt, leaving streaks of red.

"*Oh ho!*" The agent said. "I like her."

He caught Hunter giving him a hawkish glare, and his smile wilted slightly. He folded his arms and looked away.

Easton slipped on his glasses and looked at Nora with a strangely closed expression she had never seen before. A proud, hooded look, drained of warmth.

"You're welcome," he said. "For the rescue, I mean."

He cast a shifty look at Hunter.

"I know he's your father," he continued. "but I would have thought it would take more than a few hours to go running back to Daddy's arms—"

"I don't know where I'm going," Nora interrupted, "but I'm not going with you."

"I don't think you have much choice," Easton replied. "No one does, in the end."

He stepped closer and lowered his voice. "This isn't over yet," he said. "I think you'll find us much harder to judge in the end."

She glared at him. After a moment, he blinked and looked away, turning to Hunter.

"Your five minutes starts now," he said.

He gestured to McCauley, and they walked back towards the choppers. Nora felt her guards unhook their arms and step away, leaving just Hunter, Loyd, and herself standing in the open.

Hunter shot a Loyd a glare. "You heard him," he said. "Back off."

Loyd eye twitched.

"Loyd!"

It was Easton, waving him over.

Loyd narrowed his eyes and pointed at Hunter, "You're surrounded," he said. "Don't forget."

"Kid," coughed Hunter, "if you think I could run like this, I'll take it as a compliment."

Loyd turned to Nora, and she gave him a hard look.

"Get going," she snapped.

He hesitated a moment more, then turned and walked away.

Nora took a deep breath and looked down at her shivering hands. The cold covered her nervousness, but with all the murderous liars out of earshot her guilt was coming back with a vengeance.

She cleared her throat.

"Hi," she said, looking up at him—or his chest, at least. "You're not... you were shot," she said.

"I'm fine," Hunter snorted. He was pale and battered, unsteady on his feet. But he was *on* his feet, which she hadn't expected.

"Medic insisted on giving me their shitty knock off gel. Gonna give me the runs for days."

Nora almost smiled at that. She kept trying to figure out what to say, but nothing was coming.

"How about you?" Hunter said. "You hurt?"

Nora shook her head. "No," she said shakily, wiping a strong of blood from under her nose.

Hunter's voice was gentler now.

"Nora," he said. "Honey, look at me—"

"I—" she choked. "I screwed up."

"It's okay," Hunter said. "I'm just glad to see you alive—"

"Well, maybe I wish I weren't," Nora snapped. "Maybe if—"

Hunter reached out and took her firmly by the shoulders. Startled, she looked up and found him staring straight into her eyes.

"*No,*" he said. "Don't you say that. Don't you ever say that. I'd die for you right now—"

She shoved him away.

"I don't *want* anyone else to die!" she blurted. "You of all people should know how many lives I've cost. I'm *complicit* in this."

"You made a mistake," Hunter said. "We all make mistakes. *That's war*. You can't—"

His voice had begun to break. He paused and collected himself.

"I've screwed up too," he said.

Nora searched his eyes—sharp, blue orbs in the dark.

"Like Mom," she said.

Hunter was silent for a moment, then he blinked, and Nora saw a tear escape and run down his face.

"Yes," he finally replied. "Like Mom."

Nora felt something fall gently into place, and realized she wasn't the only lonely soul in the desert.

Hunter took her cuffed hands in his.

"Listen to me," he said. "This isn't the life I wanted for you—but maybe I…Well, you're in it now, so take some advice from an old soldier."

He took a breath. "Nobody deserves forgiveness—it's a gift. And if you're ever going to be any use to anyone, you've got to accept it and move on."

Nora felt him tighten his grip. "And there is *nothing*," he said, "*nothing* you could ever do, that would stop me from forgiving you."

Nora couldn't meet his eyes. She stared into his chest, his words echoing over and over in her mind.

She heard Hunter's voice. "Nora?"

"Josh is dead," she said.

There was a pause. She looked up. Hunter looked puzzled.

"The janitor," Nora said, "The—"

"Yes," Hunter said. "I remember him. I just…I'm sorry to hear that."

Nora broke down and sobbed. After a moment, she felt Hunter's arms embrace her in a bear hug.

"It's okay," he said.

"He saved my life," she burbled.

"I know he did."

"I miss Mom."

"I miss her too," Hunter replied. "It's okay. I'm sorry."

"Okay," said Loyd. "Change of plans."

McCauley's half-dozen remaining team leaders unenthusiastically turned to face him. McCauley himself stood next to Loyd, his arms folded over his chest.

Nora and Hunter watched from the wings, each with their own pair of guards hovering over their shoulders. Professor Easton stood just ahead of them, looking very nervous and out of place. After sticking his hands in his pockets, then behind his back, and into his pockets again, he glanced at McCauley and decided to imitate his stance.

"Obviously," Loyd continued. "we've suffered some major setbacks—"

"What are we, just frickin' numbers to you?" one of the team leaders snapped.

"You *stow* that shit Lieutenant," McCauley blared. "Or I'll stow it for ya, got it?"

"Yes sir, Commander, *sir!*" The NCO sounded off.

Nora grinned wryly. It didn't matter if Easton admitted he was wrong —by misuse or by malice he'd betrayed too many of his own, and it was coming back to haunt him.

"Thank you Commander," Loyd said, cracking his knuckles, "but it's a valid question, I think it deserves a valid answer."

Nora blinked. She hadn't expected that.

Loyd pulled himself up straight and flashed a winning smile.

"The Team Leader is correct—" he said. "You are all just numbers to me. Not even that really—I don't think even the Professor has a good head count on how many of you were even here at the start." He jerked a thumb towards Easton, who gave him a puzzled glare.

Nora glanced at Hunter. He looked grim, but not surprised.

"People like him," Loyd continued, "think assets like us are expendable.

Loyd looked back towards the line of still-uneasy looking agents. "And there's no more expendable asset than the kind that fails a high-risk operation like this one."

No one spoke. The rythmic thud of helicopter blades reasserted itself in Nora's awareness, and in a flash everything was made clear.

They still needed something. The men felt betrayed, and Loyd was buttering them up with a potent combination of sympathy and fear—but for what?

She turned to Hunter.

"You made a deal?" she whispered. "What's going on?"

A guard cuffed her. "No talking."

Hunter gave him a glare that could have melted glass. The guard jerked his chin at him.

"You want some old man?" he snapped.

Hunter's eye twitched, but he turned back to face the group.

Loyd was speaking again.

"If *any* of us plan on having a future," he said, "we had better start it from right here—and luckily, we have the opportunity to do just that."

He turned to Hunter.

"You're up," he said. "Tell 'em Plan B."

Nora could almost hear each eye swiveling in unison to land on Hunter. It took a moment for Easton to look around and realize he was in the way. He scowled and worked his way to the outside.

Hunter scanned the group and indulged in a wry smile.

"Evening gentlemen," he said. "I'll admit that this is more or less what I had planned for the evening, but I truly didn't expect to be doing it with you…all."

Nora let out a snort, and found herself on the receiving end of several dark looks. She cleared her throat and kept her eyes on Hunter.

"As I was saying," Hunter continued, "you bastards were stupid enough to start this mess, but hopefully you're not too stupid to clean it up—" He held out a hand to Loyd, who slapped a gas canister into his open palm.

Nora felt a sudden burst of tension in the men around her as they realized Loyd had just given him a live weapon. Hunter, for his part, ignored them and held it up for his audience to inspect.

"This canister," he said, "contains a formula specifically toxic to the creatures you just escaped. Remove the pin, and toss it into a room or large group, and this will kill every last one of the bastards in a thirty foot radius, and disorient or disable everything within sixty feet, depending on air flow. The gas is colored to enable friendly forces to identify it." He flipped the grenade in his hand and took a look at the side, "This one is green. The canister is handheld, but it also comes in forty millimeter, twenty-five millimeter, and twelve-gauge variants. It is non-lethal to humans," he wrapped up with a smile, "but it is mildly irritating, and known to cause a painful rash on eleven percent of test subjects."

"Great, fantastic," McCauley butted in. "We're going to break into freak central with three flea bombs."

"Don't be an asshole," Hunter said, turning to him. "You really think I only made three?"

"There's more than enough gas where we're going," Loyd said, plucking the canister from Hunter's hand, "This is our ticket back into the base. The primary Locust mass is heading south into the desert, but the flow out of the Monolith chamber is thinning. We've got a one-shot chance to gas the place, grab what we came for, and get out of here without all of this being for nothing—I say we take it."

"Easy," Foster said. "You're going to feel a little—"

"Oh wow," Josh groaned, sitting up on the edge of the gurney. "My head."

"Yeah," Foster said. "We'll get you something to drink, but first—"

"I've got sandbags for legs," Josh muttered.

"I know," Foster said, "but you'll feel better if you get your blood flowing, okay? That stuff we injected you with is gonna kick in after a few minutes, and you're going to feel lots better, okay?"

"Yeah, yeah," Josh said, nodding his head. "I can feel it. Okay—"

He took a deep breath, braced himself to get up, and hesitated.

"Nope," he said. "Gimme a second."

"Get the blood flowing," Foster said. "Try making fists with your toes."

Josh gave him a funny look. "Fists?"

"Fists with your toes," Foster said. "Come on, do it."

"I'm wearing shoes."

"That's fine, just wiggle your feet around, okay?"

"Okay, okay," Josh said. "Hey, I've got a question."

Foster nodded absently. "Sure. Shoot."

"You got stung, right?" Josh said.

"Yeah—but I got better," Foster said. "I had the anti—"

"Yeah, I know," Josh said. "What would have happened if you *hadn't* had that?"

Foster studied Josh's expression.

"Did you get stung?" he said.

"No," Josh said. "Nora did."

Foster's face blanched. "And you—"

"The injector," Josh said. "It had red stuff in it?"

Foster squinted at him. "Yeah," he said. "You found one?"

"In a first aid kit."

Foster looked visibly relieved. He chewed his lip.

"And Hunter knows?" he said.

"Hunter knows," Josh replied. "So that means she's fine?"

Foster looked thoughtful for a moment

"Yes," he said. "I—Yes. She should be."

Josh narrowed his eyes. "She should be?"

"She's fine," Foster said, "but…don't get stung."

When the pair limped into the hanger, the first thing Josh noticed was the noise. It sounded like a full on hailstorm was raging outside, pounding out a thousand notes a minute on the thin sheet metal walls. Josh was surprised they hadn't caved in already. Martin and Vance were hurriedly stuffing equipment into the back of a large tracked vehicle, complete with a turret-mounted autocannon and missile launcher.

"A *Bradley*?" Josh blurted. "You sure you have enough fuel?"

"With all those choppers flying around, we chose firepower over gas milage," Foster replied. "We can ditch it once we're clear."

"Clear?" Josh said. "Hold up, aren't we going after Nora and Hunter?"

Foster stopped and turned to him. "How would we do that?"

Josh stared back. "Well…I don't know. You guys have been just full of surprises up to this point."

Foster smiled wryly and looked at the floor, "Yeah," he said. "I'm glad we were able to do that at least."

"Wait," said Josh. "So...what are we doing now?"

"Packing up and going home," Foster said. "If we can, anyway. It's the best chance we've got of continuing the fight."

He caught sight of Shona striding up to them. She nodded curtly at Josh, then turned to Foster.

"Colonel Rourke called in," she said.

Foster waited for her to finish. When she didn't, he scowled.

"And?" he said.

She shook her head. "No go."

Josh flicked his eyes from one to the other.

"What was that?" he said.

"No go?" Foster said. "What do you mean 'no go?'"

"They came a few hours ago and detained half his pilots," Shona said. "He's been trying to reach us ever since."

"Shit," Foster hissed. "Can they still launch the planes they've got?"

Shona shook her head. "Not without an act of mutiny."

"What pilots?" Josh said.

"One of Hunter's old friends," Foster said. "Our ace in the hole—They were supposed to come down and carpet bomb this place to hell if the bugs got out."

"With us still here?" Josh replied.

Foster shrugged. "Well that wasn't the *plan*—"

"Shona!"

Vance dashed up to them. "Romero's on the horn."

Foster stared at him, "Romero?"

"This way," Vance said, and strode back towards the vehicle. The three followed.

By the Bradley, Dr. Martin was fiddling with a large radio pack lying on a set of tables overflowing with weapons, gear, and ammunition. Despite his determined expression, on seeing Vance's return, he immediately stood and handed him the headset.

"Here," he said. "I don't know what I'm doing."

"Are they still on?" Vance said, handing the headset to Foster, who promptly leaned forwards, flicked a switch, and cranked up the volume. Squeezing the talk button on the headset, he held the mic up to his mouth and cleared his throat.

"Evening asshats!" he said. "How's the weather out there?"

Loyd's voice crackled back.

"It's a little buggy, as long as I'm being honest," he said. "Not that I'm particularly envious of whatever hole you've managed to bury yourselves in."

"I don't know," said Foster. "It's rather homey, if I do say so myself. Which I do."

"Funny," said Loyd, "but let's cut the chit chat—Who am I speaking to?"

Foster let go of the talk button and looked thoughtful for a moment. He and Shona exchanged glances.

"He doesn't know how many of us are left," said Vance.

Foster shook his head, "He's a born liar. He always knows more than he says."

The radio crackled. "Hello?"

Foster chewed his lip for a moment, then held up the mic. "You first."

"All right," Loyd said. "This is Special Agent Loyd Romero, acting Incident Commander."

"What agency?"

"That's classified."

"Of course it is."

"Like I said," Loyd continued. "Chit chat. I've got a much better way to prove who I am to you."

"Oh?" Foster replied, "and what's that?"

"We became aware that a mutual friend of ours and his co-conspirators were preparing to bomb this facility at the behest of your boss," Loyd said. "Seeing this as a direct threat to our operation, we had them detained."

Foster was silent for a moment, "For what it's worth, you weren't the target—well, the *main* target, anyway."

"I appreciate that," Loyd said. "In fact, the presence of our buggy friends has made me appreciate a lot of things, including the deal your boss offered us."

Foster turned to Shona, who shrugged.

"Deal?" Vance muttered.

Foster keyed the mic. "What deal?"

"There's a mess that needs cleaning up," Loyd said. "Now we may not agree on whose fault it is, but neither of us is interested in having war of the worlds on our hands."

"Who's *fault*?" Vance growled. Foster held up a finger.

"Now," said Loyd, "In about ten minutes, you're going to get a call from your Colonel friend, saying that his men have been un-detained. That ought to take care of most of the Locust now making their way across the desert. In the meantime, however, we are going to meet up, go back inside the base, and shut them down at the source."

Josh noticed Martin scowling. The older man raised his hand.

"He wants the Monolith," he said. "That will be their price."

Foster nodded, and keyed the mic.

"That's uncharacteristically nice of you," he said. "What's the catch?"

"We get the Monolith," Loyd said. "That's non-negotiable."

There was a pause.

"What about their hostages?" Josh said.

"What about our people?" Foster said into the mic.

There was a pause.

"Tell you what," Loyd said, "as long as you don't stab us in the back, we'll leave them with you."

The five exchanged glances.

"Yeah right," Foster snorted to himself, then keyed the mic once more.

"Okay," he said. "Put Hunter on the line so we know this is legit."

"That'll take a minute," Loyd said.

"I've got a minute," Foster replied. "Out."

He let go of the talk button and turned to face the others.

"What do you think?" he said.

"This is crazy," Vance said shaking his head. "There's no way they're going to let Hunter go."

"True," said Martin, "but we all know Hunter would sacrifice himself to close the portal."

"We talk to Hunter," Shona said. "We wait for the pilots to be freed."

Foster scowled. "I can't see any better way," he said, "but like Vance said, there's no way they're going to let Hunter go—not alive anyway. Not any of us, if he gets the chance."

He stared hard at the radio set. "We need an ace in the hole. Something to pull out of our sleeves before the status quo changes."

"That's not so complicated," said Josh.

Foster looked quizzically at him. "Come again?"

"I'm dead, remember?" Josh said. "He shot me himself."

Shona scowled at him. "You didn't think to mention this before?"

"Well I—Should I have?" Josh replied.

With difficulty Foster managed to turn around to face Josh. He had a large grin smeared across his face.

"Ooooh, this is gonna be *good*," he muttered, a fierce twinkle in his eye. "Vance, let's put Booker's suit to good use—payback is gonna be a *bitch* today."

Nora watched Hunter talking on the radio. He was surrounded by guards, all listening in for the slightest hint of subterfuge.

In spite of herself, she found a slight smile tugging at her cheeks. She found herself remembered being bored out of her skull as her father forced her to recite duress codes and taught her how to break duct tape and cable ties. They were right to listen—not that it would do them any good. Hunter had taught her well.

Loyd's voice, startlingly close behind, shattered her reverie, bringing her back to the cold windy night.

"Stand off," he said. "I need to talk to the detainee."

The guards turned and walked off until they were about twenty feet away, and stood facing outward. Nora formed her hands into fists and tried to keep herself relaxed as she faced him.

"How are you feeling?" he said, folding his arms. "I'm cold."

Nora ignored him in favor of the guard behind him. She'd never killed anyone before, but she was beginning to wonder what it felt like.

He studied her for a moment, then jammed his hands into his pockets. "Look," he said. "I get it. I really do—"

"They didn't have the key," Nora interrupted.

Loyd stared at her. "What?"

"The people who did the experiment were working for Easton," she said. "They only set it up because they knew someone would be bringing them the key on *that day* at *that time*."

Loyd's brow furrowed. "What's your point?"

Nora stared at him for a moment, then chuckled grimly.

"What?" said Loyd. "I don't under—"

"It was you," Nora said, "wasn't it?"

Loyd cocked his head at her and blinked.

"Did Mr. E give it to you?" she continued. "Was it in the van, disguised as a computer case or something?"

"Look," Loyd said, spreading his hands, "I lied, Easton lied—we didn't think you'd understand, and I see now that was a mis—"

"A *mistake*!" Nora shouted. "Oh right, because *mistakes* aren't anybody's fault. You can stand on that pile of bodies all day and tell the whole world that it *wasn't your fault*—"

"I DON'T HAVE TO JUSTIFY MYSELF TO *YOU*!" Loyd roared back, "Everything I've done, I did because there was *no other choice*—"

"So now what?" Nora interrupted. "Are you going to shoot me—"

"I'm not finished," Loyd cut her off.

"*I don't care*," Nora shot back. "Answer the question."

"Of course I'm not going to shoot you," Loyd said. "There is literally no reason for you to think that."

"There's a *very* literal reason—"

"There is *no reason*—no reason *whatsoever* for you to think that, and I'm offended you think I would be capable of such a thing."

Nora stared at him, mouth hanging open. She had no words.

"You're...*offended*..." she repeated.

"Yes," Loyd said. "If it weren't for me, you'd be dead right now. I want an apology, and I want—"

Nora slugged him.

Managing proper form while cuffed was nearly impossible, but at this range, both her fist and the blast wave connected with his face, knocking him backwards.

She heard the guards bark, and in an instant someone had kicked her knees out from under her and thrown her to the ground. Someone cycled their weapon.

"No!" Loyd shouted. "No—pick her up."

Rough hands pulled her upright, and she found herself facing Loyd, who was nursing a gushing nose. He smiled wryly.

"I should have known," he said. "All that posturing, all that denial—you've always been your father's daughter."

He leaned in until she could feel his hot breath on her face.

"Now take a good look at where he is," he growled, "and ask yourself how much good it did him."

"Ordinarily we'd be giving you a lot more time to get used to this," Vance said, dragging a large plastic case from underneath the table, "But obviously we're in a rush, so you're going to have to learn on the go."

"I understand," Josh said, adjusting the fit of his armor vest. "Just give me the cliff notes version."

Vance unsnapped the clips, and tossed the lid back. Josh squinted the mechanized framework inside uncertainly.

"Is...are you sure it still works?"

"Yes—er, probably," said Vance, pulling the rigid chest harness open to reveal the legs folded up inside. "It's built for combat, so it's a very tough piece of equipment to start with."

"Didn't seem to help the guy who was wearing it," Josh said, noting the occasional streak of encrusted blood. He saw what looked like a name on the chest plate and wiped the coagulated grit—RONIN.

"The man wearing it did his best," Vance said, "and he didn't get a second chance."

Josh felt a pang of guilt. "I'm sorry," he said.

"I'm sure he isn't especially concerned," Vance said. "Right now it's time for you to focus."

He pulled the suit upright, and held it up like a coat. "In you go."

Josh slipped his arms through the cuirass frame, and then pushed the sides together until they locked with a solid *clack*. He tried to adjust his armor underneath and found it difficult to move.

"Feels a little tight," he said.

"Step into the feet," Vance replied, "and I'll adjust the fit."

Josh looked down and awkwardly put one shoe after the other into the open soles. Vance took a few moments adjusting the chest harness. Josh was mildly surprised that it fit over the vest at all, with all the pouches and equipment hanging from it.

Within a few moments, Vance had folded the foot clamps over his shoes, adjusted the length of each leg, and folded the integral greaves and kneepads into place. He held up Josh's bulky left gauntlet.

"You won't need gloves," he said. "There's a pair built in."

Josh furrowed his brow, "Built in gloves?"

"They're powered," Vance said. "Just like the rest of the suit—but instead of rigid joints, they use reactive fibers."

Josh stared at him, "Huh?"

"Artificial muscle fibers," Vance said. "So you can still use your fingers without ripping them off."

"Oh," Josh said. He wriggled his hand inside.

"I feel like I'm wearing steel mittens," he said.

"I haven't turned it on yet," Vance said, holding up the right gauntlet. "Put this on, then push the red button on the left forearm."

The button was on the inside of the forearm, instead of the outside, which confused Josh for a moment until he remembered the blade Hunter's suit had carried there. He pushed it and instantly felt the suit pop off his shoulders. It wasn't quite carrying him, but it certainly felt lighter than it looked, to an almost surreal degree.

"Hey," he said, "which button is for the big ass knife?"

"Booker wasn't carrying one," Vance explained. "He preferred to punch things down instead, so he stuck with just the brass knuckles."

He pointed to the armor plate on the back of Josh's glove. "Notice, the plates outside your hand use the same joint type as the rest of the suit. If you tried to punch something using just the gloves, the impact would collapse them and crush your hands."

Josh formed a fist and noted how the plates covered the knuckles. "Watch the fingers, got it."

"Especially when lifting or prying things apart," Vance said, "Push this button, and an outer set of mechanical joints will lock, making it significantly easier to—"

"Is there like, a manual or something I can take with me?" Josh said. "I mean obviously I won't have time to read it now, but—"

"You're right," said Vance. "Of course. I'll look around for one in a moment. It's really not that complicated though. There's two spare batteries in the pack, and—"

He stopped and looked up, as if listening. Over the banging outside, they heard the thump of rotor blades passing overhead.

"And now we're moving on to weapons," Vance said. "Oh, one last thing—the suit is incredibly strong, but it's sensitivity is on a curve—hit something lightly, and it'll hit it lightly—hit something hard, and it'll punch it across the room. Take it easy until you get the hang of it."

Josh nodded. "Punch with the knuckles, lift with the palms, take it easy. Got it."

"Good," Foster limped up to them with surprising speed. "Sounds like the Fuzz is here, so I'm going to make this real short. Okay?"

Josh blinked. "Okay?"

"Shona and I are going for the Monolith," Foster said. "Your objective is Nora. Grab her, then find us, and we'll all get the hell out of Dodge. BUT—" he held up a finger, "That's only if we shut down the portal. No portal, no more bugs."

"Got it." Josh said. "No, wait—how are you going to close the portal?"

"Real simple." Foster said. "The portal is generated by a big black floaty thing called a Monolith. If you remove the key in the side, the portal can't sustain itself and the whole thing shuts down. All I gotta do is pull the plug and get clear."

"That's it?" Josh said.

"That's it." Foster said. "Easy as cutting cable."

"Unless the key is stuck, Vance interjected. "Then—"

"Don't worry about it Doc," Foster said. "If that happens, we can still take it down."

"Yeah, but whoever does it is getting left behind."

"Left behind?" Josh blurted. "What do you mean left behind?"

"Monoliths come in pairs," Vance said. "One anchors each end of the —uh—wormhole, for lack of a better term. Remove the corresponding key from either and—"

"That's not gonna happen though." Foster said, slapping him on the shoulder. "And if it does, it's not gonna be you. Focus on saving the girl. I'm depending on you. Understand?"

Josh took a quick breath and nodded sharply. "I need a weapon."

Foster studied his eyes for an instant, then grinned broadly. "Right this way."

He limped over to a table next to the radio stacked with equipment and picked up a blocky bullpup assault rifle. Josh recognized it as one of the McKnight contractor's caseless weapons, but this one had a longer barrel and rail system, long enough for a *second* weapon to be mounted underneath like a grenade launcher, only it was a much smaller bore, and was itself magazine fed.

"Think that'll work?" Foster said.

"Looks good to me," Josh said. "What's that thing underneath though?"

"Twelve gauge shotgun," Foster said, "but it loads grenades too, so take your pick." He pointed at two stacks of magazines. The shells were color-coded red and green.

"Green is grenades, Red is buckshot," Foster said.

The helicopters seemed to have circled and was now coming back.

"I'll take both," Josh said, swiped a pair of mags from each stack and jamming them into a dump bag hanging from his hip, "Anything else?"

Foster looked him over.

"Gas," he muttered, "sidearm, ammo, frags, ammo ammo ammo—" He looked up and broke into a smile, "You look good. Get going."

"You've got to stop grinning like that," Josh said, pulling another magazine of caseless rounds off the table and shoving it in the bag, just in case. "The bigger you smile, the more I think I'm going to trip down a flight of stairs and break my neck."

"You're gonna be fine," Foster said, slapping him on the shoulder. "Besides, you've already died once today. Used up your quota."

"Foster!" Shona was busy slotting magazines into another pair of assault rifles. "Send the doctors on their way."

"Right," Foster turned to Martin and Vance. "Well, you can either drive the Bradley out and come back for us," he said, "or—"

"Lock us in the armored vehicle," Vance said. "It's an obvious target, but it may give you some leverage when they come inside. Besides, we don't want someone fooling around with it."

Foster thought for a moment, then nodded. "Fair point."

Shona slipped her helmet on and picked up her shield. "Let's go!"

"Right," Foster said, grimacing. "This is going to be fun."

He turned to Josh, "Uh…hide."

It took ten minutes after the Blackhawk touched down for Hunter to walk into the hangar, flanked by Loyd, McCauley, and nearly a dozen agents. Nora and Easton came with the rearguard. Through the black uniforms she could just see Foster and "Mother" in the middle of the floor, locked into their exos and loaded for bear.

Loyd casually took in the space and settled on the massive armored vehicle sitting behind them, draped in gray tarp.

"Open it up," he said. "I'm not doing this with that thing hanging over my head."

"Why not?" Foster quipped. "Dontcha trust us?"

Loyd turned his eyes to the battered fighter and looked him up and down.

"Where's everyone else?" he said.

Foster held up his hands in a time out gesture, then pointed to Hunter. "Hi Boss," he said with a grin.

"Evening ladies," Hunter said. "Foster, you look like hammered shit."

Foster shrugged. "It's Nevada sir."

Hunter glanced at Shona and nodded. She returned it, and set her shield down against the ground.

"We are ready," she said.

"Good," Hunter replied. "Break out the bug bombs."

"You got it Boss," Foster said. He turned towards the table behind him and managed to slowly lower himself down on one knee, and slowly pull a large plastic case from underneath it.

Nora saw Mother's keen eyes scanning the group. For an instant, they stopped on her. Nora felt them bore into her like a drill—but only for an instant, and then they passed on.

One of the guards next to her shifted nervously. Nora felt a bit better. She wasn't the only one who felt it.

Having successfully dragged out three cases, Foster reached over to the front of the nearest box and slowly opened it.

"This one is thrown," he said, "and that one—" he pointed at the far case, "—Is 40 mike-mike."

McCauley folded his arms, "How do we know this is the real stuff?"

"Because *I'm* going to be firing it," said Foster, letting his hand fall on a six-chambered grenade launcher hanging against his chest. "Because I'm slower than you."

He pointed at the other boxes, "There's more than enough for three thrown grenades apiece, so I suggest you all take as many as you can carry, but let us do the first couple of throws. As soon as we make contact—"

"Who are they?" Loyd interrupted, pointing to the pair of body bags next to the table.

Foster glanced at them the still figures, and then glanced up at Shona.

Shona smiled grimly.

"You should know," she said. "You killed them."

Loyd studied her for a moment, then turned to McCauley and nodded.

McCauley turned to the agents.

"Okay," he said. "Like they said—three apiece."

He pointed out two men. "2-4, 2-5—carry extra 40 mil and shadow the operator."

The men crowded past him to the cases. McCauley elbowed his way over to Foster and Shona.

"I'm gonna be watching you two," he said, a clenched grin on his face. "I don't care what the kid says—you step out of line just once, and I'll frag the two of you *myself*."

Foster flipped him off without looking up. Shona just smiled.

Nora looked around and realized she'd lost track of Hunter. Looking around frantically, she noticed Easton leading him back towards the doors. She moved, but a guard grabbed her by the shoulder.

"Dad!" she shouted.

Both Hunter and Easton stopped to look over their shoulders. After a moment, Easton moved to go—but Hunter caught his eye and rooted himself to the ground.

For a moment, Nora held her breath—and then Easton jerked his head her way, and Hunter stepped towards her.

She wrenched herself free of the guards and wrapped him in a death grip.

"Where are you going?" she said.

"I'm—" Hunter ran out of words. "It's going to be okay—"

"Where are they taking you?" she said, this time more insistent. She leaned around him and glared at Easton. "Where are you taking him?"

"Somewhere safe," Easton said. "You'll be joining him soon."

Hunter turned her face to look into his. "It's going to be okay," he said. "You're going to be fine."

"I don't care about that," Nora said. "I want *you* to be okay."

"I will," he said. "I need you to stay with Foster and Shona. They're good people."

"I—" Nora turned to Easton again. *"Tell me."*

Easton ignored her and turned to Hunter. "We're leaving," he said.

"NO!" Nora shouted. She felt an agent's hand on her shoulder, his breath as he hissed in her ear.

"Bitch, how many times do I have to—"

He was cut off mid-sentence by Hunter's hand smashing into his throat.

At least three agents pulled Hunter back as his target dropped to his knees, struggling to breathe.

"Jesus *Christ* Hunter!" Easton bawled. "I thought we had a *deal!*"

"Oh calm down," Hunter growled. "He's been roughing up my daughter all night. Don't look at me like your friggin' *surprised*."

Easton glared at him, then cuffed the back of the wheezing man's helmet.

"Idiot," he hissed, and then turned towards the door. "Let's go!"

Foster was suppressing a grin when Shona elbowed him in the ribs. McCauley was watching them. Foster nodded.

"No punchee," he said. "Got it, boss."

After Easton left with Hunter and his guards, there was perhaps a dozen uniformed agents left, including McCauley himself. After a few minutes, the Major stepped up on a nearby crate and turned to face the group.

"Okay everybody," he bellowed. "Listen up!"

He pointed to Foster, "Gas man—you're with Charlie Squad over here. You lady—you're with Delta. Both of you are on point too, so whatever happens to us, happens worse to you."

Foster raised his hand. McCauley pointed to him. "You. What's your name."

"No thanks," Foster said. "I have a question—" He pointed to Nora. "—What about her?"

"She's coming with us," Loyd replied.

"That's death," Shona stated. "She should remain here."

A murmur went through the ranks. Loyd threw McCauley a hard look. McCauley threw one back.

"Believe me, I'd want fewer guns in my back too," McCauley said, "but I'm not stupid enough to split my forces now. We stay together."

Foster exchanged a look with Shona. McCauley noticed and allowed himself a private chuckle.

"Right!" He said. "Now—show us this 'back door' of yours."

"Don't look at me," Foster said. "I just work here—Ow."

He winced as Shona punched him in the shoulder on her way past. Striding past McCauley to a large maintenance hatch by the far wall, she pulled it open.

"Follow me," she said, and dropped inside.

16

War Machine

Josh waited almost two minutes after hearing the floor grate slam shut before peeling the body bag open and rolling to a crouch, looking around carefully to make sure no one had hung back.

Satisfied, he stood slowly, made his way to the Bradley, and knocked three times on the back hatch.

Nothing happened. He was in the middle of knocking again when he heard the turret hatch open, and the tarp covering it briefly became an olive green ghost costume with Vance's voice.

"Shhhh!" Vance hissed. "Are you trying to get us all killed?"

"Can you hear yourself? Stop flapping the tarp!" Josh shot back.

Vance finally pulled the nylon canvas over his head and accidentally flopped it over Josh.

Josh ripped it off and tossed it aside.

"What is wrong with you?" he snapped.

"The rear hatch is *powered*," Vance replied. "You were supposed to knock on the *turret*."

Josh considered arguing, but decided his efforts were better served getting a move on. He patted down his equipment—rifle, launcher, suit, ammo, more ammo, gas grenades, frag grenades, gas mask—"

He looked up at Vance, who was pulling Martin out of the hatch.

"How do I look?" he said.

"Like an egg in a steel cage," Vance quipped. "Now get going!"

"Wait!" Martin said. His voice wasn't really that loud, but it made his companions wince anyway.

"Wait just a moment," he said, and pulled a small leather book from his pocket and tossing it to Josh.

Josh caught it, and immediately recognized the bullet hole in the cover. He grinned.

"It's a bit harder to read now I suppose," Martin said, "but it'll do for a good luck charm."

Josh chuckled and stuffed it into a chest pocket. "I thought you didn't believe in luck."

"I don't," Martin said. "Now off with you!"

Josh started off down the narrow tunnel at quite a pace. The exoskeleton had more or less negated the weight of his weapons. It had not altered their bulk, however, which made running difficult. His head and side were beginning to hurt, and it was becoming more difficult to breath in the cold air.

At least he still had his coveralls. They were thick, and the running kept his body temperature up.

He abruptly slowed to a walk and tried to catch his breath. Keeping up the running, of course, was his problem. The tunnel had sloped slightly upwards a quarter mile before, but Josh was beginning to realize that he must have finally reached the edge of the salt flats above, because the slope increased a few degrees about a hundred feet up ahead, interrupting the long row of overhead lights.

According to Foster's instructions, they were perhaps a quarter mile ahead of him, almost to the main access tunnel of the facility itself. This tunnel was a sort of "back door"—really meant as more of an escape route than an access point, but obviously it could serve either way.

Josh briefly slowed to a walk and patted himself down to make sure nothing was coming loose. The exoskeleton mounted several hard points allowing for weapons to be hung or stowed and keeping the weight off the operator. Josh hadn't had much time to figure them out, however, so he'd mostly hung everything as conventionally as possible. Ammunition, packed in the vest pouches, was probably the heaviest weight since it was directly on his shoulders. Foster had placed heavy emphasis on the difference between the red shells and the green shells, and making sure that he knew which mags held which—the red shells were typical buckshot, but the green shells were miniature high explosive grenades. Josh inferred the obvious health risks of using them in close quarters, and took careful note of which were which. He'd taken six or so each of the remaining ReGel and anti-toxin injectors, stuffing most of them into his pack and slipping one of each into his right side pocket for quick access.

Josh pulled at the vest and tried to settle it more comfortably on his shirt. It wasn't as bloody as the last one he'd looted, and despite his apprehension the exoskeleton didn't seem to mind the sticky red trails that had dried on its surface. Occasionally, however, something would bind up and he'd have to bend the joint a couple of times before moving on. It kept interrupting his forward momentum, which was slacking already.

He kept trying not to think about how many bugs they were liable to find inside. The spread outside had to be miles wide by now, based on the rate he'd seen them traveling—and that was hours ago. If facing them on the surface was like trying to hold back the tide, trying to fight your way through from inside was going to be like drinking out of a fire hose. Hopefully, the gas grenades would blunt that edge, but Josh wasn't willing to put his money on anything until he saw it work.

He turned up the radio. He knew better than to speak on their channel, but at least he could listen in.

All he got was garbled static.

Josh frowned. Perhaps the ground interference had finally cut them off.

A ripping series of cracks echoed down the tunnel. Josh froze.

Gunfire.

He gritted his teeth. "Shit."

Adjusting his grip on the rifle, he broke into a run.

After almost a minute of sustained running, Josh found himself coughing, and his eyes were watering. At first, he thought he was just out of shape—but a deep breath of burning air and a hacking fit proved it to be a bit more than that.

He quickly ripped open a pouch on his belt and pulled out his gas mask, pulling it over his head and blowing hard to seal it. It immediately fogged up, leaving him half blind.

"Oh, come on," he muttered.

He brought the rifle to his shoulder, clicked on the flashlight, and slowly walked forwards.

Wisps of green fog clung to the ground, falling through the darkened doorway up ahead in gentle clouds. Josh took a couple of breaths to make sure the mask was working. He listened carefully and made sure the safeties were off on both weapons.

Hearing nothing, he stepped into the tunnel and swept it with his muzzle, looking both ways.

The floor was clumped with bugs and luminescent green fog as far as he could see in both directions.

They weren't moving—Josh took this as a testament to the gas' effectiveness, though he was very surprised at the sheer amount. In the interest of being sure, however, he poked one of the bodies at his feet.

It twitched violently. Josh managed to stop himself from automatically shooting it and waited a second more. It didn't move again. Keeping his finger off the trigger, he reminded himself he wasn't supposed to exist—he wasn't sure how far a shot would carry underground, but he guessed it would be more than enough to blow his cover.

Making an educated guess as to the direction they had followed, Josh turned right and began cautiously walking towards the main doors.

After about a hundred feet he caught sight of something shining in the beam of his flashlight, and stepped towards it.

Sweeping away the fog with his arm, Josh found himself looking down on the gas mask of a black-clad body.

He was on the right track. Josh reached down, pulled a pair of gas canisters off the man's vest, and kept going.

A few minutes later he reached the entrance. The door stood wide open, nearly half choked with bug bodies. He nearly slipped on the slick mixture of brass and gore covering the floor.

Carefully working his way forwards, he sized up the sprawling pile and tried to see where everyone else had climbed over. The possibility that not everything in the stack was quite dead crossed his mind—he made note of it and pushed it aside. After a moment of carefully probing with his foot, he found what seemed a relatively solid spot, and stepped up, hiking his other foot over the tangle of stiff limbs and leaking bodies.

He put his foot down, and soon began to notice the smell.

"Aw…" he groaned in disgust. "Great."

A few more squishy steps, and he was at the top, looking towards the first building's edifice. A massive hole had been torn through the thin drywall of the first floor, leaving a messy gap wide enough for a dozen people to walk through. It too, was lined with bug corpses, but significantly fewer—

A hiss exploded from the pile next to him, and Josh shouted in surprise, scrambling forwards. He felt the pile shift outwards next to him as he leapt clear, and turned to see the a bug tear it's jaws clear of the tangle and turn to face him.

Josh waved the muzzle of his weapon towards it and pulled the shotgun's trigger. The bug's face shattered, and it slumped back, a mangled bleeding mess.

Josh took a deep breath and frowned. It had been a clean hit—almost too clean. No messy exit wounds.

He ejected the magazine into his hand and immediately remembered two things. One, that any decent military manufacturer would use some sort of safety range to their explosive munitions, and second, that he had just field-tested it.

The shells were green. Grenades.

He sighed. *Well this is off to a great start. You almost killed yourself.*

He tapped his head hard and stuffed the magazine under his arm. Awkwardly pulling back the shotgun's bolt to get the chambered shell out, he suddenly froze.

Something had moved behind him.

Before the warrior had completed it's rattling war cry, Josh had spun around and punched a dozen bullet holes in it. It hit the floor with a thud, but it was too late—Josh could hear the cry echoed down the hallway ahead.

Pulling a mag of shells from his vest—briefly checking to make sure it was buckshot—he slotted it home and tried to stuff the grenade mag back into his vest while scanning rapidly for the errant single grenade. He'd dropped it in the turn. Catching sight of it on the floor, he snatched it up and held it in his off hand as he leveled the weapon down the corridor.

The group was small and staggered. Easy prey. Josh took the first one down with three snap shots, changed targets, and leapfrogged through four others in quick succession. Bug six was crippled by the burst that mulched bug five's carapace, and took a double tap to the head.

Josh more glimpsed than saw the others in the shadows, let loose a couple of long bursts, and let go of the trigger.

Nothing moved but the gray smoke curling through his flash suppressor. He dumped the nearly empty rifle mag and pulled a fresh one from his vest.

A ragged growl from behind sent him scrambling, and he turned in time to see the bug with the broken jaw slither down to the floor and hiss at him through it's set of good eyes. Josh brought the rifle up to his shoulder and put the chambered round through it's eye.

To his surprise, it's head exploded in a thunderclap of smoke and flame.

Josh felt like he'd been dunked underwater. He opened his mouth and tried to clear the ringing from his head, and heard dozens of shrieking cries above him. He picked up his rifle and looked up to see the entire ceiling of the tunnel swarming with Locust boiling out from every side of the facade.

"No," Josh muttered, and looked straight forwards down the hall. It was clear.

He glanced behind him. The pile of bodies would slow him down anyway.

He snapped a last look at the mass crawling down both walls, and sprinted forwards down the hallway, the howling mass hot on his heels.

The storm had settled, leaving only a resonant thrum pulsing through the air. The Monolith hung in space, the scarred black rod slowly turning about it's axis. The intricate carvings on it's surface flickered like designs cut into a metal lantern, a spectrum of colored flame flickering within.

A slow, almost mesmerizing stream of debris flowed past it's surface, giving the somewhat dizzying impression that the object was ascending. Drawing back and comprehending the true image, however, was liable to disorient the viewer even more completely. A gigantic disk of earth and rock had simply vanished, expanding beyond the silo's walls until the Monolith resided in the center of a massive cavern hundreds of feet in radius. Tracing the debris trail as it sank slowly to what once had been the floor of the silo, one was instead confronted with a murky halo of dust and disintegrated matter slowly circling down, growing faster and more luminous as it went, reaching an almost blinding glow—and abruptly sinking into the most utter black Nora had ever seen.

The very light around the hole in space seemed to warp and bend, drawing her in and making war with her perception of gravity. She tried to mentally place the anomaly's epicenter in relation to the Monolith's lowest point, but it seemed to change depending on where she looked, like looking into the funhouse mirror version of a 3D movie.

She watched a vending machine as it slowly vanished into the blinding halo, warped, and merged with the black depths, sinking like a rock. Nora scowled. She waited a moment, then looked high—but not too high. It was too bright.

In contrast to the black hole below, a second sun had spawned in the space above the Monolith, and was only prevented from making it impossible to see at all because it was tucked into the hole in the ceiling that represented the remainder of the silo's length.

Watching the vending machine emerge once again from the bright ray spotlighting the Monolith, she finally put two and two together and understood the two fixtures relationship to each other.

"Up is blow," she muttered, "down is suck."

She had watched the same vending machine make it's loop perhaps three times since the agents had cleared the room a few minutes prior and moved on to clear the rooms adjacent. It usually took about thirty seconds for the vending machine to make the trip from the top portal to the bottom portal, and it was perhaps a little less than a minute before it reappeared at the top to start the whole cycle over again.

This of course, begged the question—where did it go?

A meaty *thwack* brought her back to reality in a rush as Loyd kicked a bug corpse off the ledge. Gravity lost it's tenuous hold within a few feet, and it spun gently as it approached the abyss. The debris field was choked with bug parts, as was the ledge they were standing on.

Loyd adjusted his gas mask and waved absently at the bug as it quickly gained speed.

"Don't worry." he said. "That one's not coming around again. You've got to come through on the axis, or you just fly off.

"Off to where?" Nora said.

"Nowhere." Loyd said. "The void. Hyperspace. I don't know."

"But that's not where they come *from*." Nora said.

"Of course not." said Loyd. "They're entering from the other Monolith."

"The other Monolith?" Nora said. "Where's that?"

Loyd chuckled. She felt a jolt as he placed his hands on her shoulders and leaned in.

"See?" he said. "You're coming around already."

Nora bit back a retort and turned away.

Josh flew down the trail of dead bugs and smashed doorways, the calls of the swarm always only a few feet behind. Just as he thought he was about to run out of space, he saw the open test lab doors ahead and came barreling into the open.

A digitized voice rasped from the shadows. "FREEZE!"

Without waiting for an answer, Josh was immediately showered in bullets. No less than three muzzle flashes lit the room and raked it from top to bottom.

Josh had too much momentum to stop. He threw his hands up in front of his face, sprinted through the door, swung left, and dove crashing through the window of the security booth.

After a couple of awkward, frantic seconds, he somehow righted himself and freed his weapon. He could hear the agents outside.

"Suppressing fire!" The first blurted. "Watch him! Watch him!"

"What the hell was that?"

The third apparently turned around, because all he managed was an earsplitting scream before he was cut off by a Locust roar and the chatter of hundreds of chitin feet bursting into the room.

Three bugs had burst through the entrance before Josh caught sight of the door button and slapped it. Swinging his weapon towards the mob piling through he opened fire and ripped it to pieces with a sustained burst, then switched to the shotgun. He concentrated on the nearest threats, planting three blasts in three bugs in quick succession. The door motors whined as they attempted to close, crushing the press like a living stick pile. The hole was plugged.

Josh waited an instant more, just to make sure it was slowing them down, then turned and dashed down the cylindrical hallway.

"Don't you see?" Loyd said, gesturing towards the otherworldly vista before them. "Don't you see what this *is*?"

Nora's eyes went to the Monolith and it's satellites, and then back to Loyd.

"This," Loyd continued. "This isn't like the power of the atom, or the press, or oil—this is like discovering *fire*. No one man can hold this over the rest."

"Unless it's you?" Nora retorted.

"Of course not me," Loyd said. "People like Professor Easton. People with respect for what it can do."

"Easton *killed my mother*," Nora retorted.

"Easton was weak." Loyd said. "He *let* it happen and then projected his guilt onto Hunter—who accepted it. Those two are their own worst enemies. But *us*—" he said, spreading his hands towards her, "Their time is ending. You and me, we're different. We're the next generation. We don't have to make the same mistakes—we can be the ones that turn the world around for the better."

He stepped forwards. Nora stepped back. Her eyes flicking rapidly from his face to his hands, watching for what she did not know.

"We're standing on the brink of the next great leap forwards., Loyd said, his eyes shining in the dark. "People are going to look back a hundred years from now—maybe longer—and they're going to say *this*…" he stood and looked up to the ceiling, his voice rising with every syllable, "*This* was the time. *This* was the moment. This was *IT*!"

She felt a jolt go through her as a guard's hand clapped down on her shoulder. Glancing to either side, she found herself outflanked.

"You may not like me," said Loyd, "but when it comes down to it, I'm the only game in town."

McCauley burst through the side door.

"Romero!" he shouted. "What are you doing? That thing should be down by now!"

"I need a minute," Loyd said. "What's the big fuss about?"

"The *FUSS*?" McCauley blurted, "You want to know what the *fuss* is? We're all gonna be dead in five minutes, that's what the frigging fuss is!"

Before Loyd could reply, there was the sound of crashing overhead, and a ceiling tile fell to the floor. Nora heard something scuffling in the shadowy depths.

McCauley hefted his assault rifle and jerked a thumb over his shoulder.

"Into the hallway," he said. "Move!"

Josh turned a right and felt the wind smacked out of him as a pair of bullets connected with his chest plate. He sprayed a burst down the hallway and backed around the corner.

He wheezed, trying to measure his breathing against his chest locking up, and patted himself down, looking for a wound. After a moment, he relaxed—the vest had done it's job, bruises notwithstanding.

"This way! This way!"

"Frag out!"

He heard a metallic *clunk,* and a smoking grenade skidded across the floor, bouncing off the wall in front of him. Josh jumped forwards, snatched it up, and hurled it back the way it came.

The explosion pounded through the air like a drum. Screams of pain followed.

He sucked in another painful breath, hefted his rifle, and peered around the corner. Finding it clear, he stepped forwards and hustled up the corridor, keeping his weapon trained on a body lying on the ground.

The idea that he had just killed another man rushed up, threatening to dominate his mind—and a gunshot from behind drove it away again, thrusting him back into the present.

Scrambling forwards, he rounded the corner, found it clear, and turned, backing quickly and waiting for his enemy to come into view.

Instead, he heard a crashing sound and an unhuman growl. He stepped forwards and glanced around the corner.

A warrior bug had just burst through one of the fragile hall doors and was shaking the agent in it's jaws like a rag doll. Josh hosed both of them, then turned around and kept going.

Foster adjusted his grip on the assault rifle and peeled off his gas mask, sucking in a deep breath of air.

"God!" he gasped. "I don't think I can keep this up."

Shona pulled her mask up and sniffed the air for a moment.

"Keep it off," she said. "It's not as thick here."

They were at a T-junction, Foster watching the left passage, and Shona watching the right. They had heard sporadic gunfire and what sounded like Locust calls, but that was it. Their four babysitters, stacked up behind the pair, were getting nervous.

Foster backed up a few feet, took a knee, and leaned against an open office doorframe. He glanced back at their guards, and took a moment to appreciate the view down four rifle barrels.

He waved. "Hi there."

Shona sighed, keeping her attention forwards.

Foster snorted and looked down to inspect his equipment. As he did so, he caught sight of something moving in the darkened office to his left.

He went rigid. It hadn't been black—it was wearing green.

He slid his eyes to the right and cleared his throat.

Shona's head didn't move, only her eyes swiveling to meet his.

He made a short series of hand signals in front of his chest so the agent behind couldn't see.

I See,

Friendly,

Left Side.

Nora watched McCauley slide his M4-mounted grenade launcher shut, and swallowed nervously. They had dragged her out into the hallway, which seemed to be packed with yelling agents in one direction, and in the other opened into thin air, shorn off by the edge of what was now the greatly expanded test chamber. Loyd was barking something at McCauley, but McCauley didn't seem to be especially concerned with whatever he was saying, instead taking his sweet time swapping magazines. Finally, he shouted something, and the agents steadied a bit, settling into cover behind three or four desks that had been dragged into the hall, their weapons pointed down the passage.

Nora heard thumping in the hall. A bug shrieked.

"CONTACT FRONT!"

Shots rang out and an agent dragged Nora behind a desk. Loyd and McCauley squatted behind an overturned file cabinet opposite them.

Out of the corner of her vision, Nora saw the end of the hallway vanish in a mass of black. Shona seemed to be slowing the flood using only her shield, but she was clearly backing up as Foster and their four guards used her as cover, firing to each side.

Almost inaudible over the cacophony, Nora saw a crack form on the drywall behind Loyd, and was about to open her mouth when an armored hand punched through the wall and curled back, tearing a massive hole in it.

A man wearing a gas mask and an exoskeleton pushed through the ragged opening, grabbed McCauley by his collar and, in one swift movement, flung him down the hall. McCauley hit the floor, rolled, and clawed for purchase as his feet shot out into open space.

Loyd turned in time to catch a punch that would have almost certainly caved in his skull, had he not thrown up his hands and blocked it. The air rippled as the hardened fist made contact.

Nora felt the guards next to her let go of her arms, and immediately flipped onto her back, shoving both hands upwards. The guard on her left caught the blast directly on the chin and stumbled back into the wall.

The guard on her right grabbed her arms and pulled them aside, yanking her across the floor towards the control room door. Nora flailed and tried to recover enough strength to fire again, but with a quick yank he snaked his arm through hers and pulled her upright in front of him. Nora saw his rifle barrel appear around her shoulder, waving towards her rescuer, and slapped it aside. A burst of flame cracked from the muzzle and drywall exploded.

Josh swept his leg behind Loyd's and threw him to the ground, watching the other man's eyes bug out as the air was knocked from his lungs. Turning with hands raised, he flinched as a burst of gunfire exploded from the man holding Nora and charged, swooping slightly down and to the right. He swung behind the soldier and punched him in the kidneys. It took three blows to loosen him enough for Nora to break loose and fall forwards.

"GO!" He screamed, wrapping his arm around the struggling man's throat. "GO! GO! GO!"

Instead, Nora stood, wound up both hands, and unleashed a blast that knocked Loyd backwards into the soldiers at the barricade only a few feet ahead. With that, she spun and ran past Josh as his man finally slumped to the floor.

Josh turned in time to see Nora waving him through a door a few feet beyond. He dashed forwards and ricocheted off the doorframe, following her inside. Smoothly unslinging his weapon, he turned and dashed across the room, vaulting over a desk and joining Nora, who crouched behind it.

Foster glanced behind in time to see Josh sprinting down the hall and make a hard left to disappear through the control room door as a half-dozen assault rifles reduced the walls to perforated dust.

The nearest of their four guards turned back to Foster and they locked eyes for a long moment.

Foster threw him an offhand smile.

The agent behind the first turned and raised his weapon.

Foster punched the first agent so hard that he shot back and collided with the man behind him, knocking both to the ground. A war cry tore from Foster's throat as he reversed direction and planted his shield between himself and the hallway, deflecting a hail of bullets from Shona's back.

Shona ripped a grenade from her vest and threw it high into the forest of spines. Planting her feet, she released her weapon and shoved both hands against her shield. Foster felt static build behind him as the air grew thick.

WHOOM!

Foster felt the muted blast wave slam into his back and staggered. He heard Shona shouting.

"Flash out!"

He raised the shield.

BANG!

Out of the corner of his eye, he saw Shona punch a hole through the wall into the next door office, shoving though in a shower of dust. Gathering his strength, he stumbled after her and tripped through the ragged hole, landing on his forearms. Shona was shouting again. A high-pitched shriek reverberated through the room. They weren't alone.

Josh stared at the doorway for a moment, trying to see the red dot sight past the fog washing over his visor. He could still hear the muffled roar of gunfire and alien battle cries.

His face broke into a grin beneath his gas mask, and he let out a devious growling laugh.

"I did *not* expect that to go that well," he muttered, turning to Nora. "You okay? Pat yourself down."

Nora stared at him and nodded, eyes wide with shock and adrenaline. "I'm…what's…who are you?"

"What? Oh—" Josh pulled the mask up, "It's me."

Nora looked as if she had been struck between the eyes with a large hammer.

"You're…" she trailed off.

Josh furrowed his brow. "What?"

"You were *dead*."

"Oh! Yeah," Josh said. "Uh—I got better."

Nora looked at him quizzically, then shot a glance at the door.

"So, what now?" she said. "Are the others in on this?"

"Yeah," Josh said. "No—which others?"

Nora's brow furrowed. "What?"

"We got separated," Josh said. "Why did you do that?"

"Didn't you want me to?" Nora said.

"No!" blurted Josh. "Yes! No—I have to think. Let me think."

"What's wrong?" Nora said. "Haven't you ever been *kissed* before?"

Josh was saved by a scattering of bullets punching through the wall and whizzing overhead. He huddled behind the desk and centered his sights on the doorway.

There were a couple of rapid overlapping bursts in the hallway, and then silence.

He could hear Nora breathing. She started to say something.

"Are they—"

Josh heard something rattle across the floor.

"DOWN!" he shouted, ducking and covering his ears.

BANG!

Bullets raked the desks, and Josh fell backwards, spraying fire through it.

Loyd appeared around the desk to his left, walking forwards with his arm outstretched.

Josh immediately fired a burst. The air shimmered as bullets deflected and scattered.

Loyd threw out his fist and Josh felt something slam into him. A returning bolt splashed against Loyd's face and Nora came into view, charging up a second round. Josh scrambled to his feet in time for another burst of gunfire to pin him down.

"Payback's a bitch, ain't it?" McCauley's voice called from the doorway.

Josh turned and saw Nora and Loyd going at it hammer and tongs. He pulled a frag grenade from his vest and ripped the pin clear. Popping up to mark the doorway, he hurled it through.

Nora had sparred with Loyd many times to develop her skills, learning how to apply her martial arts training to her abilities—but almost all of that time had been spent learning how to fight normal people using batons, guns, or even just their fists. The idea that she might have to fight one of "her" people had never seriously crossed her mind.

Now she was in a no-holds-barred beatdown with the man who had taught her perhaps half of what she knew, and to whom she had revealed everything else.

She was losing.

Only her reflexes were keeping her afloat now, with a complex set of hard blocks and counterattacks that bought her time, but so far nothing else. Loyd wasn't as fast as she was, but he didn't need to be so long as he knew where she was about to strike. She was on autopilot, ragged, fighting on instinct. She had to change it up before—

McCauley dove into the room and distracted her. Loyd's pulse connected with her temple and sent her reeling, and then a swift kick to the gut threw her flat.

Nora looked up to see Loyd throw a bolt towards Josh, and rolled into a crouch in time to block a shot that could have knocked her cold.

KRAK.

A grenade exploded in the hallway, blasting the door off its hinges. Loyd flinched, momentarily disoriented.

Nora concentrated, shifting her stance and lashing out in a low sweeping kick.

Loyd took the bait, launching himself upwards.

He loved to jump, Nora remembered—and a target in midair, with nothing to anchor him, was exceptionally vulnerable.

Her pulse hit him squarely in the chin. He did a complete backflip in midair and hit the floor face first.

Josh gripped his weapon, rolled into a crouch—and immediately heard the ripping crack of a dozen bullets whizzing past his head. McCauley had made it to his feet.

Josh heard the empty mag hit the floor, saw his chance, and leaped to his feet.

PLUNK.

The 40mm grenade hit him square in the chest harness and bounced off without detonation. Josh jerked as if he'd been kicked by a mule. He staggered backwards, lost his balance, and crashed to the ground.

He heard the M4's bolt snap shut.

Nora swung her fist, fired a bolt that struck McCauley center of mass, and followed up with three more that slammed into him like sandbags. McCauley stumbled, face bruised and bleeding.

Nora abruptly felt her feet dragged from under her, and fell to the floor as Loyd crouched over her, his face bleeding and eyes lit with rage. She threw her hands up to block his blow, and the air bounced like a drum as each strike pounded against her shield.

Josh saw McCauley stagger, and Loyd tackling Nora on his left. He made an instantaneous calculation, and snapped the rifle to his shoulder. A stream of bullets shredded McCauley and the wall behind him. He was dead before he hit the ground.

Josh whipped the muzzle towards Loyd, and pulled the launcher's trigger. A full-power load of twelve-gauge buckshot slammed into his vest and neck. He screamed and flopped backwards as Nora covered her face.

Pushing himself to his feet, Josh leaped forwards, locked his grip around Loyd's collar, and flung him across the room.

Loyd slammed into the wall with a hard crack, and slid to the floor in a heap.

Josh strode across the room, switched to his pistol, and pulled Loyd upright by the neck. Loyd gasped for air, but when his eyes finally focused on Josh's face, they nearly bugged out.

"You're dead," he choked.

Josh stuck the USP's muzzle against Loyd's forehead and cocked the hammer.

"Up for a rematch?" Josh snarled. "Draw."

Loyd tried to swallow. "Don't."

"Josh!" Nora shouted. "Look up!"

Josh looked up to see something fall through the ceiling tiles above his head. Letting go of Loyd, he jumped backwards as a scorpion ricocheted off Loyd and onto the floor.

Josh shot it twice. It exploded off the floor and curled into a ball, twitching. Josh heard a hissing sound behind him and spun around, leading with the muzzle, but the scorpion was already in mid-air—

WHAP!

Nora's pulse blew it out into the cavern, where it assumed a surprisingly flat trajectory. Josh spun around in time to see Loyd scrambling through the door. He leaped down the hallway after him and managed to snap two shots off before Loyd vanished around the corner.

"Oh come *on!*" Josh muttered.

17

Floaters

"Did you get him?" Nora asked.

"I missed," Josh said flatly. He stumbled towards the drop off.

"Oh," Nora said. "—Wait, really?"

Josh stopped at the edge of the cavern and keyed his radio.

"Foster, this is Josh." He said with a cough. "I've got Nora. We're safe. Where are you?"

He released the button. Static.

"So you're saying he got away?" Nora asked.

Josh keyed his mic again. "Foster? Come in man."

Nora stepped in front of Josh and tried to get his attention.

"Foster?" She said. "Who are you talking to?"

"I'm talking to Foster," Josh said.

Nora wrinkled her brow. "His brother?"

"No," Josh said. "It's—Foster's alive. It's hard to explain."

"Foster's *alive*?"

Josh stepped over to the doorway and peeked down the hall again.

"I think," he said.

He stepped over to the torn precipice and scanned the murky depths below. It was hard to see the floor, but it didn't look like anything was moving. He felt a growing sense of vertigo the closer he got to the edge.

He glanced back at Nora. She appeared to be in the process of swallowing something bitter.

"So…" She began. "Now what?"

Josh stopped at the edge of the cavern, leaned over towards a chunk of drywall, and winced, putting a hand against his side.

"So you're saying he got away?" Nora said.

"Yes," Josh replied, kneeling to keep his back straight and picking up the drywall. "But that doesn't matter anymore. You're no longer captured, and now we can get on to the real objective."

Nora blinked, and folded her arms. "What did you say?"

Josh pointed at the Monolith. "That thing. We have to shut it down."

Nora opened her mouth to say something, then shut it again.

"So what are you going to do?" she said. "Jump?"

Josh cocked his arm back and threw the drywall chunk like a fastball. Nora watched it cross the open expanse between them and the stone pillar hanging in space. There was no arc.

A pealing cry split the low reverb of the room, and a single flailing Locust fell from the murky ceiling like an awkward bird of prey. It took a vicious snap at the object, then plunged into the dust cloud below.

"No," Josh said.

"God!" Nora gasped. "How—Look at them all!"

After Josh's eyes adjusted to the harsh shadows of the jagged cavern ceiling, a shock went through him. It was crawling like a living carpet, streams of Locust climbing along the roof of the chamber towards the wide opening where they stood.

"Can you shut it down?" Nora said.

"I should be able to," Josh replied. "They told me—"

"Yes or no!" Nora snapped.

"Yes!" Josh replied. "We find the key, we pull it out, and *bip*, the whole thing shuts down. All we have to do is get *there*." He pointed to the Monolith.

Nora stepped forwards. "I can do it," she said.

Josh unslung his rifle, keeping his eyes on the crawling swarm above. "You won't last five seconds without me."

Nora rolled her eyes. "And what am I supposed to do? Carry you on my back?"

Josh turned suddenly and stared at her. She raised an eyebrow. "What?"

Josh pulled open his dump bag.

"Hold these," he said, loading her hands with grenades.

"What—" Nora looked from him to the explosives, "You want me to blow it up?"

"No, just hold them," Josh said. "Aha!"

He pulled out a roll of duct tape and held it up for her inspection. "Swap you."

Nora took the roll and stared at it. "I still don't understand."

"Have you ever flown anything?"

"Flown?" Nora said. "Like, a plane?"

"Like *Superman*!" Josh said.

Nora stared at him for a moment, then suddenly it dawned on her.

"*NO*," she said.

"*Yes*," said Josh.

"*NO!*" She repeated, "We are not just—I am not one of those people who wanted to be an astronaut when they grew up, understand?"

"Oh come on," said Josh. "*Everyone* wanted to be an astronaut at some point. Besides, you were going to do this by yourself a second ago."

He stuffed the last of the grenades back into his bag and cinched it closed. Nora held up the duct tape.

"I'm going to carry both of us?"

"There's no gravity!" Josh said. "I won't weigh a thing."

"That's not how mass works," Nora said.

"Well," said Josh. "Then you'd better grow a second pair of arms, because I bet you can't fly and shoot at the same—"

A harsh shriek whined from the darkness above them. Josh looked up.

"Look out!" he said, pushing her to the side.

A bug landed with a loud thud where they had been standing. Josh kicked it off the side and heard the rumble of feet above them. He could almost make out streams of Locust making their way across the ceiling.

Nora slapped the tape against his chest.

"I'm in," she said.

"Okay," Josh said, pressing the roll back into her hand. "Strap us together, back to back. I'll cover."

She nodded, and Josh stepped up to the edge, pointing his rifle at the ceiling.

"Make it fast!" he said, and snapped off a burst. A bug screamed and dropped out into space.

Nora backed up to Josh, pulled off a long strip of tape, and applied it to her stomach. Gritting her teeth, she pulled the roll outwards and back around Josh's side. She felt Josh grip the roll and pull.

"No!" she shouted. "Just let me do it!"

"What?" Josh barked. "What am I supposed to do then?"

"Nothing!" Nora said. "Just keep shooting!"

She reached her other hand behind her and closed her eyes, trying to feel out the roll's location—there. She had it. Pulling it around him and back to her other hand, she dragged it around her chest as it squealed in protest.

The second pass was uncomfortable, but much easier. By the third she was getting the hang of it. She pulled the fourth across her shoulder like a seatbelt, but Josh grabbed it again.

"Hey!" she blurted.

"That's good! That's good!" he said. "We gotta leave now!"

A bug slammed to the floor in front of her, pulled it self upright and spread its jaws with a hiss. Nora's eyes bugged out.

"Go!" she screamed, and shot both hands out, smashing the bug backwards—They blasted off into open space, tumbling end over end.

Nora saw the whirling glow of the portals flash past her and screamed in panic, barely able to hear Josh leaving a trail of frantic curses. A warrior bug fluttered past, twisting and flailing in freefall.

"*GOD DAMMIT FRICKING DO SOMETHING!*" Josh sqwawked hoarsely.

"*WHICH WAY IS UP?*" Nora shouted, waving her arms.

"It's SPACE!" Josh barked, "EVERYWHERE IS UP!"

Nora stopped thrashing and watched, trying to gauge their rotation. The world blurred *down* across her vision—they were rotating backwards.

"I got it!" she shouted. Bending her arms up over her shoulders, she aimed them backwards and fired a pulse. Their rotation slowed, and after a couple of spins she was able to push with and against it until they stopped facing the Monolith.

"Uh," Josh muttered, "are we upside down?"

Nora furrowed her brow. "What?"

She abruptly realized the debris stream was going bottom to top. "Oh."

"Wait, nonono—" Josh trailed off into a tense hiss as she began spinning them horizontally.

"It's okay," Nora said. "I've got my bearings now."

A burst of gunfire cracked and something slammed into them. She fought to compensate, flailing like a kid treading water in the deep end for the first time.

"What are you doing?" she shouted. "Did something hit us?"

"Yeah," Josh groaned.

"Are you okay?"

"I'm fine," Josh said. "I broke the impact with my face."

"I thought you said you were okay!" Nora said.

"I'm fine! Just drive!"

Nora steadied them and held still, reaching out behind her and slowly pushing them towards the Monolith. She blocked out everything else, concentrating on the approach. They were closing the distance much more rapidly than she had expected.

"Brace!" she called out.

Her hands and feet made contact with the surface. Losing her grip, she twisted to the side and struck the unforgiving surface with her shoulder, forcing out a painful grunt.

"You okay?" Josh said.

"I'm fine," Nora wheezed. She reached out and her hands made contact with the uneven surface. To her surprise, it was warm to the touch, almost uncomfortably so. Letting the surface slide past her fingers, she noticed it begin to rise, and realized they were slowly falling.

Throwing her arms and feet down and back, she projected a constant force, and stabilized them.

Josh nudged her. "Look out! Shift!"

Nora pushed to the side just as the vending machine swept serenely past.

"I've decided," said Josh, in a husky voice. "That I don't want to be an astronaut anymore."

Nora laughed. "I don't know," she said. "I think I'm getting the hang of this."

"Okay, okay," Josh said. "Find the key."

"I'm on it," Nora replied. "Where do I look?"

"Hexagon," Josh said. "Flush with the surface, two thirds down, on one of the sides."

"Got it."

Josh pulled his empty magazine clear and smacked a fresh one home, slapping the bolt closed with a solid *chunk*. Scanning the open room in front of him, he tried to avoid looking up or down, instead looking straight ahead to the large ragged rectangular hole that represented the control room. It wasn't much, but it kept him more or less oriented.

"How close are you to done?" he said. "Have you got the key yet?"

"I think I found it," Nora replied, "but it keeps passing me."

"Do you need a hand?"

"No, just—Hold on."

"What—oof!"

Josh grunted as he was yanked into a small orbit. Nora had obviously gotten a grip on the surface.

"Found it!"

Nora had found the key. The hexagon's surface had strata, through which a flickering glow could barely be seen. Oddly, the rock grain in the key seemed to be at an angle from that of the Monolith itself.

Nora slid her hand closer to it, and felt something like static crawl up her arm. She hesitated, not sure whether this was a sign of danger or not.

But then, she thought, she didn't necessarily have to touch it.

Curling her fingers, she held them about six inches above the surface and tried to feel out a grip...there. She braced herself against the surface and slowly pulled back.

It refused to budge.

Nora continued applying force and adjusted her stance. The static hum grew in her ear.

The key didn't move.

Nora held the pressure for a few more seconds, then let go, sucking in a deep breath.

"Did you get it?"

"One more time," Nora said.

She waited for a moment and concentrated, gathering strength. She could feel the charge growing, pulsing along with each heartbeat.

One, two, three deep breaths—she braced herself and pulled back with everything she had. Constant pressure, slowly increasing, and increasing—enough to send them both flying when it came out.

It didn't budge.

She let go and released tension, gasping for breath.

"Nora?"

"I can't get it!" Nora wheezed. "It's stuck!"

Nora's words went right to Josh's gut.

Stuck.

He gritted his teeth. "There's got to be a way."

"What do you want me to do?" Nora snapped. "There's not lock, no button, or—it's just a *plug*!"

"Turn us around," Josh said. "Let me try."

"Oh come on," Nora said. "What do you think this is, a pickle jar?"

"Just let me look at it!"

Josh heard Nora grumbling under her breath.

"Okay," she said. "Get ready."

"Okay," Josh said. "For wha—*Whoa!*"

The world spun, and he found himself grabbing frantically at the smooth black surface now in front of him.

"Easy!" Nora said. "I'm trying to keep us from flying away here!"

"I got it! I got it!" Josh grunted, digging his fingers into the carvings.

"Okay," he said, looking up and down the surface. "Where is it?"

"It's glowy," Nora said. "Probably below you. Climb around until you see it."

Shifting from one handhold to the next, Josh tried not to look out at the spinning beyond. He felt nauseous.

"Got it!" he said, looking down. "Hang on."

He inched his fingers close to the edge, through the static...and onto the smooth surface.

"I can touch it," he said.

"Can you get your fingers under the edge?"

Josh grimaced and tried to work his fingertips into the hairline crack. "I can, just barely," He said, "but it won't move."

Nora's voice was slow and cautious when she spoke. "Josh..."

Josh looked up.

At a point on the ceiling a few dozen feet from the portal, several streams of bugs had coagulated into a single seething mass that was slowly growing towards them like a living stalactite. It curled towards them in a long thick chain, closing the distance with every second.

"Back!" Josh shouted. "Back! Back! Back!"

"Where are we going?" Nora replied.

"Anywhere but the black hole," Josh said. "Evade!"

He pushed back off the Monolith, and felt the duct tape straps yank him backwards as Nora blasted off. Pulling the pin from a frag grenade, he mentally gauged the distance between him and the roiling black mass above them, and flung the hissing explosive into the tangle as hard as he could.

"Frag out!" he shouted.

"What?" Nora replied.

A skull-rattling crack boomed through the room, and Josh gritted his teeth as he swapped his launcher's buckshot mag for a box full of grenades. The living chain shuddered and twisted, swinging away from them. A thin wave of dust washed over them.

"What the hell was that?" Nora shouted.

"Me," Josh said, chambering the first shell. "Cover your ears, here comes round two."

He swung the weapon up and fired the first round just off the mass's center. The spot blossomed like a firecracker in a dirt hill, sending clumps of dead bugs spinning into open space, their shrieking comrades still tangled among them. The air filled with smoke.

"Josh! On your right!" Nora shouted.

Josh swept his weapon to the right in time to see the bug chain swinging back. Taking an instant to center the red dot, he pulled the trigger and peppered it with bullets. The chain shed limbs like a hedge being trimmed as bugs thrashed, tore, and exploded.

Josh wrangled the rifle like a wild animal, squinting his eyes against the bright muzzle flash as each round left the barrel and lanced through the incoming mass. Nora was moving, but it was curling towards them, closing the distance as fast as he could cut it.

The rifle abruptly snapped empty, and Josh was left blinking for an instant before his numbed finger fumbled for the mag release as he clutched desperately at his vest pouches. Pulling the fresh mag clear, he slammed it against the weapon only to discover his empty hadn't dropped free—no gravity.

He pushed the release again and gave the weapon a quick flip to throw the mag loose, stuffing the new one in as soon as it spun clear. He slapped the bolt home and held the trigger down, focusing his lead on the weak spot, trying to cut the snake from its head.

He felt them slow, turn suddenly, and begin to accelerate again.

"Where are we going?" he said.

"Back!" Nora shouted. "There's nothing more we can do!"

"No! Go to the Monolith!" Josh shouted.

"Why?"

"Because—" Josh couldn't finish the sentence.

"There's nothing we can do." Nora stated.

"Yes there is," Josh shot back. "Foster told me."

They came to an abrupt stop.

"Told you what?" Nora said.

Josh hesitated.

"There's not one Monolith," Josh said. "There's two. They have to maintain a connection. All you gotta do to shut them down is—"

"Go through." Nora finished.

"It's a one way trip." Josh said. "If you can get me there, you can cut me loose and—"

"I'm not leaving you behind," Nora retorted. "That's not happening. We'll wait for—"

"Either I do it, or someone else does it *for* me," Josh snapped. "Don't you understand? Look up at the ceiling—if someone doesn't stay behind, we all die—"

"Then *I* should stay!" Nora shouted.

Josh was silent. "Head for the portal."

In a few moments, they entered the overhead beam of light once again, and Josh felt them come to a stop. Josh was thinking furiously.

"We've got to go in straight," Nora said. "Or we'll spin off into… somewhere."

"Wait—hold up a second," Josh said. "You realize you don't need to—SHIT!"

Josh thrust his rifle upwards just as a diving Locust's jaws closed over them with a snap. He heard Nora scream, and saw the rough surface of the Monolith sliding past as she lost her grip.

The bug's hot putrid breath washed over Josh's senses, and he felt its lower jaws biting into his arms like knives. He had jammed the rifle upwards and crossways into its mouth. His gun hand was wrapped around the stock with no way to reach the trigger, but his forward hand, wrapped around the launcher's grip—he began tugging at it, trying to align the barrel and take a shot.

Suddenly, they jerked to a stop. Nora had found a grip and arrested their fall. The bug's body caught up with its head and flipped over, the top mandible digging into her shoulder and yanking her backwards. She screamed. If the upper pincer hadn't penetrated before, it certainly had now.

"NO!" Josh shouted. "Hold on! Just two seconds more!"

"Get it off!" Nora choked. "Get it off!"

"I got it! I got it!"

Josh let go with his gun hand and the bug chomped down. Nora cried out.

Josh caught sight of what he imagined was its eye, reached his hand up to grab its brow ridge and jammed his thumb into the soft spot. The creature squealed and loosened its grip.

Shoving the muzzle of the launcher deep into its throat, Josh aimed for where he guessed the spine connected to the skull.

"Suckit!" he hissed.

The weapon bucked and Josh felt the Locust shudder as an unexploded twelve-gauge explosive shell punched through its carapace. It jaws slipped for an instant, then clamped down on his armored shoulder with a fierce gurgle, its lower mandibles forced open wide against his vest. Josh found himself looking down into the dizzying black abyss, slowly circling the malevolent lines of the bug's form as it struggled to hang on by its neck.

He let go of the rifle now twisted against his chest, and reached down, digging his armored fingers underneath one of the mandibles. With a sharp outward jerk of his hand, he snapped it in half. The bug shifted its grip and squealed, but didn't let go.

"Josh…" Nora muttered. She sounded short of breath.

"Just a second more!" Josh shouted, trying to get a grip on the jaws.

"Watch your head," Nora said tonelessly.

A shadow fell over Josh, and he looked up.

The vending machine was bearing down on them, sinking like a rock.

Nora shifted her slippery grip on the edge of the Monolith, blocked the pain from her torn shoulder, and waited for the inevitable.

She let out a short scream as the impact ripped them loose. It flipped them completely until she was facing the abyss—she pushed away, dumping whatever energy she had left downwards as the vending machine slipped away into the blackness, the crumpled form of the bug still pinned below it.

"Up!" Josh yelled. "Up! Just a few more feet!"

Nora felt nauseous, the vortex below increasing her vertigo threefold. She felt if she blinked she'd pass out—if she didn't she'd pass out anyway.

"Come on!" shouted Josh. "I've almost got it! I can take you the rest of the way, just a foot more!"

Her left shoulder and side were on fire. Nora pushed away and squeezed her eyes shut, forcing herself not to count the eternal seconds as they slipped by. One, two…three…

"Got it!" Josh barked, a hoarse laugh tearing from his throat. "HAHA! I've got it!"

Nora let the air out of her lungs and went limp as a wet rag, nearly blacking out on the spot. She vaguely felt herself rising as Josh scaled the side of the Monolith. She began to notice pain in her side as well—oh yes, that was where the bug's hooked jaw had come down first. It felt like it was still there, lodged in her body.

The pain was a burning heat in her mind, keeping her awake. She gritted her teeth. She couldn't move, and she couldn't relax.

Initially she had felt less nauseous next to the Monolith—here at least there was some direction, even if it wasn't very strong—but now it came back with redoubled force. She felt the tape around her waist loosen, and saw the world spin until she was facing Josh. He was holding her arm with his, stopping their fall by draping them across the top of the Monolith, and was cutting loose the last of the duct tape with his other hand. She looked down at her side and found a gash trailing a swirl of red.

Josh drew a white injector from his pocket. Flipping the cap off the injector, he reached over and stabbed her in the shoulder. Within seconds Nora felt feeling return as white hot pain—then it faded to a dull throb.

She looked up at Josh. His eyes were wide, but his mouth had formed into a thin hard line. He glanced downwards, then looked up at the ceiling for a moment.

"I don't see any more of them," he said. "But you can't stay here—I don't know what'll happen when I turn this thing off."

Nora's mind cleared for an instant.

"No!" she barked. "No! I'm going!"

Josh shook his head.

Nora's eyes welled up. "No!" she snapped. "This is *my* job."

He set her fingers against the edge. "Grab the edge," he said. "I'm going to let go. Ready?"

"No!" She threw her other hand over and grabbed at his armored glove. "No! Stop! I'll stay here. I'll put the key in so you can come back —"

She found her other wrist locked in his grip.

"No," Josh said, firmly now, his voice gaining strength. "Look at me."

Nora looked down. Looked away. Down at the hole in the world. It blurred before her eyes. They were close to overflowing.

"This isn't your job anymore," Josh said. "You have to find your father. Do you understand? You have to go back. Go find Foster and Shona."

Nora's mind raced furiously. It didn't have to be this way. It couldn't. She couldn't even die properly.

"Nora," Josh said. "Nora, I need you to look at me."

Slowly, painfully, she forced herself to look him in the eye. They were strong and clear, and she wanted to hate him for it. Hate him for sparking the hope that was bubbling up inside her. She was going to live. She was going to live, and she didn't deserve it.

"Promise me you're going to go find Foster," Josh said. "Go find your father. You're not going to stay here. I don't know what's going to happen when I turn this thing off, so you need to be clear. Understand? Promise me."

She opened her mouth, tried to think of any of the million ways that surely could keep him here.

"No," she whispered.

He searched her eyes for a moment.

"Okay," he said.

He let go of her hand and grabbed her by the right foot.

"No!" This time her voice came out startled. "What are you doing?"

She scrabbled for grip on the rock surface, but his gloved fingers peeled her loose, and with a sudden tug she was flying. She was looking out at the slowly spinning world.

"No!" She screamed. "No! Stop!"

She knew what he was waiting for. They made one circuit as the Monolith slowly turned. As the control room came into sight, he let go, and she went soaring out towards it.

She tried to correct her spin, and felt the throb in her side spike like a razor. She cried out, lost control. She tried again, gritting her teeth against the pain, and nearly passed out.

Her tumble had stabilized somewhat. Through leaking eyes, she managed to look back at the Monolith. He was already halfway down the side.

"Don't," she croaked.

Josh slid down the side of the Monolith one handhold at a time, carefully picking his footing until his boots stood on the very edge of the dark oblivion beyond. He squeezed his eyes shut and focused, preparing himself to let go.

The next wave is coming. He thought. *You have to go.*

A desperate, hollow doubt clawed at his heart, trying to take shape in his mind. He opened his eyes, studying the rough black stone in front of him.

"Oh God oh God," he hissed though gritted teeth. "Please help me do this."

He took a deep breath, and closed his eyes.

Really, he thought. *Would you really go back now?*

"No," he said softly.

His mind cleared. The voices faded, and his mind was made up. In a way, he'd been making it up all day, and only just now realized it.

He was meant to be here.

He had chosen to be here.

The question rose in his mind.

How far?

"All the way." Josh replied.

He let go.

18

Katabasis

Josh was still falling.

The hole had yawned wide and swallowed him whole, leaving him lost in the pitch black void, unable to even see his hand in front of his face. All sense of motion has vanished. Sound faded away, until all he could hear was his own heartbeat and a high-pitched whine in his ears—and even that could have been his own imagination. He couldn't hear himself breathing, but he still seemed to be capable of it. It took all his courage not to panic at the idea that he'd just fallen out of existence altogether, like a sinking ship dropping into oblivion.

He was beginning to see flashes of light at the edges of his vision, splashing across his limbs and occasionally blinding him. He squeezed his eyes shut and waited for the blotches to fade, then forced them back open and tried to figure out where they have come from, twisting and craning his neck.

There—A light up above—or above his head, anyway. It was growing brighter and brighter, or he was approaching it. It was like approaching headlights, forcing him to squint and finally close his eyes as the light shone red through his eyelids. He could hear the wind rushing in his ears...

He arrived with a shock, like waking from a dream, the world warping down to meet him head-on. He gasped in surprise, his limbs tensing up, and he forced them to relax, to not throw off his trajectory. Blinking and focusing his eyes, he tried to interpret the harshly lit scene before him.

An elongated hexagon slowly turned before him, pointing resolutely to the black eye of a luminescent orange hurricane rotating in tandem. The eye warped the light around it like a lens or grain of sand suspended on the surface of a pond. Josh began to lose his bearings and focused on the approaching hexagon—which was, as he suspected, the top of the

Monolith's counterpart. He was coming down from above, exiting the "White Hole" facedown, like a skydiver.

He reached out as he slowly approached the blinding near surface of the hexagon, and carefully placed his hands on the edge, letting his body be rotated upright by the gentle downward force. Once upright, he jammed his shoes into the carvings—exactly where they were supposed to be—and tried to peer through the shining motes of dust sprinkling the air to get a look good look at his surroundings. Not much was visible through the dark and clouds of dust beyond, but there did seem to be debris floating around—he wondered how much of it was Earth dust and how much native. He also briefly wondered how it was that an alien world held the same atmosphere capable of supporting human life—and then as quickly pushed the thought away and began patting down his gear, finally gripping the rifle in his gun hand and quickly scanning the area. The lack of hostiles was bothering him. Aside from the occasional shattered limb floating past, there had been no sign of life whatsoever.

Suddenly, a sound like a titanic foghorn blew through the open space, shattering Josh's frayed nerves. He gripped the cap of the Monolith in a death grip, his eyes nearly popping from their sockets.

"Oh for the love of—*Now* what?" he muttered.

Like the trumpets of an advancing army, the harsh cries of first dozens, then hundreds of warriors rose to meet it, and Josh heard the rumble of thousands of Locust coming from every direction. Peeling one hand loose, he raised the rifle in one hand and held it stretched at arm's length, pointing off into the swirling clouds like a massive pistol.

His eye caught something, and he looked down. Curling chains of warriors reached out towards the portal—first two, then five—he finally guessed in the obscured light that at least a half dozen stretched out to meet the abyss. At first they seemed to slow as they met the warping light, then they stretched thin as they were sucked in and vanished into the darkness.

Josh swallowed hard. Reinforcements were on their way.

Trying to process the monster-sized bellow he'd just heard without freezing in panic was becoming more and more difficult the longer he waited around. For the moment nothing seemed to have spotted him, but it was obvious that as soon it happened, he was going to be catching all kinds of hell. Carefully adjusting his grip, he slung his rifle and quickly clambered down the side of the Monolith. It was tempting to let go and attempt to catch himself rappelling-style, but he knew he was only going to get one chance at this—best make it count.

He glanced down and noticed the key slot on the side to his left. He smiled grimly.

"Gotcha."

Stepping downwards, he felt his chest clench as his feet lowered closer and closer to the bottom edge. Looking down, it was almost impossible to gauge—

His toe slipped out into open air, and he yanked it back, clinging white-knuckled to the carved surface.

"*There* it is!" he gasped, squeezing his eyes shut and taking deep breaths. "*Whoo.* Okay."

After he'd settled, he let go with his left hand and moved it down to the hexagon, digging his fingertips into the crack between it and the Monolith.

Gritting his teeth, he gripped the edges as firmly as he could, and pulled.

For a moment nothing happened. He kept increasing the pressure—

His hand slipped loose and flew outwards. A shot of chilled adrenaline shot through him, and he hissed through his teeth as he steadied his grip on the Monolith.

Deep breaths.

Muttering incomprehensible curses under his breath, he looked down once more and gripped the key. Taking a deep breath, he braced himself, and slowly pulled outwards once more.

Pressure…pressure—

With a grinding snap, the key shifted outwards a full inch.

The entire Monolith shook with a low *doom*, and the abyss below rippled in the flaring light. Josh felt the hairs on his arm stand up as the air filled with static, and a chorus of inhuman howls rose all around, panicked and confused. The roar boomed through the room, echoing and crashing back on itself like a storm.

Josh blocked it out and adjusted his grip, tugging harder. It shifted again, much easier this time.

Doom. The Monolith shuddered.

Josh looked down. The black portal remained open, shimmering like a pool at night.

The next roar caught Josh off-guard—he'd expected another, but not so close. He turned instinctively to face it, his eyes stretched wide as he watched a huge black shape breach the swirling dust fifty yards in front of him. It was a freakishly elongated, frilled skull on a long powerful neck, its divided lower jaw opening wide as it let a growl rumble from its throat, a cluster of eyes embedded on each side.

Josh put his left hand back on the carvings, grabbed the launcher grip with his right, and pulled the weapon up.

Grenades. Please let it be grenades.

Approximating the distance, he aimed for the open mouth, and pulled the trigger.

Prack. The launcher bucked.

The first shot vanished into the dust. The great head shifted, as if listening.

Josh gritted his teeth and adjusted his aim. In a few seconds he was going around the back side and he'd have no shot.

Prack.

Prack prack prackBOOM!

The fifth shot hit the skull a full broadside where the right mandible contacted the jaw. The creature was slapped to one side in a cloud of smoke, as if a massive fist had slugged it. One of the ten-foot mandibles pinwheeled away into the murk and vanished. Another roar rumbled through space—this one garbled by pain.

Josh turned his attention back to the key and wrapped his hand around it, pulling as hard as he could. The rock shuddered under his fingers, and the limbs of his suit squealed in complaint. There was a grinding sound, and the drum began again, but this time it didn't stop—

the note throbbed continuously, rising, rumbling like a storm, until the last inch came loose with a thunderclap.

A pulse of light bleached the world white as the sun, and Josh shut his eyes as he lost his grip and fell out into space.

__Epilogue__

Mrs. Morrison paused as she wiped down the counter to watch the sun's warm morning glow peek up from behind the distant hills. The only thing marring her view was the totaled minivan. It had been there since yesterday morning; the owners had come back in a white commercial van before leaving the wreck double-parked on the far side of the lot, without so much as leaving their phone number. She hoped they would be back to claim it soon.

Her ears pricked up as she heard an engine approaching. She kept expecting it to pass, but there was something odd about it. It was far too deep to be a semi passing on the highway, or one of the seemingly dozens of jet fighters that had been howling across the sky all night. It sounded like someone was driving a tank.

A moment later, a once-desert-tan Bradley fighting vehicle growled into the parking lot and collided with the minivan, reducing the number of spaces it occupied to one. The tracked pseudo-tank looked like it had just crawled through a tar bath full of mutant bamboo.

A tall pink-skinned man and a tall dark-skinned woman got out, both dressed in fatigues and what seemed to be and extra set of robot limbs. The man was first inside, limping somewhat and covered in blood, sweat, and dust. He was very pale, but surprisingly energetic.

"Okay," he said, turning to the others. "Whatever you want, on me."

"I thought Doctor Vance said he could drive," the tall woman said angrily.

"Technically, he did," Foster replied, "but yes, you're driving next."

He clumped towards the restrooms. "If they've got ribs, I want ribs— Or a cheesesteak. Or maybe both. I've got to pee."

The door to the men's room shut.

Mrs. Morrison looked up into a pair of fierce black eyes set in a serious face.

"May I take your order?" she said in a small voice.

Nora stood in the parking lot, staring at the now beyond-totaled hunk of squashed metal sitting in front of the Bradley. After a moment, she wandered past it into the wide brush-dotted desert beyond. The sun was just rising over the desert, illuminating a clear blue sky streaked with a surprising number of contrails. Nora had heard the fighters overhead when they had cleared the danger zone and Foster had parked on a ridge overlooking the main swarm.

Even through night vision there wasn't much to see except a wide grainy green heat blob that blossomed into an even wider green heat blob as the bombs landed. The others exchanged smiles and sighs of relief—they were too exhausted to cheer. Exhausted and full of loss.

She closed her eyes and felt the cold wind buffet against her. A chill crawled up her spine as her body tried to compensate for the warmth being siphoned away. Her shoulder and side ached dully through the haze of drugs. In fact, now that she had stopped moving, it felt like every bump, cut, and bruise she'd accumulated all day was coming back to make its voice heard.

Or yesterday, rather, she corrected herself. Today was the dawn of a new day. A new day on a world she barely recognized.

She took a deep, rattling breath, and tried not to let her eyes overflow.

"Now what?" she muttered to no one in particular.

She felt rough fabric enclose her shoulders and pulled it close—then started, turning like a flash.

A man stood a respectful distance away with his hands behind his back, looking out at the dawn. His head was shaven, and he was dressed in olive coveralls, with aviator sunglasses concealing his eyes.

"Beautiful, isn't it?" he said.

Nora stared at him. It had hurt, moving that quickly. She tried not to let it show.

"Apologies," the man said, brushing off his coveralls. "I have a tendency to sneak up on people."

He looked up at her. She couldn't see his eyes, but she could *feel* them, somehow. They felt...restrained. Safe.

"Are you all right?" He asked.

"I'm..." Nora stopped and considered for a moment. She glanced back at the destroyed minivan and its battered replacement.

She returned her gaze forwards and took a deep breath.

"I'm surprised I'm still alive," she said, "and to be honest, I'm not sure I should be."

"The Sun doesn't mind," the man said. "It's just happy to see you."

Nora gave him an intense sideways look.

"Who are you again?" she said. "Are you—are we supposed to meet you and they forgot to tell me or something?"

"They know me," he said, "but they're not expecting me."

Nora felt a bolt of acid shoot through her. She turned slowly and took a step back.

The man, for his part, ignored her and continued staring at the sunrise.

"So...does that mean you're with us?" she said, "or them?"

"Neither," he said, turning to face her directly. "Just a messenger."

Nora tried vainly to see past the opaque lenses to the eyes beneath. She forced herself to measure her breathing.

"What message?" she said.

The man appeared to study her for a moment before he spoke.

"He knew what he was doing," he said. "Do you know that?"

Nora was silent for a moment.

"Who are you talking about?"

The man reached up and unzipped one of his chest pockets.

Nora balled her fists.

Slowly, gently even, he drew out of his pocket a small leather book.

She squinted at him. "What's that?"

He held it out to her.

"Take it," he said. "It won't bite."

Nora looked it over, but her concern that it contained some weapon was quickly dismissed. A bullet hole was torn through it.

Slowly, she reached a hand out and took it.

"I don't understand," she said.

The man glanced at his watch. "You'll have to leave soon," he said. "I'll be in touch."

Nora heard a voice call out behind her and turned around. Foster was waving her over as Shona balanced a trio of white paper bags. She turned back and stopped.

The wind scattered dust over the empty plain. The man was gone.

THE JANITOR

WILL RETURN

About the Author

John Fulton is an author and filmmaker who has made an unreasonable amount of money animating plastic soldiers on YouTube. He is also the author of the novel The Janitor Must Die, and hopes its sequels will catapult him to fame and fortune. He lives in the Darkest Midwest, where he competes with the native wildlife for basic resources like wi-fi and root beer.

If you enjoyed this book, John would highly appreciate it if you would leave a review for it on the store page where you got it.

Sign up for sequel updates:
https://www.subscribepage.com/john-t-fulton-mailing-list-fiction

Copyright © 2019 John Fulton

All rights reserved.

Made in the USA
Columbia, SC
22 April 2024